The Colour of Our Country

John Sargeant

The War Years

Copyright © 2022 John Sargeant
All rights reserved.
ISBN:9798800904710

Books in this Series

The Colour of Our Country – The Settler Years

The Colour of Our Country – The War Years

The Colour of Our Country – The In-Between Years

The Colour of Our Country –The Lucky Years

The Colour of Our Country – The Affluent Years

The Colour of Our Country – The Coming Together Years

The Colour of Our Country – The Final Years

ACKNOWLEDGMENTS

IT IS OFTEN QUOTED THAT "IT TAKES A VILLAGE TO RAISE A CHILD." I AM NOW ABLE TO TELL YOU THAT IT ALSO TAKES A VILLAGE TO WRITE A BOOK.

NONE OF THE BOOKS IN THIS NEW ZEALAND SERIES HAVE WRITTEN THEMSELVES, NEITHER HAVE I WRITTEN THEM ON MY OWN. THERE HAVE BEEN MANY OTHER PEOPLE WHO HAVE INSPIRED, ENCOURAGED, PROVIDED AND SIMPLY BELIEVED IN ME WHEN I DID NOT BELIEVE IN MYSELF. THOSE WHO READ, REREAD AND FREELY GAVE ADVICE, IDEAS, INSPIRATION AND GAVE OF THEMSELVES, I AM INDEBTED TO EACH AND EVERY ONE OF YOU. THERE HAVE BEEN AUTHORS WHOSE BOOKS HAVE PROVIDED DETAILS THAT HAVE ADDED AUTHENTICITY, GRAVITAS, AND INSIGHTS, THAT THE INTERNET COULD NEVER HAVE. IN PARTICULAR I REFER TO THE LIKES OF *THE LITTLE SHIPS OF PATEA* BY IAN CHURCH. AN OUTSTANDING VOLUME. LISTED BELOW ARE PEOPLE WHO HAVE SHARED IN THIS EIGHT YEAR JOURNEY TO DATE. WHO I WISH TO ACKNOWLEDGE.

FOR UNFLINCHINGLY PROVIDING PRINTED MANUSCRIPTS AT THE DROP OF A HAT FOR DISTRIBUTION, I THANK RACHAEL HARRIS.

FOR OUTSTANDING ADVICE ON HISTORICAL ACCURACY AND A WARM SMILE EVERY TIME I ARRIVED ON HIS DOOR WITH A MANUSCRIPT UNDER MY ARM, I THANK FORMER DIRECTOR OF THE TARANAKI MUSEUM AND SENIOR RESEARCHER, PUKE ARIKI, RON LAMBERT.

FOR READING EVERY FIRST 'DRAFTY' DRAFT OF EVERY CHAPTER STRAIGHT OFF THE KEYBOARD, AND HER CONSTANT SUPPORT, I THANK DEB STEWART.

FOR THOSE WHO NOT ONLY READ EVERY MANUSCRIPT, GIVING ME THEIR HONEST THOUGHTS AND ADVICE, I THANK THE 'REVIEW TEAM' OF: JAN MARTIN, MARY BOURKE, NIKI JENKINSON, JAN JOHNSTON, DOUG BIRD, CAROLINE BENNETT & LINDA VOGT.

FOR ADVICE WITH 'MARCO' AND 'MAC' PLAYING POKER, I THANK ABE' CHAMBERLAIN.

FOR MANY, MANY EMAILS AND EXERCISING A GREAT DEAL OF PATIENCE IN TEACHING ME THE RHYTHMS AND NUANCES OF WINEMAKING, I THANK STRAT CANNING

FOR BEING SO OBLIGING AND HAPPILY LETTING ME USE HIS IMAGE FOR 'THE LUCKY YEARS' JACKET, I THANK ANDREW GALE.

I THANK MY WIFE, TERESA, WHO SUFFERED LONG SILENCES FROM ME AS I WROTE, REWROTE, EDITED, REDITED AND STARTED IT ALL AGAIN.

THERE ARE MANY MORE, TOO MANY TO MENTION, WHO I HAVE INTERACTED WITH ON THIS JOURNEY. WHETHER YOU HAVE WELCOMED ME OR ROLLED YOUR EYES AS I APPROACHED, I THANK YOU AND IF YOU HAVE A MANUSCRIPT STILL, PLEASE KEEP IT, I HAVE A ROOMFULL!

MY FINAL THANKS IS TO THE COFFEE SHOPPES AND CAFES AROUND NEW PLYMOUTH WHOSE TABLES I HAVE TAKEN UP, DEEP IN THOUGHT AND HUNCHED UP OVER MY LAPTOP WHILE GATHERING CREATIVE ENERGY FROM THOSE AROUND ME.

HAPPY READING

CHEERS, JOHN S.

Chapter One

**

Richard Murphy sat back on the veranda of his parent's house at Llanon, exhausted after a day of repairing fences before the winter set in. He sat in silence watching Lucky who was laid out on an old settee pushed up against the wall. Richard's eyes were just starting to close just as Sean came out with a bottle of beer and two glasses. "How'd the fencing go?" he asked.
"Good. Those Ayrshires will stay in the back blocks for a while longer," Richard replied taking a stretch and sitting up.
"Thanks son, you've saved me a lot of work, Lucky too, not that he's up to it much anymore".
"How old do you reckon he really is?" Richard asked.
"Well let me see now, it's been about sixteen years, maybe more since he jumped aboard the *Cardiff* with me and your uncle Wirimu, so that's about it I reckon".
"You've been saying fifteen for the last three years," Richard remarked.
"You have a fair point," Sean smiled. "Let's call him twenty and that will do for the next three years at least."
"That's really old for a dog," Richard remarked, "especially a lab'. He's been around longer than I have."
"He has, and he's seen a few comings and goings. When you were a small lad you used to ride him around the house like a horse."
"I remember, I slipped off a few times as well."
Sean looked hard at Lucky. "I need to think about training another cattle dog, I should have done it a while ago."
Lucky raised his head and looked at Sean as if in protest, but too tired to do anything else, he let his head fall back and closed his eyes. Sean walked over and rubbed his ears.
"Finish your beer then scrub up lad," he said. "Your mother and sister will have dinner ready soon enough."

Gwyneth and Sarah were laying the table when Sean walked in, he picked up a letter lying on the table.

"Is this from your mother?" he asked Gwyneth waving the letter in the air.

"Yes, yes it is," she replied. "She's just confirming she'll be over later this week if that's alright?"

"Of course it's alright," Sarah interrupted as she laid out the cutlery. "I do miss Nana so much, I haven't seen her for absolutely ages. I miss her reading me stories the most, and the smell of lavender."

"Is she closing the tea rooms this time?" Sean asked.

"No, her friend, Dorothy will be managing while mother is away and Dorothy will have a new assistant," Gwyneth said.

"What about Betty?"

"Betty's far too old now," Gwyneth replied. "She must be seventy at least so she only calls in now and again when it's busy."

"Well your mother needs to keep the tea rooms open to keep the money coming in." "Life's not always about money Sean Murphy, my mother needs to relax as well. She works hard at the tea rooms as well you know."

"Mother?" Sarah interrupted, sensing another argument was about to erupt. "Can I read your old nursing books this evening please?"

"Of course, you've been showing some interest in them of late dear. Would you like to become a nurse?"

"Who knows, I just like reading facts more than fiction, besides you never know when it will be useful."

"Is that why you always have your head stuck in those old newspapers?" Richard asked.

"We should always know what's happening in the world," Sarah replied, "even if it is weeks or even months later."

Sarah turned back to Gwyneth. "Did you ever regret not staying in Wales and continuing with your nursing?"

"Now what sort of a question is that for your mother?" Sean asked.

Gwyneth looked at him sideways and it was enough to shut him down.

"I loved nursing" Gwyneth said stopping her work for a moment. "But I came out to New Zealand with your nana and grandpa and that was it really."
"But you did intend to go back to Wales eventually though, didn't you?" Sarah quizzed.
"What your mother really means is, she met me and fell in love so couldn't bear to be away from me. Isn't that right Gwyn?" Sean smiled looking directly at Gwyneth so she couldn't help but smile back.
"Yes. I fell in love with your father and we stayed here at Llanon. Before I knew it, the years went by," Gwyneth said, more to the tablecloth than anybody in particular.
"Don't you ever regret not going back to Wales Mother? I mean not even for a trip to see the places where you grew up?"
"No, of course not," Gwyneth lied. "Besides, staying here with your father meant we had you two beautiful children, the farm and Ballinger's Mill."
Gwyneth looked up and smiled at Sarah and Richard.
The truth was, Gwyneth was feeling more vulnerable now her mother was living in New Plymouth and with Sean and Richard working on the farm and managing Ballinger's Mill, she was feeling ever lonelier.
"What about you Father? Don't you ever want to go back to Ireland?"
"Now why would I want to go back to the land of the oppressed and the poor when all I ever wanted is right here in front of me?" Sean said taking Gwyneth's hand and giving it a squeeze which Gwyneth returned with a polite smile.
"I might go hunting at the weekend with Tama and Theo," Richard suddenly announced. "If that's all right," he added looking around for any agreement. "I might be away for two, maybe three nights."
"It's all right with me but you best check with your uncle Wirimu," Sean told him. "I know he has plans for Tama coming up soon."

**

Richard Murphy, Tama Ratahi, and Theo Twentyman were inseparable as children. They grew up together at Llanon and the neighbouring farm, Te Kainga where they played as children during the endless summers, worked the land, and hunted wild pigs in the broken hill country along the Mokau. They knew every paddock and every twist and turn in the river and every track through the bush for twenty miles around. They had each attended Murata School and were taught by Amy and Susan Tallboys. Richard was the eldest and at eighteen was as tall as his father with his good looks but he lacked his father's confidence.

Theo was the quiet one of the group. He had grown up with a strong religious background given to him from his father, George. His mother, Libby, didn't share those religious convictions so often allowed him time off from Bible studies to go and play with the other boys. Theo, like his father, had a gentle way with animals and would often be found talking to the cattle. But it's the horses he preferred. He could manage them better than anybody else. If any surrounding farmers had trouble with their horses, it was Theo they would send for. He enjoyed the company of Richard and Tama but the hunting trips brought him no pleasure. He would go along with the others but he refused to kill any animals which had been hunted down, preferring to look after the camp and make sure everything was tidy and the fire was always stoked. He always took his Bible which he read while the others were out hunting in the bush.

Tama Ratahi was the youngest. He was shorter than Richard but he was stocky and very strong which matched his nature. He was a natural leader as his decisions were well thought out and he had a confidence which people instantly recognised and were drawn to. He would often challenge decisions the group made and he was often right.

**

"What time will Nana be arriving?" Sarah asked.

"About the same time as she gets here," Sean replied. "Owen McConaghy will have caught the incoming tide, so she won't be far away now."
"I do hope she brings some newspapers with her," Sarah said. "I do so love reading about England and what's happening with the Balkan War."
"I'm beginning to think I must have dropped you on your head when you were a baby," Gwyneth told her. "I've no idea where you get all this from."
"But it's important to know these things because it can affect us here. Why would you not want to know. If the Balkan War becomes any worse, Germany and Russia could get involved, which means Great Britain as well. That in turn means New Zealand could send troops. Richard might have to go to war. Imagine that."
"What do you mean?" Gwyneth sounded startled as Sarah's comment took her off guard, getting her immediate attention.
"War Mother. If things get worse, New Zealand might go to the war, probably fighting the Germans in France or Belgium."
Richard's interest suddenly picked up.
"Do you mean go and actually fight, in a war? It sounds quite exciting."
"That's enough of that kind of talk," Sean said. "Besides, you two are not British. Your Irish New Zealanders, your place is here, not fighting for some God forsaken piece of land for those English land grabbing bastards."
"Language," Gwyneth scolded. "And the children are part Welsh as well, not just Irish."
"Irish and Welsh," Sean said. "Besides there's not going to be any war and if there was, Richard certainly wouldn't be going."

**

"Nana's here! I can hear the *Heron* arriving," Sarah shouted out as she ran down to the jetty. Sean, Gwyneth, and Richard followed.

**

After a cup of tea was made, Megan opened her bag. "I've bought you all a present," she said. "It's a Kodak camera, to take photographs of everybody and show me when you come to visit me in New Plymouth."

Gwyneth put her hand up to her mouth. "It must have cost you a fortune Mother."

"No, not really, I got it from Robertson's Photography, where we had the photo taken when you were pregnant with Richard. I bought some film as well of course. What do you think?"

"I think it's a lovely idea," Gwyneth said. "You'll need to show us how to use it. Sean?"

"I think it's a grand idea," Sean replied. "The boys are going hunting later on this afternoon. You can get a few photographs of them together."

"They may be away for a few nights. I hope you don't mind?" Gwyneth added.

"Of course not," Megan said. "They need to be out and about together, they just need to see me to say hello so then they can go and do what boys do. They've been friends for so long now."

"Ever since they were babies," Gwyneth said. "By the way, I've invited Ngaire, Wirimu, George and Libby over for dinner tomorrow as the boys are away. I thought it would be nice to have a catch-up."

"That would be good," Megan said. "I haven't seen them for almost a year now. How are they?"

"All well." Gwyneth stopped peeling potatoes and looked up at Megan. "Mother?"

"What is it Gwyn?"

"Sarah says there's a chance of a war in Europe and Britain might be involved so New Zealand would be as well. I think that may be a bit fanciful, but have you heard any talk around town?"

Megan went silent for a moment and looked down at the sink. "You have, haven't you?" Gwyneth questioned.

"It's only tittle tattle," Megan said. "Think nothing of it. You know what politicians are like. All bluster and talk."

"Sarah says Richard would have to go if there was a war which means Theo and Tama as well, and all the other young men along the Mokau come to that."

"It won't be that way," Megan said quietly. "It's just men talking nonsense, showing off."

Gwyneth went back to peeling potatoes. "I don't think I could stand it," she said. "What if… what if anything happened to Richard?"

The potato knife slipped from her grip, embedding itself in the palm of her hand, the blood immediately stained the water in the concrete sink.

"Damn, damn Mother, what if all our boys have to go to war? All the boys we have taught at Murata School, every single one of them." Gwyneth started to cry.

Megan put both arms around her and thought about what to say for a second, then she closed her eyes and summoned her strength so as not to show Gwyneth her true feelings.

"Nothing will happen to them because they will not be any war Gwyn, so put all those thoughts to one side as there's no need to worry yourself. Now I'll bandage your hand then we'll go and talk with Richard before he goes hunting tomorrow and let's have no more talk of war."

The following day was cool and the gathering clouds promised rain. Tama appeared, riding his horse along the bridle path with two pig dogs. They were muscly bull terriers bred to bail up wild pigs five times their own size and hold them down until Tama would catch up with his knife to stick the pig and bleed it to death. The dog's ears had been cut off so the pigs couldn't grip them with their teeth and they were scarred from previous encounters with wild boar.

Richard and Theo had their horses saddled and ready to go. George, Libby, Sean, Gwyneth, and Megan gathered on the front lawn to see the three young men off on their hunting trip. Megan had the camera ready. "All three of you huddle the horses together now. Sean and Gwyn, you stand in between the horses holding onto the reins."

"You go ahead," Sean said. "If you don't mind, I'll sit this one out."

"We can't have a family photograph without you in it," Gwyneth said. "Come on you stubborn Irishman."

Sean became serious. "Now, I said I don't want my photograph taken. I never have liked it, I don't know why but I really don't want to be in the photograph."

Gwyneth could see Sean wouldn't change his mind. "You take the photograph then" she demanded.

Sean looked up at Theo. "Do you have enough food?" he asked.

"Yes, thank you," Theo replied.

"We won't need much, it'll be venison for tea tonight," Richard added smiling and patting the rifle butt.

"Wild pork for me," Tama chipped in holding his knife.

"It'll be damper and sausages as usual," Theo added tapping his saddlebag. Everybody laughed breaking the gloomy mood they were all secretly feeling.

Richard could see the concern on his mother's face. He dismounted and hugged her, then Megan. "Goodbye Mum, Nana."

He gave Sean a slight hug and slap on the shoulder.

"Take care son," Sean quietly spoke in Richard's ear. "And take good care of Major, he's my favourite horse." Richard walked over to Lucky, who was watching from his place on the veranda. Richard rubbed his head. "Sorry boy, you're not coming this time."

Lucky whimpered and followed Richard over to the group then promptly sat down, not even taking any interest in the pig dogs.

"We'll be back in a few days," Richard said turning back as the three boys rode away. Gwyneth turned to Sean when the three boys were out of sight. "I do think you could have made the effort to be in the photo, flatly refusing like that hurt Richard and it hurt me a little to be honest."

Sean said nothing as they walked back to the house. Gwyneth suddenly shuddered. "Feeling the cold?" Sean asked. "No, not really," she replied, "just thinking about what Sarah said earlier."

**

After two hours of hard riding through the bush and along ridge lines, the three men stopped their horses.

"The rain will be heavy in an hour or so," Theo said. "I can smell it."

"How is it you can do that?" Richard asked.

"I don't know. I just can," Theo replied.

Tama was his usual quiet, thoughtful self. "What say we ride east for another two hours before the rain? That'll take us to good pig country," he suggested. "It's all broken hill country to get there though. It'll be hard on the horses."

"They can take it" Richard said. "Especially with Doctor Theo here, he can fix anything."

"Not anything," Theo replied. "We can't push them too hard in this weather, another two hours is about it for them today."

"Come on then," Tama said, taking the lead. "We'll make camp after that. Let's go."

The rest of the journey was made in silence as the rain began to fall just as Theo predicted. It beat against them, getting under their oilskins, cold against their flannel shirts.

The bush opened up into open hill country with no shelter. Already rivulets of water were starting down between the ridges, forming small streams. The horses had to be goaded down slippery ravines, then forced up yet another ridge only to find yet another in front of them while all the time, the clouds descended, making visibility difficult.

"Two hours you said, we've been going three now," Theo shouted out to Richard against the strengthening wind.

"Slow going," came the reply. "We'll be there soon."

After half an hour Theo stopped the group. He pointed to Richard's horse.

"Major's pulling up lame" he said as he dismounted and went over to the horse. He ran his hand down its leg stopping at the fetlock. "An old sprain I reckon. He can't take much more today, that's for sure. We need to find some bush to get some shelter and kawakawa for a poultice if you want to ride him tomorrow."

Tama and Richard knew better than to argue with Theo. Richard's head was bent down in the heavy rain. "Do you think we should go on for a while" he shouted, looking to Tama.

"No!" Tama shouted back against the wind as the rain swirled around them. "At least not eastward. We need to get down, follow a stream to the bush. Theo's right about the Kawakawa. We won't find any in this open country."

"What about Major?" Richard called out to Theo.

"You take my horse," Theo shouted back. "I'll lead yours downhill. He can't carry anybody now, the saddlebags are enough on their own."
"No," Richard insisted. "He's my father's horse and I promised to care for him, give me the reins Theo, I'll lead him down."
The trio slowly made their way down a gully with Tama and Theo riding and Richard walking, leading his horse and always picking a downhill route. The only ones not affected by the weather were the pig dogs who seemed to have endless energy running around vainly searching for any scent of a pig. For half an hour more they trudged and stumbled downhill at every opportunity, following a stream into another stream until eventually they got to some lowland forest spread out on the sides of a valley.
"There's a track," Richard shouted just as their spirits were at their lowest.
"Reckon you're right," Tama said staring into the dark and rain soaked bush. "I wonder where it goes?"
"One way to find out," Tama said with some spark of hope in his voice.
"What about Major?" Richard asked. Theo checked the fetlock over again.
"No more than half an hour if we stay on the track. I need to watch out for some kawakawa or we're jiggered. Give me a minute" he insisted.
Theo held his hand against the horse's ear and whispered into it. Immediately it held its head high with its ears forward, it snorted and seemed to have more energy.
"As I thought" said Theo. "Another half hour and that's it, we make camp where we stop."
"It bloody well scares me when you do that," Richard said.
"I've seen you do it with the cows when they hold milk. It's like you talk to them, bloody well scary it is, I don't mind saying."
"I just do it," said Theo, "nobody told me how, I just sort of knew."
"Well I bloody well can't do it," Richard said.
"Nah, me neither," said Tama smiling. "And I'm a Māori."
"No, never. Why didn't you tell us before?" Richard joked, pulling Tama's hat off and throwing it along the track into the gloom.

"Bloody pakeha's, always taking things off us Māoris," Tama laughed as he went to get his hat back.
A few minutes later his voice shouted out from the bush. "Hey, see what I've found."
Richard and Theo walked forward slowly, rounding the first bend. In the gloom they saw a dilapidated wooden hut standing in a clearing. Tama turned to them grinning.
"Not bad eh. Ask the universe and the universe will provide," he said.
"Must be a miner's hut. I reckon we're out somewhere near the Mangapapa mine. We must have come further along the Mokau than we realised," Richard said thoughtfully.
"You might just be right," Tama said. "Maryville must be well below us."
The hut was green with mould on all but the northern wall and moss and lichen were growing on the timbers, but it looked to be solid enough. There was a lean-to on the side with a few skerrick's of coal and logs scattered underneath. The rain was cascading off the corrugations from the iron roof, puddling on the ground.
"Look," Theo said with some excitement. "There's a chimney, you know what that means?"
Tama was the first to get to the door. Without thinking why, he knocked. No answer came, not that he expected any. He pushed the door open, then, without thinking, wiped the green mould off his fingers using his trousers as he slowly walked in, peering into the darkness. "There's some bunks!" he exclaimed, "and a table, what more could a man want?"
"This is a really special place, it has a good feel about it. I like it a lot" Richard said quietly.
Theo tapped him on the shoulder. "There's an old range with a few sacks of coal by the looks of it," he said peering through into a back room which served as a kitchen. Not sure I'd trust the bunks though, they look pretty rickety," he said giving them a kick. "But beggars can't be choosers."
"Who cares? There's a roof and that's all I care about. Let's get the fire going," Tama interrupted. "I'm freezing."
"Horses first," Theo insisted. "I'll go and look for kawakawa, there'll be some around here somewhere."

"Right," said Tama taking charge. "Better still, Theo, you get the horses settled under the lean-to, unsaddle them and rub them down with those coal sacks in the corner. Richard, you go and get the Kawakawa for Theo, I'll get the fire going and start the damper or we won't eat till midnight. Richard, when you get back you can help Theo with the horses and the dogs, they'll have to make do with a sausage each tonight."

**

Within an hour, the horses were stabled and dry. Theo had made a poultice of Kawakawa and put it on Major's fetlock, the damper was on its way to being cooked and the smell of sausages spread through the hut.
"I told you the universe would provide," Tama said giving the sausages a poke with his knife.
"Actually, it's not the universe you need to thank," Theo said. "It's God."
"Well then, I thank God," Tama said.
"You can thank God for all of this, but you can thank my father for these" Richard said pulling out a bag of chestnuts. "They're from the trees he planted when I was a kid, they'll make a good treat roasted up after the bangers."

**

The rain eased during the night as the southerly wind shifted to the north and the clouds disappeared as a cool breeze flowed through the valley. Richard staggered up shivering and throwing a blanket across his shoulders, he gingerly made his way outside glancing across to the bunks. Tama was buried under a pile of old grey blankets and sacks, sleeping soundly but there was no sign of Theo. Richard patted the bed to make sure. He made his way outside, almost tripping over the dogs asleep in front of the last embers of a fire. He barely recognised Theo asleep under the lean-to with the horses. He smiled to himself and turned but caught his foot on a tree root and fell into the bush. Theo woke immediately. "What's going on?" he demanded.

"It's only me," Richard said struggling to get out of the tangle of supplejack which seemed to wrap itself around him the more he tried to get out.

"Just when I was getting to sleep," Theo grumbled indignantly as Richard fell again. "But you do make an interesting sight for a hunter who can't even get out the bush," he half laughed. He walked over and held out a hand to Richard.

"How's Major's fetlock?" Richard asked.

"Not good," Theo replied. "You won't be riding him today, maybe tomorrow, but we'll have to follow the Mokau back along the valley, he won't make the hill country. It must be twenty five miles to Llanon, maybe more and it'll be a slow ride, maybe a walk for one of us."

"Damn," Richard said. "But it's an ill wind. This is good country for wild pigs, there must be a few around here somewhere. The dogs will sniff them out."

"What's a man got to do to get some sleep around here?" Tama mumbled, standing in the doorway all but covered in blankets.

"Any sausages left?" he asked after a pause as the others took in the sight.

"Half a dozen or so," Theo replied.

"There's some damper as well," Richard added.

"Right then," Tama said. "We'll have an early breakfast then hunt out some pigs. If we get a couple we could be on the way home this afternoon."

"Good idea," said Richard. "This trip's not worked out well, but we can cut our losses and still bring home the bacon."

"Ho bloody ho," Tama quipped. "I'll get the fire wound up in the range. Theo, you get the billy going, see if you can find some manuka leaves to throw in the pot as well. Don't anybody feed the dogs, we need them hungry and mean so they can take it out on the pigs."

Within the hour, breakfast was over and Richard and Tama prepared to leave the camp on foot.

"You sure you won't come?" Tama asked Theo.

"I'm sure, thanks," Theo replied. "You know how I feel about killing. Besides I want to stay here and read Exodus."

"You and your bloody Bible," Richard said.

Immediately Theo stood up and looked Richard directly in the eye.

"Richard, you and Tama are my closest friends. I enjoy your company, that's why I come along with you. I do not decry what you do but I will not stand to listen to you, or Tama come to that, swear at the Bible. It's the word of God. While you may not respect the Bible itself, I do. If you consider me to be a friend you'll do as I ask. Do I make myself clear?"

There was an awkward silence in the camp and even the bird song disappeared momentarily.

"I said, do I make myself clear?" Theo repeated louder.

"Sorry mate," Richard said, shamefaced after being taken aback. "No offence meant," he added.

"You two go and get your pigs," Theo said. "I'll stay here and change the poultice on Major's fetlock. I'll keep the fire going and scout out the immediate area. I want to do some writing."

"Well, like Richard said," Tama added. "No offence meant. What's this Exodus all about then?"

"It's Exodus twenty thirteen to be exact," Theo said. "Thou shall not kill."

"But you've already made that decision," Richard told him.

"I'm not talking about pigs," Theo said. "Killing pigs for food is one thing, killing a human being is another."

"Who do you plan on killing?" Richard couldn't help but chuckle.

"Nobody," replied Theo. "But if there is a war in Europe, we may all be going, then we'll all have to decide whether we will kill perfectly good strangers, won't we?"

"The atmosphere in the camp went suddenly cold as the realisation of what Theo said sunk in.

In silence, Tama and Richard readied themselves for the hunt. They untied the dogs and made their way to the trail leading deeper into the bush. Tama turned around at the last minute.

"Take care mate," he called out to Theo. "See you tonight, if not before."

Chapter Two

**

Sean had been quiet for a few hours just sitting on the settee stroking Lucky stretched out beside him. Gwyneth came in looking hot and bothered after spending some hours in the kitchen preparing dinner over the hot range.
"You could ask if I need any help," she scolded. "Sean, I said you could help me! You can see how busy Sarah and I are, there's a lot to do before tonight, and get that dog off the settee."
Sean didn't respond, so with her frustration building, Gwyneth walked around to face him. "I said I need some…." She stopped talking when she saw tear stains on Sean's face.
"What is it love?" she asked. Her demeanour instantly changing.
Sean's voice was faint and croaky. "It's…it's Lucky. He…..he uueerrrr, he ….he died…about an hour ago."
"Oh poor boy," Megan said sitting down by Lucky's body stroking him gently. She started sobbing. Sean put his arm around her giving her a hug to hide his own tears.
"I'll go and get the shovel," he whispered. "The one from the *Cardiff*. That would be the right thing to do. Poor old Lucky, he's been with me since those days."
"Yes," Gwyneth said. "Just after you gave him a plate of stew, you've told me enough times," she said forcing a laugh. "He's grown up with the kids. They'll miss him."
The mood at the dinner table was sombre. Wirimu was upset when he and Ngaire were told about Lucky's death and he and Sean talked about the times on board the *Cardiff* when Lucky was first with them.
"If you like I can say a prayer for him" George volunteered.
"That would be fine," Megan agreed instantly putting her hand on George's in gratitude.

"You might want to say a few words for the boys as well, especially if this weather keeps up," Sean added. "I hope they find some good shelter."

"They know what they're doing," Wirimu chipped in. "They'll build some cover if they can't find anything."

"Gwyneth, why don't you play something for us on the piano to brighten the mood?" Megan suggested. "This is supposed to be a dinner party, not a wake, maybe you and Ngaire can give us a song?"

Together, Gwyneth and Ngaire sang several songs in English and Māori with Wirimu joining in. The mood lifted with the singing with even Sean and George grunting out a few lines of Men of Harlech. "Mid the fray see dead and dying, friend and foe together lying. All around the arrows flying, scatter sudden death."

"That's it," Gwyneth said. "You see Sean Murphy, you can sing, it's only your voice that spoils it."

They all laughed and Sean winked at Gwyneth.

"What's the news in New Plymouth Mother?" Gwyneth asked as she cleared the plates from the table.

"Oh, nothing of any consequence, this and that.....you know," Megan said as though trying to avoid the question.

"Is there talk of war?" Sarah piped in.

"Sarah!" Gwyneth almost shouted out. "I've told you not to bring that up. You know how it's all nonsense."

"No, it's not Mother," Sarah replied. "We need to know what's happening in the world, don't we Nana?"

"Well Sarah love, there are some things it doesn't pay to know about too early in case nothing comes of it, otherwise we'll have worried for nothing."

"But..."

"But nothing," Gwyneth interrupted again. "I'll have no more of this talk at the table. Sean, back me up on this will you?"

Sean was silent for a moment.

"Well, it's like this Sarah. Nobody wants to go to a war which is nothing to do with them?"

George interrupted. "But it would be our duty Sean. We owe that much to Britain. Where Britain goes, we go."

Sean looked at George directly. "But what if they didn't want you but took Theo instead?" he said with some force. "Is that where you want us to go, to send our sons off to a war in Europe so the English can take more land that doesn't belong to them?"

"They're not taking land, Father," Sarah said excitedly. "They would be defending France against the Germans, because if France fell then Great Britain would be next. We must support her if the call comes. Uncle George is right. It would be our duty to fight."

"Would it be our duty to send our sons? It's the lives of young New Zealanders we're talking about. Young men, Richard, Tama, Theo, Charlie Dobson, and Ian McPherson from up the river. The young men who work at the mill. How would it be if we lost all the workers?" Sean's hand hit the table rattling the crockery, making everybody stop and look at him.

"You see," Gwyneth shouted at Sarah. "See what you've done? Why don't you just keep your thoughts to yourself?"

"We are all good enough friends to talk as we feel," George said calmly. "I agree with Sarah, it would be our duty to help Britain in her time of need. Duty is duty and what must be done, must be done."

"Well let's leave it at that shall we?" Ngaire interrupted. "War is never glorious, duty or not. I know what my people went through in the wars over this very land and how it took our men away from us. I don't think I could go through that with Tama."

"Tama would have the protection of my kuia," Wirimu added. "When she sang to me in the Patea hospital all those years ago she was telling me she wanted me to have children. We have been blessed with Tama. That didn't happen so he would be killed in a war on the other side of the world."

"I have some news," Ngaire said, desperate to change the subject.

"What is it?" Megan asked.

"Mokau is to have its very own doctor at long last." Ngaire waited for a second for the news to sink in. "Stella Ratcliffe told me when I saw her in New Plymouth last week, waiting for the steamer. He starts this week apparently and moves in today or tomorrow ready to start in a few more days."

"That's so exciting. Who is he and what do you know about him? It's not before time either. At least we won't have to go to

Awakino anymore," Libby added, peppering Ngaire with her questions?
"I agree? Do you know?" Megan joined in.
"He's Welsh, apparently, so you will like him," Ngaire said. "He's single and quite good looking, debonair even, Stella told me."
Ngaire smiled again at the other women.
"His name is, now let me see if I can remember…yes…yes, it's David, David Askill."
Megan and Gwyneth instantly looked at each other in shock as Megan took Gwyneth's hand. Gwyneth felt the blood drain from her face and she felt as though the floor would open up in front of her. She tried to speak but couldn't, instead she got up and ran to her room.

**

"Are you alright?" Sean asked Gwyneth over breakfast. "Only you went strangely quiet last night. You were fine one minute but not the next."
"I was just worried about the boys," Gwyneth lied. "All that bad weather, I was thinking of them stuck in the bush. Anyway," she said with a false smile to change the topic, "what are you doing today?"
"Just the usual, George and I are shifting some stock to go to Bailey's auction next week. Why?"
"It's just that Mother and I would like to walk over to see Ngaire at Te Kainga later today."
"You only saw her last night."
"Can I come too?" Sarah chimed in.
"No, not this time love."
"But Mother …"
"I said no for goodness sake. Have you got cloth ears? Please, just for once, do as I say," Gwyneth snapped.
"All right Gwyn. No need to be so hard on Sarah," Sean sniped back. "Sarah, you'll have to help with the milking anyway if your mother's going to be away."

**

Gwyneth and Megan walked along the banks of the Mokau in silence towards Te Kainga. After a while Gwyneth spoke. "The wind's turned to the north," she said. "It will suit the boys a lot more. They may get out hunting today, maybe they'll be safe home tonight."
"You can't wrap them in cotton wool you know" Megan replied. "They have to find their way in life sooner or later. But that's not what today's about is it??"
Gwyneth stayed silent for a while.
"Mother, I am going to tell Ngaire about David Askill."
Megan became concerned and stopped walking to face her daughter. "Do you think that's a good idea?"
"Yes," Gwyneth said. "I do. I can't manage this on my own. You'll be back in New Plymouth in a day or so and I can trust Ngaire, so I'm going to tell her about David and ask what I should do."
"But surely you don't still have feelings for David after all these years?"
"I'm not sure Mother, I'm really not sure. That's what bothers me."
Gwyneth started striding ahead along the bridle path. Megan pulled at the back of her cardigan, making her stop and turn around. She looked Gwyneth in the eye putting both hands on her shoulders.
"Gwyn, go back home and think about it for a while. You have a loving husband and two lovely children waiting for you."
"Have I Mother? Have I got a loving husband?" Gwyneth turned back towards Te Kainga determined to talk to Ngaire.

**

Wirimu saw Gwyneth and Megan walking to the house and he sensed enough to stay where he was. Whether it was the pace of their walk or the emotional distance between then, he could see it was not a social visit.

**

Ngaire poured the tea and cut some cake.

"It's two hours 'till milking," she said. "That should just about do it by the look on your face. What's happened Gwyn?"
Megan and Ngaire sat in silence as Gwyneth spoke about her life in Wales. How she had fallen in love with David Askill when he was a young doctor and she a student nurse. How she volunteered to work in the Cowbridge Road Union Workhouse, working all hours with the children just to be with David and hoping against hope that she might be noticed. Gwyneth broke down when she told Ngaire about how she realised David was engaged to Genevieve Westmorland, a socialite and only daughter of a local industrialist, and how embarrassed she was realising she had made an exhibition of herself in front of him.
"It's no wonder he never noticed me," she said. "At least not in the way I wanted him to. God knows what he thought of my pathetic advances. He must have thought me a complete fool," she said wiping her tears as she managed to gather her thoughts.
"So that's why I came here, to New Zealand, with Mother and Father, partly for the adventure, but most of all to get away from the biggest mistake of my life."
"So, Gwyneth?" Ngaire asked after some time thinking. "What are you going to do about it?"
"What can I do?" Gwyneth replied. "I can't stay here and I can't leave. I have family and friends but I can't face David again."
"Do you want to see him?" Ngaire asked.
"Yes, yes, more than anything," Gwyneth spilled out, for the moment unafraid of any repercussions. "It's not that I don't love Sean or my life here, but I just want to see David once more, God knows why but that's what's in my heart."
"You have to ask yourself how long ago it all was," Ngaire replied. "Twenty years, maybe more?"
"Something like that," Megan interrupted looking at Gwyneth coldly.
"How do you think David would feel seeing you now?"
"I think he would still see a pathetic woman who made a bumbling fool of herself" Gwyneth confessed.

"Is that right?" Ngaire asked. "Do you think he would see a love struck teenage student nurse, or a mature woman with a husband, children and several successful businesses?"
"I...I don't know," Gwyneth muttered.
"Well, I do," Ngaire said. "He will see a beautiful and confident woman who has made something of herself. I am told he is single so who knows what happened to this Genevieve Westmorland, but one thing is for certain, she's not around now."
"What are you suggesting Ngaire?" Megan asked. "I'm not sure I like the way this conversation is going."
"I am not suggesting anything improper Megan, please don't take me wrong, but time moves on. We have all made fools of ourselves over the wrong person at some stage in our lives. I am the first one to put my hand up to that, but you need put it to one side. You only have to look at the man I married. You cannot keep running from the past Gwyn. You need to go and see David Askill and talk with him. Welcome him to Mokau, talk about the past, acknowledge it and I think you will both end up laughing about your times in Cardiff, then you can both move on with your lives."
"Or you can just ignore him and get on with your life anyway," Megan added. "The past is the past, why rake up bad memories?"
"Because if you don't, they will always be bad memories," Ngaire said. "They will eat into you and you will spend the rest of your life wondering what could have been and you will never be completely happy. Take it from somebody who knows, which leads me on to something else." Ngaire looked hard at Gwyneth. "Have you told Sean about Caryl at all?"
Gwyneth immediately clasped her hands and looked down at the floor.
"I thought not," Ngaire said. "And how many years has that been now? You see how it's eating into you?" she added. "If you do not face these issues, they become who you are and other people will see that. You have to have a courageous conversation with both Sean and David if you are to move on with your life Gwyn. Take my word for it."
The walk back to Llanon was made in silent thought but Gwyneth and Megan approached Llanon, Megan spoke.

"Have you decided what you are going to do? If you take my advice you'll leave well alone."
Gwyneth thought for a moment. "Yes Mother, I have decided. I'm taking Ngaire's advice. I'm going to see David."

Chapter Three

**

Richard and Tama headed out into the bush with the dogs running ahead searching for the fresh scent of wild pigs. After an hour Richard stopped and sat on a rock thinking.
"We're still well above the river, we need to go down lower."
"No," Tama said. "If there are any pigs they'll be around here somewhere. We'll stay above the river for now."
Richard said nothing but stood up and followed Tama.
Ten minutes later, the dogs started barking and running ahead. They turned a corner catching a pig in the open. It was a large black boar with a scarred hide, the thick back bristles formed a mane which ran along from its head to its tail. It carried two large tusks curling out of its gaping jaw like tree branches. As soon as it realised what was happening, it ran into the shelter of the bush. The dogs had been well trained and soon ran it down. The brown dog wasted no time jumping on its back and biting into its ear, releasing blood down its face and shoulder. The squeal of the boar could be heard across the valley as it tried to shake the dog off.
Tama started shouting. "Bail, bail, bail boy, bail the pig for fuck's sake!"
He and Richard crashed through the bush after the boar, which was still running with the dog hanging on to its ear.
The boar stopped slowed enough to swing its head around and get a tusk under the dog, ripping its side open but still it held on.
The second dog was trying for the boar's throat but keeping out the way of the massive jaws made it difficult.
The boar broke free and ran into a blind gully where there was no escape. Richard and Tama felt the adrenalin running as they careered into the bush behind it.

The brown dog, losing blood from its wound was the first to attack again. It went for the boar's throat but the pig turned at the last second crushing the dog in its jaws.
Tama already had his knife out and without thinking he launched himself at the boar, knocking the dogs out the way.
"Stick the fucker! Stick the fucker!"" Richard screamed out but Tama never heard it, all he heard was a muffled noise as time slowed down. He saw the brown dog laying prostrate on the ground with blood pumping out of it. He slid along the boar's back, reaching out with his right arm trying to get it under the jaws. All he felt was the rough bristles on the pigs back rubbing the skin off his face in the silence of the frozen moment. As he turned his head to face the front, he saw the boars eyes rolled back trying to see as it turned to defend itself. With an horrendous squeal, the boar lurched to one side knocking Tama against a tree but he refused to let go. The boar was strong enough to attempt running with Tama on its back, half dragging him through the bush as it ran in blind terror. Tama had an iron grip on the ears as he pulled himself forward, his blood mixing with that of the boar as his trousers then his legs were ripped from being dragged over the tree roots. The brown dog came back seemingly from nowhere, snarling with its teeth bared and foaming at the mouth in a frenzied attack not an inch from Tama's face as it threw itself at the boar's throat looking for the kill.
"Get out the fucking way!" Tama shouted striking at the dog but it ignored him. With all his strength, Tama reached forward with his knife finding its first mark in one of the boar's eyes. The fated animal rolled to one side, falling down off the track, tumbling down a slope with Tama still holding with his knees and his arm firmly locked. When they got to the bottom of the gully, Tama, exhausting his strength, tightened his grip even further. Richard, running behind, arrived just in time to see Tama pull the boars head back and open its throat with his knife. He stayed rigid, locked onto the back of the pig hacking with his knife until the boar lay dead. Blood was spilling out of the animal all over Tama, even then he still didn't let go but pulled the knife down the pigs belly opening up the beast. Its intestines spilled out releasing a stench, catching Richard's

throat, and making him stand back as Tama made sure the knife went all the way to the boar's groin.

"Got you now, you fucker!" he yelled in triumph rolling off the boar, eventually standing back with the boar's intestines over his boots, steaming in the cool of the bush. Tama stood leaning on a tree gasping for breath.

"I've never seen one as big as this" he managed to say, pointing his knife at the carcass. He went over, giving it a kick. "Best we get it to the river to wash it off, then we'll get back to camp. You can take the first turn to carry it."

Tama glanced at Richard giving him a look which nobody would have argued with. "We'll need to get the dogs back and stitch them up. I didn't bring the needle with me, it's back at the camp."

"Reckon the Brownie will live that long?" Richard quizzed.

"Don't know," Tama replied. "We'll find out soon enough."

**

They arrived back in the camp with Tama carrying the boar on his back with its huge head towering above him and its front legs tied over his shoulders.

Theo stood up as Tama loosened the ropes and threw his prize onto the ground.

"I see Artemis has been good to you as Apollo has been to me," Theo commented, looking at the dead animal.

"Arte-who?" Tama demanded in no mood to play games.

"Artemis," Theo repeated. "The Greek god of...never mind, you've done well, both of you."

"The dog's ripped up," Tama said. "I've got a needle and string. Reckon you could stitch him up good enough to get him home?"

"I'll try," Theo said. "I can't promise anything."

"How's Major?" Richard asked.

"Good, he'll get you home tomorrow, but his hunting days are over."

"Right," Tama said. "Theo, you see to the dogs. Richard, go and get some tree fern fronds, the young ones, and some tips off the supplejack. Make sure you clean them up and they can go in the pan with some pork belly for tea. It's too late to leave

now, we'll camp one more night and leave in the morning. You two all right with that?"
Richard and Theo looked at each other. "All good," Richard confirmed.

**

The next morning Tama woke early and found Theo with the horses.
"How's the dog?"
"Dead," replied Theo. "Ribs were crushed too badly."
"Thought so," Tama remarked. "Bloody nuisance, it took a long time to get it trained, Shame it didn't have any pups."

**

Two hours later, the trio were riding slowly along the banks of the Mokau River.
"So what did you decide yesterday, about killing people I mean?" Richard asked Theo.
"I couldn't do it. It's wrong," Theo's response was immediate.
"So what would you do in a war then?"
"I think I would eventually like to be a doctor, so, if there is going to be a war, I'd like to think I could help the wounded in some way. What about you two?"
"Don't know," Richard said. "What do you reckon Tama?"
"It could be a good adventure?" Tama replied. "We'd get to France and Europe. Might see some of those places Miss Tallboys told us about at school. Paris, even. There must be some sort of holiday so we'd get out and look around. I can't see us getting there any other way."
"Reckon you could be right," Richard agreed. "Worth thinking about eh? If Theo here is going to be a doctor, what do you reckon you could do when you get back?"
"Haven't said I'm going yet. But a lawyer I reckon."
"A lawyer?" Richard quizzed. "Whoever's heard of a Māori lawyer?"
"You have now," Tama said with confidence. "I've spent my life listening to my mother and Auntie Atarangi. Hearing how passionate they are about doing what's right for Māori. Yeah,

a lawyer I reckon, or maybe get into Parliament. Somewhere I can make a difference. You?"

Richard thought for a moment. "A farmer I suppose. Someone has to stay and look after Llanon. Never thought I'd do anything else."

The rest of the journey was spent at a slow pace as the three men talked amongst themselves, occasionally drifting into silence. They came into familiar territory as Llanon drew near.

"You did a good job on Major, Doctor Theo" Richard said. "Reckon you're wasted on people, you should stick to horses".

Theo laughed. "Who knows what lies ahead in these times?" he said as he smiled to himself just as Sean came out the front door.

"There you are son, are you all right? That's a good looking pig you've got there."

"It cost me my best dog," Tama said. "Ripped it wide open and crushed it."

"That's the way with these boars, you don't get to be that old in the bush without learning a few tricks," Sean said. "How did Major go?"

"Pulled up lame on the first day," Richard replied.

"Thought he might," Sean replied.

"You knew that?" Richard sounded astonished. "Then why did you let me take him?"

"I wanted to see what you'd do with him," Sean answered.

"That's hardly fair," Richard started arguing.

"Life's not fair," Sean replied. "It's what you do about it that counts. You did well bringing him back in as good a condition as you did."

Theo looked up at Richard, expecting some acknowledgement for his work on Major's fetlock, but nothing came. Instead he took Sean's praise for his own.

Tama said his goodbyes as he headed downriver to Te Kainga.

"I'll hang the pig then we can butcher him," he called out to the others as he kicked his horse into a trot along the banks of the Mokau.

Sean turned to Richard. "Come inside for a minute will you. I've got some bad news to tell you, about Lucky."

**

Megan hesitated in packing her bag for the journey back to New Plymouth. She turned to Gwyneth with a face that held a long held anxiety.
"Gwyn, are you sure you are doing the right thing going to see David Askill?"
"I am even more convinced now than I was before," Gwyneth replied. "After all, what have I got to lose? Ngaire is right, I have to face up to challenges and not shrink back."
Owen McConaghy brought the *Heron* up to the Jetty as Sean, Richard and Sarah said their goodbyes to Megan and Gwyneth.
"I expect we'll get to New Plymouth over the next month or so," Sean said to Megan. "So we'll see you then and call in for a cup of tea and some of your Welsh Cakes."
"There's enough in the pantry now to last a month, though probably not enough for you," Megan laughed. She looked over to Gwyneth who was busy talking to Owen so she took her chance to take Sean to one side and spoke quietly.
"Sean, you will be patient with Gwyn over the few weeks won't you?"
"Aren't I always?" Sean remarked, surprised at the request from Megan. "What's brought this on?"
"Oh nothing much," Megan said. "You know she's seeing the doctor today, women's problems if you know what I mean."
"I wish she would let me come with her" Sean replied.
"No, she's better off on her own, a bit of solitude will do her good. Take it from another woman."
"Say no more," Sean said. "Patience is my middle name."

**

Two hours later Megan and Gwyneth stood on the Mokau wharf. The wind was cold and blew smoke down from the funnel of the *SS Kapuni*.
"Do think again about what you are doing and the harm it can cause Gwyn love" Megan said to break the silence. "It's not too late to go home and put David to the back of your mind."

"It's no use Mother. My mind is made up and that's all there is to it."
"Well, at least let me come with you?" Megan pleaded.
"No. I'm doing this on my own and that's final," Gwyneth said stepping away from Megan to close the conversation.
After the *Kapuni* left, Gwyneth walked back towards the doctor's surgery.
Moonyeen was sweeping the front veranda of the hotel with a besom when she noticed Gwyneth. She kept her head down pretending not to notice, but when Gwyneth was out of sight she quickly followed her. Once she was sure Gwyneth was going to the surgery she turned back to the hotel with a smile on her face.
The surgery was a small, modest house set back off the main road. It had plain timber panelling, painted cream with green trim and finials.
Gwyneth had occasionally, in her very lonely times in Canterbury, secretly thought of meeting David again; but that was only a dream, a fantasy. The reality before her now was never how she imagined it might be. She took a deep breath and knocked on the open door but there was no answer. She took some tentative steps into the hallway, it was dark with scrim showing on the otherwise bare timber walls. Gwyneth was taken back by the austerity. She called out in a faint voice.
"Hello, is there anybody here?"
A man's voice, deep and smooth answered.
"Hold on for a minute if you please. I'll be out very soon."
In a few minutes an elderly lady came through the door, she looked back.
"Thank you doctor…thank you. I must say it's good to have you here…in Mokau, we've waited so long for our own doctor."
"Well, it's very nice to be here" the voice replied making Gwyneth more panicky than ever. She could hear footsteps coming towards the hall and she didn't know what to do, she wanted to hide as she suddenly realised she was not prepared for this moment. She thought she would be strong but she felt the strength draining from her legs and she grabbed the back of a wooden chair. She immediately wanted to be taken away, back to Llanon, to Sean and her family, but in that same

second David Askill appeared in the doorway. Gwyneth couldn't help but stare at him. His wavy hair was still as fair and his eyes as blue as Gwyneth remembered. He was as tall but heavier with a paunch showing through his waistcoat.
"Please, come in," he said indicating to the small room. Flustered, Gwyneth put her head down and walked in. She wasn't sure if the heat she felt in her face was from the embarrassment of meeting David after a quarter of a century or from the fire in the hearth. She felt herself sitting down as David sat himself across from a large desk. He looked at her quizzically.
I…I…I don't really know…I mean to say …I don't really need to be here," Gwyneth stuttered apologetically, staring at the floorboards.
David sat back in his chair for a moment as a warm smile appeared on his face making his eyes crinkle up and sparkle. Gwyneth looked up and the years disappeared and she felt as though once again she was a bumbling student nurse in the presence of an eminent doctor.
David spoke quietly and deliberately.
"Good afternoon Gwyneth Thomas. I've travelled a long way to see you."
"You… you remember me?" Gwyneth croaked, staring at David.
"Of course I remember you, why wouldn't I. I've spent the last year travelling all over the South Island searching for you and now here you in Mokau."
"You've been looking for me? I…I don't understand," Gwyneth replied, finding her voice. "I made a fool of myself over you all those years ago. I…I loved you, or at least I thought I did, at least as much as an eighteen year old girl could love somebody. Then I found out you were engaged to be married to Genevieve Westmorland."
David pulled himself up in his chair.
"Is that why you suddenly left Cardiff?" he asked sitting forward.
"Yes, yes of course, I made such a fool of myself. I couldn't possibly stay there at the infirmary or the workhouse."
"I didn't realise that" David replied.

"My parents were planning to migrate to New Zealand, so coming here with them was an escape from the mess I had made for myself," Gwyneth admitted. She was surprised how easy it was to admit her feelings for the first time. It made her feel surprisingly liberated from her troubled past. "You must have thought me to be a real idiot?" she asked of David.
"Nothing could be further from the truth," David said. "I'm surprised you thought that. I remember you as a dedicated student who empathised with the patients like nobody else could. I remember a volunteer at the workhouse who loved those children like they were her own."
Gwyneth sat down silently listening to David's words in disbelief.
"However you felt about yourself Gwyneth, it certainly wasn't how others saw you, you can be assured of that. It's why I've been searching for you for the last year."
He changed the subject. "I hear you are married and have two fine children," he said looking down at Gwyneth's ring finger.
"How did you know?"
"Stella Ratcliffe at the hotel told me. The Chinese woman, Moonyeen Wu, told me a bit about you and your family as well."
Gwyneth held back any comments she thought about making. "Yes, yes. I'm...a...married to Sean, Sean Murphy. We have two children, Richard, the eldest and Sarah."
"And you?" Gwyneth asked David. "I don't see a wedding ring, what happened to Genevieve Westmorland?"
David sat back and gave a small laugh to himself. "Genevieve was a funny woman. Being the only daughter of a wealthy industrialist she usually got what she wanted. One of those was a doctor for a husband. It wasn't love, not really. I soon came to realise I would have been a trophy for her mantelpiece, somebody to be seen out with."
"That must have hurt," Gwyneth said quietly.
"Well it took some time to realise but thank goodness it was before the wedding so I broke off the engagement."
"How did she take it?" Gwyneth quizzed.
"Not at all well at the time, her father considered suing for breach of promise but that wouldn't have looked good in the newspapers."

"So what happened to Genevieve?"
"In less than a month would you believe, she had a merchant banker on her arm. Two months later they were married. Now they live in London, Mayfair no less, with a suite at Claridge's Hotel I hear."
"How do you feel about that?"
"A lucky escape I suppose," David said with a shrug of his shoulders.
"Has there been anybody since?"
"No. Not really. I'm married to my work you might say."
"How about the workhouse at Cowbridge Road? I really enjoyed working there," Gwyneth said gaining confidence by the minute. "There was one boy, an abandoned baby. A big lad for his age so you named him Arthur Gould after the rugby player."
David laughed.
"Yes, the captain of the Welsh rugby team in the Home Nations Championship that year," David said smiling. "Arthur went from being a big boy to an even bigger man. Except now he's heading towards thirty years of age. Like his namesake, he played rugby for Cardiff as well, not bad either. He's a dentist now, a gentle giant you might say and he volunteers at the workhouse when he can."
"That's really good to hear," Gwyneth said with a note of excitement.
"Yes, a few of the children come back as adults and help in some way. They all remember you and speak kindly of you."
"They remember me?" Gwyneth was perplexed.
"Yes, of course," David replied. "You were one of the few nurses who took the time to talk to the children, not only about what they did that day but about their dreams. You took them out of the situation they were in and helped them to realise they had a future. You didn't scold them as the others did and neither did you look down on them just because they were orphans. You helped them to believe they could be anything they wanted, an engineer, a lawyer, even a merchant banker. Not many nurses were able to reach out and touch the children as you did Gwyneth."
"I never realised," she replied, embarrassed at David's words. She gained enough courage to speak candidly.

"You said you've been looking for me over the last year."
"I have indeed," David said. "I knew you went to the South Island, Canterbury. You said as much before you left so that's where I started my search. It took some time but I stayed here and there making myself useful as doctors can. I finally found your neighbours. If you can call people who live miles away neighbours, Bill, and Anna McKendrick, they told me you moved here."
"The McKendrick's are good people. But why David, why have you wasted a year looking for me?"
David got up and walked about the room.
"The year hasn't been wasted Gwyneth. To be honest with you..." David hesitated for a moment, "I...uhh...I did want to see you again. You see it's not only the children who remember you for being somebody special. I know it's not right to say that, but it's how I feel. You see the past doesn't stay in the past does it? But there is a higher reason for finding you, apart from my own selfish reasons. The workhouse has changed and it's moving forward, but not how I want it to, not entirely anyway. We have almost a thousand children there now. All we can do is feed them and put a roof over their heads for a few days, only to send them back to the streets to beg or to be taken away for cheap labour. We can't help them like you did Gwyneth, we cannot give them hope or dreams like you did. We've got to do more, we really do."
"But anybody can do what I did. All it takes is time to listen and talk."
"No. Not anybody, Gwyneth, we've tried, believe me, we've tried."
Gwyneth was astounded at hearing what David was telling her.
"You're, you're still at the workhouse as well as the infirmary?" she asked.
"No. Sorry, I didn't tell you. Five years ago, the union offered me the post of vice chairman of the board of governors at the workhouse so I left the infirmary. That allowed me to take a year's sabbatical to find you in the hope you would come back."
"I beg your pardon?" Gwyneth said dumbfounded at the remark.

David sat down at his desk and leaned forward. "You see Gwyneth. The orphanage as you knew it is no more. The main building is still there of course but there are so many children. They are sent out to what we call 'scattered housing', separate houses all around Cardiff so it's a lot more difficult to reach out to them. We need to monitor the homes where they go and make sure the children do what they are supposed to. It's only you who can do that Gwyneth. So the real reason I wanted to find you is to ask you to come back to Wales, to Cardiff, and help grow good people like Arthur Gould. That's why I came looking for you."

Chapter Four

**

The thin timber walls of the milking shed at Llanon gave no challenge to the bitterly cold air as Richard and Sean stomped their feet on the concrete floor and flapped their arms around themselves in an effort to get their blood circulating on a frosty August morning.
"Is mother all right?" Richard asked as he blew into his cupped hands in an effort to warm them up once more for milking. "Only she's been so far away lately, like her minds somewhere else. She spends so much time talking to Auntie Ngaire."
"It's nothing to worry about," Sean replied. "Your nana told me its women's problems, so best not to mention it if you know what I mean."
"Well it's been going on for some time now," Richard said. "It's like she's always thinking of something else, and she gets mad quite quickly. I just want the normal mother back."
"You're not the only one there," Sean said. "I'll try and have another word with her soon, I can't do more than that can I now?"
The door of the shed suddenly flew open giving Sean and Richard a fright. It banged against the wall, almost bouncing back towards Sarah who stood there with her arm out, gasping in excitement and waving a newspaper.
"Richard, Father. England has declared war on Germany. Owen McConaghy just dropped off some newspapers for me. We're at war. Imagine!"
"Give me that," Richard said snatching the newspaper from Sarah.
"It's two weeks old," he said surprised.
"Yes," Sarah said. "We've been at war for a whole fortnight and didn't even know it. What are we going to do Father? Will Richard be going to war?"

"I won't have any of that talk from either of you, don't either of you say anything to your mother, I mean it, I'll tell her myself. I'll see George and Libby then go over to Te Kainga and see Wirimu and Ngaire, they won't know yet either. You two finish up here and not a word, do you understand? Not a word."

**

Richard, Tama, and Theo stood on the foredeck of the *Kapuni* facing into a bracing southerly wind. The occasional spray from the ship's bow as it pushed through a heavy swell spilled over them as it steamed towards the breakwater at New Plymouth.
"So what are we doing, are we signing up or not?" Richard asked looking to the others for a decision.
"I'm in," Tama said. "It will be an adventure, isn't that what we talked about before?"
"It's all right for you," Richard answered. "Your parents would support your decision. Mine would be against me going."
"But we'd only be going for a few months," Tama answered back. "Home by Christmas they say. Think about it, it's spring over there, we'd have two summers back to back and see a bit of the world. Put it this way, by next Christmas would you rather sit around the farm and talk about milking cows or seeing the Eiffel Tower?"
"I'll be signing up even if you don't," Tama said. "What about you Theo?"
"I'll see. I'll talk to the recruitment people first. I won't fight but I need to help Britain somehow."
"Richard?"
"I'll join if we all join at the same time," Richard replied.
The three young men all looked at each other. Tama held out his hand palm down, Theo followed putting his hand on top then Richard did the same.
"So we all sign up together?" Richard asked.
"We'll drink to it," Tama added.
They stepped on shore and went straight to the Breakwater Hotel.
"Three large whiskeys please," Tama ordered.

"Steady on," Theo said. "I've never drunk whiskey before."
"Well you've never been to war before either, so make this the first and we'll toast to a great adventure. The next time we have a whiskey together will be back in this very bar when it's all over," Tama said raising his glass. The other two raised theirs.
"To a great adventure," Tama said.
"To a great adventure," repeated Richard and Theo as their glasses touched.
They downed the whiskey with Theo coughing violently. Tama laughed and slapped him on the back. "Come on my friend, we'll make a man of you yet."
On the way out, the barman stopped them. "You lads going to sign up then?"
"What makes you say that?" Tama asked.
"You ain't the first to drink a toast like that today and you won't be the last I reckon. Any more volunteers and there won't be enough bloody boats to put them all in. I 'ope the Kaiser knows what 'e's in for, that's all I can say."
"See you in three months" Richard said.
"I bloody well 'ope so mate, I bloody well 'ope so," the barman replied.

**

Later that week, Sean, Gwyneth, George, and Libby sat around the dinner table at the request of Richard and Theo.
"I think I know what you want to talk about," Gwyneth said to Richard.
"What's that Mother?"
"You want to ask our blessing to sign up to go to the war don't you?"
"Something like that" Richard replied.
"What do you mean 'something like that'? Either you do or you don't," Sean said tersely. "Don't play with us boy."
Richard look hurt at being called a boy by his father.
"What Richard means, Mr Murphy," Theo interrupted, taking the initiative. "It's just that we've already signed up."
There was a stunned silence in the room. Gwyneth burst into tears and ran out.

"Stay where you are boy," Sean demanded standing up at the table and pointing at Richard.
"No, I won't," Richard answered back standing up surprising even himself as he challenged his father for the first time in his life. Sean ignored him and went out to talk to Gwyneth with Richard following leaving Theo with George and Libby.
"Why did you decide to do this?" George quietly asked Theo.
"We...Richard, Tama and me all agreed to sign up at the same time on the way to New Plymouth a few days ago. It's so we could stick together. We even shook hands on it."
"You'd have to kill," George remarked looking directly at Theo. "You know what the Bible says about that don't you? How do you reconcile going to war just because your friends are?"
"I haven't signed up for the same as the others," Theo replied. "Richard and Tama are in the 11th Taranaki Rifles Regiment. I've signed up for the medical corps, the First Field Ambulance to be precise. We won't be fighting, we'll be saving lives."
"So you won't be with Richard and Tama then?"
"Well initially, at the beginning for training maybe, but we'll be split up later on I expect."
"And Tama?" Libby asked tearfully.
"He's telling Uncle Wirimu and Auntie Ngaire tonight as well."
"When do you leave?"
"In about two weeks' time," Theo replied. "We'll be catching a train to take us to Trentham for military training. I'll write whenever I can of course and like Richard says, we'll all be home for Christmas. It'll be an adventure."
"You think war will be an adventure?" said a very angry Sean from the doorway. "Do you think well trained Germans aiming their rifles at you and pulling the trigger will be an adventure?"
"Well, I won't be in the thick of it Mr Murphy."
"No but Richard and Tama will be, along with thousands of other young men from the other side of the world. Bloody English."

**

The noise of the crowds cheering and waving was almost deafening as two weeks later, New Plymouth's Devon Street came to a standstill. Bunting was strewn on the shop verandas and people lined the footpaths. Megan, Sean, Gwyneth, Wirimu, Ngaire, George and Libby crowded around Richard, Tama and Theo as they prepared to march down Devon Street to the railway station with the thousand other volunteers.

"I never expected such a crowd," Gwyneth said. "I've brought the camera. I thought we could get a photograph of everybody together on such a celebration."

"This isn't a celebration," Sean said. "Our children going off to war with all the other children you have taught at Murata School certainly isn't something I want to celebrate or remember. By the looks of it every boy under twenty is leaving Taranaki. I certainly won't be in any photograph, especially today of all days. It's a day I'd rather forget and that's for sure."

"Perhaps I am getting a little carried away with it all," Gwyneth said trying to fight off the emotion. "Maybe just a photograph of the three of you boys then?"

Richard, Tama and Theo stood smiling side by side with their arms around each other for a photograph. As soon as Gwyneth pressed the camera shutter it was as though she had walked through a door to a different life. She couldn't help but cry as did Megan and Ngaire. It was only Libby who kept her composure.

"I think you're being called into line," she said pointing to the army officer shouting orders.

Still Ngaire wouldn't let go of Tama.

"Kia kaha. Stand strong, remember your turangawaewae and your tipuna. You are Ngati Maniapoto, you are from a line of warrior chiefs, always remember that."

Theo shook George's hand and George pulled him in.

"May the Lord be with you son. Your mother and I will pray for you every night, for all three of you," George whispered.

Richard turned towards Sean who walked away afraid to show his tears.

"Goodbye... Father." Richard could scarcely get the words out. "I love you," he muttered. Sean turned and rushed into Richard with a hug nearly cracking Richard's ribs as he broke down.

"Goodbye son. You are not going with my blessing but I know you are going anyway. I'll make sure there's enough work for you when you get back."

"Look lively you lot!" came the shout from the officer as the three men dissolved into ranks of other young men preparing to march down Devon Street to what they believed was to be the adventure of a lifetime.

**

Gwyneth took a break from turning the butter churner to wipe the sweat from her brow. "I wonder what Richard's doing today?" she said. "It's been over a month now and still no word."

"His time's not his own anymore with all the training I expect," Sarah replied.

"Well at least he's like his father and enjoys hard work. I've been thinking, we need to order newspapers now rather than wait for Owen to drop off the old, dog-eared copies as a favour when he can."

"Yes Mother – that would be good," a delighted Sarah said. "It sounds like a lot of the soldiers are preparing to go to France and we need to know what's happening to Richard's regiment."

"Do you really think it will all be over quickly Sarah?" Gwyneth asked. "You read the news when you can. Be honest."

"We've got a lot more soldiers than they have and we're better trained but I don't know Mother, all we can do is hope."

"And pray," Gwyneth added.

"Father will know better than me," Sarah told her

"I doubt it, he just shuts himself off to these things. All he does is bury himself in the farm or the mill ever since we lost half the workers to the war, and when he's here, he doesn't say much at all. I know he misses Richard as much as any of us but he needs to talk about it. Thank goodness I've got you."

Sarah chose not to reply but busied herself in her tasks.

**

"I'm going to see Mother this Thursday," Gwyneth announced at the dinner table. "I'll be there for a few days."
"Who's going to take your place here?" Sean asked without looking up.
"George and Libby said they could cover, the cows are almost dry now anyway," Gwyneth said. "There's enough meat in the safe and preserves in the pantry for you."
She suddenly felt the room was empty of any warmth, of any feeling or of any support for how she felt. The feeling closed in around her and she thought back to when her parents were there with Wirimu and Ngaire and the house was full of music. She got up and played a few notes of *Calon Lan* on the piano. "For you, Father," she muttered to herself before she closed the cover and walked out realising it wasn't just the house that felt empty.

**

David Askill was talking to Moonyeen at the Mokau wharf when Gwyneth arrived on the *Heron*.
"Mrs Murphy. It is nice to see you. How is Richard in the army?" Moonyeen asked.
"He is doing his duty Moonyeen, as are all the other young men along the Mokau and everywhere else it seems."
Moonyeen smiled and made her excuses to leave.
"I thought I wouldn't see you again," David said. "Will you walk along the river with me?"
"What was that woman telling you?" Gwyneth almost demanded of David as they started their walk.
"Moonyeen? She was telling me the history of Mokau and some of the people. She's had an interesting background. She was telling me of her father and brother in Arrowtown and how she had to help them survive."
"Did she say anything about Sean or me?"
"She had only good things to say about both of you."
"Nothing else?" Gwyneth asked sharply.
"No – I can't imagine there would be anything but good things."

"I'm sorry David. I've been a bit on edge lately."
"Not surprisingly," David replied. "You've seen your only son go off to war. Nobody should have to do that."
David was silent for a moment. "I did want to talk with you Gwyneth; about the job …in Wales."
"You couldn't possibly ask me to decide now David. I have too much on my mind with Richard and the farm."
"No, of course not" David replied. "But my sabbatical is coming to an end soon, but on my desk is a letter asking to extend it for another six months, I know it will be granted, but I must return when that ends or I will have been away too long. When that time comes, there will always be a place for a doctor and trained nurse if you don't mind working your passage."
"I worked as a nurse on the *Tongariro* when we left Wales," Gwyneth said nostalgically. "I didn't have to, but I wanted to do something useful you see."
"That's the Gwyneth Thomas I remember," David said. "I can't ask you to make your mind up now, I wouldn't expect you to. But can I ask you to think about it over the next few months? Enough time for you to get yourself sorted if your husband agrees of course. I'll come to your house and talk with him if it would do any good."
"No, that won't be necessary," Gwyneth immediately replied, taking David by surprise.
"Well the offer is there."
"No," Gwyneth repeated. "My mind is made up. You said last time we met that the past never stays in the past. Well, in my house it does. I don't want any of this or you on my property, it's bad enough that it's in my head. Don't get me wrong David, it's been good to see you again. I often hoped I would, it must be the romantic in me but you do belong in my past. I appreciate the job offer of course and I wish you well with your work, but it will happen without me."

**

The journey to New Plymouth was a confusing one for Gwyneth. She felt both proud and disappointed in her answer to David. She knew she couldn't leave the river and her responsibilities but she felt unfulfilled as Llanon and the school no longer held a place in her heart. She wanted to take up David's offer more than anything but she was more than aware of her duty and responsibility to stay with her family.

**

"Did you see David? Megan asked as soon as she was with Gwyneth.
"Twice actually" Gwyneth said. "When I went to see him as I said I would and again on the way here, in Mokau."
"Well, what did he want?" Megan asked impatiently.
"He wanted me to go back to Wales with him."
"He what?"
"He's the vice chairman of the board of governors at the Cowbridge Road workhouse now. There have been changes to how the children are looked after and David is concerned for them so he wants me to take over their welfare."
"What did you tell him?"
Gwyneth hesitated looking out the window of the tea rooms onto Devon Street.
"I...I told him my place was at Llanon, with Sean and he should go back home to Wales without me."
"Well I should jolly well hope so," Megan said. "But can you turn around to look me in the face and say that Gwyn?"
Gwyneth maintained her stare into the street as she quietly wept.
"No, I didn't think so," Megan told her. "There's few people who can lie to their mother. Surely you cannot think about going back now after all these years, leaving Sean and your family?"
"I told you Mother, I told David my place is here. If you're going to question me over it time and time again I'll go and stay at the hotel. Just leave me alone will you?"

**

"Another drink?" Stella Ratcliffe asked David. "On the house this time, for all the good you are doing in the district."

"That's very kind of you Stella. Just the one more then," David said. "To keep me warm on the walk back to the surgery."
"If you don't mind me saying, it's more than a whiskey you'll be needing to keep you warm tonight."
David gave her a knowing look but said nothing.
"With a good looking man like yourself, you can't tell me there's not a woman waiting for you back in Wales?"
"Ahhh. If only, if only," David smiled to himself staring at the whiskey tumbler. "It sounds like there's somebody special in mind," Stella probed.
"Well you're a fine one to talk," David said. "An attractive woman such as you, financially independent and your wits about you. What happened to Mr Ratcliffe?"
"There never was a Mr Ratcliffe" Stella said staring at her glass. "I used to own the Mokau Gentlemen's Club so I know what men, or at least what a lot of men are like, so, I leaned not to trust any of them from an early age."
"Moonyeen told me a little about the place, it sounds colourful to say the least."
"Well Moonyeen and I have been together for many years, we depend on each other to know what's going on around the traps."
"But there must have been one man for you," David said trying to pry into Stella's life. The hotel had emptied by this time and Stella was in a reflective mood.
"Well, not a professional man like yourself. But there was a man, a rogue who had a violent streak, a very violent streak at times. He used to bring the prostitutes to me from Wellington when I had the Big House, that's what everybody called the Gentlemen's Club."
David laughed quietly.
Stella went on. "No questions were asked and cash wasn't the only currency if you get my meaning. That's when he wasn't involved in crooked card games or sordid deals with sea captains to overload ships regardless of the consequences."
"You must have loved him a lot," David said.
"Yes, yes I did, though nobody ever understood why."
"That's easy," David said. "He was your villain, the man from the wrong side of town, he understood you and you understood him. That's why you both accepted each other

without judgement or tension. You could relax with him and be yourself without being judged for it."
Stella was dumbstruck.
"That the first time anybody has ever put it in words doctor, thank you. You have a good insight into people."
"Well, doing the work I do, I need to read people and see what their needs are."
"And what are my needs?" Stella pushed.
"Apart from the obvious?" David asked smiling.
Stella laughed.
"I think you are a very lonely woman Stella Ratcliffe. I don't mean just for a man but for people to care for, family. I think you have a big heart but you hide it behind the façade of a hard exterior. You want people to think that of you, but secretly, you yearn for the kind of love only a family can give. Tell me, this man you loved, what happened to him?"
"He died…he died in the fire at the Big House a long time ago."
Stella filled up the glasses.
"What was his name?"
"Marco, Marco Cacavalli." Stella started to fondle the gold chain around her neck. "This chain was his," she told David. "He wore it everywhere. It's all I have to remember him by. He'd still be alive today if it wasn't for Sean Murphy."
David stopped in his tracks and looked at Stella incredulously.
"What do you mean? Are you saying that Sean caused Marco's death?"
Stella hesitated.
"I've never spoken of this before, not to anybody," she said looking around the room. "I promised Sean I never would."
"Promised him what?" David asked. "You can tell me, I'm a doctor, I know how to keep a confidence."
"Marco and Sean never got on," Stella told David. "I said Marco was violent at times. Whenever he went to Wellington to find me girls for the Big House, Moonyeen used to go with him. Quite a few of the girls were Chinese you see, and Moonyeen used to speak with them in their own language so they knew what they were getting themselves into. Marco often made a play for Moonyeen but she always turned him

away. Secretly, she wanted Sean all along, and she got him in the end."

"Let me get this straight," David said leaning forward with all his wits about him. "Sean Murphy all but killed this Marco of yours and had an affair with Moonyeen?"

"Still is having an affair as far as I know," Stella revealed.

"Who knows about this?"

"Just about everybody…except his wife of course."

"Gwyneth?"

"Yes, the naive Gwyneth."

"So what's Marco got to do with all of this? You said he died at Sean's hand?"

"Marco attacked Moonyeen one day."

"What do you mean, attacked?"

Stella stared at the table.

"He raped her. He beat her to the ground then he raped her."

"You said he had a vicious streak but I didn't realise it went to that extent."

"I cannot excuse it, but in reality it was sometimes the price of the trade I was in. Moonyeen knew that as well."

"But to do that to somebody is inexcusable, unconscionable".

"Well it happened, that's the simple fact of it," Stella admitted. "Sean found out about it and one way or another, it ended in a fight. Sean was stabbed and nearly lost his life over it. Of course, being Irish he never forgot it. His chance to get even came one night when he and Marco were in the Big House. They had a set-to, but during the course of the fight a fire started. Long story short, Sean came out of it and Marco didn't. His body was all burned, charred to a crisp but it was plain to see his legs had been broken. Sean took off back to the wharf where he had the *Heron* moored and went home telling me to swear on a sackful of Bibles that he was never in the Big House that night. It was Joe Dickson and me who found Marco's body the next day. Joe and Betty owned this hotel then. They moved on soon after and I bought it, so, here I am now, all but twenty years later, half-drunk and spilling my soul to a complete stranger."

"Surely the police were involved?" David was totally absorbed by this time.

"For about a day," Stella said. "They wanted to see the back of Marco as much as Sean did, so let's say the investigation said that Marco's death was accidental…"
David incredulous at what he had heard.
"Thank you Stella" he said downing the last gulp of whiskey. "Thank you very much indeed."

**

"My heart tells me to go back to Wales," Gwyneth told Ngaire on her way back to Llanon. "In Wales we have an expression; 'hiraeth'. A lot of people confuse it with being homesick but it's more than that, it a longing to be at the place where you belong, where you came from and where you need to be, all rolled into one."
"It's your turangawaewae," Ngaire said. "You remember Gwyn, it's why I came back here after 'he' died. It's where I knew I had to be. Does Sean understand?" Ngaire asked.
"All Sean understands is the need to bury himself in his work. It's his way of coping with Richard going to war." Gwyneth hesitated, staring into the distance. "My god Ngaire, where have the past six months disappeared to? I've gone from having everything to virtually nothing. Richard has gone, Sean may as well be gone. All those boys we taught at Murata School are being trained for war. We taught them how to read and write, to share and look after each other, and now the world is teaching them to hate and to kill. What will they be like when they come back Ngaire, if they come back that is? And now my past is right back before me. The first man I ever loved is here as large as life and he's offering me a place in the world which I want more than anything with all of my heart. I head is saying I have to do my duty and stay here. I have to be the obedient wife and play the part of the successful farmer's wife. What's gone wrong Ngaire? What's bloody well gone wrong? Just where in the last few years did I leave the real me behind," Gwyneth blubbered, crying uncontrollably as Ngaire took her in her arms.

"I was once in the place you are now," she said. "When "he' died and I had to appear to be the dutiful wife."
"I remember," Gwyneth snivelled.
"But I let others think what they wanted to think," Ngaire said. "I followed my heart. That's all I can say to you. You need to make up your own mind to do what's right for you. That's no answer I know but it's the only one I can give."
Gwyneth broke down completely, convulsing in Ngaire's arms. After a few moments she pulled away, wiping her eyes.
"I know I have to stay" she sobbed. "That's all there is to it."

Chapter Five

**

Mother, Father!" Sarah shouted from the *Heron* moored alongside the jetty as she started to run up the riverbank with her dress hoisted up with both hands.
Gwyneth appeared in the doorway. "What's all the fuss about?"
"Look," Sarah replied, reaching the doorway, hardly able to breathe. She furiously waved an envelope in the air. "Look, it's a letter, from Richard!"
"Your father's out with the stock somewhere," Gwyneth said excitedly. "Quickly, go and get him. I'll wait here and make some tea."
Half an hour later Sean all but ran into the house.
"Where is it? The letter?"
"Right here on the table," Gwyneth said. "Sean, can I open it?"
"Of course but hurry up about it."
Gwyneth ripped the envelope open in her haste, read the first few lines to herself, and started crying.
"What is it Mother?" Sarah asked. "What's wrong?"
"Oh nothing, it's just seeing Richard's handwriting again."
"Read it out loud," Sean told her.
Gwyneth smiled and cleared her throat.

> Dear Mother, Father and Sarah
> I hope this finds you well. I'm sorry I haven't written before but the army keeps me busy day and night. I am enjoying the training. It's hard work and most of us sleep when we can. I am well, as is Tama. I don't see much of Theo now as he is with the medical corps but Tama and me see each other most days. I have seen Charlie Dobson on occasion too.
> Training is enjoyable, especially the rifle practise where I do well. Yesterday I beat Tama and I joked that he

would have to attack the enemy with his knife if he were to stand any chance. He still carries his hunting knife under his uniform where the officers cannot see it. We also train with bayonets which is close combat as I am sure you are aware, but there's no need to worry Mother as I am hoping I don't get that close to the Germans when the time comes. It seems we will never get there at this rate anyway as the departure seems to get further away if the rumours are anything to go by. The Trentham camp is large with hundreds of bell tents which are quite crowded. There are no groundsheets to speak of and our uniforms get damp so when the wind blows we are quite grateful to dry out when we can. Worst of all are the great coats which are very heavy when they are wet. I often think of my oilskins hanging in the milking shed and wish I could use those instead. They are far more practical. The food is very plain and what I wouldn't give for a leg of lamb or some of Nana's Welsh Cakes.

There are rumours that we will be leaving New Zealand for Egypt in a month or so then the real adventure will begin. Charlie Dobson who seems to know these things says there are several thousand horses being held in Wellington ready to be shipped out with us. I will try and write before we leave.

My love to you all
Richard.

"Richard's right about the horses, it was in the newspaper" Sarah said, still high on excitement.
"Of course he's right," Gwyneth added. "He's there and seeing it all firsthand."
She sat at the piano re-reading the letter all morning before she put it in the top drawer of the sideboard.
"I'll go and see Libby, she may have heard from Theo, then tomorrow I'll walk over to Te Kainga and see Ngaire."

**

Two weeks later Sarah was waiting at the jetty for the *Heron* to arrive with the latest newspapers.

"It's all on Miss Sarah," Owen McConaghy said as the boat slowed and he waved the newspaper in the air. "Our boys are heading out to Egypt all right. See, it's all in here."

"Any letters?" Sarah asked hopefully.

"Sorry love, nothing for you today, but there is one for George and Libby," he declared with a smile on his face. "From Theo no doubt. A good lad he is writing like that. You'd be surprised the families who don't get anything at all from their boys."

"Leave it with me," Sarah told him. "Uncle George and Father are out in the fields somewhere and Auntie Libby and Mother are with Auntie Ngaire.

Sarah looked at the letter, thinking for a moment. "Just imagine Mr McConaghy, Theo is going to Egypt. The mystery and romance of it all is truly incredible."

"Anybody would think you're sweet on him," Owen teased.

Sarah blushed. "Don't be silly Mr McConaghy, he's a friend, a family friend and I'm just concerned for him, that's all."

**

In the late afternoon, George and Libby made a cup of tea. Libby poured while George opened their letter and read it out.

> Dear Mother and Father
> How are you both? I am well and I have to say a lot fitter than I have ever been. I thought that farm work was hard but the training has led me to believe I have muscles in places I never knew I had, which explains my tired state. The word is we are to sail to Egypt very soon, at least by the middle of October. If that is the case this is the last letter you will have from me in New Zealand.
> I am excited to be seeing the pyramids and all the history around Egypt. I am hoping I will have time to get to the museums. If I can, I will get a piece of the pyramids, just a small piece to bring back to you as a souvenir of my travels. Just to be where Moses fought

with the Pharaoh and the ten plagues happened will be truly special. I cannot wait.

I am attached to a field medical unit as it seems even the most rudimentary knowledge of first aid is enough to have such a job.

Do not be concerned Mother but we have been training to do our work under fire. I know you had hoped I would not be involved in combat and that is true, I won't be, but even though I cannot kill another man I have my duty to the Empire and to my fellow soldiers so we will be victorious.

My decision to eventually become a doctor has been reinforced by what I have seen around me over the last month. Many of my colleagues are medical people of course and I am privileged to be with them. It is a wonderful thing to help relieve suffering. I have made many friends in the Medical Corps but of all of them, Dickie Fleming is a real chum. He and I get on well and Dickie understands that I am not versed in many medical ways so he helps me. In all, they are a good bunch of comrades and I could not hope for better.

In what spare time I have, I spend with the horses. I have never seen so many in one place at one time, some say there are over three thousand. From what I have seen, they will travel in the confines of the holds in the transport ships where there is little ventilation and certainly no means of exercise. This is a cruelty for such noble creatures and I am hoping I can help some of them on the voyage in some way.

I have not seen Richard or Tama for some weeks but we are in different units so that is expected. I am hoping we will meet up in Egypt, God willing.

I miss you both very much but please know I am in the right place and with your prayers I will be safe.

I am hoping my next letter will be sent from Egypt.

God Bless

Theo

PS Please pass my best wishes to everybody, especially Sarah.

The following week, the Taranaki Herald led with the news that the New Zealand Expeditionary Force departed from Wellington in ten troopships.
"Eight and a half thousand soldiers and three thousand horses," Sarah said. "It makes you proud to be a New Zealander, doesn't it Father? Imagine that many men and horses all going to help the Empire?"
"If you say so," Sean said biting his tongue.
The mood at Llanon was one of quiet reflectiveness over the next few weeks as everybody went about their daily lives, often stopping to think about Richard and Theo. It was the same at Te Kainga with Wirimu and Ngaire wondering about Tama.
Wirimu and Ngaire started visiting Llanon on Sunday afternoons again. They would make small talk about the farms or Murata School but would always come back to the war and speculation about what the boys would be doing. The newspapers were full of stories of the preparation for war, and hope of a 'certain victory,' but that didn't quell the subdued mood of Middle River as news of more men leaving became common place.
"We've got the last of the sheep going to auction this week," Sean told Gwyneth one morning. "That's the last of the sheep your father bred, the last of the last, you might say. I might go to the auction with them, to see how they go," he added.
"Why don't you come with me?" he asked Gwyneth as an afterthought. "Seeing as it's the last of an era. We could stay overnight at the White Hart or the State if you'd prefer. Sarah can come as well and stay with your mother, they'd both like that and it means we can go as a family."
Gwyneth hesitated.
"What's brought this on?" she asked.
"What do you mean, can't a man ask his wife out if he has a mind to?"
"It's not like you at all, that's all I'm saying," Gwyneth remarked.
"Well I don't mind admitting these last few weeks have been a drain on everybody, I think we need to get away for a few days. Seeing the last of your father's sheep off might be one

way of doing it, then we can have a drink and raise our glasses to him, and the boys of course. It'll connect your father with Richard if you know what I'm saying."

Gwyneth looked at Sean with a bemused smile on her face. "I think I know exactly what you're saying Sean Murphy and I thank you for it. It's a splendid idea."

"There's a steamer, the *Kotuku,* she's taking a cargo of timber from the mill to New Plymouth next Tuesday," Sean said. "She has pens on the top deck and the aft so she can take the sheep. She's built the same as the *Cardiff*, that's why I use her to be honest. We can get a ride on that, I'll organise it with Bill Tallboys."

Sean walked out the room leaving Gwyneth feeling wanted for the first time in a long while. Her problems seemed to wash away with his cheeky smile and any thoughts about David Askill quickly vanished.

**

Once over the Mokau River bar and into the open sea, the *Kotuku* started rolling in a big swell as she turned to port and headed into a southerly wind as the waves broke, booming against the iron hull of the ship like thunder and causing sea spray do drift across her decks.

"It's so refreshing," Gwyneth told Sean as the salt water seemed to wash away the worries of the past months. After ten minutes, Sean disappeared into the wheelhouse to talk to the captain.

"Come up here," he shouted out to Gwyneth and Sarah as he signalled them up. "I've got a surprise for you both."

For the second time in her life, Gwyneth found herself at the helm of a ship as it ploughed through the sea.

"Oh Sean, do you remember when you last gave me the wheel?"

"How could I forget?" Sean answered with a broad grin. "I was convinced you were going back to Wales after I'd done all the work to keep you here, while all the time you had decided to stay on the Mokau anyway. I don't mind admitting how pleased I was to hear that from you, Gwyn love."

"Yes," Gwyneth said laughing. "And we talked about how we felt about having children".
After a minute Gwyneth looked sideways at Sean.
"What do you mean when you just said, 'all the work you did to keep me here'?" she asked.
Sean was suddenly in a hurry to move the conversation on. "I meant all that courting, planning the piano and all."
"But that was all well before you gave me the piano."
Sean realised he had almost let slip about the situation and his conversation with Robert Robertson at the bank and how Robertson's body was found on the beach not long after. It was something he never wanted to ever think about again, but now, it came into his mind at a time when it was least welcome.
"Well to be honest, Gwyn love," he said. "All that hoping and worrying about you moving back to Wales and thinking I would never see you again seemed like hard work to me. It was the stress and strain of thinking I might lose you."
Gwyneth turned and gave Sean a kiss on the cheek.
 "Here Sarah," Gwyneth said looking at Sean who nodded as Sarah took the wheel.
"Well, will you look at that?" Sean said. "From talking about having children to seeing our daughter at the wheel of a ship full of timber from our own mill and livestock from our own farm?"
"We've been through a lot since those days," Gwyneth said suddenly sounding quite serious.
"It doesn't pay to look back, especially nowadays," Sean said.
"You told me that once before….on our very first Christmas together," Gwyneth said surprising herself how easy the memory returned.
"True enough," Sean said. "But I suppose it doesn't do any harm to think back to where we came from now and again does it?"
Sean put his arms around Gwyneth as they faced forward with Sarah at the wheel.

**

With the auction out of the way, the four of them sat down to dinner at the Red House.
"You know, I don't think I ever thanked you and your father for your decision to come to New Zealand, so I thank you now and raise my glass to him, especially on this day with the last of his sheep gone." He picked up his glass. "To David Thomas" he said.
"To David," the others called out.
"And now I'd like to return the toast on behalf of David," Megan said. "Here's to you Sean Patrick Murphy. I really don't think we would have been able to make it here without you."
"Now don't give me that old blarney," Sean said embarrassed at Megan's expression of gratitude. "But there's one thing we really need to raise our glasses to," he said seriously. "To Richard, may he be home safe by Christmas."
"Of course. Theo and Tama too," Sarah added.

**

The following morning was a Friday and Devon Street was busy as Gwyneth and Sean walked down arm in arm as they approached Robertson's Photography.
"Look," Gwyneth said. "Robertson's Photography, it's still here, do let's have our photograph taken, a proper studio photograph this time. Not like the ones I take."
Sean turned away. "As much as I love you Gwyn, it'll be a long time before I have a photograph taken."
"Oh Sean, just for me, please. I'll go inside and see how much it costs."
"That's grand, I'll go over the road and look at some boots," Sean said, keen to get away.

**

"Six and sixpence for an eight by ten studio photograph," the man said gruffly. Gwyneth didn't like the looks of him, his demeanour was cold and Gwyneth felt he wasn't interested in the business.

"I came here some years ago," she told him. "There was a young man, a Londoner, a nice young lad of about eighteen. I don't suppose he's here anymore?"

"Tommy, Tommy Robertson, he owns the business, he took it over from his father a few years back," the man said.

"Then where is he now?" Gwyneth asked.

"Same as all of 'em, on his way to bloody Egypt in a khaki suit. God knows why when he's got a good business here."

"Why did he volunteer?" Gwyneth asked starting to get impatient with the man.

"He said it would enhance his career as a photographer. Said it was a once in a lifetime opportunity. He probably got that one right."

"Well he is a very brave man for doing his duty for the Empire," Gwyneth snapped back. "It's men like him…and my son who do what's expected in a time of need." Gwyneth retorted, getting more upset by the minute.

"Well I expect your son has a rifle," the man replied. "All this silly pillock's got is a camera. Can't shoot Germans with a camera. I ask you?"

**

"How did you go?" Sean asked as he looked over some riding boots.

"Horrible man, rude and unpatriotic," Gwyneth replied. "I'll have to make do with my camera for a while longer, not that you'll ever let me take a photograph of you anyway."

"You got that one right," Sean said.

They made their way to the Britannia Tea Rooms to see Megan and Sarah.

"Top of the mornin' to you and the rest of the day to meself," Sean said as he walked in.

"It's been a while since I've heard those words," Megan remarked. She turned to Sarah and took her hand.

"Sarah has something to tell you," Megan said.

"Mother, Father. I'm glad you're in a good mood," Sarah said, turning to look at Megan for support. "Nana and I have been talking and we've, rather I, have decided…I…I want to become a nurse, a trained nurse like you Mother so I can help the soldiers."

Sean and Gwyneth looked at each other, each waiting for the other to say something.

"When did you decide this?" Gwyneth was the first to speak.

"Last night," Sarah admitted. "I've been thinking it over for some time and it's what I want to do with my life, to become a nurse."

"You wouldn't have anything to do with this would you Mother?" Gwyneth asked Megan pointedly.

"Well," Megan replied. "Sarah and I have been talking about it, and I agreed it would be a good idea."

"And where is it you would be doing this nursing, if it's a nurse you're to become?" Sean asked.

"I, I don't know but wherever it takes me," Sarah said, her confidence dwindling by the second.

"Well it will take some thinking about," Sean said looking at his daughter as though she were a stranger. "Is your mind made up?"

"Yes Father, it is," Sarah said looking father Sean.

"Well it's no use denying we'll always need nurses, but at least you'll be staying here in New Zealand."

Sarah and Gwyneth made eye contact but said nothing.

**

The *Reliance* sailed to Mokau in a following wind with Sean, Gwyneth, and Sarah in a happy mood.

"It was a good idea to get away for a few days," Gwyneth said. "It's certainly blown the cobwebs out. It was good to see Mother as well. She's getting older now and the trip to Llanon may be getting a bit much for her."

"Fair enough," Sean said. "Perhaps we could come back in a few months and see her again, before the spring flush."

"Yes," Sarah agreed instantly, "and if I am to become a nurse, perhaps it could be in New Plymouth and I could stay with Nana, to keep her company."

"You could practise your bandaging on her," Gwyneth laughed.

"That would be fun, Sarah laughed. "Although she might end up looking like an Egyptian mummy."
"We can send her over to help Richard" Gwyneth said laughing out loud. Instantly the mood became instantly sombre.

**

The ship rolled and pitched as she went over the river bar as the incoming tide fought with the outflow of the river on the shallow water. She met quieter waters rounding the bend in the river towards the Mokau wharf which appeared to be lit up in gold by the late afternoon sun.
"No sign of the *Heron*," Sean said. "I'll go to the hotel and see if there's a steamer going upriver."
"Sean, do you mind if I go for a walk, on my own, just for a while?" Gwyneth asked. "I just want some time to think."
"I'll go with Father," Sarah said. "I've never been inside the hotel before."
When Sean walked in, Stella Ratcliffe was in the reception area. There was an awkward silence between them for a few seconds as Stella eyed up Sarah. She broke into a well-used smile.
"Sean Murphy and Miss Sarah Murphy, if I'm not mistaken. This is the first time I've seen you here my dear."
"Yes...yes," Sarah stuttered. "I've never been here before."
"Not like your father then," Stella said looking at Sean while purposely fondling the gold chain around her neck. "To what do I owe the pleasure?"
"We've just come back from New Plymouth and need a ride upriver, anything going today that you know of?"
"Nothing I know about," Stella replied. "Wally will know more than I do."
Stella opened the saloon doors as Sarah stood back, surprised at the wall of noise, the smoke and smell of stale beer which swept over her.
"Wally!" Stella shouted out above the clamour. "Anything going upriver today?"
"Fuck all," came the reply.

Stella smiled at Sean and Sarah. "Wally says there's nothing today."
Sean smiled back and Sarah looked at the ground, embarrassed, but not surprised at what she heard.
"Then I'll have your finest room for tonight then please, Stella."
"For you and Miss Murphy?"
"And Mrs Murphy if you please. Gwyn's just taking a walk around to get some air."
"I bet she is," Stella muttered under her breath. "Room fourteen's free, I'll put you in there."

**

Gwyneth hesitated as she walked into the surgery. She had to wait twenty minutes but when David Askill came out, he smiled his warm smile and Gwyneth felt her resolve soften, but by now she knew what to expect and she was ready for it.
"Hello Gwyneth, I had resigned myself to not seeing you again," he told her.
"I...I've come to apologise" Gwyneth said, "for how I treated you the last time we spoke. I should never have let my temper get the better of me."
"Well now, Gwyneth Thomas with a temper, who would have thought?"
"Murphy, Gwyneth Murphy," she corrected him.
"Of course, sorry. So why are you here can I ask?"
"Like I said, I wanted to see you one last time, to apologise...so we part as, well, as friends."
"I'm pleased you came to see me. I didn't want to leave without saying goodbye," David said.
"Goodbye?" Gwyneth sounded surprised. "You're leaving already?"
"Come on through to the back," David said extending his arm towards the hallway
They went through to the living quarters. Gwyneth looked around. The sitting room was as sparse as the surgery except for a few paintings on the wall and a large photograph. Gwyneth was immediately drawn to it.
"Is this what I think it is?" she asked.

"Yes, it's the workhouse all right. The board gave it to me, as a reminder of my responsibilities I expect. It's been extended since you were there of course. These wards here are all the children's wards," he said pointing to the photo. "That's where you would have been in charge. There's about four hundred youngsters in there now and another six hundred in scattered housing. Very few have dreams of greatness you know, very few realise they have the potential to become somebody. Of course, you know what will become of them don't you? Jail fodder or labourers, perhaps at best a life of menial servitude. I know they can't all be Arthur Gould's but some of them could be with the right prompts from somebody like yourself."
Gwyneth was silent. She looked around and saw packing cases and luggage half packed.
"You're packing. Surely you can't be leaving already?" she asked.
"You sound surprised?" David replied. "After we last spoke you were so resolute in your decision I knew you wouldn't change your mind. I understand you have your responsibility as well, to be with your family and the farm."
"Yes, yes, I do," Gwyneth's reply was less than convincing. "It's just that I thought you were staying another six months."
"I was, but there is a need to get back. I only said I would stay on if I thought I could talk you around. I did so want you to come back with me Gwyneth, even if it's only for a year, for the children, to set up the systems. I...I don't suppose...?
"No, no!" Gwyneth insisted. "You have my answer. I will be sorry to see you go, the people here will be sorry to see you go too, Mokau needs a good doctor."
"Perhaps," David said, shuffling his feet. "But needs must when the devil drives and all of that. Goodbye Gwyneth".
David moved to hold Gwyneth, but she moved back rejecting the approach, then left without giving him a further chance. Gwyneth tried to gather her thoughts on the way back to the hotel, telling herself she was going back to her husband and family as a mother must.

**

"This is the same room Betty and Joe put us in the very first night we spent in Mokau, before we knew anything about the place," Gwyneth told Sean as she walked in the door. "Even before we saw Llanon for the first time, this is wonderful. I slept on the bed over there she said, pointing towards the window. It's been such a good time over the last few days. You were right Sean, getting away has done us all a lot of good."

"The walk seems to have done you a power of good too Gwyn."

"Where's Sarah?" Gwyneth asked.

"Just going to wash her face ready for dinner. She's growing up so fast now," Sean added.

"I know," Gwyneth replied staring out the window. "I think we all are."

Sean looked at her strangely but before he had the chance to say anything, Gwyneth turned with a smile on her face. "Let's all go down to the snug and have a meal there," she said.

"Like we did years ago?"

"It's all a bit 'memory lane' for me," he protested knowing all the time he would give in with good humour. "I'll go ahead and find the same table we used to sit at," he said.

On the way downstairs, he passed Moonyeen. He was stunned when he saw she had changed into a red and gold cheongsam and had put her hair up, the same as when she and Sean had spent the night together many years earlier. They stopped on the stairs where there bodies were almost touching.

"Moonyeen my lovely Chinese primrose" he said. You are looking beautiful tonight."

"Ah, Mr Sean. Top of morning to you and rest of day to me" Moonyeen said.

Sean smiled. "That dress and your hair. Twenty years and you still remember."

"Moonyeen remembers a lot of things," she said with a smile on her face as she looked directly into Sean's eyes, gently touching his shirt button.

"Ah, Mrs Murphy and Miss Murphy," Moonyeen greeted Gwyneth and Sarah as they appeared on the landing behind

Sean. She pulled her hand down quickly, but not quickly enough for Sarah to notice.

"It is good to see all Murphy family out enjoying themselves."

"Not all the Murphys if you please Moonyeen," Gwyneth told her. "Richard is sailing to Egypt, even as we speak now."

"Ah, yes of course. How is Mr Richard?" Moonyeen asked walking up to the landing.

"The same as all the eight thousand men doing their duty Moonyeen, suffering in silence as they prepare to fight the Germans so we can rest easy in our beds."

"Ah yes. Very brave men," Moonyeen said.

After they were all seated in the snug, Sarah turned to Gwyneth while Sean was away for a moment.

"Mother, I don't like that Chinese woman at all. I don't trust her. And why was she touching father when we came downstairs? I don't think she realised we were there."

"You are very observant Sarah dear. But think nothing of it, your father and Moonyeen are old friends," Gwyneth said feeling obliged to cover for Sean but didn't know why.

"Even so," Sarah said, "I still don't trust her."

"This has been a really good weekend," Gwyneth said. "Let's keep it that way Sarah."

"You don't like her either do you Mother or why would you say a thing such as that?"

Gwyneth glared at her. "Your father will be back in a minute, change the subject."

**

"Well, that was grand," Sean said sitting back and drumming his hands on his stomach after he finished his meal. "How about a nightcap?"

Without waiting for an answer he went to the bar. Sarah took the opportunity sitting forward in her chair and half whispering to her mother. "And another thing, that Moonyeen changed very quickly. I wondered why she ran back to her room

"What are you talking about dear?" Gwyneth asked in an effort to shield herself from her own thoughts.

"An hour ago she was wearing a plain black skirt and blouse. Now look at her. She's changed her hair as well, why would she do that?"

"It's no good asking me – how would I know?" Gwyneth said with a faint voice.

Sarah saw Sean coming back and she made a rash decision. "Thank you for a nice meal Father. I'm feeling quite tired and I'll go up to bed now, but you two stay here for a while and enjoy a drink together, I'll be fine."

"Are you sure dear?" Gwyneth asked.

"It would be nice to have a drink together," Gwyneth said taking hold of Sean's arm in front of Moonyeen.

Sarah went up the staircase, stopping at the top to listen for any footsteps. When she was sure nobody was behind her, she went to Moonyeen's room and tried the door and to her surprise it wasn't locked.

Her heart was pounding in her chest as she slowly opened the door. She felt scared as she went in but sensed that Moonyeen's room would hold some secrets to the past which she was determined to find. Very slowly, lest it creaked, she closed the door and slowly turned the key, locking herself in. The room was plain enough with a well-made single bed and a wardrobe by a dressing table with a small Buddha on it. A few watercolour paintings were hung on the wall with some Chinese characters written on parchments.

Sarah looked through the wardrobe with its mix of dowdy European clothing and Chinese dresses in bright coloured silks. Sarah hesitated as she looked at the drawers in the dressing table. She went over to the door again listening carefully for any tell-tale footsteps but heard nothing. She went back to the dresser and opened a small drawer directly under the mirror. She carefully looked through the contents which had nothing other than some costume jewellery and trinkets. The remaining drawers only contained clothing. Disappointed at not finding anything of interest, Sarah sat down for a few minutes, looking around and thinking. She crouched down looking under the bed where she found a very old and tattered brown leather suitcase. It was heavy, giving Sarah hope this might give her what she was looking for. It was locked so she tried to force it but stopped before anything broke. She had an

idea so went back to the top drawer in the dresser and rummaging around, found two keys on a twisted wire loop. The case was full of papers of all description. Bundles of letters mostly signed by Percy Richardson. She read through some and realised this was the story of a broken relationship. She wanted to know more but felt this wasn't what she was looking for so put the letters to one side and carried on searching.
"Nothing but letters and poll tax receipts," she said under her breath, all the time scared of making any noise as she listened out for the sounds of anybody on the stairs. When it looked like she had drawn a blank, Sarah got to a photograph album at the bottom of the case. It held faded images of Chinese people and some of Moonyeen as a young woman. Sarah couldn't help noticing how pretty she was. She turned over the last page and her eyes fixed on the studio photograph of Moonyeen and her father. She held the photograph for a moment, barely able to take it all in. She knew by the look on Moonyeen face and how she was holding onto Sean's arm there was a special connection between them both.
"Got you at last, you bitch," Sarah muttered.
Thinking for a while, she took the photograph out and carefully rolled it up and put it in her purse. She put the other papers back in the case as she had found them and slid the case back under the bed then returned the keys back in the top drawer of the dresser. She unlocked the door, checked the hallway for the last time and quietly walked back to her room. When she got back, she realised the enormity of the situation. She knew there was something between her father and Moonyeen and saw the photograph as absolute proof of a relationship. If nothing else it was the way Moonyeen was holding onto Sean with the same intimacy she had seen earlier in the evening. She resolved not to do anything hasty but to hold onto the photograph and whatever would happen would show itself in some shape, way, or form.

**

"I knew it," Sarah said reading the Herald as she walked up the path from the jetty.

"What's that you knew?" Gwyneth asked.
"The Russian's declaring war on the Ottomans, so now Britain's done the same."
"You mean the Ottomans are our enemies now, as well as the Germans?"
"Yes, that's exactly what I mean."
"And who are the Ottomans exactly?" Sean asked.
"Turks I think," Sarah replied.
"But it won't affect Richard or the others though will it?" Gwyneth asked taking a sudden interest.
"…It means the war is spreading," Sarah answered with some thought.
"But Richard will still be going to France…to fight the Germans won't he? That's what was agreed, it's why he went. It won't take long and with a bit of luck he won't be in the thick of it…will he?" Gwyneth quizzed.
"Let's hope not Mother," Sarah said as she hurriedly put the newspaper away.
"I might go and see Nana next week if that's all right. I want to go to the hospital in Barrett Street…to see about nursing," she added, deciding it was time to change the conversation.
"I'll come with you," Gwyneth replied.
"No. No thanks," Sarah said quickly. "I'd like to go on my own. It's just something I want to do. Besides, I want to get it all sorted before Christmas and Nana will enjoy coming with me. It will be like an adventure for her."
"True enough," Sean said. "You may as well let her go and make the most of it."
The reality was, Sarah hadn't stopped thinking about the photograph but hadn't thought of how to find out more without exposing her father. In the absence of anything else, she planned to take the photograph back to Mokau and face Moonyeen with the truth.
Time went quickly enough and Sarah found herself absorbed into how the conversation with Moonyeen might go. She was no clearer in her mind as to how she was going to face Moonyeen or if she did confirm there was an affair, what she would do about it? The only other person who could help her was Libby and she couldn't ask her without hurting a lot of people. In fact she was questioning if it was even her business

as Sean and Gwyneth were getting on well and there was an air of optimism at Llanon she didn't want to destroy. She was beginning to think it was all a big mistake and she should return the photograph to where she found it, putting the whole situation into the past and focus on becoming a nurse.
In the morning, as she prepared to go to New Plymouth, she resolved that would be her course of action.
"I've put out your 'New Plymouth' clothes," Gwyneth told Sarah. "I can't find your best bag, the one you always take to Nana's."
"It's at the back of the wardrobe I expect," Sarah said. "Don't worry, I'll get it."
"That's all right love," Gwyneth said, "I'll get everything ready for you, it's what mothers do."
"No!" Sarah shouted, suddenly dashing out to make sure Gwyneth was nowhere near the bag; not wanting any chance of her finding the photograph still rolled up inside.
Gwyneth was taken aback by the sudden reaction from Sarah, rousing her suspicions.
"All right," she called back. "Only trying to help."
"Sorry I'm…I'm just a bit on edge this morning. No sign of the *Heron* yet I suppose?"
"Not yet, it's a bit early, I heard him go upriver earlier though."
Gwyneth watched Sarah over the next hour and saw she was nervous and wondered if there was something about her bag to make her react so abruptly earlier so she decided to take a look.
"I think I can hear Owen now," Gwyneth called out to Sarah after a short while. "I'm busy in the kitchen, you go down and see if it's him."
No sooner had Sarah left the house, Gwyneth went straight to her room and opened her bag. Reaching in, she pulled out the photograph and her life fell apart in front of her.

**

"The lying bastard. After all these years," she found herself saying as her head started pounding and she was breathing heavily through her nose as she clutched at her chest . "The bloody lying bastard," she gasped.

After what seemed a lifetime, she heard Sarah calling for her from the kitchen. She stood up and felt giddy, having to hold on to the bed frame for support.

Without thinking she put the bag back in the wardrobe and pushed the photograph into the pocket on the front of her apron.

"You're crying. What is it?" Sarah wanted to know walking into her room.

"Oh. Just you being so grown up, off to see your nana and me being here. I should be with you, really."

"I'll be back in a few days then I can tell you all about it. I'll see if I can get Nana to agree to come back with me, if you like?"

"That would be good," Gwyneth said. "If anybody can do that, it's you, but don't forget she's not as young as she used to be. Why not stay with Nana for a week or so, it would mean a lot to her."

"Are you sure?" Sarah asked. "That would be good." She hesitated for a while thinking as she looked at Gwyneth.

"If you don't mind me asking, you are all right aren't you?"

"Of course. Ignore me Sarah. You go and find a good life for yourself. Find a good man and be happy."

Sean and Gwyneth saw Sarah off on the *Heron*, Sean turned to say something to Gwyneth but she was gone. When he got back to the house he found her packing a suitcase.

"Going somewhere?" he asked. Gwyneth didn't answer but carried on packing her clothes. "What is it Gwyn love? You don't seem yourself, you look upset. Is it Sarah?"

"I'm going to stay with Ngaire for a while if you must know, at least until Sarah gets back, that's all," Gwyneth answered sharply.

"Is it something I said?" Sean asked.

Gwyneth turned to face him. "I've got some film left in my camera" she said. "Can I take a photo of you Sean?"

"Well you know how it is Gwyn love, with me and photographs."

"Have you ever had your photograph taken?"

"Not to my recollection."

"Never?"

"No, never."

"And if you ever did, who would you have it taken with?"

Sean started to hesitate in his reply wondering where the questions were leading.

"With you. Who else?"

Gwyneth snapped.

"I'll tell you who else you lying bastard. That Chinese trollop you've been seeing for these last twenty years."

It was the first time Sean had ever heard Gwyneth curse and he didn't know how to react.

"What do you mean?" was all he could manage. "Who told you these lies?"

"Nobody told me Sean, they didn't need to. I've seen it with my own eyes."

"Now how could that be Gwyn? Don't be silly."

"I see it now Sean, right here," Gwyneth said taking the photo out and waving it in front of his face. "This photograph, it tells me everything I never wanted to know. It tells me that for these last twenty years you have been living a lie; playing me for a fool."

Sean stared at the photograph. He felt a lump in his throat and his voice dry up.

"...Oh. I'd, uh, I'd forgotten all about that. It was… it was years ago. I met Moonyeen in the street, she wanted a photo taken but not on her own so she asked me to step in."

"Look me in the eye and say that Sean Murphy. You can't can you? You lied to me then and you're lying to me now. You just can't stop it can you? Look at the photo. Take a good look." Gwyneth pushed the photo up against Sean's face so he had to turn away.

"Does she walk around town in her best silk dress? Does she always put her hair up to go shopping? Does she always hold on to the arm of a so called friend as though she was a married woman? No, there's more to this than just friends Sean. I can see the smug look on her face, she got her man all right. I see it now in the way she always makes a bee line for you, ignoring the other customers in the hotel. If a hotel it is. Is she still running a whore house for her 'special friends' Sean? "Top of the morning my eye. Top of the night more like. You've no more forgotten about this than you've forgotten you have a wife and children. How many other times did you sleep

together? How many times did you 'forget' you have a family working their fingers to the bone while you're off having fun?" Sean was totally dumbstruck. He felt the past was now the present and the time he spent with Moonyeen all those years ago could have been yesterday.
He turned and walked towards the door.
"There's no need for you to go" Gwyneth shouted at him. "It's me that's leaving. I'll tell you where I'm going and why. I'm going to see Ngaire because I don't want to see your lying face ever again."
Sean walked out not knowing what else to do. Gwyneth collapsed onto a chair putting her face in her hands, exhausted of all emotion. Her body shook as the tears came out.
Sean appeared back in the door after collecting his thoughts. "Tell me Gwyn love. If you go to see Ngaire, are you going to say goodbye to Caryl? It is Caryl isn't it? Our first child who died. Our first child you never ever told me about who's buried up by the totara. What about her Gwyn *love*?"
Just when Gwyneth thought she couldn't take any more, Sean's words brought back an avalanche of heartache and fear.
"You know about Caryl?" she sobbed. "I'm so sorry I never told you about her."
"Well, why was that Gwyn?" Sean asked walking into the room feeling as though he was back in control of the situation.
"I...I desperately wanted to, and well nearly did several times. But Father, he forbade it."
"Your father forbade it," Sean asked as he gathered confidence and his voice became louder. "You father forbade it, Gwyn? What about your responsibility to me, the father of the baby, what about my rights to know my child died?"
"Father said it would bring shame and he made me promise not to tell. So, so he told you I had pneumonia to explain why I was away."
"And I just suppose everybody else knew? Everybody else except me. Betty and Joe perhaps?" Sean snapped back.
Gwyneth didn't answer but looked down feeling the weight of twenty years of guilt fall on her.
"I'm...I'm sorry Sean," she blubbered.

"You're sorry, you're sorry? How the hell do you think I feel? I suppose I was the father?"
Suddenly incensed, Gwyneth stood up facing Sean.
"How dare you suggest otherwise. How dare you! I have always been faithful to you, Sean Murphy though god knows why after the way you've been treating me. It's not me who's been sleeping outside the marital bed, and don't say you haven't. I have always loved you Sean, from when you first took my hand to help off the *Cardiff* on the day we met. I have never so much as looked at another man since then so don't you even dare suggest it. What Father did, he did to keep this family together so we had a future. What you've done is destroy all of that with this …with this…woman."
Gwyneth held up the photograph again
"Here, take it Sean, if she means that much to you, take the damned photograph, I never want to see it or you again."
Gwyneth turned and picked up the suitcase. Even though she hadn't quite finished packing, she slammed the top down taking the time to just do up the one strap. Pushing her way past Sean she turned back for the last time.
"…and don't you dare follow me either," She shouted as she left the house heading to Te Kainga.

**

"It's always so peaceful here," Gwyneth told Ngaire. "You and Wirimu must be very happy."
"Content I think may be more accurate," Ngaire answered.
She looked at Gwyneth and gave her a smile, taking her hand.
"Don't take this the wrong way but you've been here a week now. You are welcome to stay as long as you wish of course, but don't you think you need to work out what it is you want?"
"Yes, you're right of course," Gwyneth replied.

**

Wirimu intentionally cleared his throat as he approached Gwyneth's room later that evening.

"Gwyneth?" He called out softly as Gwyneth sat on her bed staring out the window.
"Wirimu, sorry, I was miles away."
"Sean's here. He wants to talk to you…on your own, will you see him?"
"What mood is he in?" Gwyneth asked.
"He's quiet, he wants to say he's sorry. He said he just wants to talk."
"All right then," Gwyneth replied after some thought. "Give me ten minutes. I'm not sure where Ngaire is but can you let her know what's happening?"
"Ay."
"You're looking tired," Gwyneth told Sean when she walked into the parlour.
"To tell the truth…." Sean started.
"Yes, the truth would be a good start," Gwyneth interrupted. "What is it you want Sean?"
"I want you back home, where you belong," Sean said looking straight at Gwyneth.
"Home, eh?" Gwyneth said. "Right now I'm not sure where home is, that's the problem."
"Llanon, of course. Our home, the home we've built over the last twenty years. What do you say Gwyn?"
"It's not that simple though is it?" Gwyneth told him.
"I don't see why not."
"Haven't you ever heard of trust and what happens when it's broken? It's not just a matter of forgetting, pretending nothing happened. You slept with somebody else. The trust we had built with the home you just spoke of is broken. I can longer trust you any more than I can fly to the moon, and you want me to come back just because it's what you want?"
"A fresh start Gwyn love, that's all I'm asking," Sean said.
"You haven't been listening to a word I've said have you? You slept with that harlot Sean, you can't deny it."
"There's no need to bring her into it Gwyn. It's about you and me."
"Why are you still protecting her even now? You are incredulous Sean Murphy, do you know that? Do you still have feelings for her? It's not just you and me and you know it. It's

also about Mother, Richard, and Sarah. It's affects all of us, besides you haven't asked me what I want."
"Well what is it you do want?"
"Well since you've asked so nicely," Gwyneth said sarcastically. "I'll tell you. I want to have a life of my own. I want to go back to Wales, to do something that has meaning and will help others. I want to pick up where I left off, the place where I would have gone had I never met you."
"You can't be serious Gwyn. How could you do such a thing now? You've got family to consider."
"No, I don't Sean, you think I do, but there's no family for me here anymore. There's only dinners to cook and work on the farm because we can't get labourers anymore. I want more than that Sean. I want my life to mean something to others, not just a means of keeping the books balanced and the bed warm."
Sean was silent not knowing what to say. He got up and walked to the window.
"Is this the end of our marriage Gwyn? You're walking out of our marriage, is that the way of it?"
"It's not a marriage though, is it? It's you wanting me back on your terms, that's not what marriage is about. Yes Sean, you are right in one way, I am leaving you. I'm going to find a new life for myself."
"But you don't know anybody, how will you manage?"
"I'll manage very well. You see I know more than you think I do and what I don't know, I'll learn. Go now before you make a bigger fool of yourself than you already have."
Sean looked shocked and his face lost it colour. He took a few steps towards Gwyneth.
"No Sean, the door's behind you, turn around and use it, now."
When Sean came out the house he was crying. He didn't notice Ngaire and Wirimu standing at the gate, waiting to see what happened. Wirimu started to approach him but Sean waved him away walking towards the river.
"Follow him," Ngaire said. "I'll see Gwyn."

**

"I've left him," Gwyneth told Ngaire. "I hadn't even made my mind up fifteen minutes ago but seeing Sean and how he wanted me back on his terms, I realised what I wanted was to go back to Wales."

**

Ngaire saw Gwyneth off on a sunny morning. The *Heron* slowly edged to the Jetty then Owen McConaghy picked up Gwyneth's suitcase. He could feel that this wasn't the time for pleasantries.
Gwyneth took Ngaire's hand.
"Thank you so much Ngaire. I simply don't know what I would have done without you. Both you and Wirimu have been so good to me, so understanding," Gwyneth said as she held back tears. "You would think I had cried all the tears I had over the last week."
Ngaire said nothing for a while as she stared at Gwyneth as though she were reading her mind.
"Are you ever coming back, Gwyneth, to the Mokau?" she asked.
"I don't know, I barely know what's happening tomorrow to be honest," Gwyneth replied. "I know I need to be strong, Ngaire, I'll write to you, I promise. You've been a true friend, thank you."

**

Getting off the steamer at Mokau, Gwyneth headed straight to the surgery. Pleased to put the heavy case down, she knocked at the door but there was no answer. She knocked harder but still no reply came. The door was unlocked so she put her head in the doorway and called out but there was nobody there. Gwyneth turned back choosing to leave the case just inside the hallway and walked down towards the wharf. After a while she met David Askill walking back to the surgery.
"David, I need to see you urgently," Gwyneth said in a rush.

"Gwyneth, what is it that could be this urgent, you look flushed, are you all right?"

"Where can we talk David? I want to talk before I change my mind."

"Change your mind about what?"

"About going back to Wales, to the workhouse …with you. No, not like that. You know what I mean. The job offer, it is still open isn't it?"

"Gwyneth. I'm shocked. Yes, yes of course it is. What brought this on?" David said taking Gwyneth by the shoulders nit daring to believe what he was hearing.

"When are you leaving David? I need a few days, but I want to go back to help the children."

"Whoa," David said. "One thing at a time. I was leaving for Wellington next week then to England in two weeks as a ship's doctor, I could use a nurse. I'm sure it wouldn't be a problem, I can send a telegram and tell the board of governors, they will be delighted but I've got a few loose ends to tie up here first. Come back to the surgery Gwyneth and tell me what happened."

Gwyneth spent the next hour telling David about Sean and the photograph and the argument. How she felt betrayed and lied to for the last twenty years. David said nothing until Gwyneth had finished.

"So there you have it David, that's why I need to get away. I'm catching a steamer to New Plymouth this evening to tell Sarah and Mother, to tell them I'm leaving."

"That will be difficult for you," David said. "Would you like me to come with you?"

"No, thank you," Gwyneth replied. "I need to do this on my own. This is about me standing up for what I want for once, I don't need you with me…but thank you for the thought."

"Well at least you can let me put the kettle on" David said getting up to go to the kitchen.

Gwyneth looked around and at the pile of papers on the table. On the top was a death certificate. She took a glance over it. "Always a grim reminder," she muttered to David as he came back in.

"Yes, yes it is," David replied. "The poor woman died alone with nobody at her side and nobody at her funeral either apparently."
"Oh, that's terrible," Gwyneth said. "When was this?"
"Just a few weeks ago. She died in New Plymouth but was adamant she would be buried here with her husband."
"Who was she?" Gwyneth asked, becoming concerned.
"Betty somebody." David took the death certificate. "Dickson, Betty Dickson. Did you know her?"
Gwyneth gave a sharp intake of breathe and sat down breathing hard but remaining silent for some time.
"Yes, I knew Betty well" she said almost inaudibly. "It was Betty and her husband Joe who first welcomed us to Mokau, they had the hotel here, before Stella Ratcliffe."
"Of course," David said. "I knew the name was familiar."
"It was a terrible boat ride," Gwyneth went on. "We nearly didn't get over the bar. We were glad to see dry land I can tell you. I think we were all scared, me, Mother and Father of course. We'd just arrived from the South Island, we were nearly broke then and when we were at our lowest ebb, it was Betty's smiling face that made us feel welcome."
"We all need somebody like that now and then," David said.
"Betty helped me more ways than you can imagine David. I need to go and see her grave before I leave."
"Of course."
"I'll go to New Plymouth and tell Mother and Sarah what I'm doing, then, perhaps meet you there to go to Wellington. Would that work out?" Gwyneth asked.
"I think so," David confirmed. "We can work out the exact details later. You'd better be making your way to the cemetery though if you want to go today, it's quite a climb you know."
"Oh yes, I know all right," Gwyneth said more to herself than David.

**

Sweating in the afternoon sun Gwyneth was puffing as she climbed the steep hill to Mokau Cemetery. Looking to the beach far below her, she saw a family. A small boy and girl were making sandcastles while their parents watched them and she was envious of how happy they looked and how simple their lives must be. At the top of the hill, she knew instinctively to go to the town side of the cemetery. There beside Joe's grave was the freshly dug plot of Betty Dickson. Nearby was a rough timber seat and a hedge where some of the branches had reached Joe's grave. Gwyneth wrestled the worst of them, scratching her arms but she eventually accomplished what she set out to do.

"There you are Joe. Can't have you living in the jungle now can we?" she found herself saying.

She used the broken branches as a besom and swept some withered leaves and twigs from around both the graves then sat down. She could see the road below and smiled thinking of how Joe wanted to be buried there so he could 'see' what was going on.

"I need to talk to you Betty," she said. "Of all my friends, you know me most of all. I'll never forget how you helped me when I lost Caryl. You and Joe saved my life. I never really did thank you for what you did. But right now, I don't really know what I'm doing Betty love. I feel strange, scared even, I'm around people I know, yet I feel alone. It's like standing on a cliff wondering if you can fly, afraid to jump off and try, yet afraid to stay there and be safe."

Gwyneth stopped, feeling a bit awkward. She looked around to make sure there was nobody else about.

"I may be making the biggest mistake of my life Betty. I don't mind admitting I'm scared but I have to find out for myself. I have to see what I can do for the children at the orphanage. If I don't, I'll spend the rest of my life wondering what would have happened, how I could have helped them make something of their lives but didn't. I can't let them down Betty. I don't want to spend the rest of my life asking, 'what if'. I have nothing here. I feel so lonely in my own house. That's not how it's meant to be so I have to do something about it. I hope you understand."

Gwyneth felt stronger, relieved in some way as this was the first time she'd been really honest with herself. She stood up at the fence staring at a horse and cart slowly moving along the road far below. Picking some daisies from the lawn, she placed them on Betty and Joe's graves.

"I'll go to New Quay for you Betty love."
On the way out she glanced over to where Mac's grave was. There was no marker, no headstone as Ngaire requested all those years ago. There was just a small depression in the ground. How distant it seemed, yet so recent. She walked back down the hill. The family she saw earlier had left, leaving the beach deserted with only the incoming tide washing away the crumbling sandcastle the children had made.

**

"Some Christmas this is going to be," Megan said. Sarah remained silent, stunned at the news Gwyneth had just given them.
"Are you sure Gwyn love? Are you sure this is what you want?"
"No, not really if I were truly honest," Gwyneth said. "A few hours ago I was sure, but now I'm facing the reality of telling you, it's all so dreamlike so how can I be sure. But I do know I can't go back to Llanon."
"Well I suppose your father and I always said we would never hold you back from going back to Cardiff. Heavens knows though, we never thought it would be after all these years."
"You and David Askill though..."
"No Mother don't be ridiculous. I'm going back to help run the workhouse as I told you, our relationship is purely professional."
"Gwyn, I remember I once told you that you cannot decide who you fall in love with, but please don't do anything stupid will you?"
Gwyn looked at her mother. "It may be a little too late for that," she admitted.

Chapter Six

**

Richard and Tama were enjoying the army life. They were either busy on fatigues in Alexandria or training at the camp in Zeitoun on the outskirts of Cairo. That meant there was no shortage of entertainment in the souks and café's when they could get leave, which was quite often. Either way, they always managed to stay together.
"It doesn't seem like we've had Christmas," Richard said as he and Tama were resting after a morning on the rifle range.
"It was six weeks ago now, but you're right, can't say I'd recommend an army Christmas myself," Tama replied.
"Reckon we could get to Cairo again tonight if we played our cards right?"
"You'll have to get on the right side of Thunder Guts," Richard said. "Tent inspection in an hour, don't forget, mess it up and the only thing you'll get is jankers."
Tama thought for a while and turned to Richard.
"I thought we'd be in the thick of the action by now," he said. "Not stuck here. Sort out the Germans then back home for Christmas, that's what they promised us. The only action I've seen is unloading trains in Alex', swatting flies and falling off camels, that's the only difference between this place and Trentham."
"I don't remember any pyramids in Trentham," Richard said.
"Nor the heat, not many camels there either" he laughed.
"There was plenty of meningo-friggin-coccus though, I'll give you that. A lot more died after we left."
"You've got a point there," Richard said. "Cairo's pretty damned good though, you've got to give it to the wogs. Wouldn't mind getting back to the souk we went to last time, see all those women? Don't get them like that in Mokau, I can tell you that for nothing. The one you had was a looker, she

had bigger tits than the camel had humps I reckon. Hope you didn't fall off her".
Tama laughed as they both set about tidying the tent.
"I wonder what Theo's doing right now. Hope he's ok," Tama thought out loud.
"Reckon we should go and find him soon," Richard replied.
An hour later, the inspection was complete and Sergeant Major Thompson, known amongst the ranks as 'Thunder Guts,' gave them leave for the night.
Cairo was a filthy city full of ramshackle alleyways where life, love and alcohol were cheap. At night-time the darkness hid the squalor and the desperate examples of humanity were blanketed by the influx of soldiers whose only enemy was boredom as they went looking for whatever the heaving city could offer.
Richard, Tama and a dozen other soldiers walked through the squalid streets packed with Cairene's selling everything from postcards, carved walking sticks, cigarettes, trinkets, and souvenirs. They were soon confronted by a horde of Arabs, the tallest, a man wearing a dirty keffiyeh over his head had a toothless grin and a long white beard but his sparkling eyes set deep into his dark skin showed he had his wits about him. He held out a small brass pyramid and a leather camel.
"B'ery goo-od Kiwi Mr McKenzie. Mr McKenzie my friend. Kiwi's my friend. Baksiesh, Gib it Mr McKenzie, 'five piastre. Gib it?"
"Five piastre," boomed out Tama taking the pyramid. It felt good in his hand somehow.
"Two piastre," he said looking the Arab in the eye.
"Four piastre, Mr McKenzie, four piastre."
"Two piastre and no more. Mr McKenzie say you wogs rip us off."
"Gib it Mr McKenzie, Mr McKenzie my friend, two piastre good Kiwi."
Tama paid his money and put the pyramid in his pocket as he walked away smiling to himself.
An hour and several drinks later, the group walked into the Pink Pussycat bar. The noise of three hundred people all talking with nobody listening was intense. One side was the bar with a dozen or so barmen, even so, it was still five deep

with soldiers all waving money and shouting orders in the gloom over the music. Every table had a hubba-bubba pipe surrounded by circles of khaki so the air was thick with the heavy smell of dubious tobacco. Odalisques dressed with diaphanous scarves over their otherwise bare breasts and satin pantaloons, danced or draped themselves over the men who had lost all control from alcohol or opiates.

"I can feel it's going to be a good night," Tama shouted as a belly dancer, dressed in sapphire blue danced in front of him with her swaying hips taking Tama's full attention.

"It'll take hours to get a drink," Richard shouted.

"Without taking his eyes off the woman, or speaking, Tama partially opened his tunic carefully showing a full bottle of whiskey stored in a makeshift pocket.

"You bloody cunning Māori," Richard shouted.

Without averting his eyes, Tama grabbed two glasses off a nearby table and wiped them on his tunic as the belly dancer moved on to other prospects.

"Yeah, well, you gotta look after your mates eh?" Tama shouted as he filled the glasses. A second later Tama felt a hand grab his shoulder.

"Eh, Māori," a voice shouted from behind. "Aren't you going to offer a drink to a boy from Mokau?"

Tama spun around. Facing him was a smiling and very drunk Charlie Dobson.

"Charlie boy, what the hell are you doing here?"

"Same as you, drinking and rooting. Bugger all else to do. I've seen you about the place, both of you." Charlie Dobson was pointing at Richard as he swayed in his drunkenness. "I...I saw you both in Alex' last week, un-unloading fucking trains."

"Where were you then?" Richard asked.

"In the bar opposite, knocking back a cold beer," Charlie replied eyeing up a woman passing by with a tray of drinks.

"No way!" Richard said.

"Every way."

"Must have been a tough job. How come you got that?" Richard asked.

Charlie stumbled, half falling onto a chair. He laughed out loud.

"Think I'll sit down now," he laughed again. "Māori boy, pour me a whiskey!" he demanded of Tama.
Tama poured a large whiskey as Charlie tapped the side of his nose.
"It's not what you know, but who you know"
"And who is it you know?" Tama asked.
Charlie put his head down low and looked about the room in mock caution.
"Good job there's nobody else here," he laughed again.
"Don't shout about it" Charlie yelled, laughing again to himself.
"But I'm aide-de-camp to Major Williams.
"What the frig's an aide-de-camp?" Tama asked.
"A fuckin' lackey," Charlie said. "Give me another whiskey."
"Must be a cushy number then if you can sit in a bar while every other bastard has to sweat all day."
"Yup, that's about it," Charlie told him.
"What do you do then, for this Major Williams?"
"I shuffle some files," Charlie belched. "Do some paperwork…" He tried to focus on the glass but failed, pouring whiskey down his tunic.
"I..I pack the Major's bags, I brush his uniform and make sure the newspaper is ironed every morning so it's as crisp and clean as his bedsheets."
"How'd you get that job then?" Richard repeated.
"Got, got me out the line in a field inspection he did," Charlie said knocking back the remaining whiskey.
"So why'd he pick you?"
Charlie shook his head as the whiskey hit home.
"Shit, that's good. Give me another. Let's say the Major knows a good thing when he sees it," Charlie said patting his crutch.
Tama looked shocked.
"You mean he, he, and you, your homo's, you're fucking homos?"
Several soldiers who'd been listening turned around to stare at Charlie.
"Whatever it takes," Charlie said smiling.
"You're friggin sick you." Richard shouted, disgusted at Charlie's candid admission. "You won't be shuffling shit when the Germans are firing at you."

"You won't be fighting the fucking Germans," Charlie shouted. "It's the frigging Turks you want to be watching out for."
"You what?" Richard asked looking around to see who was listening.
"We're not going to France, I know, I hear these things. We're going to Turkey with the Aussies, we're all going to friggin' Turkey."

**

Theo and Dickie found themselves riding camels with Theo engrossed in a book he had kept from his early school days on the Mokau. He had convinced Dickie to come with him on a trip to Giza, intent on fulfilling a promise he made to his parents on his departure from New Zealand. Unlike Dickie, Theo was oblivious to the heat building up in the mid-morning as the sun climbed, shortening the shadows on the hot sand.
"I've always wanted to see this," he said, "the great pyramid of Khufu, the second pharaoh of the fourth dynasty and the greatest of all the pharaohs. It's one of the seven wonders of the ancient world Dickie, did you know that?
Dickie ignored the question, too busy concentrating on swatting flies and showing no interest in the pyramid.
"I've seen it in this book many times as a child but now I'm actually here," Theo hesitated. "I'm actually here, I just can't believe it. It's quite emotional really, to be standing, almost touching this pyramid built over four thousand years ago."
"It's a great piece of architecture, I'll give you that" Dickie eventually admitted. "You know Theo, I've always wanted to be an architect one day" he mused starting to take an interest in the moment.
Theo climbed down from the camel and walked towards the pyramid.
"I've got to touch it Dickie, I simply must, and then for the rest of my life, I can say I have touched the great pyramid.
Whenever I see a photograph of it, I can say I've been there and actually touched it. Imagine that."
Theo walked over and placed both hands on the stone blocks for some minutes.
"What took you so long?" Dickie asked.

"Just giving thanks for my blessings, that's all. This is such a special place."

As Theo walked back he stopped to pick up a small piece of rock.

"Dickie, do you suppose this fell off the pyramid?"

"It could have done, it's alabaster I think" Dickie replied. "You can see it's been worked on one side, all smooth and shiny. Why? I suppose you're going to take it back to New Zealand?"

"I shouldn't really," Theo said. "But it's not for me, it's for my parents."

"Fair enough" Dickie told him. "Go for it."

"I promised I would bring them back something from the ancient times."

"I might take this as well" said Theo picking us a second piece.

"For Sarah, I suppose?" Dickie asked.

"How did you know?"

"I should do by now, you've told me enough about her."

"I want to stay here for a while more, just ten minutes or so," Theo said. "To take it all in. Before you know it, we'll be back in New Zealand, and this will be a distant memory."

Chapter Seven

**

Sarah was getting ready for her first day at the Barrett Street Hospital as a trainee nurse. Her uniform, a grey cotton blouse and starched white pinafore dress with cuffs and a collar, had been meticulously prepared the night before and laid out on the spare bed beside the long cloth cap. Beside it was the plain grey over dress designed for the work of the sluice room. Megan had spent the evening reassuring Sarah there was nothing to worry about, even so, she hardly slept that night, her mind confused between nerves and excitement.
"You've plenty of time" Megan told Sarah the next morning as she brushed the uniform. "Why don't you go downstairs and make sure you've got all your paperwork in order? I'll bring your tea down in a jiff."
Sarah sat at the back of the tea rooms, her favourite place because she could look onto Devon Street yet have her privacy. The April sun rose in the sky with a light pink tinge putting Sarah in a reflective mood as she watched New Plymouth wake up to another day.
"Red in the morning, shepherd's warning Nana" she said as Megan arrived with the promised tea.
"Never mind that Sarah love," Megan told her, dismissing the comment. "Today is the first day of a brand new future for you."
Sarah didn't reply, instead stared out the window.
"What are you thinking about dear, you look a million miles away?"
"Oh, nothing really," Sarah said. "Just thinking where Mother is now and what she's doing."
"Not surprising," Megan replied. "It's normal to miss your mother at such a time, I'll leave you to your thoughts."
"Nana?"

"Yes."
"Thank you for, well, just for being Nana and being here for me."
"Think nothing of it Sarah love. I rather like all the excitement. It's like being young myself all over again."
A short time later, Megan arrived back at Sarah's table.
"Here's your lunch," she said passing Sarah some sandwiches wrapped in a damp tea towel.
"You look just like your mother" Megan said proudly all smart in your uniform. "I won't expect you back until you actually arrive and we'll see what happens from there. Now we've timed the walk, you'll be there in forty minutes, so it's best you leave soon. You don't want to start your first day all flushed now do you?"
"Thank you Nana, I don't know what I'd do without you," Sarah said giving Megan a hug.
"You've done more than you think, just by being here," Megan said. "With your mother away, Sean busy with the farm and the mill, and David gone, I was scared I'd be left well and truly on my own."
"Well you're not. I'm here and you can be my patient when it comes to practising bandages."
"Be off with you, Sarah love. I'll be thinking of you."

**

Sarah walked along Devon Street feeling happy with herself, excited about her new beginning she believed would set her up for life. Turning onto Morley Street, she started up the steep hill with the morning sun in her eyes.
"Goodbye Mummy," a voice said from behind the stone wall of a large two storey villa. In the same minute, a woman, without looking, stepped through a corner gate, onto the footpath bumping into Sarah and knocking her over.
"Oh dear," the voice said. "Are you all right? I'm most frightfully sorry."
Sarah looked up to see a woman, about the same age standing over her and obscuring the sun so she couldn't see her in detail.

"Here, let me help you up," she said. "No broken bones, that's lucky."

Sarah got up and brushed her dress down with her hands.

"I'm so sorry," she apologised. Her voice was warm and caring.

Sarah gathered her wits. "The sun was in my eyes, I didn't really see you."

"Not at all," the woman told her. "It was my fault entirely, I was in an awful rush, I didn't really look myself."

"No harm done," Sarah said picking up her sandwiches and stopping to look at the woman. She was tall with long hair tied back in a ponytail shining brown in the sun. She was wearing the same nurse's uniform as Sarah but rather than wearing cloth cap, she carried it in her hand. She smiled a warm enigmatic smile which creased her dark brown eyes making Sarah like her immediately.

"Oh look, your uniform is all dishevelled and dusty. Come inside and I'll brush it down for you."

"It's all right," Sarah told her. "I can do it."

"Nonsense," the woman said. "You have another half an hour until you report in if I am not mistaken, we can sort you out in the shake of a lamb's tail, please, in fact I insist. Come on or you'll be late and Matron will have your head on a block. 'Punctuality is a good discipline' she'll be telling you."

"How do you know?" Sarah asked.

"I should do, she's my Auntie Caroline, on my mother's side."

"Your auntie?"

"Yes, but don't let that fool you. She's harder on me than anybody else. It's more of a curse really, she can be a right old harridan sometimes," the woman laughed again holding out her hand.

"Allow me to introduce myself, I am Linda Bryant."

"Sarah, Sarah Murphy," Sarah said taking Linda's hand.

"Hello Sarah Murphy, come on in and let's get you cleaned up and we can still be early if we're quick about it."

**

With two minutes to spare, Sarah and Linda were standing in a corridor outside the matron's office. Sarah was trying to take deep breaths in through her mouth and out through her nose control her emotions but she took one look at Linda and the two of them burst into laughter. Doing her best, she adjusted her cap making sure it was on straight then, after a nod from Linda, she gingerly knocked on the door.

"Enter," came a stern voice.

Matron was a tall but slender woman. Her tightly curled hair was just visible under her cap and her pallid face showed no sign of cosmetics. She was looking at Sarah over the top of her glasses, her wise blue eyes scanning her as though looking for weaknesses, flaws Sarah thought she would find and exploit.

"Don't look so nervous. I don't bite you know, despite the stories you may have heard to the contrary" Matron said without any change of expression in her voice.

"I'm, I'm Sarah Murphy," Sarah said hardly able to breathe.

"So I understand, but what pray are you doing here Nurse Bryant?"

Linda stepped forward to speak. "I've come to explain why Sarah is later than she otherwise would be."

"Yes, you are late."

"I'm a tad early actually," Sarah was brave enough to say.

"Most trainees arrive ten minutes early, especially on their first day, therefore you are late. You will do well to remember that Miss Murphy," Matron stared stony faced at Sarah.

"Punctuality is a good discipline you know."

Linda turned to Sarah with a very slight whimsical smile.

"Nurse Bryant. Take Miss Murphy and report to Sister Pugh, you will then go to the sluice room for duties there. You will both then report back to me at one o'clock sharp this afternoon; and make sure you are scrupulously clean. Do you understand?"

"Yes Matron," Linda answered.

As they walked to the door, Matron called out. "Miss Murphy, where have I seen you before?"

"I'm not sure" Sarah replied. "My nana owns the Britannia Tea Rooms in Devon Street. I live there with her, sometimes I help if it gets busy."

"Yes, that's it. I'm rather partial to the Welsh cakes there myself."

"They're Nana's own recipe. We've grown up eating them," Sarah said proudly.

"We?"

"My brother, Richard and I."

"Where did you grow up?"

"On the river at Mokau. Middle River to be precise. My parents are farmers, they own Ballinger's Mill upriver as well."

"Your brother?" Matron asked.

"He's in the army of course," Sarah replied. "He's in Egypt now waiting for orders for the Dardanelles I expect."

"Surely you mean Belgium?"

"No, at least I don't think so. Since the British navy lost its ships, I think the army will move in to stop the Turks since they've fallen in with the Germans. There's not a lot of choice really when you think about it. We need a clear line of attack on Constantinople, to strike at the heart of the Ottoman Empire. I think it will happen quite soon."

"You seem to know a lot about the war Miss Murphy."

"No, not really," Sarah said. "I just read the newspapers a lot and work it out from there."

"Tell me. Why do you wish to become a nurse?" Matron asked.

"I just want to be of help to my brother. Indirectly of course and this is how I can do it," Sarah said.

"One o'clock," Matron told them both. "Not a minute later."

**

"I think she likes you," Linda said as they made their way to the ward and Sister Pugh. "And why didn't you tell me your parents own Ballinger's Mill? My father's a builder, he only buys timber from there. Hurry up Sarah or we'll be late, even if we're early."

"Yes," Sarah said as she started giggling. "Punctuality is a good discipline after all don't you know," she said as they both broke into laughter.

**

After two days of fierce fighting, Richard and Tama were taking shelter under a rock outcrop on the Gallipoli peninsula. "This is nothing but a bloody slaughter," Tama said. "A bloody slaughter from the day we landed, nothing but a bloody big cock up."
"You don't have to tell me," Richard said. "They got this one wrong and it's you, me and those poor bastards whose bodies are rotting on the tracks who pay the price, not those shiny arsed pricks on the ships out there. Take the forts they said, couldn't even get off the frigging beaches without being shot at. God knows how many are dead."
The New Zealand Expeditionary Force and the Australians, soon to be known as the Anzacs, landed near Ari Burnu on the Turkish peninsula some two miles north of their intended landing area and away from the allied forces at Cape Helles. Turkish guns fired heavy shells shattering the timber landing boats as they left the allied ships, and once in the bay, the men were shot or drowned after being dragged down under the weight of their packs before they had even reached the beach.
Richard and Tama, along with their regiments, had been trapped on the beach by cliffs rising vertically from the beach while the Turks, dug in on the high ground, machine gunned virtually at will during the day and fired mortars at random during the night. Neither Tama nor Richard knew how, but against the odds, they had made it inland to the comparative safety of the hills.

**

A month later, with almost catastrophic losses, the Anzacs were established on the peninsula, living, and fighting mostly within a network of trenches. Ongoing fighting continued to take its toll with many men almost too exhausted to fight.

Late one afternoon, Richard and Tama's platoon marched along McLagan's Ridge to the relative safety of the headquarters at Plugge's Plateau. They heard the distant chatter of machine gun fire so they kept their wits about them, watching out for the dust trail showing where the bullets landed.

"Don't worry about those," Tama told a frightened boy of barely seventeen years old. "They won't fire on us Māori after the haka we gave them last night. Be proud but don't be stupid. Corporal Murphy's our rangatira and he's my ehoa. He'll keep us safe. Ka pae?"

Before the boy could answer, machine gun fire opened up a lot closer with the bullets biting into the earth in front of them shredding the wild thyme and ricocheting off the rocks. Instinctively they dived for cover pushing their faces down into the ground. As soon as it started, it finished.

"Let's get out of here," Richard said. He turned to look around but the boy didn't move. Richard immediately knew why, he nodded to Tama who shook him. He didn't respond so Tama rolled him over to find his chest had been opened as though it was a carcass which had just been butchered.

"Leave him," Richard ordered. "Poor sod will have to lie here with the rest of them."

They continued to make their way back from the trenches walking through a sunken road behind Shrapnel Valley Cemetery. They had to slow down as a column of troops coming the other way trudged towards the trenches and the fighting. Their heads were bowed in silence and they neither talked nor showed any signs of interest. Their bodies, emaciated by dysentery and typhoid had been drained of any life or dignity. There was no light in their eyes, knowing that some if not most wouldn't see the end of the day.

Another column passed with half a dozen mules carrying large cases of ammunition strapped to their backs. Tama saw the last mule carried a stretcher.

"Ah mate, you're in the First Field Ambulance?" he asked the soldier leading the animal.

"What of it?"

"You know Theo Twentyman?"

"I've heard the name," the soldier said.

"Where can we find him?" Richard asked.
"Shrapnel Valley, more than likely."
"So where have you heard his name then?" Tama asked, his curiosity getting the better of him.
"He's a lucky bastard, always survives. If he fell down a sewer he'd come out smelling of roses. He puts himself in places where he shouldn't go to bring back an injured soldier, so the men follow him thinking they'll be safe as well. Has a way with the mules as well I've heard, they reckon he can talk to them?" Richard smiled. "He talks to horses as well," he said.
"I believe it, see, a few of us get close to the Turks, sorting out the dead ones from the live ones like we do, He's good at that too, but we keep it to ourselves if you know what I mean."
"Thanks mate," Richard said.
He and Tama walked ahead to catch up with the others. On the way they passed a Palestinian Arab wearing the badge of the Zion Mule Corps trying to coax a wounded mule to the front. The mule had fresh shrapnel wounds in its haunches and was barely able to stand. The motley looking beast had its ears back and refused to move as it made a terrible guttural sound sending shivers down the back of those who heard it. The driver pulled hard on the bridle rope but the mule's hooves were well and truly dug in.

**

Theo and Dickie Fleming were on the other side of the valley carrying a soldier on their stretcher. His arm had been blown off and with no bandages, anaesthetic, or even clean water at the field dressing station, he was being taken to the field hospital at Anzac Cove to be transferred to Lemnos.
"We need to give him a drink," Dickie said pointing to the unconscious soldier whose khaki tunic was now crimson with blood.
"No need," Dickie said putting his finger on the side of the man's neck checking for a pulse. "He's just run out of luck."
 "We'll ditch him here and maybe he'll get to Beach Cemetery, if he's lucky," Theo said. "If he's not he'll rot here with the others."

Theo looked about him. All around the edges of the track, bodies were piled up. Many were bloated and their skins had turned black. Hideous, contorted faces stared into space, some bodies had arms or legs missing from direct hits, some were decapitated. A great many had their brains shot out from the hundreds of lead balls which exploded downwards from the shrapnel shells the Turks favoured. Many bodies and bits of bodies were decomposing where they lay in the early summer sun. Nobody noticed the stench any more as that was normal for Gallipoli.

Theo's attention was taken by a small butterfly landing on a wildflower by his side.

"See how lucky we are Dickie?" he said.

"Lucky? Just how do you reckon we're flamin' lucky?" Dickie asked.

"See the butterfly there?" Theo said pointing.

"Yeah"

"Miss Tallboys at Murata School taught us that when butterflies come out of the cocoon, they don't have any mouths, all they can do is drink a bit."

Dickie sat back in disbelief of what Theo was saying. "So what of it?" he asked pushing his cap back and wiping his brow with his sleeve.

"Well when you think about it, our lives here are in the balance, but the butterfly's death is certain. That makes us lucky I reckon."

"Then Theo did what he had taught himself since landing at Gallipoli at such times, he bowed his head and recited the Lord's Prayer softly to himself.

"Our Father, which art in heaven, hallowed be thy name. Thy kingdom come.

Thy will be done in earth as it is in heaven. Give us this day…" Theo hesitated as he heard the braying of the wounded mule across the valley above the distant thunder of the guns.

"…our daily bread. And forgive us our trespasses as we forgive those that trespass against us. And lead us not into temptation but deliver us from evil. For thine is the kingdom, the power, and the glory, for ever and ever…Amen."

"You do that once more in open country like this and our kingdom will come all right, only sooner than you expect," Dickie said.
"You need a bit more faith in your life," Theo smiled at him.
"What's that noise?" Dickie asked. Theo lifted his head and scanned the valley as the mule cried out in pain again.
"That Dickie my friend is our next patient, come on," he said as he climbed the sides of the steep valley pulling at the dried grass and breaking off rosemary shrubs in his eagerness to get to the animal.
"You'll get us both killed, or court marshalled," Dickie told him.
"Watch out for the butterfly," was Theo's only response.

**

When they got to the mule it wasn't far from collapsing. The Arab was still beating it with a stick and shouting at it in Yiddish. Without hesitating, Theo stepped in between the man and the mule.
"How dare you treat an animal in such a way!" Theo shouted.
"Dat damned animal will get me all killed up. Damned animal won't damn move," the Palestinian shouted in broken English.
"Well, 'dat' damned animal is on the edge of death himself," Theo was shouting at the man who stood back not expecting such a challenge.
"Take the ammunition off his back and share it with the next mule train. The war won't stop because of it," Theo ordered.
The Palestinian stood silently looking at Theo.
"Do what I tell you or I'll take the stick to you," Theo threatened. The Palestinian quickly undid the girth straps letting the ammunition boxes fall to the ground.
"Now stand back," Theo warned the man. "Do what I tell you now or I'll make you carry the bloody bullets yourself."
The Arab did as he was told.
Theo got a grip of himself and walked to the mule, slowly smoothing the animal's neck and back, taking care to avoid the wounds. Slowly, amid the horrors of war and at the risk of being open to enemy snipers, Theo spoke softly in the animal's ear while rubbing its head. After several minutes the mule let Theo rub his hands over it again as it relaxed.

Theo turned to the Palestinian. "I'm taking the mule back with me."

"You pay, you pay!" the Arab shouted. Theo searched in his bag and found a tin of milk powder.

"Here have this. I'm sorry I shouted at you," he said. "I'll bring your mule back in a month or so, if I feel like it."

"As-Salam Alaikum," the Palestinian muttered as he stood in the hot sun with the tin of milk powder in his hand and looking more confused than ever.

Theo took the bridle off the animal's head so it was untethered then he walked back towards Plugge's Plateau with the mule gently hobbling behind as best it could.

"How do you do that?" Dickie asked.

"You're not the first one to ask" Theo smiled. "I don't know how I do it to be honest, I just can, always could, it's a gift I suppose, it's the same with horses."

They walked on in silence for a half a mile.

"I think I've got some dried up kawakawa from Mokau in my bag that can be useful" he told Dickie. He turned and watched the crippled mule some fifty yards behind him.

"Apollo," Theo said. "I think I'll call him Apollo…after the Greek god of music, poetry, medicine and light. There needs to be some good coming from this nightmare," he said waving his arm around.

"Hello Apollo," he said, stroking the mule's neck as he caught up. "Let's see if we can make you better."

**

Sean walked into the Mokau Hotel on his way back from the auctions at New Plymouth.

"Top of the mornin' to you Stella my love. Some of your chicken and leek pie if you would be so kind."

"Sean Murphy, what are you doing here?"

"Just on my way back from Bailey's Auctions, trying to get some fresh stock. Bugger all around now. Nobody about to sell, or to buy come to that. This war may be on the other side of the world but it's hitting us hard."

"Harder than you think," Owen McConaghy said sitting by the fireplace rolling a cigarette.

"Owen, I didn't see you there," Sean said. "You're not looking too chipper if I can say."

"Neither would you if you had to do what I do," Owen replied.

"Well pardon me for saying so, but if I ran a boat up and down the river all day maybe I'd be better off than I am now."

"Well Sean, to be honest, it's getting me down now. It's not the same anymore. I always enjoyed being part of everybody's life, it's like being paid to be a busybody, delivering people and goods, chatting along the way, you know how it is. Seeing the people move in, have kids and seeing them grow up over the last thirty years, but it's not for me anymore."

"Sounds fair enough so it does," Sean said. "So, what is it that's brought this on?"

"Because Sean my friend, over the last few weeks all I've been delivering are telegrams that break hearts and ruins lives."

Sean went quiet and Stella stopped what she was doing so she could listen.

"Killed in action is all the telegrams say," Owen went on. "Killed in bloody action. Young lives wasted and mothers crying for the rest of their lives for sons who will never come home. Fathers trying not to cry so they lash out in anger over their sons who left here for an adventure but were killed like vermin in some foreign land; and for what? The glory of the Empire? There's no glory that I can see, only death and heartbreak."

The scattering of people in the bar fell silent as Owen's words brought home the reality of the war.

"I've heard a few stories," Sean said. "The newspapers go mostly unread at Llanon, Libby reads them and that's about it. George is flat out on the farm and with me at the mill too busy to know exactly what's happening over there."

Owen stood up to leave. "Well, I know this, in the *Heron* are two telegrams. One for the McPherson's; that will be their lad, Ian who'll be dead or maimed, and there's another one for the Dobson's. That will be young Charlie of course. Both of those boys used to ride in my boat to get out of school for the day. More often than not they'd just lean over the side watching the bow cut through the water and talking. They'd finish up with sunburned faces and smiles as wide as can be. I'd give them sixpence each, but they did bugger all work of course. They were just young boys having an adventure and who can blame them for that? Now look what adventure's done for them. They're either dead or they'll have limbs blown off, but a penny to a pinch of salt they won't be coming back to work on the family farm anymore." Owen lit his cigarette and looked up at Sean. "Just hope and pray I don't have to stop at Llanon, eh?"

Moonyeen had been standing at the back of the bar and when Owen left, she came over to Sean.

"Do not worry about your son Mr Sean. He is strong and has good spirits with him."

"Owen's right," Sean said reflectively. "But it will take more than good spirits to stop Turkish bullets."

"Have you heard anything from Gwyneth?" Stella interrupted.

"Just the one letter to say she's back in the orphanage in Cardiff, busy training the staff how to look after the nippers. She seems to be happy, which is more than when she was here."

Sean moved over to a table and sat by himself, but after a while, Moonyeen came up to him, speaking quietly.

"Moonyeen help Mr Sean to overcome loneliness. Moonyeen come to the farm for a day or two?"

Sean looked around and caught Stella watching him, they held their gaze for a few seconds before she broke away, making herself busy washing glasses.

Sean thought for a moment. "It would be grand to have some time with you, Moonyeen. But I'm not sure it's right."

"But Mr Sean must face facts, Mrs Murphy has left you," Moonyeen said. "You are on your own now and you have to make choices about your future. You are not meant to be lonely. I can help if you want me to."

"There's nothing I'd like more Moonyeen. But like I said, it wouldn't feel right, especially at Llanon."
"Of course, Mr Sean. Moonyeen understand. Perhaps at hotel in New Plymouth?"
"Maybe, Moonyeen my love, maybe."
"But I have three days off in two weeks' time, perhaps then? We can go to same hotel as first time if Mr Sean wants to be there. If not, then I know Mr Sean does not want me anymore and I never ask you again."
Sean felt confused at the offer to rekindle his affair, it excited him, but he at last realised he had lost Gwyneth and secretly hoped she would come back.
Stella came out of the kitchen and put the plate of food on the table in front of Sean, then sat down opposite him.
"Sean, you and me, we understand each other. We've been friends, mostly, sometimes enemies but we've always been brutally honest with each other regardless of the consequences."
"That we have Stella, what of it?"
"Nobody's had the courage to tell you, so I will. It's no secret why Gwyneth left you, and to be honest, you damn well deserved it."
"Go on Stella, don't stop now," he said looking even more confused about what was coming next. He put down the knife and fork and looked directly at Stella.
She looked at the table, hesitating, wondering if she was doing the right thing.
"Well…. what is it Stella? What is it I need to know?"
"Well, when Gwyneth left you … to go back to Wales, she wasn't on her own."
"What do you mean by that, not on her own?" Sean asked. "Who the hell could she have been with?"
"David Askill," Stella said, "Doctor David Askill to be precise."
"And who might he be when he's at home?"

"You don't even know what's going on right under your nose, do you?" Stella said. "Typical bloody man. David Askill knew your Gwyneth well before you did, in Wales. They worked together apparently. He came here looking for her, to take her back, and you, you dumb Irishman gave her to him all wrapped up. That's why she went back. It wasn't on her own. Don't you see, it was all planned?"
"Wasn't he the doctor here in Mokau?" Sean asked suddenly realising what Stella had told him.
"He was," Stella said. "See what I mean, right under your nose. She played you like the fool you are."
Stella walked away leaving Sean to his thoughts.
After a while Sean signaled Moonyeen over to his table.
"Two weeks from Monday you say, the White Hart Hotel?"
"Yes," Moonyeen said. "Same hotel as last time Mr Sean."
"Can you make it next week? And the Red House, the White Hart's too close to the Britannia Tea Rooms for my liking."
"I think so," Moonyeen thought for a few seconds. "Yes, Mr Sean, I can be at Red House in one week if that is what you want."
"Then it's agreed Moonyeen my love," Sean said getting up to leave but not before giving Moonyeen's hand a slight squeeze. Moonyeen picked up the plate, the pie was cut and mashed and barely recognisable.

Chapter Eight

**

The summer passed quickly for Sarah as her studies and occasional outings with Linda occupied her time. Linda was a free spirit who energised Sarah, yet Sarah grounded Linda, so together they retained a sense of adventure and did well in their studies which made them both popular with their colleagues and patients. They would both study at the Britannia Tea Rooms after it was closed for the day. Megan would always bring down biscuits and cocoa at seven o'clock when they would break away from studying. That was the time they watched to see who was walking down Devon Street, sticking to the shadows and draw conjecture about what it was they were doing or where they were going.
"Look," said Linda one evening, pointing to a woman walking down the street with her head bowed looking as though she didn't want to be seen. "Over there, that's Fay Carrington, she was a charge nurse on ward two. Her father was a womanising drunkard and a reprobate who was involved in more fights than he could handle. He lost his job at the port because of it then died in a house fire soon after. This is the first time I've seen Fay back in town. Apparently, she was pregnant to a stevedore, but he was married, or so it goes which is apparently why she hasn't been seen for some time. She must have gone to the country to have the baby. No sign of a man now I see."
"She has a ring on her finger," Sarah mentioned.
"Well, it doesn't take much to do that yourself now does it, for appearances, I mean."
"Linda, you're such a gossip." Sarah laughed.
"I wonder where she's going." Linda thought out loud. "Oh Sarah, do let's follow her?"

"We haven't time, there is a test tomorrow and I need good marks. So do you," Sarah said picking up her textbook and waving it in front of Linda.

"That's what I love about you Sarah, you do keep me grounded."

"And you keep me in trouble you little minx," Sarah mocked.

"Look," Linda said after a while. "Here's somebody else. That woman, the one with the hat. She's Chinese. I've seen her before carrying that same bag. Two weeks ago, I passed her on my way in here. She'd been on the sea."

"Do get on with your work," Sarah scolded returning to her books. "Anyway, how do you know where she'd been?" Sarah asked without looking up.

"She smelled of coal smoke," Linda replied. "I know how that smell gets in your clothes. Besides, the case she's carrying looks too heavy for day-to-day things. I think she has a few changes of clothing so she must be staying here in town for a while. We could follow her, just for fun, instead of Fay. It might be a lot more interesting."

Sarah looked up and saw Moonyeen walking on the other side of the street barely recognisable under her hat.

"She comes from Mokau," Sarah said. "She works in the hotel there."

"I say, Sarah," Linda said surprised at what Sarah told her. "You know her then?"

"Oh yes, I know her. She's a special cup of tea all right. Her name's Moonyeen Wu," Sarah answered. "We won't be following her, not ever. She's bad news."

"That's seriously intriguing, do tell more," Linda was getting quite excited.

"No," said Sarah in a somber tone, afraid of what she may find out if she and Linda did follow Moonyeen. "Are we going to study or not? If not, I'll ask you to go home."

Linda took the hint from Sarah's tone and they both focused on their study for the rest of the evening.

**

Saturday morning at the Britannia Tearooms were one of regularity for many, none more than the matron. Megan always made sure two Welsh cakes were put to one side for her and she who would arrive at ten o'clock sharp without fail, so her favourite seat in the window was always reserved for her. On a cold winter's morning, she came in as usual, and Megan brought over her pot of tea.

"Good morning Matron. How are you?"

"Very good thank you Mrs Thomas…" Matron hesitated. She looked at Megan for a brief second.

'Was there something else?" Megan asked.

"Pardon me for asking - but young Sarah, she has a brother in the army does she not?"

"Yes, Richard, my eldest grandson. He's in Gallipoli doing his duty for the Empire."

"Of course dear," Matron acknowledged. "Do you hear anything from him, if you don't mind me asking?"

Megan looked embarrassed. "Well, no, not exactly. He has written to his father, he's a farmer in Mokau. He calls in when he can and shows me any letters. Not much news of course with all the censoring they do. I've seen most of what I know from the newspapers but I'm just glad to know Richard's alive."

"It's not easy, is it?" Matron asked looking at Megan. "Sarah has never spoken of her mother."

"No. Sarah lives here, with me. Her mother's in Wales, Cardiff to be exact. She's a trained nurse and was asked to go back to help reorganise an orphanage where the children are looked after properly and not treated as cheap labour for the factories and coal mines. Gwyneth, Sarah's mother, makes sure they are well fed and receive an education."

"That's absolutely fascinating," Matron said. "I had no idea."

"If you don't mind, why do you ask?" Megan enquired.

"Well, your granddaughter is a very bright young woman. You may have heard the New Zealand army nursing service has been set up to help the war effort, I am thinking of asking Sarah if she would be interested in joining so I would value your thoughts."

"That's very kind of you. I imagine she would be very interested," Megan replied. "It would be a feather in her cap and to help the wounded soldiers recuperate when they got home would be an honour and a privilege."

"No, Mrs Thomas," Matron said looking around to make sure Sarah wasn't about. "Sarah would eventually be posted overseas to a field hospital. You see some nurses have already been posted to Egypt."

Megan sat down not expecting to hear such news. She was trying to think of a reason to say no so Sarah would stay with her in New Plymouth, but she couldn't as she believed in duty above self, so her thoughts were confused. Matron looked at her over her spectacles.

"You see, if you already have one of your two grandchildren serving abroad, I'm not so keen to ask Sarah to go, if heaven forbid something should happen."

"What would the chances of that be?" Megan asked.

"Well I have to be honest, it is a war, but Egypt is relatively safe and well away from the fighting. I have to be honest and tell you it's a harsh life in the heat and Sarah would have to go to Wellington for training. With the heat you see and diseases the men have, well, lets say they are not what we experience here. I'm sure you understand, being a woman of the world."

"Yes. Quite," Megan quipped.

"There is one other thing," Matron said. "My niece, Linda Bryant, she's a bright young woman too. I know she and Sarah are good friends and they're good for each other. Well, to be honest Mrs Thomas..."

"Please, call me Megan."

"Thank you Megan, then you must call me Caroline, Caroline Bennett. Well, Linda is capable of being promoted but the board are aware she is my niece and would prefer if she worked elsewhere if she is to make something of herself. It doesn't look too good you see with me being the matron. It's not a good look for the board either if you get my meaning. I would prefer if both Sarah and Linda would go to Egypt together."

"Yes, I think I can see your point. The only answer is to ask each of the girls themselves" Megan said after some thought. "If Sarah decides to go, it will be with my blessing, but she will ask her father of course, he must have the final word."
"Of course," Matron agreed. "I was rather hoping you would understand, as a woman.

**

Theo was cleaning the wounds on Apollo's haunches when Tommy Robertson walked by with a large box camera and tripod slung over his shoulder. Noticing Theo and Apollo, he stopped.
"'ere what's all this then, a bloomin' Kiwi and a donkey?" he asked, carefully letting his camera drop to the ground as he sat on an ammunition box.
"A mule," Theo corrected him. "Apollo is a mule, not a donkey."
"All right, all right Kiwi, keep yer 'air on. A bloomin' mule it is if you say so."
"I do," Theo insisted.
"Well, you ain't no Arab and you ain't no bloomin' Indian, so why've you got a mule if you ain't one of them then?"
"I'm looking after it," Theo said.
"Why, what's 'appened to the donkey?"
"I told you," Theo said impatiently. "Apollo is not a donkey, he's a mule. If you are going to ask questions about him, at least give him the respect of using his correct name."
"Well pardon me, professor," Tommy said. "What happened to the mule then? And why'd you call it Apollo?"
"I am assuming you are a reporter since you carry a camera rather than a gun, but you lack the ability to listen very carefully."
"I'm not a reporter, I'm a photographer who can write a bit," Tommy answered holding out his hand. "Tommy Robertson at your service. Photographer to the good people of New Plymouth."
"New Plymouth?" Theo said slightly surprised. "You're on Devon Street, aren't you?"

"I am," said Tommy. "'ave I taken your photo before? If I 'ave you'll remember the quality long after you've forgotten the price. That's my motto, see."
Theo said nothing.
"So, what's with the mule?" Tommy asked.
"He was hit by shrapnel and most of his hind quarters were badly cut and some of his bones were splintered, yet his driver was still beating him."
"They usually shoot 'em when they get like that, don't they?" Tommy asked looking at Apollo who gave the appearance of listening to the conversation.
"So I've heard."
"So why didn't they shoot this one?"
"Because I bought him."
"You bought an 'alf dead mule?" Tommy looked at Theo in surprise.
"Yes," Theo said. "Although he was half alive rather than half dead. I bought the poor creature for a tin of milk powder from the Arab who was beating him."
"How you goin' to fix him then, the mule, an' why'd you call 'im Apollo?"
"Apollo was the Greek god of medicine, poetry and music, amongst other things; and since you ask, I will be fixing him as best I can as you put it with some kawakawa in my bag, all the way from Mokau."
"Well, how come you had this kawakawa stuff then? What is it anyway?" Tommy was getting more and more interested by the minute.
"It's been used by Māori for generations as a panacea," Theo explained. "I had some left over from a hunting trip with some friends a long time ago along the Mokau."
"What's hunting got to do with it?" Tommy asked. "And what's a, a panacea?"
Theo was starting to get impatient with Tommy's puerile questioning.
"Hunting has nothing to do with it, not directly anyway. I got some kawakawa, it's a bush, a herb if you like, I got it to cure a lame horse…and a panacea is a medicine which cures most things."

"This kawakawa, it fixes most things then? Horses as well?" It must be bloody good stuff!"
"It is," Theo said.
"'ave you got a girl waitin' for you back in Mokau then Mr...."
"Twentyman. Theo Twentyman. And no, there's no girl. Well yes, no, maybe."
"Well either there is a girl or there ain't a girl. What's it to be Professor Twentyman?"
"What's it to do with you anyway?" Theo replied now becoming quite irritated by this invasion into his privacy.
"Well this is a good story. See, I look out for stuff for the newspapers back home. Full of gloom and doom they are wiv our boys getting a right pastin', so the editor wants some good news stuff. This 'ere story of you sorting out the donkey...sorry...mule, is a good un. We all know about what these 'ere mules do, so a Kiwi, and a local boy saving one is a good blinkin' story if ever there was one. If there's a girl involved as well, then all the better. You see people love to read soppy stuff as well. Brings it all home it does, you could be anybody's boy. Might get on the front page, what do yer say Professor Twentyman?"
"I, I'm not sure," Theo said.
"Well, it might make this girl, the one you're not so sure about, fall for you. You'd be a right 'ero and 'spect she'll be thinking of you day and night if she sees your mug in the paper. Not that she doesn't now of course, a good-lookin' boy like you. Go on, what d' yer say?"
"I'm still not sure."
"What's this girl's name?" Tommy asked.
"Sarah Murphy," Theo said. "But she's not my sweetheart either. She doesn't even know I like her like that" Theo said turning red.
"ave you got a present for 'er. Somethin' you can give 'er, a bit of a memento? Most do."
"Yes, yes I have a piece of alabaster from the pyramid of Khufu in Egypt."
"Perfect," Tommy said scribbling down a few rough notes.

They spent the next half hour taking photographs of Theo posing with Apollo against the sandbags and the scrub covered hillside. Apollo seemed to enjoy the attention. Theo made sure all the dried mud and twigs was brushed off his hide, so he looked his best. When it was all complete, Tommy shook Theo's hand and stroked Apollo's neck.

"It's been a right pleasure to have met you it has. I 'ope to get the photographs and some other stuff over to Lemnos in the next few days and who knows from there eh Professor Twentyman?"

"I wish you wouldn't call me that," Theo said.

"Nonsense," Tommy told him. "An educated bloke like yourself should be a professor. What you goin' to do after this lot then Prof'?" Tommy asked.

"If I survive you mean? I don't know, I was going to be a doctor but now I'm not so sure," Theo said thinking inwardly for the first time in a while.

"Oh, and one other thing," Tommy asked. "When's Apollo 'ere going back to active service, carrying ammo and bodies and stuff?"

For the first time Theo realised Apollo would have to go back. He had been so absorbed in getting the animal better, he hadn't realised it would have to be taken back to the mule drivers and be led to the front where it's likely he would suffer the same fate, or even be killed. Theo's throat closed and he couldn't answer. He walked away vowing to himself he would put his thoughts down in a long letter home.

**

The Gallipoli campaign was going nowhere. Men on both sides were emaciated and thirsty as the summer sun took its toll. Fresh water was in very short supply as the few wells available to the Anzacs were targeted by the Turkish snipers. Even so, some took the risk but for the most part were shot and their bodies lay where they fell as a warning to others.

The reality was, a lot of Turks were ordinary people caught up in extraordinary times, like the Anzacs. On several occasions, Theo and Dickie came face to face with Turkish soldiers looking for those who were still alive, lying among the piles of stinking corpses. There were too many to attempt any medical aid, all they could do was to kick the bodies and if they showed signs of life they were taken away. Initially cautious of each other, they made a few attempts at sign language and swapped tins of bully beef and milk powder for Turkish cigarettes, then went back to their grisly tasks.

**

"I've heard there's going to be a big push in a few days," Tama said jumping down into a trench at the sound of machine gun fire not fifty yards away. "About bloody time if you ask me, eh Richard. The Māori Contingent's here to teach these bloody Turks a lesson. Can't let them have it all their own way."

Richard was sitting in the bottom of a trench trying to find some shade and surrounded by old bully beef tins and spent ammunition cases by the thousand. It was at the junction of another trench which led directly to the front and the Turkish trenches not fifteen yards beyond. The trench had sheer sides, shored up in a haphazard way with timber and sandbags where the sides had fallen in. Every ten yards, makeshift ladders leaned awkwardly against the walls where the troops climbed out in futile attacks against an overwhelming force. Just above where Richard sat, New Zealander's bodies lay tangled together in mute testimony to the ferociousness of the Turkish retaliations. Every now and then, officers would be looking through periscopes, watching the Turks, gathering intelligence to pass down to headquarters. Dysentery continued to take its toll on the soldiers with many voiding their bowels where they stood, shooting at the Turks with diarrhea falling through their trousers into their boots and splashing onto whatever or whoever was laying alongside, often the bodies of fallen comrades. The stench would have been unbearable other than it was just another day in the trenches so not many took any notice. With no toilets, water, or paper to clean themselves, the faeces mixed with the soil was everywhere. Flies were numerous either in the trenches or on the carcasses of the dead troops lying in the summer sun. When a fresh wind came off the sea towards the Anzac lines, the Turks would shoot the bloated corpses so the fumes and the acrid stench that came with it, fell into the trenches, reminding the Anzacs that death was only a few yards away.
"I said it's about friggin' time we gave the bloody Turks a taste of what Māori can do" Tama said.
"What?" Richard looked up. "What are you talking about?"
 "A big push against the Turks. Anything's got to be better than these stinking trenches." Tama looked at Richard who was looking dazed, holding a notepad and pencil. "What are you doing?" he asked.

"I've been meaning to write a letter home," Richard replied. "But what can I say, I'm covered in my own shite and haven't washed or shaved for weeks. I'm drinking putrid water or my own piss and there's fuck all to eat. I'm walking in a mixture of blood and shit and the bodies of my mates are rotting in front of me. How the hell do I put that into words?" Richard threw the writing pad and pencil out of the trench, then put his face in his hands to hide tears welling up in his eyes. Within seconds the writing pad attracted a hail of machine gun bullets reminding Richard once again who was in control of his life.

"Corporal Murphy," came a shout with a high-class English accent from the company commander. He was a small man surprising well-groomed who strode along the trench with a swagger stick, using it to flick tins and bits and pieces out the way. He constantly looked after his appearance, making sure his tunic and lanyard were clean and correctly presented and his cap was on at just the right angle.

"Sir," Richard said half-heartedly without looking up.

"On your feet boy. You're to report to Quinn's Post as soon as you can."

"Me sir? Why, sir?" Richard asked.

"Because you are Sergeant Murphy now, that's why boy."

"Sergeant Murphy?" Richard questioned. "Where's Sergeant Stringer?"

"Dead, boy, that's where Sergeant Alfred Stringer is. Dead as a bloody Dodo, which is what you'll be if you don't get a move on."

The captain threw a piece of khaki to Richard which he had cut off Sergeant Stringer's tunic. "Here's your stripes, I can't say you deserve them but you're the only blighter left with any stripes at all. Now get yourself to Quinn's Post just as soon as you can; or maybe you'd like a nice rest first, maybe some steak and eggs would be in order? Shall I get chef to bring something up from the kitchen?" he asked. "Now get yourself to Quinn's Post before I kick your arse so hard the echo will break your ankles. Do you hear me?"

"What about me, sir?" Tama asked pushing himself between the captain and Richard. "Me and Richard are mates, we go everywhere together."

"Oh do you now. Well let me tell you sonny, I say what happens and I say you know your place and stay here with the rest of your kind."

Tama was astounded at the way he was spoken to.

The captain turned and walked away. "Bloody Māoris, all they're good for is shit. Digging trenches and shit" he said loud enough for Tama to hear.

Tama caught up tapping him on the back of his shoulder. The captain turned just as Tama's fist swung, hitting him on the jaw, knocking him out. Several other solders saw what happened, one, a Māori, smiled and spoke to Tama. "Kia ora, ka pai. Good on you brother."

**

Richard and Tama walked through the trenches and firing lines where sandbag traverses were stacked to protect the more vulnerable sites from sniper fire. They passed British, Australian and New Zealand troops hurrying in all directions along the maze of trenches. The sound of gunfire and grenades was all around. When he could, Tama spoke to stretcher bearers when they were held up in the trenches packed with desperate waves of humanity on their way to kill or be killed.

"You know Theo Twentyman?" he would ask. The reply was always a shake of the head as the bearers went on their way, too busy to care.

After several hours Richard and Tama found themselves at Quinn's Post.

Richard thought he would be in for a reprieve from the horrors of the past months but Quinn's Post was very close to the Turkish trenches and saw some of the fiercest fighting. It was built on a hillside with eight terraces each with heavily sandbagged firing platforms and lookouts. Lengths of corrugated iron had been placed in front of some of the sandbags and there was a rudimentary roof over each terrace. Timber pathways were laid down either side with tents of various descriptions with their canvas doors hanging in the still, hot air and occupied by officers sitting around tables in the relative gloom.

Men were everywhere, either marching along the perimeter or stretched out getting some sleep in what shade they could find. Some were just sitting down, cleaning rifles, or just staring into the distance. All were emaciated and nobody cared for conversation.

"Looks like a build-up of men all right," Tama said. "Maybe those rumours were true."

Within an hour both Tama and Richard were assigned to a unit of Anzacs. Richard was singled out for a briefing and was back two hours later. He found Tama sitting with a group from the Māori contingent. They were smoking, playing cards, and laughing as though there was no war at all. Richard stopped and looked at them for a minute, envious of their predisposition to relax knowing what they were in for.

"What's the story then Sergeant Murphy?" Tama asked when Richard stood by the circle of men.

"You were right," Richard said. "An all-out offensive, twenty thousand men to take the heights and break the Turks hold on the peninsula. The British will go by sea to act as a diversion."

"Well that makes a bloody change," said one of the Māori. "It's usually us covering their arses." He looked at the others with a toothless grin and everybody laughed.

Tama and Richard wandered away from the group.

"I didn't want to say in front of the others but it's the poor bastards at Cape Helles I feel sorry for," Richard said. "They'll go over the top to face the Turks, to stop them from regrouping. We're in the battalion opening up Rhododendron Spur to hold Chunuk Bair, then we're to wait for reinforcements before taking hill Nine Seven One."

Tama went quiet, knowing Rhododendron Spur which stretched from the beach to the peak of Chunuk Bair was open to Turkish machine gun posts in the surrounding hills, exposing the men to fire most of the way.

"Better get some sleep while you can," Richard said. "We're leaving in a few hours. Orders are to capture the summit before dawn to make the most of the dark, if we're caught in daylight we'll be slaughtered."

**

"Well haven't you grown into a lovely lady?" Owen McConaghy said to Sarah as she boarded the *Heron* in Mokau.
"Thank you, Mr McConaghy, it's very kind of you to say so. This is my friend Linda Bryant," Sarah said as Linda stepped gingerly into the boat.
"Good afternoon to you Miss Bryant," Owen said.
Linda enjoyed the trip upriver but Sarah felt nervous, she hadn't been home to Llanon for some time and without her mother there, she wasn't sure of what she would find.
"You know you are getting quieter the further you go up the river," Linda told her. "Are you really that nervous of asking your father about going to Egypt?"
Sarah thought for a moment not sure whether to tell Linda about Sean and Moonyeen.
At last they arrived at Llanon and walked along the jetty and up the bank. Libby was the first to see them and she came running down the path to greet them. She hugged Sarah.
"It's so good to see you," she said as she stood back looking at her. "My how you've grown into a beautiful woman, the spitting image of your mother. I got your letter of course. Your father is at the mill today but will be home tonight. George is in the paddocks, calving doesn't stop for anything."
"No, of course not. Oh, forgive me," Sarah said standing back. "Libby, this is Linda Bryant. Linda, Mrs Libby Twentyman." The two women shook hands.
"Do come in," Libby said who leading the way, Sarah and Linda followed, smiling at each other.
The kitchen smelled of fresh baking. It was scrupulously clean with half rolled pastry on the bench.
"I've just taken a loaf out the range" Libby told the two women. "I'll make some tea. There's scones in the tin if you like and it's roast lamb for tea, I hope that's all right Linda."
"I'd say it's more than all right," Linda replied. "I've never been in such a warm and welcoming house."
"Thank you," Libby said. "George, my husband, and I live here and Sean and Gwyneth, Sarah's parents live in the big house at the back. This one's the original farmhouse. It's a lot smaller but we love it...don't we, George!" Libby said looking up as George walked in.

The girls turned around.

"Uncle George," Sarah shouted out throwing her arms around him, then he stepped back holding her hands and looked at her.

"You're the image of your mother," he said. "Has anybody ever told you that?"

"Only about five minutes ago," Sarah laughed.

"I saw the *Heron* arriving and I just called in to welcome you home. I have to get back to work but I'll see you this evening with your father," George said. "Libby here is preparing a welcome home dinner. I want to hear about everything you've been up to."

"I'm not so sure you want to hear 'everything' though" Sarah said laughing. "And Uncle George, this is Linda."

The afternoon was spent with Sarah and Linda telling Libby about their work and the gossip of the hospital. Libby enjoyed talking to the two young women more than she realised.

In the late afternoon, a steamer loaded with timber, slowly chugged its way downriver, stopping at the Llanon jetty to drop off Sean. Sarah went down to greet him.

Sean looked rough, as though he hadn't slept for weeks. His eyes were sunken in and his shaggy head of hair was uncut and with more grey than Sarah remembered.

**

The conversation at the table soon turned to the war and the three boys.

"George and Libby here get a few letters from Theo," Sean said. "But there's not a lot from Richard.

"When was the last one?" Sarah asked.

"About four months ago," Sean replied. "From the first week in Gallipoli."

Sarah looked at the ground.

"Too busy I expect," she said. "He never really was the writing sort, was he?"

"You have a fair point there," Sean said. "But a father would like to know if his son is still alive."

There was a silence at the table only broken by Libby.

"We've had to split you two girls up for sleeping arrangements. Linda, you are sleeping here with us in the spare room and Sarah, you've got your old room back in your parents' house of course."

"Yes, thank you," the two girls said almost together.

"Auntie Ngaire and Uncle Wirimu?" Sarah asked after another short silence. "How are they?"

"Both good" Libby replied. "I expect you'll be seeing them tomorrow."

"So what do I really owe the pleasure of this visit?" Sean asked after polite dinner conversation ended. Taking the cue, George and Libby made their excuses by showing Linda the way to her room. On the way out Linda looked up at Sarah apprehensively.

"So what are you buttering me up for?" Sean asked after hearing Sarah talk for a half hour about her job as a nurse and what it meant to her, how she felt rewarded by being able to do something practical to help Richard, at least in spirit.

"There's an opportunity for me, for us, Linda and I that is, to be trained as army nurses."

"And what exactly is that?" Sean asked running out of patience.

"…it means we would be going overseas to Egypt; to be of direct help to the soldiers from the battlefield," Sarah said hesitatingly.

"And how would you be getting to Egypt?" Sean asked.

"By ship of course," Sarah answered.

"And how safe is that, with a war going on I mean. I read the Germans are sinking ships."

"Oh," said Sarah surprised at the question. "They wouldn't dare torpedo a ship with nurses would they? I mean they can't be that cold hearted."

"You have a lot to learn about war," Sean told her. "So you're here to ask for my permission, is that it?"

"Yes," Sarah said quietly.

"There's a few months special training, in Wellington. There's some nurses there now, in Egypt I mean. It's nowhere near the fighting, being a hospital, but it's something I desperately want to do Father."

"You and Linda, you'd both be going together?"

"Yes, were good friends and can watch out for each other," Sarah replied.
"I'll give it some thought," Sean said. "Right now I've got some pregnant cows to see to. You know where your room is" he said with no emotion in his voice." He wiped his mouth with a napkin then got up and left.
Sarah went outside and found Linda and Libby happily talking together.
"How did it go?" Linda asked.
"He's thinking about it."
"Well that's something at least," Libby said. "You're lucky your father ate with us to be honest Sarah. He rarely eats with anybody, certainly never in his house. He's always worked hard but there are days when we don't see him at all. He sleeps in the barn sometimes, I'm sure."
"Poor Father," Sarah said. "He must miss Mother terribly."
"And Richard," Libby added. "It hurts him that Theo and Tama write home a bit, Theo especially, but he hardly hears from Richard so he fears the worst. Goodness knows what would happen if Owen McConaghy ever had to deliver a telegram. I swear it would be the end of him. I'm surprised he didn't give you an outright 'no' about Egypt, sorry but Linda mentioned that's why you are here."
Libby saw the look on Sarah's face.
"Oh I'm sorry Sarah love, I didn't mean it like that. I'm sure Richard will be all right. Have you been in your old room yet?" Libby asked.
"No," Sarah replied.
"Well don't forget you can always double up with Linda here if you wish."
Sarah was perplexed by Libby's comment but when she went into the old house she knew what she meant. The air was cold and damp, there was no fire in the hearth and the kitchen smelled of mice. Linda put her handkerchief to her nose.

"This used be such a warm and loving home," Sarah said. She pointed to her mother's piano. "We all used to pack into here when we were small with Uncle George and Auntie Libby. Uncle Wirimu and Auntie Ngaire would be over there and Mother would play the piano and everybody would be singing. *Calon Lan,* the Welsh hymn, was Mother's party piece, apparently it was my grandfather's favourite. He died the day I was born so I never knew him."

"Come on," Linda said. "Let's get the place aired."

Over the next three hours, the young women threw out old food and started the fire in the range. Sarah especially dusted the piano and rubbed in some furniture oil until it looked more like it used to, then she carefully rubbed milk onto the ivory keys. For the first time in a long time, the hammer stuck the wires and the sound of the piano once again echoed through the house.

"I wish I could play properly," Sarah said playing awkwardly on the keys.

"I can play," Linda said. "Do you mind?"

She opened the piano stool and sorted through the sheet music.

"*Calon Lan* you say Sarah? Here it is, would you like me to play it now?"

"Oh Linda, would you?"

"Not as well as your mother of course, but if you like, I'll try."

Without hesitation Linda played fluently.

Sean was standing outside and when he heard the music as Gwyneth had played it so many times, he walked across the front lawn to look in the window and watched Linda on the piano with Sarah standing by. It was like he was looking at Gwyneth as he did many years earlier when they were so in love and thought nothing could come between them. It was then Sean realised he had lost touch with his whole family. Partly because of the war, but also because of his own greed and stupidity. He realised that all he had worked for was gone other than the business he always put ahead of his family, and, for the first time, he started to wonder who he was and what he wanted. When the music stopped he stood stock still. Too full of remorse and not knowing what to do, he turned away.

**

The next morning, Sarah took Linda for a walk along the river to see Wirimu and Ngaire. They received a very warm welcome and Linda commented that she had felt as though she had been Ngaire's long lost daughter by the way she was treated. They spent some hours recounting the adventures Sarah, Richard, Tama and Theo had on the river as children. After a while, Sarah got Ngaire on her own.
"I think I know what you are going to ask about," Ngaire said. "Your mother?"
"Yes," Sarah confirmed. "I know all the reasons she gave, but what was it really about?"
Ngaire agonised for a moment as she wrestled with her conscience about how to reply to Sarah's question.
"She had to be strong," she replied. "She had to stand for what she believed in, helping the children of her turangawaewae, of her home. You must ask her yourself when you get the chance."
"And what do you think about Linda and I going to war, with the army nurses?"
"The same advice I gave to your mother," Ngaire said. "You must do what you must do."

**

"What wonderful people," Linda said on the walk back to Llanon? "I really like Ngaire, she seems so, so wise. Was it like this when you were growing up?"
"Yes, I suppose it was," Sarah said. "We often went to see Uncle Wirimu and Auntie Ngaire. Either that or they came over to Llanon on a Sunday. But all the families here lived and played together on the Mokau. It's just the way it is, or at least was. Most of the young men have gone to war now. That's why I want to go to Egypt really, to be with them in some way, helping them."
"You are a very lucky woman, Sarah Murphy," Linda said. "But tomorrow's our last day here and you still have to talk to your father."

**

While Sarah was packing her bag, Sean came into her room. "It's been wonderful having you back so it has," he said. "You and young Linda have done wonders to the house, even in the few days you've been here. I heard Linda playing the piano last night and it reminded me of your mother and how she loved to play."
"That's because you bought the piano for her, all the way from the South Island. Father, you haven't said if you will give me your blessing, to go to Egypt."
"Well a few days ago you were asking my permission, now you're asking for my blessing," Sean replied.
"Well…" Sarah hesitated.
"Go," Sean said. "You may as well. Richard's gone, your mothers gone, you may as well go too."
"Oh Father. It's not like that. We're not leaving you; we're doing out duty. Fighting for what's right."
"Fighting for those bloated lords and so called gentry in England who are too scared to get off their fat arses and fight themselves. Go Sarah, but I have to say it won't be with my blessing. Not while I have any breath in my body."

**

Sarah never spoke a word on the journey back to New Plymouth as she was too confused. Her father's blessing would have meant a lot to her but without it she didn't feel right about going even though she knew that she must.

**

By early morning, just on sunrise, the New Zealanders with Richard and Tama, were in serious trouble. The Turks had anticipated the column climbing Rhododendron Spur and had opened fire with their machine guns, taking a heavy toll. Many more Turks under the command of German Lieutenant-Colonel Hans Kannengiesser had dug in at the summit, firing at will on the allied offensive. Tama was separated from Richard and he was one of the first to get to a small, sheltered plateau called 'The Farm' just below the summit. He ran in and threw himself against the earthen wall, totally exhausted, hardly able to think about what he had been through, let alone take into account what to do next. He had seen many good men gunned down around him. As it was, Tama was trying to keep his wits about him while others desperately sought shelter from the bullets and shrapnel flying around them from both sides. They tried to dig in, but the hard, stony ground made it all but impossible and as more men arrived they were even more exposed to gunfire.

A young man lying on the ground wounded and in tears started to crawl towards Tama holding his hand out for help. Tama was a second away from taking his hand when bullets raked the man's back causing his flesh to explode, exposing the man's spine and ribs shining white for a brief second in the pale light of dawn.

A voice shouted out. "Ready men, attack!" Hardly able to breath, Tama, without question started running again, firing blind as he and several hundred others made it to the next sanctuary, 'The Pinnacles'. It was just another rocky outcrop but half the men made it but were once again pinned down by Turkish fire as they hugged whatever cover they could find.

"What do we do now, sir?" Tama shouted at a young captain stooping besides him with his pistol, shooting at whatever he could. The captain, a young Welsh officer turned and spoke in a calm voice. "We wait for orders soldier, we wait for orders." Encouraged at the captain's manner and grateful for a chance to take stock of what had happened, Tama looked himself over and noticed blood showing through his tunic sleeve.

"Shit, I've been shot," he said to himself.

"Sure you ain't dead?" came a sarcastic reply from a soldier behind him.

"Take more than a bullet to kill me," Tama shouted back. He checked himself again and found a hole in his sleeve, revealing a flesh wound.
"Never felt a bloody thing" he said.
"Better get it seen to all the same," the captain advised. "As soon as you can soldier. We need all the good men we can if we're to take Chunuk Bair."
"Are you Welsh...sir?" Tama asked.
"Cardiff," the captain replied. "What makes you ask?"
"Nothing. Only my auntie's Welsh. Well, she's not really my auntie, my mate's mum and neighbour."
"Where is it she comes from then, in Wales I mean," the captain asked.
"Llanon, they called their farm Llanon after her hometown."
"There's nice," the captain said in his lyrical voice. "It's good to know there a little bit of Cymru in New Zealand."
Tama immediately recognised the tone of a man who was proud of who he was.
"Kia ora," he said holding out his hand. "Tama Ratahi, Private. Wellington Rifles. Ngati Maniapoto."
"P'nawn da," the captain replied taking Tama's hand. "Gareth Jenkins, Captain. Fifteenth Battalion, Welsh Regiment. It's a pleasure to know you Private Ratahi."

**

For three hours Tama never moved. Captain Jenkins had disappeared but eventually came back to his position where he could see the Turkish defences at the summit.
"What's the guts?" Tama asked
"We're to stay where we are," was the reply. "Lieutenant Colonel Malone says he's lost enough men today. We're to continue the advance after dark."
"On our own?" Tama asked desperately.
"No, Private Ratahi, at least I hope not, the Western Division and the Gloucester's and maybe what's left of the Welsh Regiment will be helping us with a bit of luck." The captain looked at Tama. "You've got a good man in Malone, a damned good man."

It was a long day for Tama. At one stage he took cover and went back looking for Richard but after an hour of searching, couldn't find him. There were many wounded soldiers, some died where they lay and were pushed to one side to make the way clear, some were severely wounded but all were exhausted and traumatised after fighting against overwhelming odds. They were starving and dehydrated and few had any resolve to go further, at least that day.

Tama went back to his post not wanting to miss any further action. Putting his head against a rock he closed his eyes for a few seconds. He woke with a start, ashamed of himself for falling asleep, he looked at the captain.

"Go and get that arm seen to soldier," was all he said could say. "The First Field Ambulance are coming up behind the reinforcements. Get a dressing on your arm at least."

"Yes sir," Tama said.

He went back down the track again only this time there were more soldiers than before. He stopped some of them, more than happy to see fresh faces.

"Where are you from boys?" he asked a group of soldiers who were humming in unison.

"We're from the valleys you see boyo," said a young soldier. "From Wales you see, all the way to bloody Gallipoli just so we can teach these Turkish blokes how to sing properly. A real din they were making until we got here they were."

"Ay, that they were," said another Welshman. "And the thing is you see, if they don't sing good enough, well we bloody well shoot 'em."

The others in the group laughed and Tama almost cried with relief.

Half an hour later he noticed some stretcher bearers and stopped in his tracks.

"Theo? Theo Twentyman? Is that you?"

"Tama, Tama Ratahi, well if you're not a sight for sore eyes. I thought you must be dead," Theo said.

Tama rushed over and hugged him. "God it's good to see you Theo. Me and Richard have been looking for you ever since we arrived in Egypt."

"Yes," Theo replied, "Richard just told me."

"You've seen him?" Tama stood back in surprise.

"Yes. He's just down the track. Not too good, he has a bullet in his chest," Theo said going quiet. "He's lost a lot of blood Tama, my mate Dickie Fleming's with him. We put some dressing round his chest to stop the bleeding, he'll be taken back down the spur soon."
"Not before all three of us get together Theo. Come on, we need to see him."
Theo hesitated. "I've got a job to do here Tama."
"Come on Theo mate," Tama pleaded. "Me and Richard have been together all the time through this hell hole. Just two minutes eh? Just to be together again, like at Mokau for all those years. It would mean a lot to him, and me."
"All right," Theo agreed. "But we'll have to be quick."
Richard was semi-conscious when the two men arrived.
"Richard mate, wake up, this is no time for a nap," Tama said with a fake smile hiding his concern.
Richard roused himself.
"Wakey-wakey hands off snaky," Tama said. "You're not in Egypt now Richy boy."
"He's lost a lot of blood," Dickie said.
Theo gently lifted the dressing on Richard's chest and blood spurted out onto the ground. Theo looked back at Tama and gave his head a gentle shake.
"Richard! Richard! Wake up!" Tama shouted." Don't forget we've all got to have a whiskey together… at the Breakwater Hotel, like we promised ourselves … when we left. Remember that Richard?"
"Of course I do," Richard rallied, doing his best to smile. "And you're bloody well paying," he whispered.
Tama smiled.
"Too right I am," he replied, "after you get the first round in".
Richard put his head back and lost consciousness altogether.
"Fuck it," Tama said.
Pulling back the dressing he plunged his finger into the bullet hole in Richard's chest. Within a few seconds the bleeding stopped.
Theo looked startled. "You can't do that."
"I just damn well did it," Tama replied. "What do I do now?"
"What can you feel with your finger?" Theo asked.
"Just wet flesh, warm blood. Hold on. Here's something hard."

"Might be a rib" Theo suggested.
"If it is, it's a bloody funny shape."
"Must be the bullet," Theo said. "Can you wiggle it around?"
"Ay".
"Can you grip it?" Theo asked.
"Not with one finger, it's too slippery," Tama replied.
Theo was stuck for a reply.
"I know," said Tama. "Theo, I'm going to pull my finger out and you're going to put yours in very quickly, to stop the bleeding, all right?"
"I suppose."
"There's no fucking suppose about it. Richard's bleeding to death," Tama said.
As soon as Tama had his hands free he reached into his tunic and pulled out his hunting knife.
"What are you going to do with that?" Theo asked.
"Just watch, and for God's sake, keep your finger still."
Carefully, Tama slid the back of the knife down Theo's finger into Richard's chest until it found the bullet, then he brought the blade forwards along one of Richard's ribs, opening up the wound.
"Now put your other finger in and grab the bullet" he told Theo. "But do it quickly, he can't have much blood left."
"Wait!" Theo suddenly shouted out, giving everybody a fright. "Dickie, get my bag. In the bottom, there's the last of the kawakawa leaves I used on Apollo. It's only a few old dried up bits but rub it in your hands to break it up and put it all on the wound when I pull the bullet out. It's all we have for disinfectant."
Dickie fetched the leaves and crushed them in his hands.
Theo and Tama looked at each other.
"Our Father which art in heaven…" Theo started reciting as he quickly pulled his hands out of Richard's chest.
Dickie threw the crushed leaves on the wound.
"Give us this day a decent bandage," Tama said as he immediately stuffed the already blood soaked muslin in the gaping wound as fast as he could until no more would go in.
They all waited, watching, but there was no more bleeding.

"It's up to you now," Tama told Theo. "You and your mates need to get Richard to help as quickly as you can. I've got to get back and God willing we'll all meet up at the Breakwater Hotel for that whiskey before we know it."
"May God be with you," Theo said.
"I reckon God will be busy enough without having to look after me," Tama replied.

**

At three o'clock the next morning, the British navy bombarded the summit of Chunuk Bair for half an hour before the reinforcements were ordered to advance on the enemy. The Wellington Regiment were the first to reach the summit virtually unopposed and Tama was one of the first to stand on the top. Surrounded by darkness, he felt elated and exhausted at the same time. He could see the rocky ground was pock marked from the bombing and the whole area was strangely silent in stark contrast to what he expected. Before he knew it, the allies were swarming over the summit.
"They've all scarpered," a soldier shouted out. "They've all bloody well scarpered."
"They'll be back soon enough," said a nervous voice from the darkness.
"Dig in lads, we'll need all the cover we can from both the north and the south, make walls from the rocks if you have to." The familiar and calm voice of Captain Jenkins was close to Tama.
Tama worked trying to loosen earth and rocks with his bayonet and stacking rocks until his fingers bled. By five o'clock, the Turks opened up with machine gun fire from the nearby Hill Q and Battleship Hill which the allies had failed to capture.
By the end of the day, the allied position on Chunuk Bair was strewn with the dead and the dying. The Turks had crept up to within two hundred yards of the summit without being seen, such was the steep terrain. Tama used his own rifle and any other he could find from his dead comrades. His hunting knife found the bellies and the throats of Turks when his rifle was too hot or had jammed.

The following day was no different. More allied soldiers died in close hand to hand fighting as well as machine gun fire as, in the total confusion, the battalion of Gurkhas ordered to take Hill Q, had been wiped out by fire from their own side. The New Zealand machine gunners on the Apex, killed as many of their own men as Turks for the same reason.

After relentless attacks, the Turks eventually took the eastern side of the summit giving them a foothold to launch an offensive in massive numbers, almost annihilating the two thousand remaining allied soldiers. As Tama backed down from the summit, he turned for a last look. The enduring image put in his mind in that instant was the piles of bodies, three or four deep in places and now left in the hands of the enemy. He did what he could to help the pitiful line of wounded and dying as he virtually crawled back down Rhododendron Spur. It was less than a mile from Chunuk Bair to the beach but it took three days for the wounded to be cleared out. Those who died, were pushed to one side to make room for the living. All the time, Tama, half dazed from trying to take in what had happened, asked about Theo or Richard but found no sign of either.

**

Dickie looked up at the shattered figure of Theo as he entered the tent two days later, totally exhausted. "You all right?" he asked. "Apollo's at the back somewhere. He's been waiting for you, refusing to leave." Theo went out and found the mule grazing amongst the rocks. Putting his arms around the animal's neck, he cried until his body convulsed and there was nothing left to give.

**

On his way out of the tent on the following morning, Theo caught sight of his reflection in a broken mirror. He had to look twice as he didn't recognise himself and was genuinely shocked at what he saw. His face was gaunt and filthy. His lifeless eyes had sunk back into his face as though they belonged to another man. He rubbed his chin as he tried to remember what he used to look like and wondered whether he would ever see that youthful face again.

**

Theo and Dickie spent the next week doing what they could at what passed for a medical station at the beach or taking bodies to be buried. The operating theatre consisted of no more than a square of sandbag walls. There was no roof and the operating tables were packing cases stashed on top of each other, where surgeons amputated limbs with virtually no anaesthetic or fresh water.

**

Beyond physically and emotionally spent, early on a Sunday morning, Theo couldn't sleep. As the sun was just rising, he decided to take a walk to the hills for prayer, but first he went to the beach to bathe and wash himself. He was surprised to see a dozen or so other men already there and throwing a rugby ball around in full view of the snipers. One of the men threw the ball to Theo as he walked by.
"C'mon Kiwi" he called, "we need another man on the team to take on this bunch of Aussie sheilas."
Theo laughed and threw the ball back.
"Got to scrub up first, might come back later."
"What about your mate?" the man called back pointing to Apollo who was following behind.
"He'll be back too" Theo laughed. "We're a team."
After washing himself down in the sea, he swam a few strokes and enjoyed the feeling of the water on his body in the morning sun. He walked back up the beach waving out to the hills acknowledging the Turkish snipers he knew were watching.

Back at the tent he shaved as best he could then combed his hair.

Dickie stirred in his bed.

"Where are you going?" he asked.

"Church," was Theo's reply. "Or at least to the hills for prayer and to see if I can make some sense of this mess."

"Say one for me," Dickie said.

"You can come with me and say one for yourself if you like," Theo replied.

"You sound chipper this morning," Dickie mumbled pulling a sheet back.

"It's times like this I turn to God all the more."

"Fair enough, but what will you pray for today? There's a pretty long list you know."

"I'll just give thanks for being alive Dickie. I don't need to do any more. God knows what's in my heart already. Psalm one hundred and twenty one. I will lift up mine eyes unto the hills from whence cometh my help," Theo quoted. "My help cometh from the Lord, which made heaven and earth."

"Well like I said, say one for me," Dickie said pulling the sheets back over his head.

Theo found Apollo grazing on a half dead shrub and gave him a rub between the ears and the two of them walked along with Apollo still limping badly but trying to keep up. They made a strange looking pair but there was an understanding, a reliance on each other they both needed for survival of their minds and their bodies.

Theo had a new enthusiasm for life, refreshed in his hope for a future as he found himself thinking of Sarah for the first time in a long time.

Together, Theo and Apollo walked along a strangely silent Shrapnel Valley to Plugge's Plateau, then on towards the hills. They were invigorated by a breeze of fresh air coming off the sea and the only sound of fighting was sporadic machine guns or snipers in the far off hills. A quiet day for Gallipoli.

"Just a bit further boy and then we'll rest," Theo told Apollo as the ground started to rise up in the foothills. "We don't want to get too close to the front on this narrow ledge."

They walked around a bluff where Theo knew the track widened out and the rocks gave cover and there was a good view of the hills which had cost so many lives.

A harsh rattle of a machine gun was louder than the others. Theo knew immediately something was wrong. Apollo let out a deep bray which almost ended in a scream. Theo put his hand on Apollo's shoulder and called out.

"Our Father who art in heaven, Hallowed…."

Time slowed right down to a seemingly glacial pace as Theo turned to look at Apollo whose ears were back and he looked scared. Theo clearly saw five bullets following one another in the air before they exploded into the side of the bluff.

"…be your name. Thy Kingdom come…"

The next six bullets went deep into Apollo from his haunches, along his back and into his neck.

"…Thy will be done in earth. As it is in heaven…"

Theo watched as Apollo fell in slow motion, trapping Theo's feet as three more bullets hit Apollo's jaw, shattering the bone.

"Give us this day our daily bread. And forgive…"

Two bullets exploded into the rocks between Theo and Apollo. Theo saw them catching the sunshine and he knew what was going to happen next.

"…us our trespasses, as we forgive them that trespass against us…!" he shouted as four more bullets went through his tunic, ripping his liver, spleen, and a kidney before coming out of his back.

"And lead us not into tempta…"

Five more bullets entered his body smashing his pelvis and spine.

His torso was separated from his legs by six more bullets going through the rest of his body. His intestines exploded out of his rib cage landing on Apollo's body.

In the hills a Turkish gunner smiled. "Piç olduğunu almak" he said under his breath as he spat out a cigarette butt, then leaned back putting his hands behind his head, content with his work.

An hour later a reconnaissance party approached. The captain looked at the shattered bodies of Theo and Apollo.

"Unusual to see a mule up here," he said. "Push the bodies over the edge. We need to keep the track open."

**

"You need to go and see your father before you go to Wellington," Megan told Sarah one evening. "You don't know how long it will be until you see him again."
"Yes, I suppose you're right," Sarah said. "Will you come with me Nana? It would make it the best family gathering we can muster until the boys get back."
Megan smiled and thought for a while. "Well I suppose I could. It's been so long since I've been to Llanon, I hope the trip won't be too much for me."
"Nonsense Nana, I'm sure you'll be all right. Auntie Libby will make us most welcome. You can teach me how to make Welsh cakes properly. Do you mind if I ask Linda? She's an absolute whizz on the piano and Father likes her."
"No, not at all dear" Megan replied.
 "Good," Sarah said. "I'll write a letter to Father tonight to tell him we're coming. Hopefully the house will be looked after better than last time."
Megan looked up at Sarah and smiled without saying a word.

**

Two weeks later, in late August, Megan, Sarah and Linda were on the *Reliance* sailing towards the Mokau River bar. Megan remained silent, staring out to sea with a tear in her eye.
"What is it?" Linda asked when Sarah was still in the saloon.
"Oh nothing really, just the wind and the sea spray," Megan lied.
"You know you're allowed your memories, Mrs Thomas," said Linda rightfully guessing that Megan was reliving the past.
"You are an insightful woman," Megan smiled. "I was just thinking of the first time we came here, with David, Sarah's grandfather and her mother. All the things that have happened since then. Sometimes I wish I could turn the clock back."
"Well none of us can do that Mrs Thomas. All we can do is be grateful for the good times we've had. It's like a rose that blossoms, then fades, but leaves a beautiful memory"

"Yes, you're right of course. I've got lots of good memories when all is said and done. It's just this war pulling families apart."

No sooner had Megan finished talking when the ship listed as her bottom scraped over the bar. The two women grabbed a rail to steady themselves making Megan laugh. "What's funny Mrs Thomas?" Linda asked rather startled.

"Just more memories Linda love, just more memories."

As they headed towards the wharf they passed two steamers loaded with timber making their way towards the bar.

"Oh look Nana," Sarah said appearing from the saloon. "That timber must be from Father's mill."

Another steamer was tied up at the wharf with its funnel belching out smoke, ready to make its way upriver with some supplies for the farmers. At Megan's request the captain accepted the passage for the three women and within an hour they were leaving Mokau. At the last minute, before they went inside to get away from the smoke from the funnel, Linda tugged at Sarah's coat.

"Look, over there Sarah. There's the Chinese woman we saw from your nana's café a while ago. You said she worked here, there she goes walking along the bank, Moonyeen somebody wasn't it?"

"Yes," Sarah said. "Wu. Moonyeen Wu. And I also said she's bad news if you remember."

Megan and Sarah looked at each other, then they both turned their backs and went inside.

**

The welcome from Libby was as warm as the first time Linda arrived at Llanon. Sean had taken an afternoon off work to make sure Megan was welcomed and at Libby's insistence, dinner was held in her house. She had spent almost the whole week cleaning and baking. The table was laden with meats, winter vegetables and pies of all descriptions. Libby wouldn't accept help from anybody other than Linda, leaving Sean, Megan, and Sarah in the front parlour.

"Have you heard from Gwyn?" Megan asked at the first opportunity. "It's just that we haven't seen you in New Plymouth for a while."
"A man gets busy running two farms and a mill virtually on his own," Sean replied. He stood up and walked over to the sideboard. Opening the top drawer he pulled out a letter and passed it to Megan.
"It's four months old," Megan exclaimed.
"There's a war on or have you forgotten?" Sean replied sharply.
"Oh I haven't forgotten Sean, how could I with Richard, Theo and Tama fighting."
Megan started reading.
"What does Mother say?" Sarah asked.
"Not a lot more than before really," Sean said. "It seems the orphanage is a great success and your mother seems to be held in high regard. There's no mention of Doctor David Askill of course."
"It's not like that Father," Sarah said. "It's purely platonic."
"Call it what you want Sarah love, it's all the same to me."
"Dinners ready," Libby called out.

**

Two days passed and there seemed to be a peace at Llanon for the first time in a long while. Sarah and Sean talked a lot about Sarah going to Egypt and life after the war. Linda played the piano and Megan and Sarah sang *Calon Lan* almost moving Sean to tears.
"Oh Nana, let's have a picnic on the front lawn like we used to? We can do it at lunchtime, before we go back, before Owen McConaghy comes for us" Sarah pleaded on the last day.
Libby overheard the conversation. "Oh yes, that's a good idea. George and Sean can take out the old table and chairs out on the riverbank."
No sooner was it said than done and when everybody had sat down, Sean stood up and proposed a toast.

"I know it's difficult for us with the boys away and I miss them more than words can say. I have to admit there have been times when I have shed tears for my boy, not knowing where he is or what he's doing. But if there's one thing George and Libby have taught me, it's to have hope. So as this is the first time we have all sat down together since I don't know how long, I'd like you to raise your glasses and drink to hope. Hope the boys will be back safe and be back soon."

Amidst tears and smiles, the others raised their cups. "Hope" they all called out.

The family gathering was all Sarah hoped it would be. She caught Linda's eye and smiled at her, Linda quietly raised her glass as everybody chatted sitting in the bright winter sun. Sean was telling her stories embarrassing Sarah. Sean retrieved his battered old shovel from the milking shed to proudly show off to everybody, telling them how Wirimu had thrown it at him at the New Plymouth breakwater when he left the *Cardiff* after a fight with Bill Walsh.

"If I had a penny for every time I've heard that story" Megan laughed.

Nobody heard the *Heron* approach Llanon, neither did they notice Owen walk up the bank until Sean spotted him.

"Owen, you're early," he said. "Come and join us for a drink."

Owen's face was white and he looked troubled.

"Cheer up Owen McConaghy for goodness sake, you look like you lost five pounds and found sixpence," Sean said. "What is it man?"

Owen looked down at the ground, otherwise remaining still. After a moment he slowly held up his hand holding a brown envelope. A sudden silence fell and the winter chill found its way back to Llanon as the sun disappeared. Ngaire took Wirimu's hand. George put his hands on Libby's shoulders and fell into prayer. Sean stood resolute.

"Who's that for then Owen?" Sean asked. "Is it for me? Is it young Richard? I expected as much." Sarah ran over to Megan crying.

Owen cleared his throat. "It...it's says Mr and Mrs George Twentyman," he said with a break in his voice. "I'm sorry George, Libby." He walked up to George and passed the telegram over to him.

Ngaire went over to Libby holding on to her as she started convulsing with her head in her hands and crying out loud. George picked up a knife from the table and slowly opened the small but significant envelope. He wiped his eyes with the back of his hand and read the telegram to himself. He looked at Libby who by this time was inconsolable. He hesitated, looking at the others, nobody moved or spoke so George cleared his throat and read the telegram out loud.
"Regret to inform. Theo Twentyman killed in action. Dardanelles."

Chapter Nine

**

Sarah and Linda heard about lodgings over Jimmy Brown's cobblers shop on Adelaide Road in Newtown, about half a mile from Wellington hospital. When they walked in, the smell of leather and polish was almost overwhelming as the November sun shone through the shop front window onto the display of boots and shoes.
Jimmy Brown was a small man with remnants of silver grey hair around an otherwise bald head. He wore a leather apron and his shirt sleeves were rolled up.
"Good morning ladies," Jimmy greeted them, looking over the top of his wire rim glasses, Linda picked up a twinkle in his eye she didn't quite trust.
"What is it I can do for the both of you?" He looked down at Sarah and Linda's boots. "No, let me guess. New heels for you both? Half a crown each and a good polish thrown in for free. How's that?"
"Half a crown," Sarah gasped. "The same thing would be one and six in New Plymouth."
"Well pardon me for saying so, but you're not in New Plymouth are you miss?" Jimmy said, looking at Sarah.
"Are you Irish by any chance? Jimmy asked.
Sarah was taken aback. "Well… part Irish, and part Welsh," she said proudly.
"Thought so," Jimmy said.
Linda could see Sarah heading into an argument so she interrupted.
"Well actually, Mr Brown, we understand you have lodgings for nurses over your shop."
A smile appeared on Jimmy Brown's face.
"Well assuming you two ladies are nurses, I think I can find a vacancy for you both" he said looking them both up and down.

Sarah looked at Linda and rolled her eyes.
"How much?" Linda asked.
"A pound a week, each, with two weeks in advance, each," Jimmy said without hesitation.
"A pound a week, each," Sarah blurted. "That's far too expensive."
Linda grabbed Sarah, pulling her out of the shop. "We need to talk a minute" she told Jimmy over her shoulder.
"I don't like him, not at all," Sarah said as soon as they were out of earshot. "He's no better than the others."
"But this is the fifth place we've tried this week," Linda replied. "And we have to be out of the nurse's home by Friday, we're running out of options."
Sarah hesitated so Linda went back in the shop.
"We want a look first," she said.
"Of course, follow me ladies,"
"I had a girl from New Plymouth in last week, happy as Larry here she is", Jimmy said leading them up a creaking, narrow wooden staircase.
"Who's that?" Sarah asked.
"Fay Carrington" Jimmy replied. "Do you know her?"
"Vaguely" Sarah replied looking at Linda.
"You'll have to share a room," he said. "There are two other rooms so that's four other nurses. Ablutions are down the hall and no men visitors. I'll leave you and Irish here to think about it," Jimmy said looking at Linda. "But be quick about it, there's not many places like this around with more and more nurses arriving by the day."
"I'm not sure," Sarah said after Jimmy left. "It's not that clean and I'm not at all sure about 'him' either."
"We can handle him all right," Linda assured her. "Besides, it's only for a few months until we get to Egypt. Goodness knows what we'll find then and all of this will seem like the Ritz."
"I suppose you have a point," Sarah thought out loud, hesitating for a moment. "All right then, but let's see if we can get the rent down."
They found Jimmy Brown back in his shop hammering tacks into the sole of a boot.
"How long have you been doing that?" Linda asked.
"Oh about half an hour," Jimmy chuckled.

"You know what I mean," Linda said giving him a scornful look.
"Only all my life," Jimmy relented.
"How can that be when you haven't had all your life yet?" Sarah questioned.
"Northern or southern Ireland? Jimmy asked.
"Southern Ireland. My father's from County Kerry, near Tralee."
"Thought so," said Jimmy. "So are you taking the rooms or not?"
"Make it seventeen and six a week and we have a deal."
"A pound" Jimmy responded.
"Eighteen shillings and we'll pay a month in advance" Linda said confidently. "In cash."
"We have a deal ladies" Jimmy said holding out his hand after he spat in it."
"I hope you don't think we carry that sort of money around in our purses," Sarah told him. "We'll be back later this afternoon with the money. In the meantime you can prepare the rent book."
"Yes Irish, whatever you say Irish," Jimmy said winking at Linda. They left Jimmy Brown's cobblers and walked along Adelaide Road.
"I need to wash my hands before I do anything else" Linda insisted.

**

Newtown was full of small, busy shops and seemed to attract more than its fair range of foreigners. Both Sarah and Linda enjoyed the hustle and bustle it offered and they linked arms as they pushed their way through the crowds. The streets were full of the smells of food they had never seen or smelled before. Cigar smoke wafted across on the air and the occasional young man walking by, would tilt their hats at the women with a cheeky smile. They heard languages spoken they had never heard before and the mix of nationalities became a game between them, guessing where the people came from and who they were.

They found some respectable tea rooms beside a shop selling Chinese herbs and medications on one side and a barber shop and tobacconist on the other.

"It's like being back in your grandmother's tearooms, only more exciting," Linda said. "All these people from all over the world, all with their stories to tell. It's all so new, almost intoxicating, hedonistic even."

"Yes," Sarah agreed. "It makes you wonder what the rest of the world is like.

"Imagine being in Egypt," Linda said tapping Sarah on the shoulder and adding to the anticipation of the occasion. "I wonder how that will be?"

"All we'll see will be the inside of the wards and the sluice room I expect. It's our duty to look after the men regardless of the temptations of foreign lands."

"Yes…I know," Linda said. "But there must be occasions when we get some time off."

"I do admit to being rather keen to see the pyramids" Sarah answered. "I remember Theo telling me about them, they always fascinated him at school."

The mood between the two women became subdued until Linda broke the silence.

"Oh Sarah, let's go to Oriental Parade on our day off tomorrow, we can get a penny section on the tram, walk the promenade at Oriental Parade, or maybe get the ferry to Days Bay for afternoon tea or an ice cream perhaps. Who knows when we'll get the chance again?"

"Yes," Sarah muttered as she stared into the distance.

"You haven't heard a word I've said have you? Thinking of Theo?" Linda asked.

"Richard, Theo and Tama of course. Theo was a stretcher bearer, not supposed to be in the thick of it, but thinking back, I suppose he would have to have been to get his job done. He didn't want to kill anybody, and now look. It's times like this I miss Mother, and Nana of course."

Sarah's eye's welled up.

"Well you'll just have to make do with me Sarah Murphy. Come on," Linda said taking Sarah's arm. "Let's go and get the money for Mr Brown and get the rent book sorted then we can see about moving out of the nurse's home.

**

The next month saw Sarah and Linda work, study and only occasionally go to Wellington city where they would get a tram to the railway station then walk back through Lambton Quay and Willis Street. They would make sandwiches and stop at Pigeon Park where they enjoyed watching Wellington go about its business. Often soldiers, on leave from Trentham would walk by and on occasionally whistle at them. The young women would giggle then Sarah would become sad, as, again, she thought of Richard wondering if he walked the same streets with his friends as these boys did.

**

When Sarah got the opportunity, she would be pouring over the Evening Post getting whatever information she could about Gallipoli.
One evening she came running back into the common room from her walk to get the newspaper. She burst in the door, "Look. Look Linda," she said waving the newspaper as she burst into tears.
"What is it Sarah, whatever it is, it can't be that bad."
Sarah pushed the table clear spreading out the paper.
"Look, here, Theo's on the front page."
"Your Theo, you said he was dead."
"He is. You were there when the telegram arrived. This must have been taken a while ago." Sarah started to shake and her eyes welled up.
Linda poured over the photograph of Theo posing with Apollo. She read out the headline. "Mule's life saved by Anzac. Private Theo Twentyman of the First Field Ambulance changing the bandages on a wounded mule. Oh, Sarah. I don't know what to say."
There was a silence as Linda read it.
"It says here that Private Theo Twentyman has a sweetheart back in Mokau and he has a present for her. Now, I wonder who that could be." Linda smiled nudging Sarah in the ribs then stood up and hugged her.

"What a wonderful memory to have."
"I wonder if it's in the Herald so George and Libby will see it." Sarah thought out loud.
"Maybe we can go to the newspaper office and ask, see if we can get a better photograph, a real one. We could get a copy and send it to George and Libby," Linda said. "I'll come with you tomorrow before the afternoon shift if you like."

**

The next morning, the women headed off to the newspaper offices. Sarah carefully explained what she wanted to the man behind the counter. He listened patiently then went out the back to see what could be done. The door was left open and the two women heard men's raised voices in the corridor.
"We simply cannot keep printing these stories about how well our boys are doing in Gallipoli. We're being beaten by the Turks hands down and no mistake" said the first voice.
"Maybe so," said the second. "But we can't keep printing that or God knows where the morale of the country will be."
"Well you can't keep pulling the wool over people's eyes much longer," the first voice retaliated. "The *Tahiti* will be docking here in Wellington next week with the first casualties. How do you think people will react when they see those boys all blown to bits? What are you going to print then? Ah?"
"All right, all right," said the second voice. "Give me some ideas then. It's no good complaining unless you can come up with something. You're the sub-editor, what's your idea?"
"Damn," said the second voice just before its owner looked through the doorway to see if anybody heard the conversation. He was a small, middle-aged man wearing a waistcoat and a white shirt with the sleeves rolled up. His spectacles had very thick lenses and he was balding with a few lines of dark hair on the side of his head. He took a drag on a cigarette while he sized up the situation.
"Good morning," he said with a false smile, puffing out smoke all over the two women.
"Good morning," Sarah and Linda said in unison.

Sarah took a chance. She never knew where the courage came from or how it was that she said what she did, but it changed the course of her life from then on. She stood up straight and pushed her shoulders back.
"I have an idea for your newspaper" she announced.
"What?" the man asked.
"I heard you talking … in the corridor. I have an idea to show the country how brave our soldiers are. How they are paying the price for democracy, the price to stay in the Empire with their lives."
"Who are you?"
"Sarah Murphy" she said holding out her hand.
"Reginald Harris, editor of the Evening Post," the man replied. "And are you a writer Miss Murphy?"
"No. I'm a nurse, along with my friend here, Linda Bryant."
"And why is it that you think you can do this Miss Murphy when you are not even a writer, let alone a journalist?"
"Because Mr Harris, I have been through what a lot of women have been through," Sarah said passionately. "Look, look at this," she insisted shaking the copy of the Evening Post she had brought in. "This man, this man on the front page of your newspaper was a lifelong friend of mine, Theo Twentyman. We were neighbours on a farm on the Mokau River, We grew up sharing, exploring, learning, and playing together. Theo wouldn't hurt a fly, now he's dead. I know because I was there when the telegram arrived at his parents' house, the telegram every woman dreads. Imagine how his mother and his father feel? I know what it's like Mr Harris to have a hole punched in my heart and not being able to do a damn thing about it."
Sarah found herself shouting and crying as at last she released her emotions.
Linda pulled up a chair and pulled Sarah down onto it. She stood up again and looked Reginald Harris in the eye.
"I can write your article for you Mr Harris but it will be the voice of a thousand sweethearts as you call them. Sweethearts who have had their futures shot to pieces in the defence of the Empire."

Reginald Harris was silent for a minute as Sarah sat back down with her head in her hands. He drew on his cigarette again, coughing a little, then turned back towards the door. Halfway he stopped and looked back.
"Can you write a thousand words by Thursday, five o'clock?" he asked.
"Yes," Sarah said. "Yes I can do whatever you want Mr Harris if it means Theo died with a voice."
 "Bring it in, and don't be late, five o'clock at the latest, otherwise don't bother."

**

"Just what came over you in there?" Linda asked when they got outside. "What the hell have you done?"
"Don't you see? I meant what I said about Theo not harming a fly. He went to Murata School and received the same education we all did, but he knew so much more. He was intelligent, curious, and nobody had a better friend. How many more Theo's are there being killed in a hopeless situation defending the indefensible. Without a voice those men will have died for nothing. I have the chance to be that voice, at least for one newspaper article and if that can bring some comfort to the women of New Zealand who dared to hope for something they can never have, then it will all be worth it."
Linda thought for a moment, teary eyed.
"Oh Sarah," she said hugging her. "I'm so proud of you."

**

A late summer sun shone on the Cowbridge Road workhouse in Cardiff. Gwyneth Murphy walked into the main quad' of the gothic, four storey building. A messenger had been sent from the chairman of the board of governors himself inviting her to an extraordinary board meeting at eleven o'clock.

She walked along the lawn looking at her watch; a quarter to eleven. As she was early, she took the opportunity to sit on a bench to make the most of the sun. She enjoyed the warmth on her face as she tried to relax in preparation for the meeting as the late arrival of the invitation had sent her in a spin. She struggled to get some cover for her rounds but she managed so she could change into her best blue pinafore uniform and white apron. She felt flattered as she knew her six month probation was about to end and she felt she had made a good job of organising the orphans. Her systems had been put in place to make sure the children were well housed and fed with some basic education so most of them could at least read and write.

Her mind went to Bronwyn Evans who was her favourite. Bronwyn was an undernourished, pale-skinned girl whose only comfort was sucking her thumb as she had been completely overlooked for all of her five years. Gwyneth recognised her loneliness immediately so when she first met her on a cold winter's day, without speaking herself, she sat Bronwyn by the fire, gave her some warm toast and jam and simply brushed her hair. Then she gave her a kiss on the forehead and an understanding smile.

From that day, anytime Bronwyn saw Gwyneth she would run up to her and hold on to her skirts with one hand while sucking her thumb on the other and wouldn't let go of either. For weeks, she never spoke but only drew rudimentary pictures of terrible things happening to people so Gwyneth spent many hours drawing pictures for Bronwyn. Pictures of her life at Llanon and Mokau with the river, the sea, and a distant Mt Egmont. She never expected Bronwyn to speak, but after a month or so, her pictures turned from ones of hate to ones of trees and the sun and rainbows so Gwyneth decided that was better than words.

**

Sitting in the warm sun in the quad, Gwyneth suddenly remembered why she was there and glanced at her watch. Five past eleven. She was late and the blood drained from her face.

Rushing up to the boardroom, she knocked on the heavy oak door. After a minute the door slowly opened and the clerk who reminded Gwyneth of a weasel with his pointed face, looked at her as though he was about to turn her into stone. He slowly turned to the board and cleared his throat.

"Mr Chairman, Mrs Murphy is here, at last," he declared.

"I…I apologise for lateness Mr Chairman," Gwyneth said entering the room. "Pressures of the job you understand."

The chairman, a heavy man with a thick black beard and a slow, gravelly voice spoke.

"You were seen sitting in the sun for the last twenty minutes. Is that what you mean by pressures of the job, Mrs Murphy?"

"No, Mr Chairman," Gwyneth said, getting flustered. "I was merely collecting myself you understand, preparing to meet the board."

Gwyneth looked around the table stopping at the space usually occupied by David Askill. David's smiling face was missing and in his place was a small solid man with thick grey hair brushed back and a salt and pepper beard. He sat at the table with a nervous expression on his face and wringing his pale and clammy looking hands. The other board members were all present. To the right of David's replacement was the clerk who constantly wrote without ever looking up. Next to him was the auditor, the workhouse master, the workhouse matron, the schoolmaster, the surgeon, and the chaplain. The Chairman looked anxious, always turning to David Askill's replacement for some kind of assurance.

The Chairman played with some papers for a few minutes, when Bronwyn could clearly hear the large clock on the wall tick, tick ticking. He cleared his throat, then looked up.

"Mrs Murphy. Thank you for attending this meeting at such short notice. The board appreciates how busy you are." He cleared his throat again. "Mrs Murphy, the board is aware that your probationary period is coming to an end and is duty bound to consider you for a post as a permanent employee of the Union Workhouse."

"Yes Mr Chairman. I understand that" Gwyneth said starting to feel a little better.

The Chairman spoke again.

"This is not easy for any of us Mrs Murphy so I will come to the point. The Union Workhouse is above all, a Christian organisation. We uphold all that is right and proper in society for the benefit of those less fortunate than ourselves. This is especially so with the care of the children as I am sure you are well aware."

"Of course," Gwyneth said. "I wouldn't have it any other way."

"Then Mrs Murphy, you will appreciate the predicament that your future employment would put us in?"

"I'm sorry Mr Chairman, I don't understand," Gwyneth said. Her feelings were quickly turning to alarm.

"Let me speak plainly," said the Chairman. "When you first came to us, we heard rumours that you were having an improper relationship with Dr David Askill, the vice chairman."

Gwyneth was finding it difficult to understand what was being said.

"I'm sorry Mr Chairman. I'm totally unprepared for this. Are you saying that David…Dr Askill and I had an improper relationship?"

"You need to know that Dr Askill is working his notice, but please Mrs Murphy, let me finish."

"When you first came here we heard rumours you and Dr Askill were in a relationship which was dubious to say the least. Dr Askill actually travelled around the world to find you and bring you back here for professional reasons but we are to believe it was also for personal reasons as well."

"Well, yes, I suppose he did in some respects," said Gwyneth. "It's true that we knew each other before because of our work here. But that is clearly recorded, in fact that was the point of his sabbatical surely?"

"Then is it true Mrs Murphy that you left your husband of twenty years in order to travel with Dr Askill?

"Yes, I mean, no," Gwyneth spoke out. "I had been married for twenty years at that stage. Sean, my husband, and I have a son Richard who signed up for king and country. Our daughter, Sarah is a trainee nurse. Both our children had left home for the good of the Empire Mr Chairman. I'm sure you will appreciate what that means coming from the other side of the world as we did."

"Your children were simply doing their duty Mrs Murphy, as many have."

"So what are you telling me Mr Chairman?" Gwyneth asked looking around the table for a friendly face but not finding any.

"The Union cannot afford to be involved in any hint of impropriety Mrs Murphy, I am sure you understand that?"

"Of course I do but rumours are all they are at the very worst, surely I have the benefit of any doubt?"

"Maybe so if rumours were all they are, but you need to know that we are in the possession of a letter. A very damming letter giving an account of your relationship with Dr Askill which outlines the romantic link between you both, including you visiting him in his surgery in New Zealand."

Gwyneth's head was spinning.

"A letter?" she asked. 'From whom?"

"Your husband Mrs Murphy, the injured party in this distasteful matter."

"From Sean?" Gwyneth replied totally bewildered.

Gwyneth turned to the chaplain. "Fetch me a Bible sir," she demanded, "and I will swear that nothing improper happened between Dr Askill and myself on the voyage, nor at any time before that. Our relationship was purely professional."

"But even so, you left your husband to be with Dr Askill did you not?"

"I left New Zealand to help the children of Cardiff Mr Chairman. You will know that from my work record and all I have done in the time I've been here. Doesn't that count for something?"

The chairman looked at the chaplain then back at Gwyneth. "That is not the point Mrs Murphy."

"Then what is the point Mr Chairman?" Gwyneth was now getting emotional as she could see how vulnerable she was becoming.

"The point is that the Board will not be offering you a post at the Union workhouse. On the contrary, you have five days to find work elsewhere."

Gwyneth couldn't believe what she was hearing. She became quickly incensed as her whole world was being taken away from her. She drew her shoulders back and gripped the arms of the chair as she pulled herself forwards.

"Mr Chairman!" she burst out. "I have worked my fingers to the bone for the children day and night. I have travelled halfway around the world to do that and I continue to hold the love for them which I had while volunteering as a student nurse. Do you honestly think I would jeopardise all of that for such a ridiculous affair as you suggest?"

The chairman was taken aback by the outburst but managed to hold his composure. He looked at Gwyneth over the top of his spectacles.

"Five days Mrs Murphy" he reminded her. "In recognition of your work here, the board are offering you the opportunity to resign your current post and you will receive a record of employment outlining your work. But you will also appreciate that we cannot attest to your character."

"And if I don't resign?" Gwyneth demanded.

The chairman hesitated. "Your employment will be terminated immediately for reasons I have just explained."

"You're sacking me?" she asked out loud as she stood up.

"Yes Mrs Murphy, to put it bluntly, we are sacking you. Whether you go with grace, or in shame, is entirely up to you."

Gwyneth couldn't remember leaving the boardroom or how she got back to her lodgings. Her head was spinning with the words which had shattered her world. She couldn't gather her thoughts so she just fell onto her bed and convulsed in tears.

**

After a wretched night of half sleep and half nightmare, Gwyneth was woken early the next morning by a loud and persistent knocking on the door. She was in no mood to see anybody so ignored the intrusion.

"Gwyneth," came a voice from the door. "Gwyneth, it's me, David."

She thought for a moment and realised that she needed to talk so she opened the door.

"I've been so worried about you," David said as he rushed in, putting his arms around her.

"What happened David, where have you been?" Gwyneth demanded as she pulled away. "You obviously knew what was going on. Why didn't you warn me?"

"I couldn't. When I asked to see the agenda, they refused to show me and I was told in no uncertain terms not to attend the meeting. Nobody told me they were sacking you until just now. I honestly had no idea."

"But they cannot do what they've done David. It's just not right. Nothing happened between us, we both know that, so why don't they believe us?"

"It's the perception they are cautious of. They'll do anything to protect the name of the workhouse."

"What are we to do then?" Gwyneth asked. "We have to fight them surely."

David stepped back and looked sheepish.

"I'll be leaving in a few weeks" he said. "I have to sign off some papers first while I still have the authority. There's no shortage of work Gwyn, there are many hospitals, military and otherwise with broken men where you can easily find work. You can always come and work with me."

"You don't realise do you David. I came here to work with the children, not to be with you. If I can't do that then I need to go back home, to Mokau and to my family."

"Even when you're not sure about the welcome you'll get from your husband?" David said getting quite agitated.

"Yes David, even to my husband, I'll cross that bridge when I get to it." Gwyneth looked at David. "Is there something you want to say?" she quizzed.

"Did you know your husband was implicated in the death of Marco Cacavalli?" he said desperately thinking on his feet, trying to give Gwyneth a reason stay close to him.

"Marco Cacavalli?" said Gwyneth in genuine surprise. "What do you know about him?"

David told Gwyneth everything Stella had told him about Sean and Marco and the leading to the Big House burning down with Marco inside. Gwyneth was stunned, not wanting to believe what she was hearing.

As bad as what Gwyneth was hearing, she felt uneasy about David trying to stop her from going back to Mokau and her family. For the first time, she saw him in a different light and didn't like what she saw.

Going to the door and quite adamantly holding it open, she summoned up all the courage she could muster. "Be that as it may, that it is something I will deal with when I get there David, I think you had better leave now," she said.

**

Over the next three days, Gwyneth went on her rounds in a daze saying her goodbyes to the children, feeling lost and after her conversation with David she felt as though she belonged neither in Cardiff nor in Mokau anymore. She had resigned from her position as directed and told those who asked that she was going home to New Zealand to be with family. She felt bad seeing the children she had come to love, for the last time. Some of them didn't understand, some of them were sad that Gwyneth was leaving their lives and some simply wanted to know about New Zealand, asking why it was better than Cardiff.

It was the last house that Gwyneth was dreading going to, it was where Bronwyn Evans lived.

As soon as Bronwyn saw Gwyneth she ran to her, wrapping herself in Bronwyn's skirts. Gwyneth picked her up and sat her on her knee. She had a piece of paper in her hand. It was a picture of two people smiling and holding hands.

"Bronwyn, that's a beautiful picture," Gwyneth said. "Is it the two of us?"

Bronwyn smiled and nodded shyly.

Gwyneth took a deep breath. "Bronwyn, I've come to say goodbye. I'm going home to New Zealand. I have to go and see my family so I won't be able to see you anymore, do you understand?"

Bronwyn's smile faded immediately and she looked directly at Gwyneth with a puzzled look on her silent face.

"I have to go Bronwyn," Gwyneth repeated trying to hold back the tears. "I have to go all the way to the other side of the world. Remember? I've told you about New Zealand before."

Bronwyn looked back at Gwyneth and started shaking her head and getting agitated.

"I really have to go," Gwyneth repeated, trying to hold herself together. "I have to go, love."

Bronwyn looked hurt as she climbed down from Gwyneth's lap. She turned to Gwyneth crying then screwed up her picture and threw it on the floor. "No" she shouted. It was the first time Gwyneth ever heard her speak and she was devastated that Bronwyn's first word was one of hurt and disappointment. Bronwyn repeated "no" before she ran down the hallway in tears.

**

Gwyneth had arranged to meet David Askill in town the following day.
"What are you going to do David?" she asked.
"I have a job offer in Dorset, as a locum in Sherborne. I called on a few friends. Most of them have signed up so there's certainly enough to keep me busy."
"Why Sherborne?" Gwyneth asked.
"It looked to be the most attractive to be honest. It's an old medieval town with two castles and an abbey no less. You'd like it."
"It sounds nice," Gwyneth said.
"Do you have any plans Gwyn?"
"No. I have no idea what to do David, no idea at all. I have the lodgings here for another week then I have to leave."
"Why don't you go to Weymouth?" David suggested. "The Anzac Convalescent Depot is there. It's full of New Zealand and Australian troops injured in Gallipoli I'm afraid. There's more and more arriving each day I'm told."
"How do you know that?" Gwyneth asked eager to know more.
"Friends told me at the interview for Sherborne. Weymouth's only about twenty five miles from there."
"I'm still thinking of going home to Mokau," Gwyneth told David, "but that sounds perfect in the meantime, at least I can make myself useful."
"I can phone them for you this afternoon," David said. "I still have an office and the use of the telephone until the end of the month. It's the least I can do."
"Yes. Yes thank you."
"Are you all right Gwynn?" David asked.

"We have to clear the air," Gwyneth said. "When I said I didn't come to Cardiff to be with you, that much is true but I still respect you for your work. You know that don't you?"
"Yes, of course I do," he replied. "I'm sorry for what I said before…about Sean and Cacavalli, I should never have said anything."
"There's no need to be sorry," said Gwyneth. "Nobody has to apologise for telling the truth. It is the truth isn't it?"
"As far as I know. But it was such a long time ago Gwyn, maybe it's best to let sleeping dogs lie?"
"You said you still have some authority for a while," Gwyneth said changing the subject.
"Yes, until the end of the month, about three weeks away. Why?"
"I want one massive favour from you, if you can do this for me I won't ever ask anything of you again."
"What is it Gwynn, you know that I'll help if I can."
Gwyneth hesitated.
"I can help at Weymouth for a short time until I get a passage home, that will take a few weeks, but after that I want you to sign Bronwyn Evans over to my care. I want to take her back to New Zealand, I owe her that much."

**

Sarah almost ran to the Evening Post building, clutching her purse containing her story of one thousand words. She had worked tirelessly on the article, well into the small hours after a week of night shifts and studies. Nevertheless she was proud of what she had written.
Mr Harris sat down with her in his office, the air was thick with cigarette smoke.
"This is good," he said after he finished reading it. "I like the perspective. I'll use it for the Saturday edition."
Sarah felt a thrill to think her words would actually appear in a newspaper.
"We pay ten shillings for an opinion piece."
Sarah had never even expected to be paid, it had never even entered her mind.
"You'll pay me?" she almost laughed.

"Yes, of course," Mr Harris said half smile and passing a ten shilling note to her. "Can you write another one for a weeks' time? This Wednesday morning, the *Tahiti* is due in with the first casualties from Gallipoli. As a nurse you'll be in a prime position to talk to the men, I can't even get my reporters in as close as that. Only this time I want two thousand words. I need another hero Miss Murphy, Can you find one for me?"

"Yes," Sarah immediately agreed. "Two thousand words by next Thursday, five o'clock sharp."

"Good girl" Mr Harris said. "If I use it, I'll pay a pound."

"And if you don't? Sarah asked.

"Then I pay nothing."

Sarah couldn't believe that her work would appear in the Evening Post. How many times had she read the newspaper and now her story, with her name would be read by thousands of other people? She almost ran all the way back to Adelaide Road to tell Linda.

**

Both women changed into their uniforms early on the Saturday so they could get a copy of the Evening Post and still be in time to get to the hospital for the late shift.

"Here it is," said a very excited Sarah as the delivery van chugged its way down the street and towards the dairy. They stood by the van as the bundles of newspapers were unceremoniously throw onto the pavement, Sarah had her money ready in her hand.

"Can I please have a copy of the Evening Post," she asked barely able to contain her excitement.

"You're keen miss," the shopkeeper said.

"She has an article in it," Linda said smiling broadly.

Sarah stood in the dairy, desperately searching through the paper with Linda looking over her shoulder.

"There it is," Linda shouted.

"New Zealand Sweethearts Sacrifice for the Empire" Sarah read out then mumbled a few lines more to herself than anybody else. "That's not all my work, it's been edited."

"Yes but your name's there isn't it?" Linda told her. "There, SM Murphy it says as plain as day, and you're smiling like a Cheshire cat."

**

The following Wednesday, Sarah and Linda reported in for a double shift. It was the day the Gallipoli casualties were due to arrive on the *Tahiti*. The ambulance they travelled into the Wellington wharves in, was an open cab truck which had been converted with a simple timber framed plywood body on the back. There were six wooden slat beds, three on either side stacked above each other. There was a small hatch at the front end for the stretcher bearers to get out allowing room for one more bed on the floor.
It made its way down Cambridge Terrace towards the wharf.
"I wonder how they'll be feeling; the casualties I mean," Sarah said
"Happy to be home I would imagine," Linda replied, putting a handkerchief to her mouth against the acrid exhaust fumes billowing into the back.
The news of the arrival of the *Tahiti* had spread and many people were walking through the city to see the 'war heroes' for themselves.
"Look at them all," said another nurse peering out the forward hatch. "They must think it's a bloomin' circus, poor sods."
The ambulance eventually turned into Queen's Wharf where Sarah and Linda climbed out. Instantly they found themselves in a busy crowd of people lining the wharf alongside the *Tahiti* with its battered black hull. The air was thick with orders being barked out and the ship was prepared for the casualties to disembark.
"Nurse Murphy," said a stern voice from behind.
"Yes Sister," Sarah said as she turned.
"There's work to do. You are stationed at the bottom of that gangway over there. When the casualties get to you it's your job to smile and welcome them home."
"Is that all Sister?"

"Yes nurse. You must remember these brave men have been at sea for over six weeks. Now they're back in New Zealand, they'll want to see a nurse to know they're in good hands and to be assured they are home safe. It's your job to do that. Do I make myself clear?"
"Yes Sister."
"Nurse Bryant, you come aboard with me and help the walking wounded.
As Sarah waited by the gangway, she looked up at the *Tahiti*. She noticed the single grey funnel giving out a small wisp of smoke contrasting against the fresh blue sky. Sarah caught a faint smell of it which took her back immediately to the many trips she took to New Plymouth on the *Reliance* as a small girl. The sheer sides of the *Tahiti's* hull seemed to dominate everything, blocking out the views of the harbour and only allowing some view of the water, sparkling in the late winter sun. Sarah noticed the rivets holding the hull plates together. Every one of them seemed to stand out in the crisp light.
She was brought out of her daydream as the first stretcher bearers appeared on the gangway. She smiled at the face of the first young man as he passed by. "Welcome home" she said but the words had barely escaped her lips when she saw they weren't heard. She knew because of the look on the soldiers faces. There was no sign of expression, no life in the eyes which simply stared up into the sky. The next soldier's eyes were completely bandaged. Sarah could see scars from burning all over his lips and his nose, the next had an arm and a leg missing but at least he smiled back. "Good mornin' nurse. I'm sure glad to see you and no mistake," he said as he was carried along.
Sarah looked at him as he was pushed onto the back of an open lorry.
"Do you know Richard Murphy?" she called out; but the soldier never heard above the clamour and pushing bodies so Sarah turned for the next casualty. Over the next four hours she became more and more disturbed at how broken the soldiers spirits were. Many had limbs missing, or were burned, and some had no obvious signs of injury but were openly crying. All looked emaciated, strikingly gaunt with pale skin accentuating their dark eyes and reluctance for life.

After the stretchers, the walking wounded started to disembark. They slowly made their way down the gangplank. Sarah smiled and welcomed them. If her smile was returned, she would always ask after Richard or Tama but if there was an answer, it was a confused stare or a shrug of the shoulders.

By lunchtime Sarah was fully realising the human cost of war. She heard it in the low moans and empty stares of the young men as they were helped off the ship. These could easily have been the same young men she saw parade so proudly in New Plymouth only a year before, full of energy and pride for the Empire. She couldn't get her mind off Richard and wondered where he was and whether he was even alive so she moved down the line of casualties, asking each in turn.

Two hours later, she was sitting in a dark corner of a warehouse crying and found herself being shaken by Linda. "Thank God I've found you Sarah. Sister sent me looking for you, what's wrong?"

"I never imagined people could be tortured in so many ways. These are the survivors Linda, the lucky ones. Imagine what happened to those who will never come back. I need to find out about Richard somehow."

**

The following week, Sarah's second article appeared in the Evening Post. It reflected on the realities of those who she had seen disembarking. More than that, Sarah wrote about the void she felt through not knowing whether her brother was dead or alive. She wrote about the bravery of those men who could still manage a smile despite losing a limb or their sight. She also questioned the moralities of going to a war on the other side of the world, especially if the cost was going to be a lost generation of men needed so much in a young country.

**

The next morning, the matron of Wellington hospital sent a message for Sarah to appear before her. She was standing behind a large desk in her office when Sarah entered

"Tell me Miss Murphy, just exactly what was it you hoped to get from writing such an atrocious article in last night's Evening Post," she demanded. I assume it was you, there are few people with the name 'SM Murphy' who had such close access to the men.

"I told the truth," Sarah said confidently not at all threatened by the matron's overbearing demeanour.

"Whose truth" Matron asked? "Because if it's the truth of the men you are meant to be caring for as a nurse, then you have done irreparable harm? You see Miss Murphy, their truth is they are injured in the body and the mind. The truth is many of them will never be better, if they survive that is. The families of all injured men will see your article and the fears you expound will spread. You are a nurse, you are meant to be caring for people, not spreading fear and dread."

"But my truth," Sarah retaliated, "and that of a nation of women, is we too are injured. Not in the way the men are, but we are left home or on the farms working hard to keep our vulnerable country alive. If New Zealand were a soldier it would be lying in a bed with its legs missing and barely breathing. Yet we are still sending men over to Europe and will be for the next three or four years if I am any judge. Where will they come from, our factories, our farms, and our fledgling industries? I know it's for the so-called glory of the Empire but we need to think ahead. When it's all over, we as a country will have a missing generation of men. Where will we be then?"

Matron sat down in thought for a moment, shocked at Sarah's passionate response.

"You raise valid points Miss Murphy, and I admire your spirit, a luxury of your young age perhaps," she said reflectively. "But I have to remind you, first and foremost, you are a nurse training here in Wellington with the hope of going overseas to look after our brave young men. What you have seen here is nothing to what you would see in Egypt where the men's wounds will be raw and their mental states equally so. My concern is whether you are suited to the job or would I be better sending somebody who is more dedicated to the task at hand. On balance, given your political viewpoints and your ability to spread dissention, I have no choice but to advise you will not be going to Egypt with the New Zealand nursing corps. You will be returned to New Plymouth as soon as possible."
"You can't do that," Sarah retorted.
"I am not saying you are not a good nurse Miss Murphy. What I am saying is you lack the professional detachment required of every nurse. You allow yourself to become emotionally involved with each and every patient. There is a difference between empathy and sympathy which you have yet to learn. That and your left wing political viewpoints are not that of the government and we need nurses who will focus on the men, not on the nation. I suggest Miss Murphy that you think hard about your future and whether you want to be a nurse at all." She hesitated. "As your matron that is my decision. What I am going to say next Miss Murphy is simply as a woman. You have a spirit that isn't meant to be contained within you. At the same time you are a caring and patient person, I have seen it for myself in the way you care for people. But you are outspoken and have a vision for the country which is not needed here and now, perhaps in the future and I say that guardedly, but at the moment we need nurses, not politicians. There may well be a different path in life for you to follow but that is for you to think about. Right now I will be completing the paperwork to send you back home. In the meantime you have some work to do. Good day Miss Murphy.

**

Sarah worked through the next few days strangely enough feeling quite excited.

"I like Matron," she told Linda as they walked down Adelaide Road one evening. "She's right you know. Perhaps there is something I am more suited to, something that will help our country in a way I never thought possible."
"Well it's not difficult is it," Linda replied.
"How do you mean?"
"You should be a reporter, Sarah. You are perceptive, you have a good head for politics and a gift for writing, all you need is a job to put those skills to work. Maybe you should go and see Mr Harris at the Evening Post to see what he can do?"
"But we should be going to Egypt Linda. We agreed to stay together, especially now the training is coming to an end."
"But you won't be going to Egypt Sarah, that's very clear. At least your father will be pleased, I'll write to you every at opportunity when I get there. I can be your foreign correspondent" Linda laughed. "Only don't tell Mr Harris."

Chapter Ten

**

Richard knew very little of the journey from Gallipoli through Lemnos to England other than it was a never-ending nightmare full of darkness and sharp pain where he often hoped for death to come and take it all away. He struggled for breath every minute in his cramped bunk well below decks with only a faint light coming from a partly obscured porthole. His bunk was the middle of five with the next one only a foot and a half above him. There was little air and even less conversation and the heat was oppressive. The nights were the worst as it seemed to highlight the pitching and rolling of the ship causing nausea until what passed as daylight arrived. In reality, it was only a three day journey, but it seemed a lifetime for Richard as he fought his dark, hellish dreams, not wanting to live but neither wanting to die. He could remember leaving Chunuk Bair, seeing the Turks climbing over the hill like ants on a summer's day and he had faint memories of talking with Tama and Theo, but the more he tried to remember, the more the memory faded and he started to wonder if it was a reality or just a dream.

After what seemed an eternity, Richard became aware the ship was barely moving and the vibration and humming of the engines he had become so used to, had stopped. There were men shouting orders and he heard the word 'lines' being shouted out several times.

"Welcome to Blighty," said a voice from around the corner. "We'll have you off this old tub as soon as we can, so in the meantime prepare yourself to be shifted. Those of you who can walk sort yourselves out. There'll be stretcher bearers on board soon enough for the rest of you."

After several hours Richard was shaken by an orderly, a big, red headed man with a beard and a friendly face.

"Righty-o soldier, can you swing yourself round or shall we lift you out as best we can?"

Richard just stared at him as he was lifted onto a stretcher and carried off the ship and onto the docks.

The fresh air was as intoxicating as wine to Richard. He immediately felt better. He had to close his eyes from the sunshine but after a while he managed to see clouds scudding across the autumn sky as he was carried off on a stretcher. He wasn't sure whether he heard guns or not and he suddenly felt scared.

"We'll have to leave you here for a few minutes mate" the orderly," told him. "There's a bit of a queue for the lorries, sorry?"

**

Gwyneth arrived in Weymouth when the convalescent home was in chaos with wounded arriving in more numbers than could be managed. She stood back in wonder at the waste of life. It was the first time she had seen the results of war firsthand and it eclipsed even her worst nightmares about Richard and the young men she remembered from Mokau. She was immediately put to work, washing and disinfecting wounds, some were infected with the flesh, cut to the bone. She learned to look for the insignia of the Taranaki Rifles, hoping for news of Richard but it was all in vain.

After a busy day, she took her evening meal outside to be on her own for a while but was interrupted by a young doctor out for a quiet smoke. A tall and rakish man with thick, fair hair and a boyish face.

"Nice evening," he said acknowledging Gwyneth. "Sorry, I can see you want to be alone."

"No matter," Gwyneth said. "I just wanted to gather my thoughts for a while."

"Yes, me as well," the doctor replied. "Sorry" he said holding out his hand, "Don Plumtree, pleased to meet you."

"Gwyneth Murphy," Gwyneth said taking his hand.

There was a moment's silence.

"What a waste of young lives," Don said.

"Isn't it?" Gwyneth replied distantly. "I used to teach in a primary school in New Zealand for some years, now I see what could be the same boys lying here".

"I've heard New Zealand's a beautiful country," Don mentioned as he drew on his cigarette.

"Yes. I suppose it is, though when you live there you get used to it."

"Where about's in New Zealand?"

"Middle River, near Mokau."

"What's it like then, this Mokau?"

"It's lovely. The river's our road. There's some settlement as the land's been divided off, mixed farming mostly, some dairy and dry stock."

"Dry stock?"

"Beef and some sheep. You can get a steamer to New Plymouth or north to Kawhia then on to Auckland if you want. If you go to New Plymouth you'll see Mt Egmont right on the coast. Covered in snow it is in the winter."

"A mountain right on the coast?" Don asked. "That's unusual."

"Yes, I suppose it is" Gwyneth replied. "My husband and I have a farm there, and a timber mill."

"You must miss it?"

"Yes, yes I do," Gwyneth said surprised at Don's perceptive comment, "but working here with the Kiwis is where I'm meant to be right now. I have a son in the army, along with his friends and our neighbour's sons and so on. They may well be here in this carnage though I can't find many from Taranaki.

"Taranaki?" Don asked.

Gwyneth smiled. "You pronounce it well."

"I've heard the word before. You could do worse than to go over to the east wing of the annexe, there's a lot of New Zealanders there, some from Taranaki maybe? I really have to go now," Don said looking at his watch and throwing his dog-end away, grinding it into the ground with the front of his shoe. "Good night Mrs Murphy. I hope you receive good news about your son."

"Thank you Don, and thanks for the tip, I'll go over while it's still light."

Don hesitated for a while. "Can I ask a favour of you please, before I go? It may sound odd but please don't take it the wrong way."

"Of course," Gwyneth agreed.

"It's just that I've seen at least a dozen young men die today, just as they have reached the land of their birth and carrying hideous scars. Any one of them could have been my brother. I would love to ask you if I can have a hug, just a simple hug from a kindred spirit. That's all."
Without speaking, Gwyneth did as she was asked and put her arms around Don as though he were her son. "May God be with you" she barely uttered.

**

The annexe was a large red brick, single storey building Gwyneth hadn't been in before. It was strangely quiet and she heard her own footsteps as she walked down the polished hallway.
"Can I help you?" another nurse appeared out a doorway. "Were just getting the patients settled down for the evening."
"I've been sent over to help," Gwyneth said thinking quickly. "I'll start by drawing the curtains shall I?"
"Yes," the nurse said. "That will be fine. You can start down this end."
Gwyneth walked into the first room. It was small with just six beds. She looked at the soldiers, none of them showed any interest, they just stared at the ceiling or had pulled a sheet over themselves. Gwyneth drew the curtains across the white painted metal framed windows and went into the next room. Several men were alert and she spoke to one but there was no response. The next was the same and Gwyneth realised these men were all shell shocked. There were little signs of injuries as they were all morose, traumatised by what they had been through.
Gwyneth shook some of them gently.
"Richard Murphy, do you know Richard Murphy?" she asked. Some shrugged their shoulders and others just stared or cowered away.

In the last bed lay a man with his back to the door. Even from just a glance at his tussled hair poking out from under a grey blanket, Gwyneth immediately recognised him. With a sharp intake of breath she gently reached out to him, not daring to speak. Very slowly, she reached out and touched his shoulder. He jumped when he felt her hand and pulled the blanket down as he turned to stare at her.

"Oh Richard!" Gwyneth cried out. Every maternal instinct in her came to the fore as she saw her son lying on a bed looking absolutely terrified as though she were a total stranger.

"Richard is that really you?" she asked, crying her eyes out. Richard never said a word but turned his back on her then pulled the blanket up and buried his face in the pillow.

**

"Miss Murphy! Miss Murphy! Where the hell are you?" Reginald Harris was shouting down the corridor from his office.

"Here I am," Sarah said appearing from a doorway.

"Get to the boardroom in five minutes and tell the others to come. We're holding the front page, we don't have much time."

"Why?" Sarah asked.

"There's no time to ask questions, not yet anyway."

Anybody who was anybody at the Evening Post were gathered in the boardroom.

Reginal Harris entered and there was an immediate silence. He stubbed out a cigarette in the ashtray on the desk and cleared his throat.

"A ship, the *Marquette*, possibly a hospital ship has been torpedoed by the Germans in the Aegean Sea. There were around thirty New Zealanders on board including nurses and some members of the medical corps. It's coming off the wires now.

"Good God, no!" Sarah exclaimed putting her hands to her face.

"That's exactly what we want in words people can understand Miss Murphy. You're a nurse, or at least you were. I want a piece explaining just how you feel now. Go and make a start, the rest of you listen to me."

In less than ten minutes the boardroom was empty as everybody went about their tasks. In an hour Sarah had her work to Mr Harris.

"No, not good enough" he said hurriedly. "Make it more emotional. Pretend one of your friends was on board. I want raw emotion, now go back and do it again."

"Some of my friends probably were on board," Sarah told him.

"Then make it read like that, like you were there, write it as a nurse."

Sarah sat down in a corner of the main office sitting in front of a typewriter. This was one piece of news she didn't want to write about but she knew she had to. She hit the keys angrily, trying to rise above the emotion and all the time wondering who the nurses were and if she really did know any of them.

"That's a lot better," Mr Harris said reading through the second draft.

"Take it straight down to the typesetters" he said scribbling his name on the bottom.

Ed White, the chief typesetter grabbed the paper off Sarah with his ink stained hands.

"Couldn't have left it a bit later could you?" he shouted sarcastically above the noise of the newspaper presses and conveyer belts as they were gearing up for what was going to be a late run.

"Well it's certainly too late for those poor souls on the ship isn't it?" Sarah shouted in return.

She went back to the main office for an hour or so and watched people dashing about, then she picked up her handbag and walked through town to pass some time on the warm balmy spring evening which seemed to directly contradict the high drama of the last few hours. She found herself in Courtney Place where a delivery van was dumping bundles of newspapers on the street outside the Criterion Hotel and she wondered where the time had gone. Beside the piles of newspapers stood a young boy dressed in a dirty white shirt several sizes too big and tweed shorts held up by braces. He put one unshod foot on a bundle of newspapers to cut the string while the driver put the poster on the advertising board.
The boy turned and yelled "Eeeev-nin' Po-ost!" at the top of his lungs as he expertly swung a wad of newspapers under his arm. "Eeeevnin' Po-ost. Read all abart it. British ship sunk by German torpedoes. Kiwi nurses killed. Read all abart it." Sarah bought a copy and caught a tram to Adelaide Road.
Linda started to shake and cry as Sarah read the news. Sarah never finished reading it out as Linda was in no state to hear it anyway. She sat beside Linda on the sofa and took her in her arms and stayed like that for over an hour.
"I'm going home to New Plymouth for a week." Linda eventually whispered.
"Why?" Sarah asked her.
Linda spoke with a croak in her voice. "I'm going to Egypt Sarah. I heard today, there's fifteen of us leaving for Egypt in two weeks' time."

**

Megan was shaken out of her thoughts by a wave hitting the side of the *SS Raglan,* a tramp steamer heading back upriver to the mines to take on coal needed to run the boilers at the expanding Waitara freezing works. It was the only ship she could find that would take her directly to Llanon without having to stop at Mokau. She didn't want to run into anybody, least of all Stella Ratcliffe or Moonyeen Wu.

She sat at the table in the modest saloon deep in thought, much as she had been ever since Gwyneth's letter arrived saying she was coming home with Richard and Bronwyn. She knew she should tell Sean but had put it off, not knowing how he would react. Now it was time to tell him his estranged wife was returning home after a year away. Not only that but she was bringing back Richard who sounded in a bad way as well as a small girl.

In a last minute decision made from caution more than anything else, she asked the captain to stop at the Te Kainga jetty, suddenly desperate to speak with Ngaire.

**

"Hello, it's only me," Megan shouted out down the hallway.
"Morena, come in," Ngaire said from the kitchen.
When she saw Megan she rushed down the hallway drying her hands on an apron. "Megan!" she called out throwing her arms around her. "What are you doing here? Not that you're not welcome. No, that's not what I meant," she laughed. "It's been so long since I've seen you."
"I know what you mean," Megan said smiling broadly. "It is good to see you too Ngaire. I had no idea how much I have missed you. How's Wirimu?"
"Wirimu's fine, he's out in the milking shed at the moment, we've just taken on a new worker, Paul Herring. Wirimu's showing him the place. Come on in," Ngaire said untying her apron. "I've just finished some baking, you're just in time."
"Any news of Tama?" Megan asked.
"Yes, yes. We've had a letter…from Gallipoli. He's keeping all right, given the circumstances." Ngaire hesitated. "Have you heard anything from Richard?" she asked, not sure what Megan's response would be.
"Yes, that's why I'm here ," Megan replied.
She spent the next hour telling Ngaire about the letter from Gwyneth. Ngaire asked more questions than Megan could answer so they both drew conclusions.

"I can't believe she's taken on a small girl," Megan admitted. "According to her letter, the wee girl, Bronwyn has taken to Richard, neither of them speak at all but they seem to find comfort with each other drawing pictures of all things. Maybe that's their escape?"

"How's Richard, really?" Ngaire asked.

"Shell shocked according to Gwyneth," Megan replied. "He was shot in the chest. Lucky to be alive by all accounts." Megan rubbed her eyes with her handkerchief.

"His left lung collapsed so he only has the right lung now. I think he's all right physically, or as right as you can be with only one lung, but his mental state is one of confusion to say the least."

"Megan. I know about Richard's wound," Ngaire said solemnly. "In the letter Tama sent, he told us Richard had been shot. He wanted us to know so we could help you, but it wasn't our place to break the news. I hope you understand. All three boys were together at Chunuk Bair, Tama, Richard and Theo."

"All three?" Megan asked surprised at the news."

"Yes. All three," Ngaire said. "It was the first and the last time since they left New Zealand".

"It must have been just before Theo…before Theo was killed," Megan said. "How did George and Libby take the news?"

"About how you would have expected?"

"Yes, of course," Megan responded. "A silly question."

"They are more philosophical about it now. Their religion helps them but news of our boys being killed or maimed is commonplace now. You know Ian McPherson and Charlie Dobson are dead?"

"Yes. Yes I heard," Megan replied, her head bowed.

"Well perhaps some Mokau sun and home cooked kai will get Richard right," Ngaire said enthusiastically.

"Well that's the point Ngaire. Gwyneth wants to stay with me, in New Plymouth. At least until she's spoken with Sean."

"I can see why," Ngaire agreed. "Both Richard and this girl will need a settled place and there may be a way to go with Sean before that can happen."

"How is he, Sean?" Megan asked.

"He's good. He's been busy lately. Listen Megan, it's not for me to say but you really need to see for yourself."
"Has he been drinking?"
"Men drink don't they? It's their way of coping sometimes and Sean's no different really. When were you thinking of going to see him?"
"This afternoon. I must tell him about Gwyn and Richard. I owe him that."
"Then have something to eat here first and talk with us. I'll go and get Wirimu, Paul may come as well, you will find him interesting, he used to work for Sean."
"Used to?" Megan asked.
"Yes, he left because Sean never paid him."
"Really? That is news. The Sean that I know of would never do a thing like that," Megan said in genuine shock
Ngaire let out a sigh. "Sorry to say that Sean left a while ago and you may not like the one whose taken his place. But that's better coming from Paul himself. Did you know Owen McConaghy's left the river?"
"No, how come?"
"He said he'd had enough, can't say I blame him. He took every one of those telegrams to heart. He sold the *Heron* to a young man, David Stockford. Poor boy's deaf in one ear so couldn't join up."
"Murata School?" Megan asked,
"Amy and Susan Tallboys are still there of course." Ngaire told her. "Susan does most of the work now. Amy's getting too old to teach all week."
"And Bill Tallboys, is he still at the mill?"
"Yes," Ngaire said. "He's still there, there's nobody to take his place as most of the workers have gone off to be soldiers of course."

**

Paul Herring was a tall man with fair hair and an honest way about him. As they all ate lunch, Paul described how he was expected to work for Sean seven days a week but the pay Sean promised never eventuated.

Megan was embarrassed that her son-in-law should treat somebody so badly. After a long conversation, Megan left for a few moments. When she got back she pressed a ten pound note into Paul's hand.
"This may not make up for everything," she told him. "But it should help."
She turned to Ngaire and Wirimu. "I need to go to Llanon now," she said.
"Are you sure?" Ngaire asked. "Wirimu, you go with Megan."
"Bless you but no, thank you for asking. You are always so thoughtful."
"I insist," Wirimu told her. "This spring has been very wet so far and the banks are muddy. There's more rain to come if I can read the cows right."

**

Sarah waited at the Wellington Railway station for Linda to arrive back from New Plymouth. The train was due in at four thirty and while Sarah could almost count on it being late, she still arrived at four o'clock just to watch the people going about their business, something she loved to do. Her eye was drawn to a ship berthing at Queens Wharf across from the station. Even as she walked over, she could smell the coal smoke drifting across on a lazy breeze. She loved that as it always took her back to her childhood. Noticing the ship was laying low in the water, she was intrigued as to what the cargo was. A stevedore wearing a flat cap, a black woollen jacket and baggy brown corduroy trousers was leaning casually against a warehouse wall. Sarah didn't notice him until he moved to light a cigarette
"What's she carrying?" Sarah called out pointing to the ship. The man was taken aback at her interest.
"Locomotive parts. For the workshops out the Hutt Valley" he called out giving Sarah a cheeky grin, "are you interested in buying any love?"
"Not today, thanks all the same" Sarah called out smiling back. "I have enough at home for the time being but thanks for asking!"
"Well if you ever need any more, you know where to come".

"That I do Mr Stevedore. That I do," Sarah laughed out loud enjoying the brief encounter.

It was a clear sunny day and the harbour was like glass sparkling in the spring sunshine. She looked along the wharf and saw a shoal of herring breaking the surface of the sea like a thousand sparkling diamonds. As soon as it started it stopped again as the shoal dispersed.

Sarah looked up and could see across the harbour to Oriental Parade. She watched a tram trundle slowly along and people promenading on a relaxed Saturday afternoon.

Sarah loved Wellington. She felt the war wasn't going to last forever and although many people said it would be the war to end all wars, Sarah didn't believe that. She had a firm belief in the future so was excited to be in the capital city of a young country. She turned and looked across the front lawns of the railway station to where the new Parliament buildings were being built. Like everything, they were held up by the war with a shortage of labour and supplies but even so, to Sarah it was a symbol of a new beginning, a fresh new start. She realised there were opportunities that it would bring and she wanted to be a part of it all. She wasn't sure how but she knew she would have a part to play.

She was startled by a whistle as Linda's train drew into the station, so she hurried back across the road just as the train came screeching and hissing to a halt in a cloud of steam. The carriage doors were all flung open at the same time and people filled the once empty platform in an instant. Sarah stood on her toes looking over the crowd for Linda. In a few minutes she appeared carrying a heavy case and as soon as she saw Sarah, she dropped the case and ran up to her.

"Good grief Linda, you hug like a bear" Sarah said standing back to take a good look. It's only been a week you know."

"It seems like an eternity" Linda replied. "Let's get back home Sarah, I've lots to tell you."

**

They let themselves into the rear of Jimmy Brown's shop and met Fay Carrington running down the staircase.

"Oh, hello Linda, welcome back, how was it all?" she gabbled, not waiting for a reply. "Can't stop, late for my shift and sister will have my guts for garters if I'm late again. I hope you're all set for Egypt, only a week to go. I can hardly wait"
Fay ran out the door only stopping to shout out. "Oh Sarah. A letter arrived for you at the hospital yesterday after you left, I brought it back, it's in your bedroom, hope that's all right? Must dash." And with that she was gone.

**

Linda threw her case on the bed.
"And are you ready for Egypt Linda?" Sarah asked hesitatingly.
"Well that's just it" Linda replied. "That's what I have to tell you. I'm not going anymore."
Sarah sat back for a second. "Well to be honest Linda I thought something was up, you hardly spoke in the tram on the way back here. What's made you change your mind?"
"Well its Mother really, and Father. After the news of the *Marquette* being sunk, Mother doesn't really want me to travel. It's not so much Egypt itself, although that doesn't please her too much either, it's just the risk of me being killed on the way by a German torpedo."
"And what do you really want to do yourself, in your heart?" Sarah asked.
"I want to go, I really do. I've had all the training but really, when all is said and done, I'm really nervous about going."
"It's perfectly understandable" Sarah said quietly.
"I still want to be a nurse" Linda replied, "and look after the patients, like the ones we helped off the ship, the men from Gallipoli, but I don't really want to travel to Egypt. Is that selfish of me?"
Sarah thought for a moment. "Well I'm not the best person to judge am I?" she said after a while. "We both came here to train to go to Egypt. I left that behind, for different reason of course, but in reality, I bowed out of doing my duty of caring for others just to be a journalist. At least you'll still be a nurse."
"If they let me stay" Linda said.

"I'm sure they will. Besides it looks like Fay will be going so it will be her job to tell us all about it."
"Thank you for understanding" Linda said putting her arms around Sarah.
"Think nothing of it" she said. "Fay mentioned a letter for me. I wonder what that can be" she said going into her room. She took the letter recognising Megan's handwriting. "It's from Nana. I hope she's all right."
"God," Sarah called out. "It's Richard, he's alive and he's coming home."
Linda jumped up and threw her arms around Sarah "I'm so pleased to hear that, I really am."
"Thank you. It is a massive relief to be honest," Sarah told her going back to the letter.
"Richard?" Linda asked afraid of what she may hear.
"Yes. He's alive thank God. He's been seriously injured but he's coming home, back here to New Zealand. Can you believe it? Mother's with him on board the hospital ship, the *Maheno* with a little girl Mother is looking after. That doesn't sound right but it's what Nana says in her letter."
"Richard's all right though, isn't he" Linda was sounding concerned.
"According to Nana he's lost a lung and has shell shock."
"I completed a full day's training on shell shock before I went home" Linda said. "I may be able to help if you like."

Chapter Eleven

**

For the entire voyage from Southampton to Auckland, Richard slept in his clothes, often on the floor of the cabin crying himself to sleep. When he wasn't doing that, he would sit down in the corner of any room, depending on where he was at the time and remain there for a day, sometimes more with his knees drawn up to his chin and rocking backwards and forwards groaning to himself, flinching at any loud sound. Nobody took much notice because he wasn't the only one doing it.
At the beginning, Gwyneth spent a lot of time looking for him, but when she found him, she couldn't do anything other than call a doctor only to be told he was shell shocked and would eventually come out of it himself, either that or he would need to keep a stiff upper lip.
It was Bronwyn who became his only true friend as although she didn't speak, she understood Gwyneth's concerns seemingly able to understand Richard's plight. One evening, just before it was time to sleep, Bronwyn appeared in the cabin with Richard, holding his hand and making him lay in his bunk. They made a strange pair, a diminutive five year old girl leading a grown man by the hand. After a week they became inseparable and at mealtimes, they would appear with Bronwyn making Richard wash then eat. If Richard stopped eating, Bronwyn simply pushed the plate closer towards him pointing to the food. So it was Gwyneth learned to trust Bronwyn and her care for Richard so she could work tirelessly looking after the casualties.

**

The *Maheno* sailed into Waitemata harbour on a stunningly beautiful day. As the ship slowed her engines, Gwyneth, dressed in her finest clothes of a white lace blouse over a full skirt and a wide, black belt, stood by the rails. She held Bronwyn in one hand and turned to Richard. "Welcome home son, welcome home, she said as Richard simply gazed to the front, oblivious of what was happening."

She picked up Bronwyn pointing over to Rangitoto. "Look, that's a real volcano over there. You don't get those in Wales." Bronwyn shaded her eyes from the sun as she looked around her. Hundreds of small boats and yachts were sailing out to meet the ship knowing it was bringing home the wounded. The armada trailed the wake of the big ship and every horn and siren that could be, was relentlessly sounded and the air was filled with a celebration of life. It seemed every person in every boat was waving out, welcoming back their sons from the war that was to end all wars. Gwyneth found herself smiling more than she had for a long time. She felt elated that she was somewhere where she belonged and no matter what happened in the future, she had done the right thing by her son. She pointed out some people in a small boat right below them waving frantically. "Welcome home to Zealand and God bless our heroes!" one man shouted out, standing his boat, and waving out his arms.

"Thank you, thank you! It's good to be back," Gwyneth returned the greeting. Just as she said that the ship's siren let out three long blasts that seemed to shake the air itself.

It took a full hour for the *Maheno* to cross the harbour before the tugboats could get alongside. As the ship approached the wharf, Gwyneth turned to take Richard and Bronwyn to gather their possessions and prepare to disembark.

Another three hours passed as they waited in the crush of people on C Deck. Eventually the hatch opened and they started the walk down the gangway and back onto New Zealand soil.

It took several more hours to get through all the form filling. All the time a very patient Bronwyn held onto Richard, quietly talking to him, almost whispering, telling him how excited she was and how she was looking forward to meeting everybody. As they eventually pushed their way through the crowds, Gwyneth heard a familiar voice.
"Mother, Mother, over here."
She looked over to see Sarah jumping up and waving for all she was worth on the other side of a fence, beside her was Megan holding back tears. Gwyneth took a quick look around but couldn't see any sign of Sean. Her relief was immediate. She gathered up Bronwyn and Richard as they pushed their way through.
Sarah hugged Gwyneth and moved to hug Richard, but Bronwyn threw herself in between. Sarah took a quick look at Gwyneth who just indicated to pull back.
"You must be Bronwyn," Sarah said holding out her hand. "I've heard a lot of things about you. Good things."
"Hello Richard," Sarah said, not knowing what to expect. Richard stared at her intently.
"Sarah… Sarah," he said. "Is that you?"
"Yes, Richard, it really is me, Sarah, your sister."
Sarah looked around to Megan. "Nana's here as well, we've come to take you back home, home to get better…at Llanon." Richard cried for the first time since leaving Gallipoli. "Tama. Theo. Where are they?" he asked.
Everybody looked at each other not realising that Richard didn't know anything about Theo's death, or Tama for that matter.
"We'll find out about everybody once we get you home," Megan said quickly.
"We need to have something to eat and get to the railway station," Sarah added. "The train leaves in a few hours."

**

Sarah's job as a cadet journalist was going well. Mr Harris recognised her intelligence, giving her stories to write on the events of the war. It was going well for her, but it brought home the realities of the politics and how lives were being wasted at the whim of politicians which didn't sit well with her. Sarah and Linda left Jimmy Brown's boarding house and had taken lodgings in Hataitai on Moxham Avenue just up from All Saints Church. The rooms were run by Mrs Chard, a diminutive but determined widow who ran the boarding rooms with an iron hand.

"No noise, lights out at ten o'clock sharp and absolutely no gentlemen callers," were her first words to both Sarah and Linda before they hardly put a foot in the door. Mrs Chard cast a beady eye on Linda. "It's bad enough you being a nurse coming in at all hours, but as you are looking after our brave boys I can make an exception. But if you break my trust, either of you, you'll be out so fast your feet won't touch the floor. Do you understand?"

"Yes," they both agreed, trying not to smile.

Their rooms were austere with the barest of furniture but they was scrupulously clean, and after the rooms above Jimmy Brown's, it was a welcome relief.

As Sarah got off the tram that evening and walked down Moxham Avenue, she felt comfortable enough in herself but still felt as though something was missing. She slowly unlocked the front door and collapsed into an armchair in the common room but, unable to relax, her mind fell into turmoil as she became drowsier. The letters from her mother told of the problems with Richard, how he couldn't settle at anything. He was still sleeping on the floor and cringed when he heard loud noises.

Sarah started to drift away to a troubled sleep just as Linda arrived back from her shift at the hospital.

"Sarah. I didn't expect you would still be up, did I wake you?" she asked. She took a long look at her. "You look worn out, you need to get to bed for a proper sleep. Are you all right?" Sarah rubbed her eyes. "Hello Linda. Yes. I'm fine thanks, just tired."

"What's wrong?" Linda repeated. "Is it family? Richard? I've been meaning to ask, how is he now he's been home a few months?"

"Well that's just it," Sarah replied. "I'm not sure he is back really, not even now, not in his head at least."

"Still shell shocked?" Linda asked.

"Mother writes in her letters that it's like his mind is elsewhere. If he hears a loud bang or something he still cowers down and puts his hands over his head, and he cries a lot of the time."

"But that's good in some ways, isn't it?" Linda said. "Crying I mean. It's good to let it out."

"I'm not sure," Sarah replied.

"I knew he would have changed of course, but it's like the physical injuries of being shot in the chest doesn't matter. It's his mental state that worries me. Fairly soon it will be the first anniversary of the landings so I might go home for that. It may help to clear Richard's mind but I fear Mother will need more help, especially with Bronwyn. I can understand why she took the girl on, but at her age it's probably tougher than she imagined."

"You'd better be careful all the same," Linda remarked. "Anniversaries can be powerful triggers; it could go either way."

Sarah thought for a moment. "Linda, would you come back with me, to Llanon? Richard is still with Mother above the tea rooms in New Plymouth. It's pretty packed with Nana, Mother, Richard, and Bronwyn but they go to Llanon sometimes and Father puts Richard to work on the farm which he apparently enjoys. I'm sure Uncle George and Auntie Libby wouldn't mind the company as well. It's not like you haven't been before and you've worked with shell shocked casualties at the hospital. You may have some ideas to help Richard."

"Of course, I'd love to help if I can," Linda agreed.

**

Several weeks later Megan and Gwyneth, holding Bronwyn's hand on a wet and blustery evening, met Sarah and Linda at the New Plymouth railway station.

"Where's Richard?" Sarah asked immediately almost shouting against the noise of the rain on the iron roof.

"He's with your father at Llanon," Gwyneth replied.

Linda went down on her haunches and looked Bronwyn in the eye. "You must be Bronwyn," she said smiling and holding out her hand.

Bronwyn immediately turned away and pulled herself into Gwyneth's coat as though to shield herself.

"Don't worry Linda, she'll soon get used to you" Gwyneth said. "It's all right Bronwyn. This is Linda. Remember I told you about her lots of times. She's Sarah's friend. You remember Sarah who met us at the railway station when we got off the ship?"

Bronwyn just buried her face in Gwyneth's coat again.

"Come on, let's get out of this weather and head home," Megan suggested.

**

"I thought we could all catch up here for a few days," Megan said the following morning. "Then see how the land lies about going to Llanon."

"That's a good idea," Sarah agreed. "Mother, Linda here works with shell shocked soldiers in Wellington. We thought she might be able to help Richard."

"Only if it's all right with all of you," Linda interjected. "I understand it's a sensitive family matter and I'm not family… but as Sarah says, I have had some training and I am working with many soldiers who are in the same circumstances as Richard. If I say so myself, I do seem to be able to bring them out of themselves to a small degree somehow."

"Yes I suppose a pretty girl who is able to listen may have some advantage depending on the level of damage to the brain," Gwyneth said. "It's worth a try. Tell me Linda, how would you make a start?"

"Just by being around quietly for a while. Let Richard get used to me and see if I can draw him into some simple conversations. Soldiers with those injuries need a gentle hand, somebody to talk at rather than talk to, initially at least. Sometimes a stranger can do that more easily than family…with all respects of course. You see, Mrs Murphy, their brains are scarred. Their memories they have of the horrors of warfare has erased the good memories they had before. Those bad memories need to be aired so they can be put to one side. Not everybody shares my views of course and some see them as radical, but I have seen many occasions where these men are told to keep a stiff upper lip and it doesn't do them any good. It just locks the demons and the nightmares in their heads, but I find the opposite helps. The men have suffered enough and the last thing they need is to be told to ignore the hurt they feel. If it was a physical injury it would be treated immediately, but because it's the brain that been damaged and it's not visible, people ignore it. A lot of the men turn to the bottle for help I'm sorry to say. I think women understand this a lot more than men as we have been hurt many times, not by the war of course, but because of the times we live in… well, and by men to be completely honest, and we can only turn to ourselves to express that, just as the soldiers turn to themselves. So the longer we leave Richard, the more deep seated the problems will be."

"You speak wisely," Gwyneth said.

"Well if you would give me the opportunity Mrs Murphy, I would like the chance to help bring your son back to you." Gwyneth put her hand on Linda's. "Linda love, there is nothing I desire more than that in the whole world."

**

When Sean told George and Libby that Megan, Gwyneth, and Sarah were coming home with Linda as well, there was great excitement. Libby wasted no time walking along the river to pass the news onto Wirimu and Ngaire. "That's excellent news. Should we all put on a dinner? A gathering to mark us all being together, as best we can in the circumstances." Ngaire immediately suggested. "It can never be a celebration given Theo…will never …well, you know."
"That's a good idea," Libby replied. "We've all been so pre-occupied with everything, we need to come together again. You're right, Ngaire. Nothing will bring Theo back, at least not physically, but he would be here in spirit. I need to ask George of course but let's do it if he, and the others agree."
Libby hesitated. "I have had a bit of a surprise Ngaire, a letter."
"How do you mean?"
"You must promise not to say anything, but a letter arrived several weeks ago… I don't mind admitting that it rocked us. It's a… a letter from Dickie Fleming."
"That name sounds vaguely familiar," Ngaire said looking puzzled.
"Dickie Fleming was a stretcher bearer at Gallipoli, with Theo. They worked together a lot and learned to depend on one another. Theo mentioned him a few times in his letters, he held him in high regard."
"And what does his letter say?" Ngaire asked eagerly.
"You must promise not to say anything as George would be angry. I promised not to say anything just yet but it turns out both Theo and Dickie made a promise to each other. A promise that if something happened to one…" Libby hesitated as her voice broke.
"That if something happened to one," she started again throwing her head back, "the other one would visit their family and bring back their effects."
"So this Dickie Fleming, he's coming here?" Ngaire was almost beside herself.
"Yes. Yes Ngaire, he's coming here soon."
"Oh Libby, that is such a blessing. When is he arriving?"

"I don't know exactly," Libby replied. "He wrote from Auckland, where he lives. He was shot in his groin just after Theo was killed so he's been discharged. We wrote back immediately asking him to come as soon as he could. I cannot tell you how much that would mean to us. Theo's death has affected George so much, well, both of us but it has caused George to question his faith, he wanted to keep the letter private for a while, which is why you must keep this to yourself."
"Yes of course," Ngaire readily agreed.
"Like I said before," Libby said, "Theo will never be back but to meet this Dickie Fleming, Theo's best friend, could be the medicine we need to move on with our lives."

**

David Stockford slowed the engine of the *Heron* as it pulled up alongside the jetty at Te Kainga. For a brief second, Megan was taken back to the first time she and David had met Ngaire years earlier. It was when they first journeyed along the Mokau to look at the farm which became Llanon. Now here she was, a widow, with a family who were anything but happy. She was broken from her daydream by Ngaire waving and calling out from the jetty.
They all greeted each other with hugs, Wirimu held back letting Ngaire, Gwyneth, Megan and Sarah greet each other. He smiled at Bronwyn who was also holding back, temporarily forgotten about. Wirimu smiled as she unashamedly stared at his prosthetic leg. He gave a small wave and got a thin smile for his trouble. Gwyneth turned around noticing. "That's more than most get," she said to Wirimu. "Oh Bronwyn love," she said scooping her up. "These are my very best friends, Mr and Mrs Ratahi. Ngaire, this is Bronwyn." Bronwyn buried her head in Gwyneth's chest.
"She's adorable," Ngaire said.
Megan turned around and introduced Linda.
"Naumai, welcome," Ngaire pressed Linda's hand.

**

Walking along the bridle path in single file with the river on their right, Llanon came into view. "The old place hasn't changed much," Gwyneth said as she stopped to take it in. "Still the same old jetty I see."
She was disappointed but not surprised to find no sign of Sean or Richard to welcome them. On the way up the path to the house they heard a loud shout from Libby who came running down the track with George close behind.
"Oh Gwyn, Megan, Sarah. It's so good to see you again. I cannot tell you how glad we are that you are here."
"Where's Richard?" Gwyneth asked. "Is he out working?"
Libby looked at George.
Gwyneth immediately sensed that something was wrong. "What is it Libby, tell me?"
George interrupted. "He's been drinking."
"You mean he's drunk… now, in the middle of the day?"
"I'm afraid so," George confirmed. "He found Sean's whiskey. Today of all days."
"You mean it's happened before?" Gwyneth demanded.
"A…a few times more recently. The first few weeks he was all right, but now…well."
"Come in. Come into our house," Libby invited them.
"Not the welcome I was hoping for," Gwyneth said under her breath as she walked in.
"You've kept the house very well," Megan said. "Linda, this was the first house we lived in when we bought the farm."
"Yes. I know," Linda replied. "I was here before."
"Where's Richard now?" Megan asked becoming more assertive.
"He'll be in the shed out the back," Libby answered.
"That's…that's where he eats and sleeps."
"And drinks?" Megan quizzed.
"Yes, it is," George said. "It's no use trying to hide it," he told Libby. George looked at Linda not knowing how she would react. "It's all right," Sarah told him picking up his concern. "Linda here works with similar men, those who are shell shocked, she knows what happens."
Linda looked at Megan who gave a barely discernible nod. "I've seen a lot worse than this," she told George. "A lot worse."

"Linda is going to try and help Richard if she can," Megan interrupted.

"I'm going to see Richard now." Megan declared, heading out to the shed. "Libby, be a love and take Bronwyn for a while will you?"

Megan walked into the darkness of the shed. It was a simple structure made of old bits of corrugated iron and oddments of timber with just one door and two small windows up high. There was no order or anything that even indicated it was lived in. No bed, no furniture other than a small table and single chair in the corner by a pile of filthy rags and old sacks. Once inside Gwyneth scoured the tiny space looking for Richard but he was nowhere to be seen.

"He sleeps here?" she asked, pointing to a shallow part of the dirt floor Richard had scraped out.

"Yes," George replied.

"You said he was here, I can't see him anywhere," Megan said.

Saying nothing, George walked over to rags and pulled them to one side. They revealed Richard curled up asleep. He was covered in dirt, barely distinguishable from his filthy surroundings, his hair was matted and he was laying in vomit. Beside him was an empty whiskey bottle.

Gwyneth, Megan, and Sarah gasped.

"He was never this bad, even when I found him in Weymouth," Gwyneth said as her anger started to rise.

"Pardon me Mrs Murphy, but that was before the bottle found your son," Linda spoke. "I can assure you this is quite normal for a lot of men. They may have survived the actual war but it's still going on in their heads. They cannot leave it behind as they did Gallipoli."

"But what can we do?" Gwyneth asked. "We can't leave him here."

"Yes you can," said a voice behind from the doorway.

Gwyneth spun around to see Sean standing behind her.

"Sean. I didn't hear you come in," she flustered as the moment she had been dreading was thrust on her when she was at her most vulnerable.

"He's been like this for two days," Sean said. "There's nothing I can do. He won't listen to me and neither will he work, he just mopes around and drinks."
"How much has he had?" Gwyneth demanded.
"That's the second bottle in as many days," was Sean's relaxed reply.
"Don't you care about our son, Sean Murphy? Why have you let this happen?"
"Oh it's not me Gwyn love. It's nice to see you by the way. It's the bloody British taking our men away for a useless war nobody wanted. They're the ones who have done this to your…our son, not me."
"Don't you start that talk again? Its action that's needed now."
"Well," Sean said, running his fingers through his hair in anguish. "If it's action you want, it's action you'll be getting when he wakes up and finds out there's no more whiskey. Then you'll be wishing he was flat out on the floor again."
"I would never wish that on my son," Gwyneth snapped.
"That's what you say now," Sean told her as he pulled up a shirt sleeve. "You see these bruises here on my arm. That's what he did when I told him there was to be no more drinking. This wretch laying on the floor in front of you isn't our son Gwyn. He's a total stranger and I don't mind telling you, he scares me."

**

The tension between Sean and Gwyneth meant the evening meal was spent mostly in silence other than Sarah encouraging Linda to tell stories about the soldiers she had worked with. Sarah had thought that it would encourage some skerrick of hope that Richard would get better but it didn't seem to work. When the meal was finished, there was a very awkward silence in the room.
After ten minutes Gwyneth suddenly slammed the tabletop.

"Right. That's it. I just cannot sit here and do nothing while my son rots in a drunken stupor inside outside. Sean, George, you two are going to get Richard, then you will strip him naked while I run a bath here in the parlour by the fire. I'll scrub him clean and he can sleep in the back room, on the floor if need be but he will be in his own house and not in a filthy shed I wouldn't put a dog in."

"It won't make any difference," Sean said. "He'll end up the same way again in a day or two."

"It will make a difference!" Gwyneth shouted. "It will make a difference to me. I cannot accept what's happening to Richard and even less do nothing about it. George? Are you with me, after all, cleanliness is next to godliness isn't it? Sorry," Gwyneth said. "I didn't mean it like it sounded."

"That's all right," George smiled a false smile.

"Yes, that's a good idea Gwyn," Libby said. "George, do as Gwyn asks. We have to do something. I'll put the kettle and some pots on the range for hot water."

The men went out the back while Gwyneth and Libby brought the zinc bathtub into the parlour. Half an hour later and with the bathtub steaming and everything prepared, Gwyneth shouted out to the men in the shed. "Is he ready yet?"

"As ready as he will ever be," George shouted back.

"Bring him in. I need you men to stay with me just in case Sean is right," Gwyneth demanded.

"What does she mean?" Sean said under his breath, "In case I'm right. Of course I'm bloody well right."

With the bath prepared, George and Sean brought Richard in, naked except for a sheet draped over his body. He was semi-conscious but didn't struggle.

"I'm surprised he didn't wake up properly," Megan said watching from the other side of the parlour.

"If you had several bottles of whiskey inside you, you wouldn't wake up either," Sean muttered.

The two men lowered Richard into the bathtub, Gwyneth pulled the sheet off at the last moment and gave a sharp intake of breath as she put her hand over her mouth when she saw Richard's chest.

"Good God almighty," she said taking in what she saw. "Look what they've done to our son. What kind of hell has he been through for this to happen?"

"I've never seen scars like that before, at least not on a living man," Sean said quietly. "It looks like half his chest is missing. It's as though he's been blown to bits and put back together all wrong. No wonder he's turned to the bottle."

Megan nodded to George as Richard was settled into the bath and they left Gwyneth and Sean with him.

In the failing light of the front parlour, Gwyneth wept in silence as she cautiously washed Richard. She was careful to keep the soap out his eyes and made sure when she washed his hair, he didn't get his face wet.

"Remember? That's something he never liked as a toddler," she said to Sean quietly. "He used to get so angry with me if I got water on his face."

She washed his scarred chest with the sensitivity of a mother washing her newborn baby for the first time as she gave a slight smile. "I used to get upset when he grazed his knees, now look at him."

"It's no use torturing yourself Gwyn love." Sean's words pierced the darkness. "We're lucky he's alive. Look at Theo and the thousands of others. Over thirty thousand dead so far Sarah tells me. Over two thousand from New Zealand and they're still sending in more. I said it before and I'll say it again, it's those bastards in the British government, Churchill, Hamilton, and their cronies. You won't see them getting their arses shot at, I can tell you that for nothing."

"Well if it wasn't for you writing that terrible letter to the orphanage resulting in me losing my job, Richard would probably be dead by now."

Sean was stunned by what Gwyneth said not knowing what to say.

"No need to apologise" Gwyneth said. "It all turned out for the best."

"Weren't you angry?" Sean asked.

"Of course I was at first, you took my life away from me which is what you wanted out of spite more than anything else. You couldn't stand losing me to somebody else, not that there was anybody else of course. But then, when I found Richard, I realised everything has a plan and your spiteful ways were oddly enough a part of it. It's like everything happened to get Richard out of that hell hole he was in. So to answer your question now Sean, no, I am not angry. I am disappointed but I know that what we both want, either with or without each other will happen somehow."

Gwyneth remained quiet not wishing to disturb Richard, he looked normal while he was laying in the water, his scars all but submerged in the grey soapy water and no sign of mental anguish.

After several minutes of silence broken only by the water splashing as Gwyneth gently bathed Richard, Gwyneth turned around to Sean.

"We used to be so happy farming, building up the herd, getting Murata School started. We did so much and still had time for each other. Remember the Sunday afternoons around the piano. Mother and Father, Wirimu and Ngaire. You went to all that trouble bringing the piano up from Dunedin. Had you given me the crown jewels I couldn't have been happier. We used to bathe Richard after that, just like we are now. What happened Sean? Where did it all go so wrong? What's to become of us?"

Sean couldn't look at Gwyneth and he thought for a few minutes and started to speak, more to break the silence than anything else.

"Life was a lot simpler then, that's for sure. Everything was on the up and up. Your father was alive, him and his sheep eh? Building the school, dealing with old Jacob Ballinger. He said we paid too much for the mill and I said that one day it would be a bargain. I got that right, with the new trade the mill's doing well so it is. One day it will be a good inheritance for Richard and Sarah, along with Llanon."

"You're avoiding the question," Gwyneth declared. "I asked what's to become of us, you and me Sean and our sham of a marriage. There's Richard to think about, and now Bronwyn of course."

"You can't put young Bronwyn on me," Sean said. "It was you who decided for whatever reason to bring her back from Wales. What were you thinking of Gwyn? You knew how much work she'd be."

"If only you knew the work the little mite's put into surviving" Gwyneth answered. "We grew close in Wales, I was her protector and she came to rely on me. I couldn't desert her. And for your information Sean, I'm not 'putting' her on you as you put it. I'm quite prepared to do the work to bring out the bright young girl that's in there somewhere."

"But you're too old to be bringing up a kid like that. She'll be hard work Gwyn, damned hard work."

"I can do it on my own," Gwyneth replied. "After all, I wasn't planning on coming back to you."

"We're still married Gwyn," Sean spoke quietly as he stepped towards her.

"You call this a marriage?" Gwyneth asked tersely. "And don't 'love' me either. We don't know what to say to one another, we're awkward in each other's company. If it wasn't for Richard we wouldn't be here now and you still cannot see behind these tears can you?"

Richard groaned and stirred in the bath briefly. Gwyneth shushed him and put a warm towel across his shoulders as he settled back into his stupor.

"You know what the difference is now Sean, what's missing from this…from this marriage?

"I…I don't really know," Sean managed to stutter out.

"You don't know? That's incredulous Sean, even for you. I can tell you what's missing, it's trust. I lost trust in you the moment I saw that photograph of you and that… that Chinese woman. When you lied to me about that I knew our marriage was over. That's what happened, Sean. It was you who let the stranger in to our marriage and it's you who destroyed us. It's no use denying it."

Sean got up and walked about the room. In a thin voice he called "I'm sorry Gwyn love, I truly am."

"Then tell me this, Sean Murphy," Gwyneth reacted immediately. "Are you still seeing her, Moonyeen Wu? Look me in the eyes and tell me you're not."

Sean shuffled about on his feet and said nothing.

"No, I thought not," Gwyneth said.

"Contrition isn't spelt with Chinese writing I've seen on the jars and packets in the pantry is it? Even I know that. It's no good looking back on the faded glory that was once our marriage Sean."

"Contrition," Sean said. "That's an interesting word and not one I've heard you use before. Is it one your fancy doctor man taught you after you left the marital home?"

Gwyneth was incensed by Sean accusation. "Don't you dare…"

But she was interrupted as Richard stirred again, only stronger this time. His body was wet and Gwyneth's hands were soapy so she couldn't hold him in the bath. He slipped causing the water to spill out the other end. Richard grabbed the side of the bath as he leaned over and vomited onto Gwyneth's lap.

"There, there, Richard. No need to worry, we'll look after you now," Gwyneth said as she took him to her chest and gently kissed the back of his head. Gwyneth looked up at Sean. "I know what you are thinking, Sean Murphy, he would be better off dead. Well he won't be because I will bring him back to health even, if it kills me."

Chapter Twelve

**

Stella Ratcliffe was washing glasses behind the bar of the Mokau Hotel when Sean walked in.
"Top of the mornin' to you Stella Ratcliffe and the rest..."
"Don't be giving me that Irish bullshit Sean Murphy," Stella interrupted. "How the hell are you anyway?"
"Oh you know Stella, always the same me," Sean said walking up to the bar and leaning on his elbows.
"And how's that son of yours doing? I hear he's getting about a bit more."
"Well nothing escapes you does it Stella my love? He's doing a lot better since Gwyn moved in with Libby and George last month. I have to give it to that wee lass Bronwyn though, she doesn't say much but she's a bright kid and she has Richard wrapped around her little finger. Gwyn only tells her what to do with Richard and she's onto it. They go everywhere together so they do. I give Richard jobs to do at Llanon, with the wee girl keeping him company so he keeps out of harm's way. It's the booze he misses though. I've hidden most of it, but he gets the tremors something shocking."
"And young Sarah?"
"Sarah and her friend Linda are back next week for this Anzac service, they think it'll be good for Richard."
"Do you think that's a good idea?" Stella asked.
"I'm damned if I know but Linda seems to think it will do Richard good and she works with these men, if men they are. More shadows of men really, but your son is your son no matter what."
"Well, I've certainly seen a lot more of Moonyeen in the last while now she's not been traveling upriver," Stella quipped.
"It's not my business Sean, but is there any hope for you and Gwyneth?"

"I think there's more chance of the moon being made of cheese if you know what I mean. We see each other of course, with Richard being about, but we don't say much unless it's about Richard or Sarah."
There was a brief silence for a minute.
"Where's Moonyeen now?" Sean asked.
"She's out the back washing some sheets. I've no doubt you want to go through."
"Just for the minute. I'm off to New Plymouth on the *Kapuni*. Just waiting on the slack tide in an hour or so. I'll go through to the back if you don't mind."
"If I did, I would have said so a long time ago."

**

Moonyeen was standing at the front of a double concrete sink pushing a cone shaped agitator through the load of sheets.
"Moonyeen," Sean called out as he approached her from the back, placing his hands around her waist.
"MMmmm. Mister Sean."
"I've no time to be stopping, I'm heading off to New Plymouth for a few days if you're thinking of heading over that way yourself."
"No Mr Sean, I am not sure that's a good idea."
"Why ever not my Chinese primrose?"
"Mrs Murphy. She is back home. It is not right anymore."
"It's no more right nor wrong than it's ever been. Mrs Murphy isn't living in the family home, but with Libby and George in the old house. We are no more together than we have been over these last few years or ever will be."
"Yes," Moonyeen said. "But you will be back together one day, Moonyeen knows this. I have seen the look in Mrs Murphy's eyes when she looks at you, ever since you first met. It is the same as it has ever been. You must go to your wife, Mr Sean. It is the honourable thing to do."
"You talk of honour Moonyeen when you have been sleeping with me all this time. Me and Gwyneth were together when I first slept in your bed at the White Hart."

"That was different," Moonyeen pleaded . "I seduced you. It was a foolish thing of me to do and I said it could not happen again at the time."
"What do you mean? That was years ago, how many times have we slept together since then?"
"Many times, but no more. You must be with your wife. It is honourable I give you up now I have seen Mrs Murphy and how she loves you. This I didn't know before. Now I do."
With that Moonyeen turned her back on Sean. Stella, who'd been listening intently, heard the back door slam hard as Sean left. She went to Moonyeen who by now was a shaking mess.
"Are you all right? I heard every word you said. What's happening Moonyeen, what have you done?"
Moonyeen took a minute to compose herself.
"Mrs Ratcliffe. You have known me for many years, I hope you know I have honour and belief in the right thing."
"I know you do," Stella said. "But you and Sean Murphy. I'm the last one to say anything with my background and I know Sean is married, at least in name, but you've both been happy, you especially after all you've been through. I don't understand."
"No. you do not understand Mrs Ratcliffe, even after all these years. My happiness does not matter to me, maybe it does to you but you know I have no rights to Mr Sean. I am a woman. I am second class to most people and to make it worse I am Chinese. Life has taught me to neither expect anything nor deserve anything. Only you have extended the hand of friendship when you come and find me in Arrowtown long time ago. I have no right to expect anything else, especially a man like Mr Sean. I know that no happiness will ever come while Mr Sean has a wife at home. It is not right I should expect otherwise."
"Well more mug you," Stella said. "None of us are getting any younger and sometimes you have to take happiness where you find it."
"Yes but happiness has not been found with Mr Sean. It has been taken, stolen by me from another who has a right. To take what does not belong is a bad thing to do."
"Well, Moonyeen. There's no denying that, but I wonder if you are doing the right thing for yourself."

**

Dickie Fleming sat in the *Heron* holding onto two brown paper parcels Theo Twentyman had wrapped so casually less than a year ago after their adventures in Egypt. It was Theo who had the idea that if he or Dickie were killed, their meagre possessions would be returned in person by the other. "Make sure you give this one to my father and this one to Sarah," he carefully explained as he pencilled 'Father' and 'Sarah' on each respective package. Just after that simple act, Theo didn't return from his Sunday morning walk to the hills at Gallipoli. Dickie knew in his gut something had happened and that was confirmed a few days later, so he collected Theo's belongings and put them with his own. Now he was on the last leg of his journey to make good on his promise. Although it was only early winter, the weather had not been kind and three days of heavy rain and flooding eventually made way for some meagre sun which shone half-heartedly on the water. It was a journey he knew he had to make but was reluctant as he felt an imposter in the world Theo loved, only there by invitation from the vagaries of war.
"Next stop for you," David Stockford called out to Dickie. "Be about ten minutes."
"Thank you," Dickie said somewhat startled as he was deep in thought and hardly able to talk. As the *Heron* pulled into the jetty at Llanon, he unnecessarily checked the bag as he had done for many times, just to make sure Theo's parcels were still safe.
"I'll tie her up tight," David Stockford said. "The jetty's not too clever and you with your gammy leg, you'll have to be careful. You hop off, pardon my words but you know what I mean, and I'll pass your bags to you. The house is only a hundred yards from here, I can take them up for you if you want."
"No. No, that's all right," Dickie replied immediately. "Sorry but I need a moment to gather my thoughts first. This is the last part of a long and painful journey you understand."
David Stockford had seen enough shattered men over the last six months to know not to ask any questions.

"As you want it mate," he said putting Dickie's bag down on the jetty.

**

Libby was working in the kitchen when she heard the *Heron* pull away.
"Who that can be," she muttered to herself as she looked out the window towards the path, but nobody came up. She waited a few moments then went looking.
As she walked towards the riverbank she looked down and saw Dickie picking up his bags. Immediately recognising one as Theo's, she called out. "Theo, Theo."
Dickie looked up and seeing his face, the bitter reality of Libby's loss hit her again and she fell to her knees sobbing. Dickie climbed up the bank as quickly as he could.
"Are you all right?" he asked. Libby looked up at him wiping her tears away with her apron.
"I'm sorry," she sobbed. "It's the bag, it looks like the one my son had."
"It's the one Theo had," Dickie replied. "My name is Dickie Fleming. Are you Mrs Twentyman?"
Libby nodded.
"I wrote to you a month or so ago. I am Theo's friend and comrade at Gallipoli. I promised Theo I would come and see you, and now here I am. I'm sorry to have frightened you. I shouldn't have used Theo's bag, it was thoughtless of me, I didn't mean to give you such a shock."
Libby wiped her tears away again and tried to get up and Dickie held out his arm to help her.
"No. It is me who's sorry" Libby managed to speak through her tears. "I have embarrassed myself Mr Fleming."
"Please, call me Dickie. And no Mrs Twentyman, you haven't embarrassed yourself. In this war, it isn't only those who fight who are hurt."
Libby immediately took to Dickie. "Come up to the house and meet everybody," she told him. "You have timed your visit well."

**

The next day was spent with Dickie recounting stories of his times with Theo while everybody sat around listening. While he was solemn in his approach to what he and Theo saw and did, he was careful not to give too many details of what the two men had been through.

When he felt the time was right, he excused himself for a few minutes, coming back with Theo's bag. Libby took one look at it then took George's hand and clenched it tight.

"Mr and Mrs Twentyman, my purpose in coming here to Mokau, to Llanon, was to fulfil a promise I made to Theo. As I told you in my letter, we promised each other that if one of us didn't come back and the other did, then we would personally deliver what little belongings we had. There is nothing of value of course, at least not in a monetary sense but there are two things, presents Theo went to a lot of trouble to collect and it's these he would have wanted me to bring to you if, well... you know."

The room went deathly quiet as Dickie reached into his bag and pulled out a heavy looking parcel wrapped in a dirty piece of calico.

"When Theo and I were in Cairo we had a day's leave. Theo was keen to go exploring. I can see him now sitting on his camel reading his book, looking at the photos then looking up reliving the history as though he were a part of it. He fossicked around, eventually picking this up, he was so excited to find it as I believe he promised to bring you something from the land of Moses and the Pharaohs."

"Yes. Yes he did indeed," George said barely able to speak.

"So I hand this over to you now," Dickie said. "I know Theo is here, watching this so it is from him to you both."

Dickie passed over the parcel and George slowly unwrapped it as everybody watched. George passed the stone to Libby. Its white translucence seemed to shine on her face, highlighting her tears.

"It's alabaster," Dickie said. "From one of the statues of the great pyramid of Khufu, hand carved by the Egyptians over four thousand years ago."

"I also have something for you," Dickie told Sarah. He reached into the bag and took out a smaller parcel. "Theo wanted me to make sure you got this as well," he said passing it over. Linda took her hand, smiling at her. "He was thinking of you all the time," she whispered.

Richard had been sitting quietly at the back of the room, in the dark with Bronwyn but at that moment he leaned forward and whispered. "Theo was a good man, bloody useless in the bush, but good with animals," he said making everybody turn around.

"Linda got up to join Richard but Bronwyn cuddled up to him even more as though to stop Linda from approaching. Linda took the cue and sat down again.

Sarah didn't open her parcel. "I'll look at it later," she said quietly, not being able to hide her smile.

"We owe you a great deal Dickie," George told him. "A great deal indeed."

"I have delivered everything as I promised ," Dickie said. "But there is one thing more. Mr and Mrs Twentyman, Theo wrote a letter to you both, a very long letter just after he was interviewed for the newspaper, along with Apollo, his mule. He never got around to sending it and when I collected his things I found it addressed to you both. I have it here. I remember Theo was amused by the photographer, a Londoner working in New Plymouth, he thought it quite a coincidence."

"Robertson's Photography!" Sarah shrieked loud enough to frighten everybody. She reached over to her bag and started rummaging through it.

"It must have been Tommy Robertson," Gwyneth said.

"Mother, you remember him. He took the photograph of you and I years ago in Devon Street. You played 'Calon Lan' on the piano in the studio."

"Yes," Megan said. "It was a Marshall and Rose, the piano I mean. We were in town to buy some drapes for the school."

"There nothing wrong with your memory" Sean said wanting to get into the conversation.

"There's nothing wrong with mine either," Gwyneth interrupted looking sharply at Sean, shutting him down immediately.

"Here it is," Sarah declared holding out a folded newspaper clipping, showing it to Dickie. "Here's the very article with a photograph of Theo and Apollo."

"Well I never did," Dickie said. "That brings it all back like it was only yesterday. You know he told me so much about you Sarah. He wanted to take you to Cairo one day to show you the pyramids himself."

Sarah blushed deeply.

"I'm sorry," Dickie said realising what he implied. "I didn't mean to embarrass you. Here Mr Twentyman, here is the letter."

The conversation flowed around the many times Dickie and Theo had, from the training at Trentham to their adventures in Cairo and to Gallipoli.

After a very long and tiring day Libby got up.

"Well, Dickie Fleming, as George said earlier, we have a lot to be grateful to you for. Nothing can bring Theo back but you have helped us come to terms with his death more than you can ever know. We will always be indebted to you for being a good friend to Theo. You took him under your wing at Trentham, through to Gallipoli and now your duty is finally discharged. Thank you. If you will all excuse us now it's time George and I read this letter in private so we can give the last word to our son."

With that Libby and George went into their room. George handed Libby the letter opener and she carefully and slowly took the letter out.

> Dear Mother and Father
>
> Well I finally left Trentham and found myself in Egypt. I left on 13 June on board the Maunganui. Many men were seasick but fortunately after a few days I was all right which sadly I cannot say the same for the horses. We had over two hundred cramped into the holds and with poor ventilation and no exercise, many succumbed to illness and died. There is nothing sadder than to see such a noble creature's body being hauled out the hold on a winch and dumped unceremoniously into the sea; or so I thought at the time.

While in Cairo I tried to find Richard and Tama but my duties kept me busy as did theirs so I am afraid we never met up.
I have kept my promise and I have safely stored away a piece of stone taken from the great pyramid of Khufu. It is alabaster so could have fallen from one of the great statues themselves. To think it was carved and placed there by the ancient Egyptians two thousand years before Moses walked the earth and stayed there for another two thousand years after. I also have a smaller piece for Sarah, I hope you don't mind. I think she might like it but please do not mention it to her as I would rather like it to be a surprise for her on my return.

I have to say that I was excited to hear we were being sent to Turkey to take the Dardanelle Strait. To be near the ancient city of Troy after being in Egypt would have been a double pleasure. The land of Homer and the Trojans would have been the icing on the cake but the circumstances I found on the Gallipoli peninsula have erased any pleasure that would have brought.
I arrived on the Foxhound with C Section. At first sight I thought there were rocks in the surf, but once we neared them we saw they were bodies horribly shot up. We were pinned on the beach for half a day but eventually made our way inland and made headquarters at a place we call 'Plugge's Plateau'. I am sorry to say many of my comrades-in-arms never made it off the beach alive.

It seems we have been under constant fire or attack from the Turks ever since the first day.
My good friend, Dickie Fleming is a comfort to me in these troubled times as he is a cheery soul. He and I work together carrying the wounded to the dressing stations or the lucky ones to the field hospital at the beach for transportation to Lemnos. How that must be like heaven to them after Gallipoli.

I have made another friend, a mule. He was injured and I cared for him for a while. Luckily, I kept some of the kawakawa from the last hunting trip with Richard and Tama when Major went lame. Although dried, up the Kawakawa revived in some of the last clean water I have seen for a while, so I was able to make a poultice of sorts. It was worth it as the poor creature is now much revived. I have named him Apollo after the Greek god of poetry, music, medicine and light so he may bring what little inspiration there is on this bitter land.

Seeing the faces of the dead rouses both feelings of revenge and compassion within me. Revenge which I am trying to quell, as to be fair, the Turks are good men fighting for their own land so in some ways I cannot blame them, but their savagery in combat is unrelenting. I have learned there is no glory or bravery in war, only the will to survive and pure luck. There must be a better way as both sides of this war have paid dearly for no benefit that I can see. The blood-stained soil will remain, as will the bodies of the men who will never ever come back to New Zealand. Many lay where they have fallen and remain there even after a month.

Surely men have been butchered in every way possible. The beaches, the trenches and all around are piled with bodies and parts of bodies, and the heaps of rotting flesh are black with flies, New Zealanders, Australians, and Turks alike and the stench is acrid and stings my nose.

I found a young man yesterday; he couldn't even have been sixteen and had been shot in the stomach. There was nothing I could do other than stay with him as he screamed out for his mother until he died in my arms.

We have had an armistice to bury the dead. I could not walk along Lone Pine without having to step over bloated black and hideously contorted bodies every step of the way. After eight hours, the shooting started again.

There can be no victory in this hell we call Gallipoli, a land once crossed by the conquering Persian armies of Xerxes and Alexandra the Great but it is now the graveyard of the Anzacs.

This is why Mother, and Father I am giving up my plans to become a doctor. I used to think I could relieve physical suffering, but nothing can relieve the physical torment, anguish, and utter pain I have seen in the last few weeks. I think there is a higher cause. My plans are now to become a priest. I have seen the work these men do, how they can help the most tormented of souls. Healing the body is one thing, but healing the soul is another and that is the path I will take when I return. This is what keeps me sane, knowing that I can please God in some way and perhaps make some sense of this depravity and carnage. I hope you understand this is something I feel I must do.

I pray for you all in Mokau and for Richard and Tama as well of course. I pray the three of us will meet up again in peaceful times and we can be with you all on the banks of the Mokau once more as a family. How I ache to be back, but until then I must do my duty and face my tasks knowing I can help others less fortunate than I.

Please pass my regards to Sarah.

Your Loving Son

Theo.

Chapter Thirteen

**

David Stockford tied up the *Heron* at the Te Kainga jetty and walked the path to the house.
"Kia ora," he called out.
Ngaire stood in the kitchen, stock still, her face frozen in anticipation.
"It's all right. There's no telegram," David immediately reassured her, holding his hands up in front to show her he carried no such news.
"Thank God" she said noticeably relieved. "What brings you here then?"
"Is Wirimu about?" he asked.
"He won't be far away, why do you ask?"
David reached into his jacket pocket and pulled out a letter. "I have this for you. "Thank God. Our prayers have been answered," she said seizing the letter and ripping it open there and then. She was pouring over it just as Wirimu walked in.
"What is it?" he asked seeing Ngaire.
"It's a letter, from Tama," she sobbed. She looked up at Wirimu, smiling as she wiped the tears away with the back of her hand. "He's all right. Hardly a scratch he says, just a bit of a cut on his arm. Here, see for yourself," she said holding out the letter.
"It's short enough," Wirimu said. "But it's the news we needed to hear thank God. He's been made up to sergeant."
"That will be the Maniapoto coming out in him," Ngaire said proudly. "Atarangi will be so honoured. I must write to her".
"Thank you David, thank you for bringing us such good news," Ngaire said. "Please excuse me but you will know it is the first letter for some months and we've been so anxious to hear. You have no idea how we listen for you coming upriver hoping you have something for us."

"Well this time I have, so it's good news," David said. "But I know how Owen McConaghy felt at times. The telegrams are the worst part of the job all right."
"Kai?" Ngaire asked. "Shepherd's pie, just out the oven."
David smiled. "I wouldn't like to upset you with a refusal" he said sitting down at the table before he had even finished speaking. "But I can't be long. I have a letter for Sean and Gwyneth at Llanon, from Sarah by the looks of the writing on the envelope."
"David?" Ngaire asked. "Can I seek a favour from you? After we've eaten, Wirimu and me can walk along the river to Llanon. We haven't done that for so long without a heavy heart have we Wirimu?" she said turning to seek his agreement.
"Now we've heard from Tama. we can tell everybody our good news and deliver Sarah's letter if that's all right? She's such a bright soul, her letter will be good news as well."
"Of course," Wirimu agreed. "We can go now. Wrap the rest of the kai in a towel and take it with us; we can all eat together at Llanon. David, you don't mind eating on your own do you?"
"No, of course not," David said, eager to get back to Mokau.
"Close the door on your way out then, we're leaving now," Wirimu said smiling at Ngaire.

**

Gwyneth was in the kitchen standing in a cloud of steam as she drained a pot of boiled cabbage when Wirimu and Ngaire knocked on the door.
"Kia ora Gwyn," Ngaire called out.
"Ngaire," Gwyneth said clearly flustered by the surprise visit.
"It's all right Gwyn," Ngaire reassured her. "We have good news we wanted to share straight away. News from Gallipoli."
Gwyneth almost threw down the pot. "What is it?"
"He's all right Gwyn. Tama's all right." Ngaire couldn't help but hug Gwyneth as she let out a flood of tears.
Gwyneth took it.
"Well he certainly doesn't waste his words, but this is the best news. I'm so happy for you, so very happy. A sergeant as well, you must be so proud?"

"We've brought some kai" Ngaire said. "It's just that we wanted to share our news straight away."
"Of course," Gwyneth agreed. "Why don't you go over to the old house and tell George and Libby and I'll finish up in here."
A short silence fell.
"Don't worry Ngaire," Gwyneth said. "They will both be as pleased to hear your news as we all are. Since Dickie's visit, they're a lot more settled about Theo."
"Oh!" Ngaire said suddenly. "I almost forgot in all the excitement. I have a letter here for you, David Stockford asked me to pass it on, well, actually, I asked him if we could deliver it ourselves."
"That'll be from Sarah I expect," Gwyneth said. She looked at the envelope. "Yes, thought so" she said putting it on the table. "I'll read it later."

**

"Is Richard still eating in the shed?" Wirimu asked at the dinner table.
"Yes, he spends most of his spare time in there. He's made a kind of a camp bed on the floor," Sean added. "He's keeping off the bottle too, mind you I still have to hide the whiskey, but I have to give it to him, he's a hard worker. He'll work on the farm all day with hardly a break. Not the greatest conversationalist I have to say but he puts his back into it. In fact there's times I have trouble keeping up with him."
"Well none of us are getting any younger are we?" Gwyneth asked rhetorically looking at Sean.
"The recent floods did a lot of damage," Sean said. "They tell me the slips have closed off the top of the river and so many trees have fallen in, the snags are making the rest all but impossible to get the steamers in. No doubt it'll slow down business at the mill."
"A week of solid rain has to do some damage," Wirimu added.
"It'll slow up the surveying," Sean said "which means the river won't be settled as we hoped. It's taken Lands and Survey long enough to open up the country north of here. It'll take a damn sight longer now. They've only just surveyed the land next door."

"I expect the mill will survive. It always seems to," Gwyneth added.

"How's Megan?" Ngaire asked.

"She's getting along well enough," Gwyneth replied. "The tea rooms keep her busy but she's slowing down a lot more."

There was another short silence where Sean felt as though he was a stranger in a group of friends.

"We'll have to start preparing for Christmas soon," George said recognising the tension building up in the room. "We've a lot to be thankful for; especially with your news," he added, looking over at Wirimu and Ngaire.

"And we need to be grateful Bronny's with us too." Gwyneth chimed in. "You have settled in really well and enjoying school as well, aren't you Bronny?"

"Yes," came a quiet reply from Bronwyn as she struggled to dig her spoon into some mashed potato.

Sean got up and took some empty plates. "I'll take these back for you," he said putting his hand on Gwyneth's shoulder, not sure what to expect in response.

"Thank you" she offered as Ngaire gave Wirimu a quick glance.

**

Sarah jumped off the tram even before it stopped and strode angrily down Moxham Avenue to her boarding house. Bursting into Sarah's bedroom in a frenzy, she sat on the bed and waited for a reaction, but she didn't get the listening ear she was hoping for.

"What is it for crying out loud," Linda demanded. "I'm just back from a double shift and just got off to sleep after a day from hell."

"You'll never guess what's happened" Sarah erupted angrily. "The news came off the wires this morning."

"Then why don't you tell me exactly what it is you're talking about?" Linda replied, resentful at being woken.

"We've pulled out of Gallipoli," Sarah declared. "It's over."

"Come in why don't you?" Linda said sarcastically. "Gallipoli you are saying, it's all ended then?" she relented seeing the look on Sarah's face as she gathered her thoughts. "The slaughter's over?"

"Yes. It's over, at least in the Dardanelles. But more importantly, it means the Turks have won, we've failed to stop the Germans using the straits so we can't control Constantinople."

"So our boys will be home, or at least in England for Christmas?" Linda asked.

"No, you don't understand," Sarah said. "The war itself has barely started. But the point is our lads have died for nothing. Richard and all those young boys have died in vain. Doesn't that make your blood boil?" Sarah shouted as she paced round Linda's bedroom. "You know I'm starting to think Father was right about those politicians in England. It's Churchill who's to blame, and Massey and his damned reformists for sending our boys over on a fool's errand. I could give them a piece of my mind I can tell you."

"So you are your father's daughter after all," Linda quipped.

"No. It's not that?"

"What is it then?"

"Well, don't you think it's time we, New Zealand that is, has a stronger voice in the world? It's time we grew up. I know we have a duty to follow Britain but do we have to blindly follow the mother land?"

Sarah looked at her scornfully.

"Father was right in one thing," Sarah went on, "as a young country we have been severely weakened, and if I'm right, this war has a long way to go. We haven't even been to France nor the rest of the continent and that's where all the fighting is. Gallipoli was just an experiment by bloody Churchill and his cronies. An experiment which has cost us three thousand good men plus all the wounded and ruined men, and their families. Some Christmas this will turn out to be."

"Have you heard from Dickie?" Linda asked.

"You're keen to change the subject," Sarah said.

"Well," Linda goaded. "Have you or haven't you?"

"Not lately," Sarah replied giving in to Linda's questioning.

"You've grown quite attached to him since you first met," Linda said, pushing her luck.
"No. Not really. It's just that…well, we get along all right and he was close to Theo so we have a lot to talk about."
"You are turning red Sarah Murphy," Linda teased, pleased she got a rise.
"Yes, well Christmas is here now and neither of us can get away. I hope Mother understands, I haven't had a reply from my last letter. I just hope she got it in time."
"Now who wants to change the subject?" Linda said laughing.
"Your Mr Harris at the newspaper is a right old slave driver though."
"No more than the hospital is to you. Needs must when the devil drives Linda. We all have to do our bit."

**

On Christmas Eve, Sarah was sitting at her desk waiting for inspiration to hit her, but it didn't. She sat staring at the latest letter from Dickie which arrived just the day before. It was inside a Christmas card with a picture of a robin sitting on a spade handle in a snow-covered field. Sarah looked outside onto Lambton Quay and noticed the air shimmer off the road in the baking hot sun and she smiled at the irony.
She started tapping at a few keys on the typewriter, but they didn't make any sense
so she reached out to Dickie's letter again. Noticing a movement through the window in the door to Mr Harris's office she hastily put the envelope back in her bag and started typing again.
"What are you working on?" Mr Harris demanded as he strode out the door.
"Nothing much."
Mr Harris dismissed Sarah's terse reply.
"How long have you been with us now?" he asked.
"A little over six months."
"Come into my office," he demanded.
Sarah could feel the blood drain from her face and her chest thumped as she was ushered in.

"I won't beat about the bush," he said lighting a cigarette. "I've been watching you and I like what you're writing. You did a fair job with the retreat from Gallipoli, and you seem to have a knack for guessing what's going to happen next."

"With all respects, Mr Harris, it's not guessing, well not really. It's all a matter of adding up all the events of the day and putting them all into one big picture."

"Yes, exactly," Mr Harris said. "Politics, you are very good at politics Miss Murphy. You seem to have a natural aptitude for it."

"Now, when the House sits in the New Year, I want you to take more of an interest. I'll be giving you some smaller, lighter jobs of course but nevertheless I want you in the House more than you have in the past. Is that clear?" He hesitated to take a long draw on his cigarette. "You'll have to write under a nom-de-plume of course, the public aren't ready to hear the news from a woman yet, and you certainly won't be in the press gallery either, so you'd better get used to it. What do you say?"

Sarah hesitated for a moment.

"I would say thank you for showing confidence in me, but I certainly don't agree with the falsehood of using a nom-de-plume. Just because I am a woman there's no reason why I cannot write as well as a man. You yourself said I had a feel for what's happening."

"So what is happening, with the war I mean?" Mr Harris asked suddenly becoming very serious.

"The western front, Mr Harris. I think the western front will make Gallipoli look like a cake walk."

"You really think so?"

"I know so," Sarah said confidently. "All indications are the two great armies will meet there, in far bigger numbers than they already have and with more effective weapons. You and I have both seen the stories we're not allowed to publish, the atrocities and the horrendous deaths on both sides of the war in Flanders, the gas attacks on our soldiers and the flamethrowers we use to flush the Germans out. All the stories the government doesn't want the public to read about."

Mr Harris looked sideways at Sarah

"German mothers love their children too Mr Harris," Sarah added.

"I'll pretend I didn't hear that," he scolded.

"We've already seen two great battles on the Ypres Salient," Sarah went on. "There has to be more as the Germans build up in western Flanders while we have to push through if we are to liberate the continent. It's two immovable objects facing each other, and one side will eventually have to give way at a very heavy cost of lives. There is nothing more certain."

Mr Harris was silent for a minute, deep in thought. "Tell me Miss Murphy," he said eventually taking off his glasses and cleaning them with his handkerchief, then holding them up against the light. A habit he developed when he was nervous. "You have a brother at home, injured at Gallipoli wasn't he?"

"Yes," Sarah answered. "Richard, why do you ask?"

"When are you seeing him, and your parents next?"

"I'm not sure, I don't have any leave."

"Well take a few days off now. It's quiet, there's no news to speak of and there's no paper tomorrow anyway. Take some time off but get back for Monday week."

Sarah was visibly shocked at the unexpectedly generous offer. "I can't do that" she protested. "There are more senior people than me who can't get away at all."

"Nonsense," Mr Harris said finally putting his glasses on. "Between you and me, I have a daughter about your age, Annie. She's bright and curious but I've seen her held back just because she's a woman. She wants to be an architect but there's no chance of that in this life. We fell out a year or so ago … and I haven't seen her since. I cannot help thinking how I would feel if she walked in the door right now, at Christmas especially. You go and see your family; you'll miss Christmas Day of course but you'll make it for just after. I'll tell the others you're sick. I'll square it up. But be sure when you get back you will be in the thick of it, real name or not."

"Mr Harris? Pardon my asking, but seeing as we are talking about family, you have several sons, don't you?" Sarah asked sensing there was something more to Mr Harris's offer. She was feeling as though she were imposing but her curiosity got the better of her. Mr Harris looked down at the ground and fumbled in his pocket for his handkerchief again. He didn't talk for a moment. "Those are the sorts of questions that will make you a good reporter Miss Murphy."

"It's, it's just that I sense a sadness with you of late. I hope I'm not imposing?"

"No, you're not imposing. I'm pleased I can talk to somebody outside of my family for once. My wife and I have, or rather had two fine young boys, both at Gallipoli. Brian got off but we found out just recently that Edward was killed just before the evacuation, on his twenty first birthday."

"I am so sorry," Sarah said. "How is Mrs Harris?"

"About how you would expect, totally inconsolable. She cannot bear me touching her, let alone talk."

Mr Harris turned his back and Sarah could see he was fighting tears.

"You know Mr Harris, it's perfectly all right for a man to cry. My father holds in tears, angry tears about my brother and its turning him bitter. I can see it. Don't let that happen to you."

Mr Harris stared at Sarah for a few moments then turned his back on her. "Please leave now," he said through a breaking voice.

Sarah walked towards the door and all she could do was to put her hand on the shoulder of the tweed coat as she walked out the office. "I'm truly sorry," she murmured.

"What's your middle name?" Mr Harris asked just as she got to the door.

"Megan. After my grandmother."

"Very well" Mr Harris replied. "As you wish then. No nom-de-plume, you will write under SM Murphy as usual. Nobody will know you're a woman so that'll be fine."

"Thank you," Sarah said, about to say something else, but thought against it.

**

Two days later, on a hot afternoon, Sarah found herself walking up the pathway from the Llanon jetty along the track. It was lined with tall, dried out grass and the hills were browning off as the summer started to take effect.

She was going to send a telegram of her intended arrival but the words of Mr Harris resonated with her and she wanted to give her parents a surprise. She thought she would probably beat the telegram anyway. Gwyneth was the first to see her. "Sarah!" she called out. "Sarah!" "Mother, Sarah's here and in a short time Megan appeared.

"Well bless my soul," Gwyneth said as she started running down the pathway. "I thought I heard the *Heron* slowing down. What are you doing here Sarah love? We only got your letter a few days ago saying you couldn't be here?"

"Mr Harris gave me a few days off, long story Mother," Sarah said hugging Gwyneth, then breaking off to hug Megan.

"Bronny love," she said stooping down to look at Bronwyn who was dressed in a green gingham dress with her hair in plaits. "What a pretty girl you are turning out to be."

"And she's doing so well at school," Megan added. Bronwyn smiled a toothy smile.

"Bronwyn love, why don't you go and get Richard?" Gwyneth said. Bronwyn turned and ran back to the house.

"Are George and Libby here?" Sarah asked.

"No. they've gone to see George's father in the Waikato. He's not well at all. It must be serious as his mother sent a letter. Apparently, George's father was asking for him and Libby."

"That doesn't sound too good," Sarah said, "given what happened when they first met."

"Is Linda not with you?" Gwyneth asked.

"No, she can't get away from the hospital," Sarah replied.

"Of course not, sorry, it's just that Richard might look for her as you are here, that's all. Linda seemed to make an impression with him."

Just at that moment Richard appeared led by Bronwyn. He looked un-kept, his hair was greying prematurely and looked greasy. His clothes looked as though they needed a good wash and his face and neck were covered in a rough beard. He walked slowly as though he'd just woken. He approached Sarah cautiously staring at her as though she was a stranger.

Sarah was taken aback but managed a greeting. She hugged him but it was difficult as Richard didn't respond, he just stood there with his arms at his side looking at Sarah.

The awkward silence was broken by Gwyneth. "Come on in Sarah love. Your nana's been baking Welsh cakes, just the thing with a cuppa after a long journey. It's so good to see you. Your father will be so pleased to see you when he gets back."

"Gets back? Where is he? I thought he might be here for Christmas."

"He was," Megan said as though to justify Sean's absence, but Sarah's curiosity was already aroused. She looked at her mother, but she knew not to say anything, not then.

**

That evening after everybody else had gone to bed, Gwyneth approached Sarah. "You've been acting as though you want to ask me something," she said. "What's on your mind?"

"Am I that transparent?" Sarah asked.

"You're my daughter, I know that look where you bite your lip. Is there a man involved?"

"Well…sort of. There is and there isn't. It's Dickie Fleming."

"I thought you were sweet on him, beyond his connection with Theo.

Linda even said as much a while ago. So?" Gwyneth asked pointedly. "What's happening, or not happening, as the case may be?"

"That's just it," Sarah said making sure nobody else was in earshot. "I like Dickie, more than that, but I don't really know how he feels about me. He's sweet, thoughtful, and funny in his own way. He's very intelligent and he cares for people. But the problem is I don't know if he cares for me, no, that didn't sound how it was supposed to."

"Let me guess," Gwyneth said. "You care for him and want to see him more, but he's in Auckland. Are you thinking of going to see him? Is that it?"

"No, that's not it at all," Sarah said getting a little anxious. "Quite the opposite. He's thinking of moving to Wellington, he doesn't say it's to be near me but I can't help hoping it would be, but it might not be. Oh I don't know," Sarah said throwing a book onto the settee in frustration.

"So Dickie wants to move to Wellington? What would he do for a job?" Gwyneth probed.

"He's been offered a position in the Public Works Department as a trainee draughtsman. He has an uncle there, a Stephen Popplewell who's set it up for him. Apparently, Dickie has always wanted to be an architect so this is one way of getting a step on the ladder so to speak."

"So why is this causing you upset?" Gwyneth asked. "If you like Dickie and he's moving to Wellington, surely that would be a good thing?"

"Ordinarily yes," Sarah said. "But he's written telling me all of this and also asking if it's all right with me. He'll be living with his uncle in Miramar, possibly getting the same tram as me to work."

"Mm. That could be awkward," Gwyneth nodded in agreement.

"It's as though he's asking my permission to do something which will change the rest of his life," Sarah said with almost a desperate tone in her voice. "If I agree to him coming to Wellington, I will appear too forward and possibly commit myself to something I don't know the outcome of. If I say no then I would be holding him back from a career he's always wanted."

"I see what you mean," Gwyneth said thoughtfully. "Maybe you need to put all of this down in a letter to him," she said after thinking for a while. "You said yourself he's thoughtful so he'll understand he's put you in this position unintentionally, a bit over caring of him if anything. You can't let him down by doing nothing, but you are right, you cannot be too forward either. Perhaps if you tell him you cannot hold his career back but also that you hope he will make friends and perhaps go out with you in a group, after all you have your job to think of, not that should get in the way of course."

"Why not? Can't a woman have a career?" Sarah demanded. "I'm surprised you would say such a thing. More and more women are making careers for themselves, especially since this hideous war started, you were a nurse, weren't you?"
Gwyneth chose to ignore Sarah's remark.
"You could invite him to some of those 'do's' your newspaper people have from time to time. Don't be too obvious but let him know you still want to be friends, then if something comes of it then all well and good. If not, then that's something you both have to deal with. You are both adults now, it's a part of life after all."
"Yes. Yes perhaps that's the best way," Sarah said calming down again. "Make him welcome to come to Wellington but it needs to be his choice after all."
"You know," Gwyneth said, "one time, many years ago, your nana told me you cannot decide who you fall in love with. It just happens. Whether it works or not is something only you can find out if you put time and effort into it."
"Nana told you that. Why?" Sarah questioned. "Whatever made her say something like that"?
"Always the reporter," Gwyneth said. "Not now though, it's too late and I for one am going to bed. Your father will probably be back tomorrow. He needs to put Richard to work as soon as he can."
"That's a bit harsh at New Year," Sarah said.
"It's either that or Richard will spend all day looking for a bottle. Your father has his precious Jamieson's whiskey hidden away and if Richard finds that, there'll be trouble."
"How do you mean?" Sarah asked. "Father wouldn't be that mean surely, he wouldn't hurt Richard."
"No, not like that. I mean if Richard gets his hands on it, then one of us will have to spend the rest of the week looking after him."
"Is he that bad?"
"I'm afraid so. We even have to keep little Bronwyn away from him if he gets that way or God knows what would happen."

"Surely not with Richard, he's my brother for heaven's sake."
"Your brother, my son, it's all the same if he's on a bender. Gwyneth dabbed her eyes with her handkerchief. "It's not like a few drinks, one over the eight or whatever. He'll have a bottle of whiskey; upend it and it's gone in less than half an hour. He's not Richard when that happens, he's somebody who's bad, evil almost; and to be honest it's somebody none of us here likes at all."

**

Sean arrived the following afternoon, surprised to see Sarah. He went to give her a hug, but she immediately pulled away as she picked up on the very faint smell of perfume on her father. It was the same scent she remembered from when she was searching through Moonyeen's belongings at the Mokau Hotel where she found the photograph of her father and Moonyeen together.
"Well if it's not top of the mornin' to my only daughter and you treat me like a virtual stranger. What is it they're teaching you in the big city Sarah love?"
Sarah could barely speak through her anger.

**

The week at Llanon passed quickly enough for Sarah as she avoided her father and talked with her mother and Megan reminiscing or talking of the future and the changing times, the war and what lay beyond. She visited Wirimu and Ngaire who spoke of the few letters they had received from Tama, how he was alive and well and had been evacuated from Gallipoli safely.
"I'll come with you to Mokau when you leave tomorrow, Sarah. I'll bring Bronwyn as well" Gwyneth said over breakfast.
"Around New Year I like to go and tend to Betty and Joe Crawford's grave. There's a hedge on Betty's side which always needs cutting back."
"That's thoughtful of you," Sarah said.

"They were very good friends to us. They made your nana and grandfather, and I very welcome on our first night in Mokau. That was before I even met your father," she said looking at Sean with a thin smile on her lips. Sean smiled back and Sarah saw her father again for a brief time. "We were all very frightened in our own way. We nearly lost all our money in the south island and Mokau was our last hope of a life in New Zealand. We crossed the river bar on a stormy night and the captain nearly lost the ship. We were glad to be on land after that I can tell you. It was Joe who sat us down by the fire in the hotel and Betty brought us over a bowl of stew."

"Betty was a breath of fresh air all right," Megan said walking in with a plate of Welsh cakes fresh from the oven. "But it was your mother here who made the biggest sacrifice," she said taking Gwyneth's hand. "Three times we offered to send her back to Cardiff and three times she refused. In the end she made us spend her ticket money on dynamite, fencing materials and a few cows so we could make a fresh start here at Middle River." Megan sat with Gwyneth and Sarah. "So now," she said, "now it's time I made a small sacrifice for my family. I'm going to sell the Britannia Tea Rooms. If it's all right with you I'll be moving back here, to Llanon, permanently."

A silence lingered as Sarah looked at Gwyneth and Sean.

"It all makes perfect sense," Megan said breaking the silence. "I'm getting too old to run the tea rooms now. You said so yourselves only the other evening when you thought I was asleep. I might be dottery but I'm not deaf," she said looking at Sarah with a twinkle in her eye. "Besides, with young Bronwyn and Richard taking up more time when he's… when he's not well, you need all the help you can get. The money from the Britannia Tea Rooms will go into a special account for Richard and Sarah to be shared equally when Sarah reaches the age of twenty-five, unless she gets married first, by that time Richard will be well I'm sure. I was going to leave the tea rooms to you both in my will anyway, but if I am reading things right Sarah, your future lies in Wellington one way or the other," she said pressing Sarah's hand into hers. "You'll be better off with the money".

"Nana? Are you sure this is the right thing to do?" Sarah questioned even before the others had time to react.

"I am quite sure my dear. I know you'll spend the money wisely when the time comes and Richard, well Richard will be better one day and then he'll need some financial help for what he decides to do with his future."

"But why Nana?" Sarah asked

"Well to be perfectly honest Sarah. I'm getting lonely in New Plymouth. My eyesight isn't what it used to be either. I get confused between a florin and a half crown at times. I'm getting forgetful too, sometimes I even forget the names of our regulars. I need to be around my family, so if anything, you would all be doing me a favour."

"Oh Nana," Sarah exclaimed. "Why haven't you told us before?"

"Well nobody likes to admit to getting old do they?"

"Megan," Sean interrupted. "I can buy the business off you now for a good price and put a manager in."

"No Sean," Megan said immediately brushing his offer away without any further thought. "That's very good of you; but you're a farmer and with the mill keeping you busy, I'll sell to the highest bidder. My mind is quite made up. I'll see my lawyer and get the place on the market and set up a trust fund."

"Thank you Nana, thank you, thank you, thank you." Sarah said hugging Megan.

**

In the evening as Sarah was packing her suitcase for the journey back to Wellington, Gwyneth knocked on the door and walked in carrying a rag doll.

"Sarah love, I've just come to see if there's anything else you need to take back with you. Remember this?" she said holding up the doll. "Maggie, you called her, she was your favourite. You took her everywhere."

"Of course," Sarah said taking the doll, holding it against her face for a moment then putting it in her suitcase.

"You know there's a bedroom full of your things here which will need to be sorted one day."

"Yes, I know," Sarah replied. She hesitated before making her next remark. "But that's not all that has to be sorted, is it?"

"I don't understand Sarah, what is it you mean?" Gwyneth replied.

"You know very well," Sarah said.

"Why do you put up with father's infidelity? When he came home, I could smell that Chinese woman on him. He hadn't been to New Plymouth, he would never have gotten any further than Mokau, surely you realise that? Why do you put up with it?"

Gwyneth hesitated, choosing to look out the window with her back to Sarah.

"You have grown up haven't you?" she remarked. "It's not easy keeping a family together. Compromises have to be made for the sake of others."

"Compromises are one thing, but Father sleeping with a whore rather than his wife is something else."

"Sarah do not for one moment think I want your father in my bed. I too have my pride you know. Anyway, Moonyeen Wu is not a whore, although many think believe she is. Besides, it's complicated, more than you can ever know."

"How can wrong be complicated? Wrong is wrong and that's that. And why are you defending her?"

"This is life real Sarah. I need to keep the family together, for the sake of Richard if nobody else."

"There's a lot you are not telling me," Sarah said with a tone Gwyneth didn't care for.

"Sarah. Life is difficult enough for me without you raking up the past. Do you think I enjoy seeing your father disappear for days at a time, Richard drinking himself into oblivion and a little girl to look after? Now Mother is coming to stay I'll have to look after her as well no doubt."

"So why did you bring Bronwyn back from your mysterious trip to Wales?" Sarah hesitated for a moment. "Oh my god mother" she said almost falling down onto her bed with her hands over her mouth. "Is that what you talked about the other day when Nana said you couldn't help who you fell in love with? Is that it? Has there been somebody else in your life?"

Gwyneth moved over and sat beside Sarah.

"Sarah, what I am about to tell you is the truth, whether you choose to believe me or not is up to you, but I swear on your grandfathers grave it is the entire truth, you deserve to know. You had a photograph of your father with Moonyeen Wu taken in Devon Street some years ago. I found it in your bag in the wardrobe. When I saw the photograph, it was the first time I knew your father was having an affair. I could tell by the demeanor of Moonyeen that she had slept with him. She had a look of having got her man, the way she was holding onto him, I can still picture it. How that photograph got into your possession I don't know."

"I stole it," Sarah said quite brazenly. " You said we are being brutally honest so I am telling you some facts. I broke into her bedroom and went through her things until I found the photograph. I'm not ashamed of what I did and I remember saying to you at the time I didn't trust her. I never knew what it was I was looking for but I knew I would find something, women like that always have something tucked away as a secret pleasure. Once I found the photograph, I didn't know what to do so I put it in my bag and left it in the back of my wardrobe where you found it."

"It was the time we went to New Plymouth to see the auction where the last of your grandfather's sheep were sold," Gwyneth said. "It was a good few days, your father was his old self, and the man I fell in love with and was proud to have married. Little did I know what was really going on?"

There was a brief silence broken by Gwyneth clearing her throat.

"Sarah, when I was a student nurse in Cardiff, there was a doctor, a David Askill who was in charge at the orphanage where I worked as a volunteer. It's a long story but to cut it short, he travelled halfway around the world to ask me to go back to Cardiff to help him run the orphanage. He even went to Canterbury and found we had moved here, so he came to Mokau, such was his determination. I felt very flattered really as he almost begged me to come back, but I flatly refused. My place is here with all of this," Gwyneth said standing up and facing Sarah as she gained the courage to speak openly. Sarah remained silent almost scared of what was coming next.

Gwyneth cleared her throat again. "You said you wanted honesty Sarah. David eventually accepted I wouldn't be going back to Cardiff with him so he resolved to return on his own. I went to see him that night, it must have been the same time you went to find that damned photograph. I went to say goodbye, after all, we were friends and it was the least I could do after such a noble effort on his behalf."

"Mother," Sarah said with concern in her voice. "You're not going to tell me…"

"No, no Sarah, nothing like that ever happened with David, It was purely a professional and very much a platonic relationship."

"Go on," Sarah said.

"A week or so later I found the photograph in your bag and, and as you know, that's when I left your father. I knew David hadn't left yet so I went to see him to say that I had changed my mind and I would go back to Cardiff with him. I found him just a few days before he left to go to Wellington for his ship. I was talking to David when I found out Betty had died, I remember finding her death certificate on David's filing cabinet."

"But why did you suddenly decide to leave Llanon? If your sense of duty was here, what made you change your mind so quickly?"

"I wanted to get back at your father I suppose. You see all the time we've been married I've had nothing that I can say is mine. Everything is in your father's name, I don't even know what we have in the bank for God's sake but I do believe we are not as well off as your father would like us to think. The mill's been taking up a lot of his time lately. Anyway, this was one way I could make my own decision, no matter how it went, it was my choice. I can well remember how exhilarating that was, to be in charge of a situation for once and not having my mind made up for me. It was truly liberating Sarah. A great sense of freedom. I think that's where you get your determined streak from, your sense of justice, especially for women. Your nana was just the same in many ways."

"But when you went to Cardiff you didn't stay long. Why?" Sarah asked pushing for more.

"The board of governors decided David and I had breached their rules around impropriety, because we left New Zealand together, we were assumed to have slept together."

"But you didn't, did you?" Sarah asked totally captivated by the story.

"No. I told you Sarah, ours was a professional relationship. We both worked our passage on the ship and barely had a minute to ourselves for the entire journey. But the rules were rules and David and I were asked to resign. That's when I went to the convalescent home at Weymouth to help as a nurse for a few weeks until I could sort a return passage, and that's when I found Richard."

"How did you feel about everything at the time?" asked Sarah.

"Annoyed my new career had been taken off of me but happy I was still independent. Confused mostly I suppose," Gwyneth pondered with some distance in her voice. "I was without a purpose, a reason for everything that had happened, so I doubted myself again. I didn't want it all to be for nothing but that's how it seemed at the time. When I found Richard in the hospital, I knew what the reason was. Maybe it wasn't the one I wanted but it was enough to know I could save my only son from a hell he would otherwise have been consigned to."

"That all makes some sort of sense," Sarah said, "it must have been a terrible time for you."

"Frustrating, mostly," Gwyneth said, "and emotionally draining. There wasn't one night I didn't cry myself to sleep as I tried to make some sense of the whole mess. I have never been as lonely in my life as I was then, before I found Richard that is."

Sarah leaned forward in anticipation of the next confession.

"But where does Bronwyn fit into all of this?" she asked.

Again, Gwyneth hesitated and turned away from Sarah.

"This is my shame, Sarah," she said through a broken voice. "Before your father and I were married, I lost a baby to him. I had a miscarriage."

"That must have been awful," Sarah said barely able to talk.

"It was at Mokau cemetery, walking up the hill at Mac McAllister's funeral. Mac was Ngaire's first husband. I was taken back to the hotel on the back of the wagon which had carried Mac's body. They took me to the hotel where Betty looked after me as best she could. But even they couldn't do what was needed. I nearly died that night, Sarah," Gwyneth looked pleadingly into Sarah's eyes holding on to both of her hands. "The nearest doctor was in Awakino and despite Betty's best efforts, the person who saved my life that terrible night was Moonyeen Wu,"

Sarah let out a gasp. "Moonyeen Wu, Father's Moonyeen Wu?

"How many Moonyeen Wu's do you know?" Gwyneth snapped.

"Sorry," Sarah said. "So we all owe her a debt of gratitude?" she muttered.

"To some degree I suppose," Gwyneth said. "But Moonyeen wouldn't say that. I did go to thank her personally, but she wasn't there. I finished up speaking candidly to Stella Ratcliffe and that was an education I can tell you."

"That madam, and I use the word literally," Sarah said.

"That's not the point," Gwyneth told her. "Moonyeen did what she did for genuine reasons, she would have done the same for a perfect stranger. She's experienced in these things so because of her, I survived the night. So you see I owe Moonyeen my life, I always have and up until tonight I have never told anybody about it."

"But what about the baby, the one you lost?" Sarah asked eagerly wanting to know more.

"A wee girl," Gwyneth said. "Caryl, I called her. She would have been your sister of course."

"And umm… where did you…"

"Where did I bury her?" Gwyneth said to confirm Sarah's thoughts. "Initially Betty buried her in Mokau, but we exhumed her wee body and now she's buried by the totara tree not two hundred yards from here. That's why I had the kitchen window put in when we built the new house – so I could see the tree where Caryl is."

"So Bronwyn…?"

"Bronwyn is Caryl's substitute I suppose," Gwyneth admitted. "You must admit she's an adorable child. When I was in Cardiff, we became very much attached to each other and when I told her I was leaving to come back to New Zealand she wouldn't have it, she was so very upset. So anyway, I asked David for one last favour, to have Bronwyn put in my charge so I could bring her with me. I knew at the time it wasn't the most practical of ideas but it felt so right somehow."

"So you didn't actually adopt Bronwyn?"

"No, I couldn't. There are no formal adoption laws anyway," Gwyneth replied. "So legally she's not even mine. I've never even thought about it really. I just didn't want to let her go, I couldn't let her go."

"So now how do you feel now?" Sarah asked.

"Resigned to my life here," Gwyneth said with a flat voice. "Looking after Richard, and now your nana and Bronwyn of course as well as putting up with your father's ways and not being able to do anything about any of it. Don't get me wrong. I don't begrudge Richard or your nana but it's not the life I hoped for and my biggest regret is how disappointed I am in myself."

The tears started flowing as the release of the emotions she had subdued for years were lifted. "But I am happy I can talk to at least one family member," Gwyneth said putting one hand on Sarah's shoulder.

"What is the life you imagined for yourself?" Sarah asked.

Gwyneth was struck dumb by the simplicity and the strength of the question.

"Do you know, Sarah, nobody has ever asked me that, probably not even myself," Gwyneth reflected.

"Go on Mother, let loose, what would you do if you had the absolute choice? Richard, Nana and everybody to one side, what's the one thing you want to have the opportunity of doing just for yourself?"

"To sing. To sing on a stage one day, a proper stage" she said sitting up bolt upright and with a bright light in her eyes. "To sing, with a good tenor. The songs of Wales and of New Zealand. Ngaire and I used to sing a lot together, in the old house where George and Libby are now. Your uncle Wirimu taught me waiata while I was nursing him after he lost his leg and Ngaire and I would sing them when we all met on a Sunday afternoon. Those were good days, good days," Gwyneth said with the light in her eyes disappearing. She hesitated and brought herself back to the present time.
"You have grown so much Sarah love. Not only physically of course, but as a woman, a strong woman. I hear you've joined the National Council of Women as well?"
"How did you know?" Sarah asked.
"Oh, just heard it around," Gwyneth replied.
"Around where?" Sarah asked indignantly. "You don't go anywhere to be just 'around."
"Don't say it like that."
"Sorry, I didn't mean it. It was Linda wasn't it?" Sarah asked.
"Still it wasn't a state secret I suppose, it's just that it's...well it's..."
"It's a sophisticated city thing?" Gwyneth offered.
"Yes, I suppose so Mother. It's difficult enough now for women to find a voice, the NCW is something that gives us a collective voice, although we are seemingly less effective than we used to be. Sorry, this is no place for politics."
"As I said, you are a strong woman Sarah," Gwyneth repeated. "What I really wanted to say is you need to think your life through, make good choices and don't put up with second best or you will never be who you were born to be. You have a bright future; you can be somebody. Don't tie yourself down too early in life like I did."
"But you married Father for love, didn't you? How could you have stopped that happening?"
"I couldn't Sarah, of course not, but sometimes love isn't enough. If I looked hard enough maybe I could have seen how things would have turned out. Love takes all that away. It makes you blind in so many ways."
"Who else knows all of this?" Sarah asked.

"Your nana … as well as Ngaire and Wirimu but just bits and pieces really, you're the only one I have told the whole story to, in my own words. They only know the facts, they don't really know my feelings, maybe Ngaire does as she's been my best friend and confidante, but she has the sense to let me speak when I want to, when I feel it's right."

"Well it's obviously right tonight, mother. I am so, so very proud of you."

"Proud?" Gwyneth questioned. "Proud?"

"Yes, proud, because you had the strength of your convictions and followed your heart to help the orphans rather than spending the rest of your life wondering 'what if'. Yes, mother, I am proud of you."

"But all that was for nothing Sarah, don't you see, I still ended up back here, I still don't know how much your father and I have in the bank, what's really changed after all that effort?"

"You have" Sarah said. "So will Richard. Imagine if you hadn't had gone to Wales, Richard would be in a sanatorium in God knows where with the rest of the shells of men. Your time will come Mother, it really will."

Chapter Fourteen

**

Tama's platoon was a part of 'A Company' which was allocated to repairing trenches and digging a section of 'Turk Lane' on the edge of Delville Wood in the Somme. Snaking over five miles, Turk Lane was a major communication trench which would eventually lead directly to the front line. Here, the company faced increased sniper fire and enemy shelling, while all the time digging in heavy rain and knee deep mud sapping their energy and making progress glacial at best. Not one of them had so much as a wash or a shave for the fifteen straight days of digging.

Almost unrecognisable in the mud and with the frigid damp chilling his rain and sweat soaked uniform to his skin, Tama took in the scene of utter desolation. Two years of fighting and bombardments along with continual heavy transport had made the road to the nearby village of Montauban all but impassable. Remnants of trees caught in bomb blasts and bomb craters pockmarked the ground as mute testimony to the utter destruction of the countryside from the fighting for the salient. Fighting which cost twenty thousand British and South African lives.

The sound of a shell screamed overhead and slammed into the ground half a mile ahead. Tama knew it had been fired to get a new mark so was quickly followed by a barrage as his men automatically stopped digging and hugged the side of the trench. He pulled his helmet over his face as seconds later shrapnel whistled over the heads of his men, falling in the mud where they had been digging only seconds before.

"Hey, Serge. We'll have to dig faster or we'll be blown to bits at this rate," said a voice from a hunched up figure only yards away. "If we don't drown in the bloody mud first," a second voice shouted out.

A mortar shell landed close to the trench. The men knew one landing close was better as the shrapnel would go high above them. It was the shells landing further away they were more scared of.

"Stop complaining Nepia or the Hun will send over more shells just to shut you up. Ngati Porou eh? Always bloody complaining," Tama said smiling at the man next to him but loud enough for Private Kepa Nepia to hear.

The banter was interrupted by the roar of more heavy shells coming in, closer this time as the Germans found their mark. The men huddled into the trench as close as they could, and a few fell into muttering prayers. Some muddy water spilled away from the sides of the trench and into Kepa Nepia's mouth making him turn to spit it out. Just as he did, he heard a loud whirring noise as a piece of shrapnel the size of a fist landed just in front, splashing him with mud. He wiped his eyes and stared blankly at the red hot, jagged metal shard not a foot away from his face. It made a small crater and the mud momentarily boiled as the half buried shrapnel cooled off. Kepa stayed silent for a minute stunned at his luck and the reality of what could have been.

The bombardment ceased as quickly as it began but the sound of the shells and explosions rang in the ears of the men as several minutes of anxiety passed with no one willing to move.

"All right men," Tama shouted out. "Smoko's over, back to work. It's Pozierés and Givinchy's turn to take a pounding now, poor bastards."

The men rose slowly out the trench scraping mud off their uniforms out of habit more than practicality as they looked nervously about them, expecting sniper shots at any moment. Men's bodies which had been full of life only minutes before, were lying scattered and broken beside the line of the trench. Stretcher bearers appeared tending to the wounded. The scene was made almost ethereal as the late autumn air hung damp and a freezing fog started rolling in, obscuring the distant view, and muffling the sounds of the artillery.

"Start digging men, repair the trenches around you…again, leave the wounded to the medical corps," Tama ordered noticing the men watching the wounded knowing any attempt to get to them would attract sniper fire. A soldier, not one hundred yards away lay groaning, holding his blood-stained chest. Tama was immediately taken back to Gallipoli and Richard. He focused on his platoon. "Put some shoulder into it Nepia!" he shouted. "You're not digging kumara at Tolaga Bay now, do you good to lose some weight anyway."

Kepa Nepia smiled and turned to the next man. "You know him?" he asked pointing to Tama.

"No sir," said the man. "I only arrived yesterday with the reinforcements."

"I heard there's some coconuts come over as well."

"You mean Samoans?"

"That's what I said."

The man ignored the comment. "Is he the boss, sir?" he asked pointing to Tama.

"He is," Kepa said. "And don't 'sir' me boy. I'm a private, the same as you. That's Sergeant Tama Ratahi. You stick with him and you'll be right. He's a lucky bastard. Been through Gallipoli with barely a scratch. Some men are like that; they fall in a shit hole and come out smelling of roses, lucky bastards, you stick by him and you'll be right, mark my words."

The fresh-faced man, almost a boy looked across at Tama. He was scared and was trying to glean some assurance from Tama he would be alive, at least to the next day but he got none. All he saw was Tama seemingly larger than life standing stock still, looking back holding a shovel with both hands and covered in mud.

"What are you waiting for?" Tama demanded, almost startling the boy. There was no reply.

"You scared?" Tama demanded taking one step towards him.

"No… no sir".

"You're a liar," Tama told him. "I'm scared and I've been through a lot more than you. What's your name?"

"Jim, Jim Manuel, Private Jim Manuel …sir," the reply came.

"How old are you, Private Jim Manuel?"

"Sixteen, sir."

"Sixteen? Are you sure?" Tama questioned staring at him. "You don't look sixteen to me."
Jim looked to the ground. "Well... nearly sixteen ...sir."
"Where are you from?"
"Ham... Hamurana ...sir."
"Where's that?"
"Awahou ...Ngongotaha?"
Tama looked puzzled.
"Rotorua...sir" Jim said.
"Ah. Te Arawa?" Tama asked.
"Ay. Ngati Rangiwewehi and Tuwharetoa. My kokara's from Taupo".
"Tena koe, Jim Manuel," Tama said as he walked up for a hongi.
"Tena koe, sir," Jim Manuel said, his shoulders dropping a little after the greeting put him at some ease.
"If I went to Hamurana, what would I see?" Tama asked.
"Springs ...springs, sir," Jim replied, surprised at the question.
"Springs?" Tama questioned.
"Yes sir. Springs. Te Puna-a- Hangurua. Sir. Water fifty feet deep yet so clear you can see the bottom," Jim said proudly.
"Is that so?" Tama asked unbelievingly.
"Yes, sir. The manuhiri throw in coins, pennies mostly...sir, they think it's lucky." "Why don't you get the pennies out for yourself?" Tama asked.
"Water's too deep and the springs too strong," Jim said. "Nobody's ever been able to get to the bottom. Can get some pennies, the ones at the edge of the banks of the awa. My father took one and gave to me for luck before I left," Jim said taking out a leather pouch attached to a woven flax cord from under his tunic. He tipped out a copper penny. "See here, sir...in this keti. A new penny. I have to take it back ... to Hamurana and put it back in Te Puna-a- Hangurua, the springhead, so all is well on my return home."
"And you can see the pennies...at the bottom of this fifty foot spring?"
"Yes sir, clear as day," Jim answered gaining some confidence.
"You said springs, more than one?" Tama demanded.

"Ai" Jim said. "Kauaenui as well. 'The spring of dancing sands' we call it so the manuhiri understands. Water so clear you can see the sand moving at the bottom."
"Must be a sight to see," Tama said. "Crystal clear water eh? Must be good kai?"
"Ai" Jim agreed. "Koura and kokopu. And inanga, freshwater cray's as big as your feet. Vegetables too. Gardens along the banks of the awa. We trade vegetables with Māori from Tauranga and Whakatane for kaimoana; snapper, hapuka, any fish really. Kina too."
Jim was getting excited telling Tama about his home
"Might get there one day," he said. "But your vegetables won't beat to the ones we grow on the Mokau. But Hamurana sounds a good place, Private Jim Manuel. You show me around one day?"
"If you want, sir. It won't take long, not a big place you see," a faint smile appeared on Jim's face.
"Kia ora boy," Tama said. "Well the faster you dig now boy, the quicker you can get home to Hamurana to put your penny back in the spring, Ka pai?"
"Ka pai," Jim said, nodding in agreement.
"S…sir?" Jim asked just as Tama turned away.
"What is it, Private Manuel?" Tama asked, turning back.
"I am scared, what I want to know is, how do I survive?"
"You know what an octopus is?" Tama asked.
"Ay sir."
"Well we have a saying, *Kia mate ururua. Kei mate wheke.* Fight like a shark not an octopus. That's how you survive Private Manuel."
Tama went back to swing his shovel as did Kepa Nepia as Turk Lane crept incrementally towards the front line.

**

"Got a smoke?" Kepa asked of Jim after an hour of digging.
"No," Jim replied. "I don't smoke."

"Can't get a bloody fag anywhere," Kepa muttered as he used his pick on some stubborn ground. "Five bloody months we've been in France and all we've done is dig, dig, bloody dig," he mumbled to anybody who would listen. "We've been shoveling mud for fifteen days from dawn to dusk without a break, shit food and shit all smokes. I came here to fight like a man, not dig like a bloody dog. I could have stayed home and dug kumara as the serge says, not fight this white man's war."
Jim Manuel threw him a disapproving glance. "Serge says the faster we dig, the faster we get to go home," he argued.
"That's a joke," Kepa retorted. "More like the faster we get to the front line."
"Then you'll get the chance to fight, won't you?" Jim said bravely. "But it's not about us is it?" he added thoughtfully. "It's about being a part of an Empire. About making sure other men get to the front safe so they can kill the Hun. We are kaitiaki, fighting for the Empire."
Kepa gave a sarcastic laugh. "Get to the front quicker, so we can be shot quicker more like?"
"That's enough of that talk," Tama shouted so all his men could hear as he suddenly appeared behind Kepa.
"Half hour break men," he shouted without taking his eyes off Kepa. "You two," he ordered pointing to two men. "Freshen up the billy, open up the bully beef. Be quick about it," Tama ordered. The men could see he was in no mood to be trifled with. "Nepia, come with me, I want a word."

**

By the time Kepa Nepia got back to his position, he was sullen and didn't speak. Jim Manuel threw him some bully beef on a chipped enamel plate. "What did Serge want?"
There was no response.
"Where's he now?" Jim asked.
"Full of questions aren't you boy? Ever heard of minding your own fuckin' business?" Kepa snapped.
After ten minutes, Tama reappeared. "Listen up men, good news, HQ's pulling us back for a few days' rest."

**

Tama's platoon arrived in the village of Longeuval, there was nothing to speak of other than a few rows of bombed out grey stone houses with shattered slate rooves. The main road had been cleared of rubble to make way for the endless streams of horse drawn artillery on the way to the front. Tama's platoon marched through the village square surrounded by civic buildings and a nearby church miraculously left intact.

Three old women dressed in heavy coats and head scarves over their age worn faces sat on a bench in the square, solemnly watching the soldiers trudge by.

Tama's platoon was allocated a half bombed out barn on the outskirts of the village. One end of the barn had been completely blown off with the stones that had been laid in place by hands two centuries earlier, lay scattered and broken. The surviving end of the barn had some straw stooks built up into a stack in a corner covered by the remnants of a shingle roof. A few chickens scattered as the men walked in. Hardly speaking, they threw their helmets off, shifted some hay bales to use as beds then closed their eyes in absolute relief.

Tama saw Kepa Nepia eyeing up a chicken. "Hands off," he shouted. "We're under orders not to touch the villager's livestock. If you think we've had it tough, think about these poor sods. This is their turangawaewae, their home. They are the tangata whenua. We need to respect that, Ka pai?"

Kepa looked across at Tama from the corner of his eye. Just then, a soldier at the other end of the barn lit up a cigarette and Kepa Nepia immediately made a bee line for him.

"Shame about the chickens, a hangi would go down well with the men right now," Kepa said returning with a packet of Gitanes in his hand.

"How'd you get those?" Tama demanded not totally trusting him. "Ngati Porou," was all Kepa said touching his nose.

After a few hours rest he called Kepa over. "What you said about a hangi before, that's not a bad idea. Reckon you could do something with your mates? Without touching the villager's animals of course."

'You're too slow Serge," Kepa said. "They're onto it already. They've seen a few pigs a mile south of here, in a wood, feeding on chestnuts. Big fat pigs Serge, just right for a hangi."
"So what's the score?" Tama asked instantly excited by the thought of a hunt.
"The Ngati Porou boys are digging a hangi pit " Kepa replied." Away from the village."
"Get some men and tell your mates we'll help. What about hangi stones for the fire?" Tama asked.
"Cut up railway tracks," Kepa answered immediately. "Better than bloody Belgian rocks. Begging your pardon …sir."
"I'll authorise it on two conditions," Tama added thoughtfully.
"Sir? Kepa asked.
"One, you reassure me none of the villagers owns the pigs..."
"And the second, sir?" Kepa asked.
"I come on the pig hunt," Tama said feeling the hunting knife he still carried under his tunic. "But no shooting. Don't want to scare the neighbours eh? No need for them to know what's going on."

**

Two hours later Tama and Kepa with half a dozen men were stalking pigs in the chestnut wood. Just before midnight, a pig was spotted rooting through some mud. Tama could barely make it out as it was black with white blotches along its back.
"Could do with the pig dogs right now," he muttered.
"Nah. They're Belgian pigs" Kepa told him, "not like ours, they're used to people. Don't think you'll get much sport here, plenty of pork though," he said smiling up at Tama. At that point, Kepa's foot became caught on a tree root and he fell, accidentally firing his rifle. The pig immediately ran off with two men chasing it through the bracken. They were shouting to each other, trying to turn the animal back to the main group. Eventually the pig turned, but at the last minute, headed to a gap between Tama and Kepa.
"Shout. Shout!" Tama yelled. "Push it towards me."

Kepa shouted as loud as he could and waved his arms and the pig turned towards Tama. With his knife in his hand he launched himself on the terrified animal, grabbing its ear as he was dragged off his feet. He managed to swing his body around, plunging his knife in its throat. The pig slowed as its blood oozed from the gaping wound. For a second, Tama was back with Richard and Theo on their pig hunt before signing up, but the noise of the men cheering as he opened the pig's stomach with the knife brought home the reality of where he was.
"Ka pai," said one of the men holding out his hand. "Not bad for a Maniapoto. Tama took it with a broad grin on his face.
"Best we bury the guts quickly," he said.
Just as the offal hole was being dug, some men's voices were heard, and torches were seen shining through the wood.
"It's ok," one of the men said. "They're locals, they're speaking Flemish."
"What do they want?" Tama demanded.
"Their pig back I expect," Kepa replied.
"What do you mean, Nepia? You said the pig didn't belong to anybody."
"It don't," Kepa said. "At least nobody in particular, it sort of belongs to the whole village."
"Just what the hell have you done?" Tama demanded.
"It wasn't me who stuck the knife in the pig's throat was it?" Kepa said trying to back out of the situation.
"It was you who said... Oh never mind that now. We need to get this sorted, the villagers are getting closer."
"You stay here," Tama ordered pointing to three men. "Wipe some blood on your arm and tell the villagers there was some German sniper fire and you've been grazed. We're taking the pig back to the village...now."
Tama and Kepa picked up the carcass and ran as best they could. Ten minutes later they came to the outskirts of the village, behind the church, but there were more people milling about wondering what was happening.
"Don't they ever sleep?" Tama asked rhetorically.
"Quick, in the church," Kepa said. Tama looked around seeing there was no other choice. Short of breath and starting to panic, they dragged the carcass up the aisle to the altar.

Out of options and not knowing what to do, they stopped and looked at each other.

"So what's next?" Kepa asked.

Never one to give up, Tama looked about him. Along the sides of the aisles were stretchers used by the villagers to carry the wounded.

"Quick, grab one of those," he demanded.

With the stretcher on the altar, the men threw the pig onto it. Tama noticed a pile of sheets used to cover corpses. He threw one over the pig seconds before the church doors were flung open and a priest, carrying an oil lamp, stood in the doorway.

"What's the meaning of this intrusion into this holy building?" he shouted in broken English.

Without flinching, Tama took off his helmet and put it on the pig's head where the blood immediately soaked through the sheet.

The priest stood aghast.

"I am sorry gentlemen. I did not realise…"

Kepa immediately caught on to what Tama was doing.

"Snipers," he said simply. "In the woods."

The priest slowly walked up to the body taking his Bible out from his pocket and started speaking in a low tone. "Per istam sanctam unctionem ignoscat tibi Dominus quicquid peccaveris sive delinqueris."

Tama and Kepa bowed their heads unsure of what was happening, then beads of sweat formed on their brows as they realised the priest was giving the last rites to what he thought to be a dead soldier.

Kepa could barely contain a smile. Instead he looked over to Tama nodding towards the door and raising his eyebrows.

Tama gave a slight nod in agreement.

"Thank you Father," Kepa said quietly. "But you'll appreciate our need to get back to the platoon with our fallen comrade."

"But of course," the priest replied.

With that, the men carried the pig on a stretcher out the church.

"The hangi's over this way," Kepa said between his laughter as soon as they were out of earshot. "I believe holy pork is on the menu."

"That's the last time I ever go on a pig hunt with Ngati Porou," Tama said laughing with him.

Chapter Fifteen

**

"So how was it with George's family?" Gwyneth asked Libby when they were alone in the kitchen. "We got your telegram about George's father dying, very sad of course but where did that leave you?"

"Very much in the background," Libby replied. "George's mother was very distraught as you can imagine. She had at last accepted me as a part of the family but nevertheless, I was still very much on the outer. Nothing was ever said, she just tolerated me."

"It must have been awful for you?"

"In some ways, but George is ever the diplomat and bridged any awkward gaps. As you know, we were only meant to be there for a week or two so I put up with it for George's sake, but with George's father failing like he did, it became six weeks. 'Mother', insisted we stayed for the reading of the will, I think she just wanted to see the look on my face when George's father made good his threat to disinherit us."

"I can't imagine you would give her the satisfaction," Gwyneth said eagerly taking it all in.

"No," Libby said with some hesitation. "Well to be honest, I didn't have to as it turns out."

"Why ever not? Didn't you stay for the reading?"

"Well the drama started before all of that. When we first arrived at the railway station, George's brother Ian, met us off the train. He was with Michelle Watts, she was George's betrothed."

"Yes. Yes I remember," Gwyneth said. "He turned her down for you."

"Well, to cut a long story short," Libby said. "Ian married this Michelle only a month before we got there."

"And George never knew?" Gwyneth interrupted.

"No. Not a clue. There was no way he could have known as true to his father's word, there has been no contact from the family over the years, only George continually writing unanswered letters to his father, as he said he would do. He's kept them up to date with the news for all these years, as well as birthdays and Christmas cards and so on. He's never failed in what he saw as his duty, as a son."

"So what about Ian?" Gwyn asked moving to the edge of her chair.

"Ian had been married before, but his wife died in childbirth. Michelle had waited all these years in the hope that George would return one day. Of course that day never came so she eventually married Ian. More out of convenience, I'm sure. Not to mention the inheritance."

"So Michelle turns out to be a gold digger," Gwyneth said. "That must have been awkward all round".

"Well, to be fair, Michelle did have an affection towards George, but it was never meant to be. She took it hard when George finally rejected her."

"I bet she did."

"Apparently, she considered suicide at one stage. It hurt her to be passed over for a … well you know my past Gwyn."

"How did you manage all of this? It all sounds very awkward."

"Well not really. Both George and I accepted the situation for what it was. George knows he did what he believed to be the right thing and what others think didn't really come into it."

"So how did the reading of the will go?" Gwyneth asked totally absorbed in Libby's account.

"We all met in the library. The atmosphere was quite tense as you can imagine, and George's mother had a such a smug look on her face. Nobody knew any details of course but everybody expected Ian would inherit the farm, lock, stock, and barrel.

"And did he?" Gwyneth could barely contain herself as Libby's face started to light up.

"You must promise to keep this to yourself," Libby said taking Gwyneth's hand.

"Yes, of course. What is it Libby?"

"Well, a lot of smaller items, paintings and so on went to some distant relatives and so on, but when it came to the farm …it was split evenly between George and Ian. Old Mr Twentyman never disinherited George at all."

The two women were sitting down facing each other. Libby's face was radiating with excitement.

"So George has a half share in the family farm?" Gwyneth quizzed just to make sure she heard it right.

"Yes. Yes he does. The will is being challenged of course. George's mother has put a QC on the case but George has taken sound legal advice too."

"Which is?"

"Which is the will is ironclad and there is no case for a challenge."

"Libby, that's excellent news. What made George's father change his mind?"

"Through the will he said he regretted the falling out and he learned to admire George standing by his principles, putting me ahead of his inheritance. But it was the letters he received from George over the years which really did it. Hearing about Theo growing up and how Llanon was going. How George was helping with the stock…and of course saddened by Theo's tragic death. He said…through the will… that he knew more about George from his letters than he knew about Ian, who apparently, did the bare minimum believing that one day he would inherit the lot."

Gwyneth was silent for a moment taking it all in. "So what I am hearing, Libby, is that George, or rather you and George have some money behind you at long last."

"In a way Gwyn. But it's not just 'some money' as you put it, the farm has been extended over the years along with interests in a horse stud in Cambridge. Once the dust has settled, George will be a very wealthy man."

**

The next several months were spent with George working long hours at Llanon while Sean spent more and more time at the mill. The long summer dried out the paddocks and a drought started biting as grazing was becoming a problem for all the farms at Middle River. Gwyneth and Libby, and even Bronwyn, worked almost as hard as the men with fences to be mended as well as the usual washing and housework. It was a difficult time as the long summer days seemed relentless. It was only rarely Gwyneth, Megan and Libby took Bronwyn and found themselves walking to Te Kainga on a Sunday afternoon to simply get away and socialise with Ngaire and Wirimu. It was on such a Sunday afternoon when even the air along the river seemed heavy that they decided to go.

"How do you manage to keep the farm going?" Gwyneth asked Wirimu. "We struggle so how do you two manage?"

"I'm not surprised you struggle," Wirimu said looking at Ngaire. He hesitated. "Paul is a good worker, we're looking at investing in a few stationary engines to pump water onto the paddocks and help with the milking. Even so, I work more hours than Paul so we keep on top of it all."

Wirimu took Ngaire's hand.

"I can't help noticing Gwyn, Sean spends a lot of time at the mill leaving all the work to George, and let's be honest, Llanon hasn't had that much spent on it."

"I suppose you're right," Gwyneth replied. "We could do with more help but it's just that Sean has to spend so much time at the mill lately. The main boiler's had to be replaced and a lot of the bearings and belts are on their last legs, they had quite a few injuries lately and with no men around, productions behind. It all seems to soak up the money, not that I know how much of course. Added to that, Bill Tallboys is about set to retire too, the poor old man must be seventy if he's a day anyway. School Farm's the same as Llanon, it needs time and money."

"Why don't you talk to Sean about it?" Ngaire asked. "Surely he must tell you something?"

"When did Sean last tell me anything?" Gwyneth said. "George can't do everything. Even wee Bronwyn's growing muscles from fetching and carrying all those pails of milk and churning butter. She never complains either."

"And Richard?" Ngaire asked.

Gwyneth looked at the floor and cleared her throat. "I know he's my son, but right now, he's either sat in the corner of his shed rocking backwards and forwards and staring into space or striding over the hills for two or three days at a time. God knows where he goes or what he eats. Without Sean, he's left to his own devices and I'm sorry to say they are not good."

"How's he been since we saw you last, it's been a while now?" Ngaire asked.

Gwyneth lowered her gaze. "Well to be truthful, I am more scared of him as time goes by. He used to be my son who was taken over by a stranger. Now he's a stranger who occasionally lets me see my son."

A silence fell on the house broken after a few minutes by Gwyneth.

"I'm scared of him Ngaire. I don't mind admitting it. He has such a temper set off by almost nothing at all. A bang or sudden noise, on the farm that happens all the time as you all know. Last week I dropped a pot and he jumped a mile and looked at me like I was the enemy, then ran away but not before he stared at the knife drawer, I could see his mind fighting something, terrible thoughts and memories locked in his head." Gwyneth looked around the room at her friends but felt as though she was on her own.

"He's totally unpredictable in how he behaves, even to Bronwyn. She could manage him in a sweet and gently way and he recognised that, but not anymore. Whatever's wrong with my son is getting worse Ngaire. I know they call it shell shock and they say he needs to get over it, but somehow, I don't think he will."

"Not everybody if I remember right," Ngaire said. "Linda, Sarah's friend, seemed to be able to get through to him by listening, gaining his confidence. Isn't that worth a try?"

"I suppose, but how? She's in Wellington, Richard's here, there's nothing that can be done."

**

Mr Harris kept his word sending Sarah to the House as a political reporter. What irked her was she would still not be accepted into the press gallery, so she missed out on being given titbits of information which made all the difference between a good story and a great story. Instead, she was forced to sit in the public gallery with her work signed off as 'SM Murphy' so readers assumed she was a man. But her mind was on the long game. She loved politics and absorbed the machinations of government like a sponge.

**

On a wet and windy morning, Sarah bowed her head against the wind as she jumped off a tram on Lambton Quay and headed for Parliament. Her coat was already soaked and the southerly wind she was fighting, made it hard going only made worse by motor traffic driving through the waterlogged street splashing her with no regard for her gender or comfort. Turning right into Whitmore Street, she crossed the road barely looking up as a car drove around the corner nearly hitting her. A claxon sounded out in anger and the driver shouted out but with her mind deep in thought about on Mokau and her family, she never really heard him.

It had been some months since she heard from anybody as her letters went unanswered, so she was thinking it was time she went to visit. Shaken after the near miss with the car, she walked into the government buildings. Although it was lauded as the largest timber building in the southern hemisphere, its austere interior was dark, and many places were unlit. The labyrinth of offices and even darker corridors held many secrets and meetings that 'never happened'. Sarah was well aware of the cloistered halls she often thought of as the 'dark and satanic mills' of Parliament. Many times she wondered how many deals had been struck by the bearded old men she had grown used to seeing around the catacomb like building. While the men noticed Sarah, she was rarely acknowledged as she walked through the clouds of cigar smoke and patriarchal stares. But somehow, it all added to the intrigue which fascinated Sarah and she became even more determined to undermine it, dig out its underbelly and expose it for what she thought it really was. She was bemused by how the bloated and pompous men controlled people's lives without a second thought. It was the definitive men's club to which Sarah was an alien, a total stranger, and an unwelcome visitor.

She strode into the lobby and took off her coat giving it a good shake then did the same to her hat. She put them both over her arm and approached the young man at the reception desk. He was about twenty, a tall man wearing a double-breasted suit half a size too big. His dark hair was smarmed across his head and stuck down with Brylcreem giving his ears the appearance of sticking out too far. His redeeming feature was a ready smile and a happy nature, unique in the mens world she was entering.

"Good morning, Ronnie. How are you today?" she asked.
"Good morning, Miss Murphy. I'm good. Thank you for asking."
"How's your leg? You must find it worse in this cold weather," Sarah asked as she rummaged through her bag.

"Getting better every day it is," Ronnie replied. "Must be the New Zealand rain rusting away the shoddy Turkish shrapnel, not like the decent British stuff we gave them, eh?" He held out several sheets of notepaper. "Pardon me Miss Murphy but will you be needing some dry writing paper again today?"
Sarah smiled. "Yes please. You know I don't think this rain will ever cease."
"Just your smile is enough to bring the sunshine," Ronnie joked handing over the paper.
"Looks like a busy day today," Sarah said looking over the order papers for the House.
"Question time mostly," Ronnie said. "About the six o'clock closing I expect. Some of them inside just realised if it goes ahead, the pubs will be closed by the time they finish for the day."
"Good job they've got Bellamy's then eh?" Sarah quipped.
"Cheap whiskey and good food to put them in equally good humour. They'll be pleased the elections have been put back so they can remain in the style to which they want to become accustomed?"
"I don't half wish the rest of the public were as keen as you Miss Murphy, about Parliament and stuff I mean. I reckon you know more than some of them inside 'ere."
"Dear Ronnie, you are always so cheerful," Sarah complimented him.
Ronnie looked down at the desk smiling.
"There's no need to be embarrassed," Sarah told him. "You really are a cheerful soul, there's no doubt of that and it's a tonic just to talk to you.
"Well working here helps."
"How do you mean?"
"Well. I'm a part of the future ain't I? I know it's only a desk job and anybody could do it. But I'm a part of building a fresh future for a different New Zealand. When they finish the new Parliament buildings over the road, I want to be a part of that as well, then we'll have a real future, when the war's over I mean. How exciting is that?"
Sarah stood still for a moment, taking in exactly what Ronnie was telling her.

"You are a true inspiration, you really are. A few more 'Ronnie's' and we will lead the world in no time."

Sarah started to walk down the corridor deep in thought. She walked up the timber stairs to the toilets on the third floor where she knew she wouldn't be disturbed. It was the one place where she felt she could relax away from the suspicious gazes of the old men. On the second floor she stopped to look across Lambton Quay to the half-finished Parliament buildings with white marble blocks looking like a row of teeth with some missing. The scene was dominated by a crane which hadn't moved for months as the building was dogged by costs and labour shortages caused by the war.

Sarah hung her hat and coat on the peg at the back of the cubicle door before locking it. She sat down to go over the order paper in detail, making notes in shorthand and looking for anything out of the ordinary but there was nothing which stood out for her enquiring mind.

**

The debating chamber was as crowded as the rest of the building. Sarah found no interest in the banal questioning and looked across at the members sitting back talking amongst themselves, some of them argued minor points of order to stretch out their arguments. Sarah's thoughts turned to what Ronnie had said earlier about the country needing a fresh start after the war. Deep inside her, there was an ever growing realisation that what she saw in front of her now must change and she wanted to be a part of that more than anything else.

**

"You've been quiet all week," Dickie said to Sarah on a Sunday afternoon at the Oriental Bay Tea House. "You've hardly touched your tea cake."

"Sorry," Sarah replied, taking Dickies hand, and giving it a light press.

"Something on your mind?" Dickie questioned carefully.

"No. Well, yes, but I just need to think things through."

"It sometimes pays to talk you know".

Sarah remained silent, preferring to stay with her thoughts.

"Sarah? I need to ask. Is it me, or rather, us?"
"Heavens no Dickie. It's just work, well more than that, it's the war dragging on and what it's leading to."
"But we will win. We have to."
"No Dickie. That's not what I meant at all. Sorry. Of course we will win, but what happens then? Most of our men will be dead or wounded. The government will split away from the coalition and go back to their squabbling party lines. You haven't been in the House. You haven't seen the likes of who'll be running the country regardless of which party gets in. We need women in the House to have a balance, a diverse opinion, women who care for a future our children want to be a part of, not tied to the apron strings of the Empire. But of course, women aren't allowed to be in Parliament, did you know that Dickie? Sorry, of course you do. We women are expected to cook, clean, breed and know our place, that's all."
Dickie looked around nervously. "I say Sarah, keep your voice down, we are in the tea rooms you know. What does Linda think?" he asked, stuck for a response.
"Oh she agrees with me, of course. But Linda confuses empathy with sympathy and spends all her time on individuals that she feels sorry for, so they suck all the energy out of her."
"Well, she is a nurse," Dickie said.
"Yes, I suppose so," Sarah agreed, giving out a disparaging half-hearted laugh.
"And there's home. I haven't heard from anybody for a while. I've sent two letters with no answers to either. I guess I have a lot on my mind really."
"Not to mention questioning who you are as well," Dickie said.
Sarah went quiet. "You are insightful sometimes, even for a man," she laughed. "I love being a reporter; of sorts but it's always behind a cloak of anonymity just because I'm a woman. It's so unfair."
"So what would Sarah Megan Murphy be if she had a choice of anything regardless of the shackles of our times?
Sarah thought for a moment.

"I want to be a politician Dickie. I want to sit in the House, elected by the people as a woman as well as a politician. I want to bring change to our young country. We need to recognise the past but move on to the future. That's what I really want."

Chapter Sixteen

**

The smell of lavender polish filled up the house at Llanon as Megan was busy polishing the piano. In one hand she held a rag and with the other she was vigorously rubbing polish over the walnut veneer; the movement shaking her tiny body as though she was having a fit.
"I thought I smelt polish," Gwyneth said walking into the parlour. "A bit early for spring cleaning isn't it?"
"It's never too early to clean a house," Megan replied.
"But you polished the piano yesterday," Gwyneth told her.
"And the day before that."
Megan hesitated.
"Well you know it's clean then don't you? Cleanliness is next to Godliness you know. Besides, I still have to rub the keys with some milk…from the Jerseys. It's got far more cream in it, nothing like cream for bringing out the ivory."
"If you polish those keys once more I swear they'll disappear, polished to oblivion."
Megan stopped and looked at Gwyneth as though she was looking at a stranger.
"Nonsense …" Megan couldn't finish her words.
"Gwyneth, Mother. My name is Gwyneth."
"Yes… yes of course dear. I was just thinking of something else. No need to be sarcastic. Anyway, Theo and Tama will be here soon to go hunting with Richard and then, then…" She threw down the cloth and started to walk away. "I'll be back later to polish the piano," she called out.

**

"Mother's getting worse," Gwyneth said to Sean at dinner.

"If she's not polishing the blasted piano, she's looking for Richard. She thought Theo and Tama were coming over this afternoon to take Richard hunting. Yesterday she asked where Lucky was."

"She's just getting old," Sean muttered. "It'll come to us all one day."

"Not like that I hope. I'm starting to worry for her safety," Gwyneth said. "Who knows what she's up to when we're not around?"

"Talking about not being around" Sean said. "I'm heading out to the mill tomorrow for a day or so, then New Plymouth."

Gwyneth gave him a sideways glance.

"Care to tell me why?" she asked.

"Just business," Sean replied.

"Does that mean you'll be calling in to Stella Ratcliffe's? Visit Moonyeen Wu maybe?"

It was Sean's turn to bite his lip and remain silent for a while.

"If you must know, I have to see the bank manager," he said eventually.

"Why?" Gwyneth asked, surprised at Sean's candid explanation.

"You need to know we're overextended on the mill," Sean said quietly. "The new steam plant cost more than I thought. That, and business has been slow lately with not much going on to speak of, orders are down. It's not only me, but other mills are also slow as well."

"So what do you mean, 'the plant costing more than you thought'? Just how much have you borrowed? And what do you mean when you say, 'we', are over extended?"

Sean stood up and paced the floor.

"How much?" Gwyneth demanded.

"Fifteen thousand pounds," Sean admitted.

"Fifteen thousand pounds?" Gwyneth gasped. She was livid, "You've borrowed fifteen thousand pounds? Against Llanon no doubt and you didn't tell me! Our home, our farm, everything we've worked for, and everything my father worked for. You're putting it all in jeopardy and now you want to borrow more!"

Gwyneth stood up becoming more anxious by the second.

"Calm down Gwyn. It's not that bad, we can pay it back in a few years once the mill picks up."

"We! Once the mill picks up!" Gwyneth was shouting again. She walked up directly to Sean and shouted in his face. "And don't you dare tell me to calm down. In case you hadn't noticed, there's a war taking all our men away. All our builders, our customers. Their women and children are being left behind and they can barely scratch a living some of them. You've seen the shells of men coming back. Men like Richard. Just when do you think the mill will be picking up Sean? I can tell you now it won't be soon like you seem to think it will be, if at all. Just what have you done to us?"

Libby couldn't help but hear the shouting from the house. When she saw Sean storm out, heading for the back blocks with his shotgun she made her way over to Gwyneth. "Are you alright?" she asked through the open door." She could hear crying coming from the back bedroom.

"Are you all right Gwyn!?" Libby called out again.

"Yes, yes I'm just bloody fine," came Gwyneth's voice. Libby cautiously entered the bedroom.

"What is it?" she asked. "Is it Bronwyn, or Richard?"

"No," Gwyneth answered with a note of desperation in her voice. "Bronwyn's outside playing with her imaginary friends again, thank God. I think Richard's in his shed staring at the wall so as you can see, everything's just bloody fine."

Gwyneth put her hands up to her face and cried desperately as Libby put her arms around her.

"What is it, Gwyn?" she asked. "I've never seen you like this before."

"Just Sean being Sean as usual." Gwyneth turned to the window so she didn't have to face Libby. "He's only borrowed fifteen thousand pounds from the bank without telling me, and now he needs to borrow more so we are even further in debt. He's borrowed a king's ransom and not a word to me about it."

"Whatever for?" Libby asked.

"Oh, the mill and Llanon. He's spent too much upgrading the mill or something, so he's borrowed against Llanon with virtually no hope of paying it back. The bank will take our home and our livelihood, just as it did with the Tallboys before we came here."

Gwyneth wiped her eyes and dabbed at her nose with her handkerchief. "You know Libby, one thing I always thought was that we were secure after all the years of back breaking work, starting Murata School and bringing up the children. Now it's all up in the air, how we'll ever pay the loan back is beyond me, it really is."

"Where's Sean now?" Libby asked.

"He's going to shoot some old cattle on the back paddocks, I think he'd rather shoot me to be honest," Gwyneth said between her tears.

"Gwyn. George will be home in a minute. I'll go and see him as soon as I can, but there's something you need to know before Sean goes to the bank. I'll make a cup of tea for us both now and you can tell me all about this bank business, then I'll go and see if George is in. He has something that you and Sean need to hear about. Is it all right if we come over for dinner?"

"Not more bad news Libby, I don't think I could bear it," Gwyneth pleaded.

"No Gwyn, not bad news, at least I hope not, now I'll go and make that cuppa shall I?"

**

The dinner was a stilted affair. The air was heavy with expectation and unease. Gwyneth looked around as she joined the table after taking a meal out to Richard in his shed. After a few minutes, George broke the silence.

"Did you shoot those two cows this afternoon?" he asked,

"No. They wouldn't go over to the gully," Sean replied.

"Reckon they knew something was up. Damned if I was going to shoot them in the paddock and get the bullocks to drag their useless carcasses fifty feet. They can wait for next time, anyway, I'm almost out of cartridges, I'm sure I had more somewhere."

With that, only the noise of knives and forks on the plates broke the silence except for Bronwyn who sat by two empty chairs. Each had a table setting with a plate and cutlery where she served some carrots, mashed potato, and a slice of mutton to her imaginary friends. She cut up the food, chatted quietly to herself and made eating noises, then she ate the food herself.
"Your friends are hungry tonight," Libby said trying to lighten the atmosphere. "What are their names?"
Bronwyn ignored the question. "They've had a busy day," she said.
"Really, what have they been doing?"
"Looking after everybody," Bronwyn replied. "Especially Richard and Auntie Gwyneth."
"Do they need looking after?" Libby asked, interested in Bronwyn's reply.
"Oh yes," Bronwyn replied. "Both of them need help."
Sean smiled but said nothing.
Gwyneth looked up in surprise turning to Megan.
"Eat your meal Mother," she scolded as she watched Megan for pushing peas around the plate with her fork.
"That's all right dear," Megan said. "I'll finish this, then I'll polish the piano."
Gwyneth slammed her knife and fork on the table. "For God's sake Mother, never mind the bloody piano, just eat your dinner will you?"
Bronwyn looked up at Gwyneth who immediately regretted her outburst.
"I'm sorry."
"That's all right," Megan said. "No harm done. Anyway, there'll be pork tomorrow when the boys come back from hunting."
Gwyneth raised a wry smile at the perversity of the situation, then looked around the table. Sean hadn't touched his food and Gwyneth could see that nobody was in the mood to eat except Bronwyn who just finished sharing her dinner with her 'friends'.

"Go and wash up then brush your teeth Bronny love," Gwyneth told her. "Say your prayers then I'll come and brush your hair." Bronwyn smiled a sweet smile at Gwyneth. "My friends said to say thank you for dinner and that everything will be all right for you."
"That's nice," Gwyneth said taking no real notice. "It's very kind of them to be so concerned."
"They said you have to practice your singing Auntie Gwyneth as you will need your beautiful voice one day, they miss hearing you sing."
Gwyneth was momentarily taken back with Bronwyn's comment as the hairs on the back of her neck rose up and she got the goose bumps.
"What do you mean?" she asked.
"Nothing. That's all they said really."
Once Megan and Bronwyn had left, the awkward silence was again interrupted by a polite offering of a drink from Gwyneth.
"Don't worry about that Gwyn," Sean said. "I believe George here has something to say."
George cleared his throat.
"I'm not sure where to start," he said looking around the table.
"The beginning is usually a good place," Sean said. Gwyneth glared at him.
George looked around nervously. "Well, as you now know, my father passed away a while ago and although I'd thought he'd disinherited me, he had in actual fact left me half of the farm and horse stud with the other half going to my brother Ian."
Sean looked twitchy and was clearly restless.
"George. Let me stop you there. If it's your good news you've come to tell us about, well, I'm happy for you, I really am, but this isn't really the best time if you get my drift."
"That's why we're here," Libby interrupted. "Hear us out please Sean." She turned to George. "Go on love."

George looked around again. "Well I've had a letter from the lawyers, and it seems that everything is in order. The challenge to the will from my family failed and to cut a long story short," he said becoming more nervous and hesitated. "Well, to cut a long story short, the money is all but in the bank". George looked at Sean and Gwyneth. "This is the awkward bit. I know you need money and I'm, or rather we, are willing to help you out, financially I mean."

Sean was sitting back in his chair but now he leaned forward after taking in what George had said.

"So George, let's get this straight. You are offering to lend us money to help us out. Do you have any idea of how much we're talking about?"

George cleared his throat again. "Well, I understand it's in the region of fifteen thousand pounds," he said.

"You have that sort of money George?"

"Well not right now, but we will have it in about a month's time when the estate's been settled."

"And you'll take the risk of lending us this money?"

"No, I didn't say that" George told him.

"But didn't I hear you say you are happy to help us out?"

George remained calm and kept a clear head. "And so we are but it's not a loan Sean." George became a bit more relaxed. "What I am proposing is we clear all your debts, here at Llanon and the mill, in return for a share in both."

Sean sat back in his chair again. "And how much 'share' are you expecting?" he asked incredulous at George's offer.

"Half of Llanon and half of Ballinger's Mill," George replied.

Sean got up and paced around the room.

"You," he said looking directly at George. "Both of you are offering to buy into my businesses for fifteen thousand. Let me tell you it'll take a bit more than that."

"Then we'll pay more," George said calmly. "I want to modernise Llanon, get some stationary engines in, big ones. A lot of the farms are modernising. Wirimu and Ngaire are talking of doing the same to work the separators and pumps and as we share the milking shed with School Farm, we need to pull our weight. I want to make that happen sooner rather than later. That's the way farming is going Sean. What do we have here? All hand operated equipment which has seen better days. It's the same for School Farm." He looked at Libby. "We want to modernise School Farm as well so the kids get more learning rather than having to work on the farm most of the time."

"All very fancy and good," Sean said. Gwyneth thought she noticed a sarcastic tone in his voice.

"Is there anything else you'd be wanting?"

"Well yes actually. A telephone would be useful, the wires are coming along the Mokau so it won't be long unto we get the chance to have a telephone installed."

"Now what would we be wanting a telephone for?" Sean asked.

"Don't be difficult" Gwyneth admonished him. "It's obvious isn't it?"

Sean ignored her. "Just how much did your da' leave you?" he asked directly.

"Enough," George replied. "He had a successful horse stud in Cambridge as well as the farm, plus a few other investments in the stock market and so on. He left my mother very well looked after so there's no worries there. Ian and I agreed rather than split the farm and the stud, I would have the farm as Ian had no interest in it, so he kept the stud. Both were valued equally so it was all squared off. The thing is mother couldn't stand to see me get the farm; because..."

"Because of me," Libby interrupted. "So she offered George a good price to keep it in her side of the family so it wouldn't get in the hands of a former prostitute."

"Don't put it like that Libby dear," George said taking her hand.

"Well if some people don't have all the luck," Sean said sitting down again.

"George's father dying isn't luck" Gwyneth said quickly.

"That's not what I meant," Sean replied.

"So you want to be my business partner is what you're saying?" Sean asked George.

"Yes. Yes I suppose I do."

"Why, when you can have a damned good farm in some of the best land in New Zealand? Why would you want a small farm in what's mostly broken hill country?"

"Because I love the place…and the people," George answered.

"That includes you two," he said looking at both Sean and Gwyneth. "You took me on when I was looking for work and you've always been fair with me. If it wasn't for you I would never have met Libby."

"You can say that again," Sean muttered.

"Our children grew up here," George said ignoring Sean's comment. "I know every hill and valley, every sod and every fence. The sweat of my brow is in the soil here Sean, it's a part of me. I know you're in financial trouble so what I am offering is a way out so you keep the farm and the mill but it's also an investment in our future as well." George took hold of Libby's hand again. "You are not in this mess through bad management Sean, you are a victim of the times, we all are. Nobody knows more than Libby and me with Theo and you with Richard. It's just that we have to make the best of what we have, it just so happens we now have money so let's use that and look to the future, The war can't go on for ever and we need to plan for that." Sean remained silent. "There's no need for any immediate decision" George added. "The estate won't be settled for a while so give it some thought over the next few weeks, that's all I'm asking."

"But I wouldn't be keeping the farm would I," Sean replied. "I would only be keeping half the farm."

**

A week later Libby walked slowly over to Gwyneth while she was putting out the washing. "Bronwyn looks happy playing with the tea set on the lawn."

"Yes, she's having morning tea with her so called friends again," Gwyneth said.

"I'm not surprised on such a lovely morning," Libby replied. "The river looks nice today with the sunshine making it sparkle. The breeze and a bit of sun will dry the washing quickly, a good day to open up all the windows too," she smiled at Gwyneth. "How's Richard? I only said to George the other day we haven't seen him for a while."

"He's spent several weeks in his shed mostly, oblivious to anything happening outside. The sunshine started to bother him so he's collected sheets of iron from around the farm and nailed them over the windows and the door. He's left a small gap at the bottom to crawl out or for me to slide a meal into."

"That's terrible Gwyn, can't anything be done?"

"Not that I know of. I'll never give up on him Libby, but to be honest I just don't know what to do anymore. I'm out of options so Richard being alive is the only thing I can hang on to. I might ask Sarah to come over for a while if she can get away from that newspaper of hers and bring Linda too, see if that would do any good. I still have several letters of Sarah's I intended to answer, but you know how time slips away" Gwyneth said, knowing what was coming next.

"Has Sean said anything about George's offer?" Libby asked.

"No. But he's thinking about it," Gwyneth told her. "He cancelled the meeting at the bank on the strength of George's offer, so that's something I suppose."

"Yes, that's a good sign," Libby agreed.

"He's wandering around the paddocks today looking for his shotgun."

"His shotgun?" Libby asked.

"Yes. He put it down somewhere when he came back from culling the herd yesterday. He can't remember whether he brought it back or left it in the paddock somewhere. There were a few people on the riverbank a while ago now word's got out about Lands and Survey putting a few more pegs in, opening up some more land at last. He thinks one of those may have taken it."

"Surely not," Libby said as she shuffled her feet around in the grass. "George has to be at the lawyers in a few weeks to sign all the paperwork so the money can be transferred to our account."

"So very soon you'll be a wealthy couple?" Gwyneth asked.

"Yes. I suppose so," Libby said. "Who would have thought it? After all those years working for Stella Ratcliffe and Marco Cacavalli and it turns out like this."
Gwyneth put the clothes pegs back in the basket. "I'm really happy for you both, I really am. But you are lucky in more ways than that. George talks to you, you share everything, and you both talk about things and come to an agreement. I have no idea where Sean is, who he's with nor what he's thinking even."
"I've got a cake in the oven," Libby said. "Come on over for a cuppa in a minute."

**

Rain was beating against the saloon windows of the *Heron* as it struggled its way upriver towards the jetty at Llanon, fighting against the current swollen by heavy rains. Sarah turned to Linda. "Mother will be pleased to see you, seeing as how you and Richard get on. She seemed so desperate in her letter."
"I don't think it's that Richard and I get on," Linda said looking through the steamed-up windows at the bush passing by on the riverbank. "It's just that he talks, and I listen. I know a few words that seem to resonate with these men. It seems to get through somehow like a key opens a door."
"Well let's hope it works, and this weather clears," Sarah said, "it looks as though we may get a few more days of rain."
The two women were greeted by Gwyneth watching out from the house, running out to meet them in the rain.
"Come inside Sarah love, you too Linda, you must be soaked to the skin."
"No more than you are now," Sarah said as they all rushed to the front door. Once inside, they hung up their wet coats and went into the kitchen to sit in front of the range to dry off.
Gwyneth opened the door of the bread oven to let some heat out. Instantly two women could feel the dry heat warm their faces, drying their skin, making it prickle. Gwyneth took the kettle off the range and made a pot of tea.
"Where's Father?" Sarah asked suspiciously.
"He's out separating the milk, he's had to fix the separator a few times. It takes so long to do it now."

"You need to modernise a bit," Sarah commented.
"Well funny you should say that as there is an opportunity. But that's a long story I'll tell you later," Gwyneth said.
"What do you mean?" Sarah asked.
"Tell you later," Gwyneth repeated.
"How's Nana"?
"She's here physically but she's all over the place in her head," Gwyneth replied.
Sarah glanced up. "Is she demented?"
"I'm afraid so," Gwyneth admitted. "She's doing all sorts of strange things. She remembers events from years ago, like when you and Richard were small, but she can't remember yesterday. She spent the last two weeks looking for Lucky."
"Poor Nana," Sarah muttered. "...and Richard?"
"In his shed. He's boarded it up from the inside with roofing iron."
"You said as much in your letter," Sarah replied.
"You must be very lonely, Mrs Murphy," Linda interrupted.
"Yes, yes I am since you put it that way."
"Is Richard the same as you described?" Linda asked. "Sarah read out the parts of your letter… about Richard. I hope you don't mind?"
"No, not at all, quite the opposite. Yes, to answer your question, he's about the same, but to be honest we rarely see him nowadays. He roams around at night mostly, we've seen him stalking about the place in the moonlight. Sean thinks he's back at Gallipoli looking for Turks and he's probably right. Bronwyn has imaginary friends as well. Sometimes I think I'm the only sane one here," Gwyneth laughed. "If it wasn't so sad it would be funny."
"We have patients at the hospital like that," Linda interrupted. "They have left the war but the war hasn't left them."

**

Sarah couldn't sleep that night. The wind was up and the rain was beating relentlessly against the side of the house. She looked out the window looking for any sign of Richard and was soon joined by Linda.

"Couldn't sleep either? I'll go and make some cocoa," Sarah whispered.

Five minutes later she came back putting two cups down on top of the dresser.

"Seen anything?" she asked.

"No," Linda replied, "nothing. This is all a bit like how we used to watch out for people at the Britannia Tea Rooms, and at Newtown. It all seems like a lifetime ago. Remember when we saw Fay Carrington? I wonder where she is now."

"Still in Cairo I suppose," Sarah muttered.

"The wind's even stronger now," Linda said after a while.

"There's a few small branches blown across the lawn."

"Look!" Linda burst out, pointing with her finger. "Over there, by the shed, someone's there. I saw somebody move. I'm sure of it."

"Where?" Sarah asked, craning her neck to see any sign of anybody.

"There, by the shed, there's somebody crouching, over by the door."

Sarah squinted and rubbed the windowpane with her sleeve.

"Good God, it's Nana," she yelled at the top of her voice. "Get Mother and Father," she shouted out to Linda. "I'll get Nana back inside."

**

"Lucky!" Megan shouted out as she wandered around the yard unaware of the rain. "Are you there Lucky?" She ran across the clearing towards to the chestnut grove just as Sarah got outside.

"Lucky!" Sarah heard her call out again just as an ear rending crack filled the air as one of the chestnut trees split in two. Its heavy branches crashed to the ground, missing Megan by inches.

"Lucky!" Megan called out again totally oblivious of what had just happened. "Where are you, you naughty dog. Come here boy."

As if from nowhere, Richard jumped out from behind a tree with Sean's shotgun set against his shoulder. He swung it around in front of Megan, aiming directly at her face. Without any hesitation, he pulled both triggers.

In the nightmare blast of red, yellow, and black which lasted only a split second but lived forever in the minds of Sarah, Sean, Gwyneth, and Linda, they witnessed Megan's life end violently as her frail body exploded in a red haze of blood.

Sarah let out a scream and Richard span around and aimed directly at her. She stared, frozen in terror at the crazed face of her brother.

"Richa..." she called out but before she could finish, Richard pulled both triggers again, but this time there was no answer from the shotgun and Richard was gone in an instant.

Chapter Seventeen

**

The II Anzac Corps moved north from Armentières into Belgium, among them the Pioneers with Tama and his platoon. They were soon put back to digging trenches in the bright sun but the northerly wind stole any warmth and the mud stuck to their shovels in spite of recent dry weather.
"See the world," Kepa said. "See the world and become a man they told us. All we've been seeing is the sides of bloody trenches, mud, mud, and more bloody mud. We may as well have joined the tunnelling company. At least they never got their arses shot at or had fuckin' bombs and gas dropped on them, Bloody good life if you ask me."
"Well we're not asking you Nepia, so give it a rest eh? You don't know when you're well off," came a comment from a nearby soldier.
"Well off? You call this well friggin' off?" Kepa Nepia questioned.
"You're alive aren't you? Not like those two poor sods this morning," said a second man.
"Hey Serge," Jim Manuel interrupted. "Is it right that if we don't get Ypres then we can look forward to another winter digging trenches?"
"Reckon so," Tama said. "Won't be easy boy, the Germans are well dug in and the British had two cracks at it already."
"So what's the difference now then?"
"Well this time around we've got something they don't," Tama said.
"What's that?" Jim asked.
"We've got Maniapoto, Ngati Porou and Ngati Rangiwewehi. The Hun have reckoned without us," Tama said winking at Jim. "But right now, we've got to get these trenches dug."

For three days, Tama and his platoon worked alongside several hundred men of the Pioneer Corps, often through heavy bombardments. Soldiers were shot at randomly by snipers, others lay where they fell with their lungs burned out from the gas. The digging wasn't easy as tree roots often made the going tough and the cold wet mud became stickier with each passing shower. But under Tama's leadership the men stuck to their task.

Tama had been reconnoitring up ahead and running back, he jumped into his section of the trench as bullets from sniper fire bit into the mud not ten feet away. He slipped on the timber duck boards falling onto Kepa who was busy rolling a cigarette.

"For frig's sake," Kepa yelled out. "Can't a man have a quiet smoke in peace? That was the last of the baccy too."

"Sorry I disturbed you, but at least I had something soft to land on," Tama said smiling. "Shall I knock next time?" he mocked.

"What's up Serge?" Jim called out.

"Word is we're being attached to the First French Army to lay telephone cables."

"Frogs should do their own friggin' spade work. I'm gonna get some smokes," he said climbing up the small ladder.

"Use the trench," Tama called.

"Looks good to me," Kepa said gingerly peering over the top.

"I said use…" Before the words were out of Tama's mouth, a shot from a sniper found its mark shattering Kepa's skull. His body slumped back in the trench, sitting grotesquely against the far wall with half the head missing and the brains exposed.

**

"What's wrong boy?" Tama asked Jim the next day.

"Nothing…sir."

"You're lying again, Private Manuel. It's Kepa isn't it?"

"Might be."

"You've seen enough men die to get used to it. What's so different about him?"

Jim said nothing choosing to stare straight ahead.

"It's just luck, isn't it?" Jim asked after a while.

"What is?"

"War. Whether you live or whether you die. It's only luck."
"Depends on what you believe," Tama replied. "Some men think they're being saved for a special purpose. Like you, some believe it's just luck and some believe in guardian angels."
"What do you believe Serge?'
"Well that's a story for another day. But you've got your lucky penny…from the spring at Hamurana?"
"Ay."
"Didn't you get through the attack at Messines Ridge without as much as a scratch?"
"Ay."
"Didn't you kill some Germans before they killed you?"
"Must have."
"Well that's a sort of luck isn't it, keeping you alive."
"I suppose" Jim said. "That and the massive explosion from the mines in the tunnels killing thousands of the Germans on the ridge."
Tama smiled. "Ay, maybe that had something to do with it."
Jim took the pouch from around his neck and took out the penny. "But it's not this is it, making me lucky," he said holding up the coin.
"What is it then?" Tama asked.
"Don't know," Jim replied putting the penny back in the pouch. "Back at Hamurana, I had an Uncle, Uncle Jimmy. I was named after him see. He was fat like Kepa and he always complained about work, like Kepa. But when it came to helping the whanau or doing anything on the marae, he was the first to turn up and the last to leave, usually drunk, but he looked after me and my whanau cos he didn't have any kids himself. Really, he treated me and my older sister like we were his own."
"You've got a sister?" Tama asked. "You've never mentioned her."
"I've got five sisters," Jim answered. "Wikitoria's the oldest, then there's me. She was called Wikitoria after Queen Victoria 'cos my dad liked her. He said she was strong for a wahine and she led the Empire good, so when my sister was born, she was called Wikitoria…after the Queen."

"You say you 'had' an uncle?" Tama asked intrigued by Jim's candid story.
"Uncle Jimmy was kicked in the head by a horse at the stock sales at Ngongotaha. Cracked his skull wide open it did; killed him stone dead, just like Kepa was shot. Nobody saw it coming. Alive one second and dead the next. I liked Kepa. I thought he was sent by Uncle Jimmy to look after me, like a guardian angel, only now they're both dead."
"Well now you've got two guardian angels as far as I can see it," Tama said. "Your Uncle Jimmy will be watching over you to make sure you get your penny back to Te Puna-a- Hangurua. That's important boy, understand?"
Jim hesitated for a second.
"Understand?" Tama asked again.
"Ay," Jim said quietly.
"And there's only one person you can rely on to do that," Tama said putting his hand on Jim's shoulder. "Jim Manuel, that's who," he said before Jim could say anything. Jim gave a wry smile. "I've never seen so many men before today, not in one place anyway," he said changing the subject. "Tanks as well, like huge steel monsters, and nothing seems to get in their way. They make the air and the ground shake"
"Reckon the Hun know something's happening so we're upping the ante, pushing through to the Gheluvelt Plateau."
"Must be an important place?" Jim said.
"Must be," Tama agreed. "Now go and get some kai. There's some bully beef and spuds around somewhere, might be a few barkers if you're lucky."
"Thanks, that'll make a change," Jim said making Tama smile.

**

Several days later, the deep rumble of tanks and heavy transport still filled Tama's head as he looked about him. Heavy trucks as well as horse drawn artillery were on the move en-masse now the ground was firming up and there seemed to be a determination on the faces of the endless columns of soldiers marching by.
"Looks like the whole army's on the move" Jim said.

"Reckon it must be," Tama agreed. "We're moving out tomorrow ourselves."

"Digging more trenches?"

"Ay. Digging more trenches, with the French."

"When do we get back in the fighting Serge?"

"Soon enough boy."

"But there's fighting all up ahead, we should be in on it?"

"Well somebody's got to keep the communications open or the top brass would have to be at the front themselves, can't see that happening, can you? Just be grateful the weather's picked up and the bloody rains stopped for a while at least. Makes for better digging if nothing else."

"So where's this place anyway? The one you said about the other day?"

"The Gheluvelt Plateau?"

"Ay."

"Over the ridges you see ahead of you," Tama said. "It's flat, high country, not a long way but it's crawling with Germans shooting at anything they can see. The Aussies have made a start already."

"Have you seen a map then Serge?'

"Ay."

"So what's between us and the high country?"

"Not a lot. We've got to get to Ypres first, over a big ridge just over from a village called Passchendaele."

"What's at Passchendaele?" Jim asked.

"Nothing I know of," Tama said. "A quiet little village by all accounts, something like Hamurana I expect."

"Some of the men say they saw aeroplanes yesterday," Jim commented. "I've never seen one before, have you Serge?"

"A few, high up looking at what's going on I expect, don't know who they belonged to. You'll see them soon enough I expect judging by the build-up of men and guns, let's just hope they're British. Now eat your kai while you can."

**

Each day brought more men and more artillery to the front, often fanning out past the Pioneer Corps who were still busy digging trenches often under fire from an enemy determined to break the allied communications.
"Aussies," Jim commented watching the men trudge by.
A soldier turned around staring at Jim with a gaunt face, devoid of any expression.
"It never stops does it Serge?"

**

On a surprisingly clear and sunny day about five miles southwest of Passchendaele, the platoon were sheltering from sniper fire in a trench when a French soldier suddenly jumped in next to Jim and Tama.
"Bonjour," he said, leaning against the trench wall, gasping for breath.
"I see I 'ave the 'onour of being with Kiwi's." he said after a minute. "Now I know I am safe eh, monsieur?" Tama looked at him closely, his dark hair, clear blue eyes and solid jaw showed strength of character and Tama instantly liked him.
"Bonjour..." Tama stuttered. "Tena koe," he said holding out his hand more confidently. The Frenchman took it and smiled.
"Now monsieur I need your help. I have to take this wire and connect it to the other wire by the tree for the telephones to work, no? I need you monsieur to make sure I come back alive. You see I like being alive, a lot," he said smiling.
"We'll cover you mate," Tama said nodding to Jim and the others in his section, "You just do what you've got to do."
"Merci monsieur, I see you are a good man, you are a Māori, oui?"
"Oui," Tama replied smiling broadly. "Tama Ratahi, Maniapoto, from Mokau."
"Man...eeee...errr...po...toe. Moe...cow," the Frenchman said slowly still smiling.
"Oui, kia ora," Tama managed through a wide grin. "Close enough mate."
"I go now to fix the wires over by the tree, you keep your promise to me, Henri-Émile Dechambeau, and keep me safe from the Bosche."

"Henri-Émile… Dechambeau," Tama uttered.

"Oui, very good. I was called that after the French artist Matisse. You see 'e also was a Henri-Émile, oui? We were both born at Le Cateau-Cambrésis. No, per'aps? Never mind eh. You look after me, I go now."

Tama signaled to his men to give covering fire as Henri-Émile climbed back out the trench and ran towards the tree as several German machine guns immediately opened up. Tama and his platoon returned the fire as best they could as the Frenchman ran for his life. The tree's tortured limbs and burned trunk, blasted by weeks of heavy artillery offered scant protection but he was able to get some cover. Tama saw he looked perplexed after a while as he looked back to the trench. He held up his end of the wire and pointed forward, then back to his wire again.

"What's he doing Serge?" Jim asked.

"Not sure," Tama replied. "I think the other wire's moved. It must have been dragged along or something."

"He'll never make it alive."

"He has to," Tama replied. "Keep firing at anything as soon as he makes his move." Tama waved out and gave the thumbs up and Henri-Émile waved back. "Merci," came across over the noise of the battle.

No sooner had Henri-Émile made his move when an ear-piercing roar came from the air. Tama and Jim turned and looked up instinctively to see a British biplane almost fall out the sky in a steep dive and levelling out less than fifty feet above the ground, not two hundred yards away. A German triplane, bright red with the black symbol of the German iron cross on the fuselage and tail plane was in hot pursuit. The scene took the full attention of the men on the ground. The British plane was flying erratically towards them as the pilot was struggling to keep control. Tama noticed he wore a black leather helmet, but it was the pilot's eyes clearly visible behind his goggles that took Tama's attention, he looked scared Tama thought.

In a split second towards the end of the dive, the German plane opened fire and the machine gun, missing its target, spat death on the men below. Tama immediately turned to protect himself as best he could against the side of the trench. As soon as the planes had passed, he turned to see them go into a steep climb with the pitch of the two engines almost screaming. The British plane was slower and the German was able to climb steeper, gaining on his quarry. Again the German machine gun sounded but this time, Tama saw a smoke trail from the British plane. Then for a brief second it appeared to stop in mid-air as the engine and the pilot became engulfed in flames, the pilot's body jerking in a vain attempt to get out. In a matter of seconds the plane plummeted into the ground leaving a plume of smoke wafting up into the air.

"Henri!" Jim said out suddenly. He looked over the top of the trench and saw a body lying in the mud.

"Damn." Tama said. "Looks like he never got past the tree." He looked down the trench. Many bodies lay where they fell with hideous wounds from the aeroplane's machine gun. Some men were conscious and their cries filled the air.

"Anybody able to get up?" Tama shouted.

"Ay," said a voice behind him, "I can still shoot."

"I'm all right," said another pulling himself up from the mud. With a few other men able to get up, a half dozen sat against the trench wall looking around at the devastation.

"Help the others and do what you can," Tama ordered

In the sky were a half a dozen other planes in a 'dog fight', the noise of their engines swamped by the machination of war making them appear almost silent. Jim spotted them. "It's like they're in a different war. Like it's not our war at all, something far away."

"War's different for everybody," Tama said.

Jim looked at Tama. "We got to do it eh? Connect the wires so the phone's work."

"Ah," said Tama looking down the trench. "Nobody else boy, just us." He turned to his men. "Cover me," he ordered. With that he went over the top and ran to the tree as just as before, machine guns opened fire. Tama dived under the bullet ridden body of Henri-Emille, freezing as bullets came precariously close and wood shards from the tree trunk flew as bullets bit in with a solid thud. Tama waited for a second, wondering whether he had been hit and with his face being pushed further into the mud from the weight of Henri-Emille's body, his mother's words came to him. "You are a warrior of the Maniapoto, make me proud son." Wriggling out from his precarious position, Tama took a grab at the wire and crawled on his belly, going forward, past the tree. He looked all around but couldn't see any wire to connect to. He felt isolated as the noise of gun fire was all around him. All he could see was a shattered landscape of bare, muddy land, with twisted tree stumps and coils of barbed wire spread for miles separating the two great armies. He crawled around looking desperately for any sign of a wire, the bullets seemed to be getting closer and for the first time he knew real fear. He thought about his mother's words again and forced himself to move on. After what seemed an hour, but in reality was only several minutes, he noticed more covering fire coming from further along the allied trench from his own section, he suddenly gained more strength and confidence. Keeping low he crawled around and eventually he saw a tangle of wire lying half buried in the mud, looking more like a bird's nest than anything else. He grabbed at it fumbling for an end to connect to. He spat on it and wiped the mud off, connected the ends, then still under heavy fire he crawled his way back to the trench.

**

Two weeks later, Tama's platoon had been combined with a mix of New Zealand and Australian troops. They marched through heavy rain along 'K track' which ran alongside the Ypres to Zonnebeke road. Massed artillery and heavy transport continuously rumbled by in a seemingly inexhaustible line on the hard road in the hope of not getting bogged down. The noise of their engines and smell of exhaust fumes was a constant reminder of the scale of the allied forces building up for the attack the men knew was coming.

'K track' was nothing more than three miles of timber duckboards barely wide enough for two men weaving its way through the Zonnebeke bog. In bitterly cold winds and under continual bombardment from randomly fired German shells, the battalion of men several thousand strong, kept marching. Once the quagmire was crossed, they faced the Zonnebeke to Langemarck road which had been heavily targeted by the enemy so was nothing more than a crater field, which, in the heavy rain became a sodden maze of small lakes and hillocks. Many men slipped off the muddy boards and were left to drown in the mud as orders were to keep moving regardless of circumstances. Their cries for help could be heard in the bleak and desolate night. Some pleaded to be shot by their comrades rather than be left to drown such was the hopelessness of their situation. The line marched all through the night with each man striving to keep sight of the man in front as a guide lest they lose their way and fall victim to the mud. They had no idea of their task or where they were going, they only knew this was a living nightmare they couldn't escape from and what lay ahead would not be any better. They were continually being pushed to keep going but they were hungry, cold, and soaked to the skin from three days of continuous heavy rain. There was no conversation between the men and morale was the lowest it had ever been.

Every now and then the men would see orange flashes on the skyline, followed by a loud crescendo like distant thunder and not knowing whether they were British or German.

Eventually the ground became firmer, and the division found itself in a cemetery. Exhausted they fell to the ground, many not caring if a German bullet found them such was their exhaustion and state of mind. An hour passed and a weak and watery sun rose over Belgium, showing the scene of utter decimation and carnage. The countryside was nothing more than a landscape of deep mud. What looked like rivers of grey water was in fact vast tracts of barbed wire stopping any advance. The skyline was flat other than remnants of trees which were once woods and the sound of the enemy artillery was louder now and more constant, reminding the men that their fate lay ahead. Bodies could be seen laying half submerged, the more the men looked, the more bodies they could see. As the light improved, a high ridge appeared a mile ahead of them where the main action was.

"All right you lot, on your feet, rifles at the ready, bayonets fixed, prepare to attack," came the call from a Scottish officer striding along the lines of exhausted men with his arms behind his back looking for all the world like he was on a parade ground.

"You got to be joking, mate," came an Australian voice out the darkness. "We're fair knackered."

"Attack before sunrise, that was the order sonny, you shower are two hours late already because you were too bloody slow getting here. Now your turn has come sunshine. We need all the help we can get if we're to take Passchendaele."

"Passchendaele?" Jim said to Tama. "You said Passchendaele was a quiet village."

"It was," the officer said overhearing Jim. "That's the trouble with these Germans, they ruin everything. Now get to it laddies."

Red flares rose high in the sky above the men, giving the signal for the artillery to open fire. Immediately, the ground shook, hurting the ears of those who were nearest as the closest thing to Armageddon was released against the Axis forces. For an hour the big guns continuously roared. Jim looked from side to side as he marched with the other men, sometimes stumbling over German or Allied bodies.

Tama turned to his left and looked at Jim.

"Have you got your lucky penny boy!" he shouted above the roar of what was to become his end.
"Ay sir," came the reply from a surprisingly aminated Jim.
"Good, you might need it today, if this is indeed day."
The first they heard of an enemy shell coming in was a strange whistling noise they hadn't heard before. It exploded to their left and every man for a hundred yards in both directions fell. Tama was one of the first to get up, checking himself over and not believing his luck at not being injured. Looking about him, he saw bits of men, arms and legs torn from torsos, heads blow off and bellies ripped open from the shrapnel. He could taste the blood in the air and he was immediately reminded of the smell of bleeding a live pig. Physically stunned and with his ears ringing, all he heard was the muffled noise of men groaning as all around him they were seemingly dying in slow motion. "Jim!" he heard himself shouting. "Jim!" he screamed but all he could hear of his own voice was a muffled noise. He beat his ears with his fists but it didn't make any difference. He staggered over to a pile of body parts, the exposed flesh wet with blood, he looked up and could see what was left of his section advancing up the hill but all he could think about was Jim.
He looked around everywhere, but the bodies and bits of bodies were too numerous.
"Jim!" he shouted out for the last time. Confused by not being able to hear and not knowing what was happening, Tama turned to start up the hill again when he noticed a bright copper coloured metal shard catching the morning light. It took his attention and he picked it up. Looking closely he realised it was all that was left of Jim Manuel's lucky penny.
Despite witnessing the atrocities and butchering of men over the past three years, for the first time, Tama cried. His body shook uncontrollably as his tears fell, but soon enough, the realities of open warfare opened up before him once again and he was forced back into being the person he never wanted to become. He wiped his eyes with his muddy sleeve and picked some khaki material off a strand of barbed wire from the uniform of some poor wretch. Wrapping the remnants of the coin, he carefully put it in his pack vowing to return it to Jim's family one day.

Chapter Eighteen

**

The Murphy family, along with Linda, George, Libby, and Wirimu and Ngaire with some friends were gathered at Saint Leo's Church in Mokau for Megan's funeral.
"Is there anything you'd like me to say in particular?" Father Michael asked Sean.
He looked at Gwyneth. "I'm no good at this sort of thing. Gwyn love, you're going to say a few words aren't you?"
"Yes, George will say a few as well, won't you George?"
"It's the least I can do," he replied.
"Fair enough," Father Michael said looking at everybody.
"Life's a funny old thing when you think about it," he said trying to encourage a bit of conversation. "Look at Megan, a lifetime of travelling the world, setting up home for her family and starting up the farm with David as they did, then at the time of her life when she should be resting, she's taken away from us with such a simple but cruel misfortune."
"Indeed," Sean agreed. "The tree falling on her was a terrible thing, make no mistake. It was horrible finding her there like that with the big chestnut bough laying on top of her and with her head like it was. At least it must have been quick."
"Yes, I suppose that's a blessing in some ways," Father Michael said looking Sean in the eye. Sean held his gaze but Gwyneth remained silent and looked as if she didn't know quite where to put herself.
Gwyneth was close to admitting the truth about Megan's death but she knew George would then know about how Richard shot Megan and the authorities would become involved. It was Gwyneth who suggested the lie about the tree falling on Megan to protect her son, something she would do at any cost.

After a while, Gwyneth had to walk away, knowing Sean was telling lies to a man of the church which made her feel uncomfortable.

"Are you alright?" Libby asked walking after her. Once around the corner, the two friends stopped "This must be such a trial for you," Libby said.

"More than you can imagine," Gwyneth replied, wanting desperately to tell somebody about the deceit, but too scared to tell the truth.

Libby put her arm through Gwyneth's as they walked along the side of the church and around the back. "Well you know George and I are always here to support you through this don't you? It's not that we're going anywhere now Sean has agreed to sell forty nine percent of Llanon and the mill to George. He really made his mind up very quickly once we got back from New Plymouth with the lawyer."

"I think he's letting go in some ways," Gwyneth replied smiling wryly.

"You think so?" Libby asked.

"Yes, the problem is, what will take its place? I know none of us are as young as we were but I wouldn't be surprised if he had something up his sleeve. It's not like Sean to just let go like that, he'll be up to something."

George, and Wirimu stayed with Sean making small talk with Father Michael as Ngaire went looking for Gwyneth and Libby.

"There you are," she said as the two women rounded the church and walked back to the entrance.

"I'm ready whenever you are," Father Michael told the group.

**

The bright winter sun shone on the track leading up to the Mokau cemetery, a place which brought back mixed emotions for Gwyneth. She looked down from the sheer cliffs to the crisp white waves breaking on the beach far below and took in the fresh salty air. Without any reason she was aware of, a feeling of loneliness, somehow mixed with guilt fell on her and she somehow felt incomplete and confused. The years melted away and she remembered when she lost her baby at Mac's funeral and the nightmare which followed. Her thoughts were brought back to the present by the sound of the ropes holding Megan's coffin take the weight as the horse, straining against the collar, started the trek up the steep hill.
"It makes you wonder when your turn will come," Gwyneth muttered.
"When your name's in the book and not a day before," Ngaire said taking Gwyneth's arm, "that's when. Stand strong Gwyn, we're here to support you, don't you ever forget that" she said tilting her head back towards Sean.
As soon as the party arrived in the cemetery itself, Gwyneth looked over to Betty and Joe Dickson's grave. She surprised herself as her private thoughts went back to David Askill, wondering what he was doing.
"I should have cut the hedge back," she said trying to break her train of thought. "Joe won't be able to see what's happening on the road." The other's laughed quietly. "Well if he can, then somebody's in trouble," Libby said.

**

The evening was spent at the Mokau Hotel. Stella Ratcliffe reserved the snug bar so privacy was given.
"Well, what are we to do now?" Gwyneth asked nobody in particular.
"We go home tomorrow and carry on as usual," Sean replied. Gwyneth watched him closely as Moonyeen approached with a tray of drinks as the atmosphere in the group went to one of cautious tension.

"And what exactly is 'usual'?" Gwyneth asked making sure Moonyeen could hear. "What exactly are you saying Sean. What's 'usual' for you may not be exactly what others want to accept?" Moonyeen disappeared quickly.

As the tension grew, George cleared his throat more to get attention than anything else as he stood up. He made a dramatic figure caught in the firelight. "I'd like to ask you to raise your glasses to David and Megan Thomas. Megan, together with David, led us all here to a good life and a good land. Without them both, goodness knows where we would all be."

"I'm glad somebody's having a good life then," Gwyneth muttered. "I'm sorry everybody but it's been a long day so I'm going to bed." She turned to Sean and spoke clearly. "I'll see you in the morning Sean. I expect you'll be sleeping with your trollop tonight, and quite frankly I don't care."

"She's all confused with the funeral and all," Sean said to the others after she left. There was no reply from anybody, only an awkward silence. Libby and Ngaire got up to follow Gwyneth. Libby looked at George raising her eyebrows and George nodded in response.

"I'll come with you," Sarah called out. Linda followed.

Sean looked over to the bar. "Stella my love, can you bring over a bottle of Jameson's. We'll have a real drink now."

**

At Llanon, on an overcast and grey afternoon when Gwyneth and Libby were bringing in the washing, Libby hesitated and looked at Gwyneth to get her attention. "Gwyn, do you mind if I have a quick word, before the men arrive? It's just something George and I have been thinking about."

"Of course not, what is it?"

"Well tell me to mind my own business if you want, but we can see the problems with Richard. It seems he's heading for a miserable life to be honest and with the farm and all, well, neither you nor Sean have the time to spend with him."

"Well that's a fact," Gwyneth admitted.

"Well we've noticed Linda has a way with him and …to be honest she's the only one Richard likes to spend time with."

"Sadly, that's true enough," Gwyneth reflected.

"Our idea, well, George's idea really, is we pay Linda to stay here, as a nurse for Richard. George will pay her what she gets at the hospital in Wellington, but the idea is she lives here for a while at Llanon to help Richard while you and Sean can take a breather and get some peace of mind that he's in good hands. We need to talk with her of course and it'll be a big ask, but that's the idea in principle and like I said, it's not really our business but…."

"No, I understand," Gwyneth interrupted, staring at Libby for a while thinking. "I need to talk to Sean but are you sure? That's a very generous offer."

"No, not really, with George's inheritance we can afford the money, but it's the toll it's taking on you that we see the most, and, if it's one more thing we can do to help with you and Sean, then so much the better. You forget we have seen Richard and Sarah grow up and we feel for Richard almost as much as you two."

"I'll give it some thought but I'm not so sure really."

"Well, why not? You'll still see Richard around, more than you do now probably. Sean won't mind I'm sure."

"Oh you're right about that, Sean will snap up your offer if it frees up more of his time for God knows what."

Libby took Gwyneth's hand.

"Tell me you'll talk it over with him and if you both agree then we can ask Linda, if you don't think it's a good idea then enough said about the matter. Will you do that Gwyn?"

"I will, Libby, and thank you."

**

Gwyneth spent a great deal of the time walking on her own by the river or talking with Ngaire and Libby over the next few weeks. The spring sun not only warmed her body but helped her clear her mind and crystallise her thoughts. Occasionally she caught sight of Richard wandering around Llanon hunting rabbits or making a fire by the chestnut grove where he often slept in the warmer nights.

Sometimes she called out his name and he would stop and look over. Occasionally he smiled and that was enough for Gwyneth, just knowing there was some of the Richard she loved was still there.

"Have you thought of our offer about Linda?" Libby asked one morning when Gwyneth was making bread.

"Yes. I was going to come over to see you both later. Sean thought about it for a while and eventually agreed, if it's still all right with you two of course."

"Yes, of course it's all right. We've seen Richard out and about now the warmer weather's here, he looks better with a bit of sun on his face I must say."

"Yes, he does," Gwyneth instantly agreed.

"Are you really sure Libby, about Linda?"

"I shan't tell you twice Mrs Murphy, you write to Linda as soon as you can and we shall see what she wants to do. She may not want to come of course. It's a big ask of her."

"No, I won't write" Gwyneth said. "I've been thinking about this a lot. I thought I'd get the train to Wellington and see Sarah and Linda myself, as you say it's a big ask and I think it's better face to face." Gwyneth hesitated for a moment. "Why don't you come with me Libby? You should do, it will be better coming from you and it'll be an adventure in some ways."

"I've never been to Wellington. I was always an Auckland girl," Libby blushed.

"Do you think Ngaire would like to come with us? I know it's spring and milking is busy, but with all the pumps and modernisation that's been happening, she may be able to get away for three or four days, I'm sure Wirimu won't mind. Our telephone will be going in a few days, you could call Sarah at the newspaper, imagine that, and she'll get such a surprise."

**

A few weeks later, Linda welcomed Gwyneth and Libby into the Hataitai boarding house in the late afternoon.

"Hello, how are you? Was the journey comfortable?" Linda asked.

"We are well thanks. The journey was surprisingly comfortable," Gwyneth answered thinking how awkward Linda both sounded and acted. "

"How's Bronwyn? She's turning into such a sweet girl."

"She's fine," Gwyneth told her. "We were hoping she might come along as a treat but she was determined to stay with her two friends, so Ngaire let her stay at Te Kainga so she could look after her."

"It's good she has a few friends though."

"Yes, but they are only imaginary, all kids have them of course."

"And Richard, how's he?" Gwyneth turned and looked at Libby then back to Linda.

"He's… he's all right, but it's because of Richard we are here really."

"Yes," Linda said. "Sarah mentioned your phone call. She was rather surprised that you have a phone at Llanon. That's good to see."

"Yes," Libby said eagerly. "It's so wonderful to be connected to the outside world now."

"I hope we didn't get Sarah into trouble," Gwyneth interrupted.

"No, of course not. She uses a telephone for her work. She'll be here soon," Linda explained still nervous. "It's the newspaper you know, it's a tough master and the balloon's gone up apparently, the war's not going too well of course. Sorry. You'll know already."

"Know what?" Gwyneth asked. "We don't get much news, you know what Sean's like about it all. We heard there was a bit of a setback from a few overheard conversations on the train but everybody was so sullen, we felt awkward asking."

"Well, 'a bit of a setback' is one way of putting it," Linda said. "There's a big push and we're not doing at all well. It's still building up apparently. Sarah knows everything of course, it's better she tells you herself."

Just then Sarah came bursting through the front door.

"Mother, Auntie Libby, it's wonderful to see you. I'm sorry I couldn't get here earlier, I hope Linda here saved the day."

"Yes, she did well. You look thin, and so tired Sarah love. Are you all right?"

"Oh, it's nothing, just the newspaper is keeping us on our toes at the moment, the war and all that."

"Linda was saying. What's happening?"

"Well. It's not good I'm afraid. Mr Harris held the press again today because of the news, the battle for Ypres, well it's been lots of separate battles, but it's all ended up at a place called Passchendaele." Sarah's voice went sullen and she looked awkward. "We lost a lot of men, the worst day of the war it seems."

"How many?"

Sarah hesitated and looked down. "Well like I said, it's not good."

"How many Sarah?"

"About eight hundred dead, plus two thousand casualties."

"My God Sarah. Over how long?"

"What do you mean?"

"Weeks, months, how long has it taken for our men to die in such terrible numbers?"

"One day, a matter of hours really!" Sarah replied

"A day? A single day?"

"It's hard to believe that many men can be slaughtered so quickly," Sarah said, "but that's modern warfare for you. That's not the British either, it's just the New Zealanders."

"Tama?" Gwyneth asked.

"Who knows?" Sarah replied. "We don't deal in single names, not with numbers like that."

"God, you said it wasn't going well but I didn't realise…"

"How many British dead?" Libby interrupted.

"About three hundred thousand, dead or injured over the campaign so far. Only God knows really."

Libby looked back at Gwyneth with a stunned look on her face. "Three hundred thousand men. That cannot be true, can it? It must be most of the British army surely," she said unbelievingly.

"Not sure," Sarah said. "We know the Germans have lost almost as many as well. I know it's hard to believe isn't it? Half a million men all told, just for a few miles of mud. When it's coming off the wires, we have to write it out quickly so I don't really take it in, but when I think about it afterwards, it makes it all the more real somehow. It sounds cruel but I have trained myself not to think too much or I can't do my job. When I think of Richard, I'm not sure whether he's lucky or not."
"All those young men, dead," Gwyneth uttered still trying to take it in. "All those mothers and families suffering, as we suffer now with Theo and Richard." Tears welled up in Gwyneth's eyes.
"The whole newspaper, the press and the offices did all their work in silence mostly today," Sarah said. "The clatter of the press never sounded so loud, everybody's affected whether they have family in the army or not, everybody knows somebody fighting and nobody knows who's dead and who's alive anymore. I'm sorry to say it but these are surely our darkest days."
"But we won, didn't we?" Libby asked.
"Nobody's won Auntie Libby, the fighting for Ypres still continues and is likely to do so for another month, the losses at Passchendaele are just a part of it. More men are being sent out now, the same for the Germans. Don't forget that German mothers love their sons as much as we love ours," Sarah said.
"Is it wise saying things like that?" Gwyneth quizzed.
Sarah saw the affect her words were having. "Sorry, I'll make a cup of tea shall I, then I'll show you your room? Mrs Chard has given you the large room on the eastern side so you'll get the morning sun. You must be worn out, both of you. I have the day off tomorrow. We can talk then, have a good old catch up eh?"
"I'll see you in the morning as well," Linda said. "I start night shift tomorrow so I'll be around most of the day."

**

By the end of the next morning, Gwyneth and Libby had explained the situation at Llanon with Richard and had asked Linda to consider staying on as a nurse to Richard.

"So that's really why we're here," Gwyneth said when she had finished explaining. "You'll have full board at Llanon of course and still get the same pay you do at the hospital now. Libby and George have been kind enough to make this offer to you Linda, for Richard's sake as much as anybody else's but I don't mind admitting it would be a blessing. Oh, and there's Bronwyn of course, I'm sure she would be happy to help, she and Richard get on so well, or at least they used to. I don't know what I would have done without her on the voyage back from England."

"It needs some thinking about," Linda said. "It would be a change. I like Llanon and I've enjoyed being there before. I don't mind admitting that I am scolded at the hospital on a few occasions for spending too much time with the men. It's so difficult because I seem to be able to get through to some of them and they open up. You can see the difference in them immediately, it's like a kettle letting off steam, if they can't do that, then one way or the other there'll be trouble."

"How do you mean?" Gwyneth asked.

"We have had a few lose their tempers, shockingly so. They are very strong then and take some holding down or they could cause considerable harm to themselves and others. Sometimes they think they are back in the war, in the fighting and try to do all sorts of things, including attacking people."

"That's terrible," Libby said.

Linda's comment caused Gwyneth to make eye contact with Sarah. She ached to tell Libby the truth about Megan's death but remembered her promise to Sean and the others. It was only now she realised she had betrayed the trust of George and Libby, the two people who had helped them the most and she felt ashamed, so she resolved to tell Libby. As though reading her thoughts, Sarah looked over and nodded.

She brought her focus back to Linda. "I think I would like to spend all my time with Richard," Linda said. "It would be a good opportunity to put my skills to use. It would take some time though."

"That's exactly what we thought," Gwyneth agreed.

"I'll have to think about it and talk with Mother and Father of course."
"That's all we can ask," Gwyneth replied.
"Linda, would you mind if Sarah and I spent some time with Libby, alone?"
"No of course not. I have some washing to do anyway."
"Libby?" Gwyneth asked nervously looking at Sarah.
Sarah guessed what was coming next and nodded.
Libby smiled "What is it you two?".
"There something we have to tell you, it may change everything but I cannot bear to keep it from you anymore."
Sarah moved over and took Gwyneth's hand.

**

"But why didn't you tell us immediately?" Libby asked when Gwyneth had finished explaining what really happened the night Megan died.
"Because…because in the heat of the moment we all agreed to it, to protect Richard. Don't you see Libby, he murdered Mother, as good as anyway."
"It would be manslaughter surely?" Libby said getting agitated realising her best friend had been holding secrets from her.
"To get the police in and then have to go through a trial would mean Richard would be on remand regardless. How do you think he would react to that?" Gwyneth raised her voice desperately hoping Libby would understand. "Being put in a cell would be the end of him. Don't you think he's been through enough already? It wasn't really Richard who pulled the trigger. It was a madman, a product of the war."
"But we deserved to know the truth all the same," Libby said starting to get angry. "How do you think George will react when I tell him our trust in you has been betrayed?"
"That's just the point Libby, had George known the truth he would have told the police because it would be his duty, even if we pleaded with him. We protected Richard, that was all. Putting him in prison wouldn't bring Mother back, all it would do is kill what remains of my son. At least he now has some hope if Linda agrees to stay with us."

"I'm not sure, not sure at all," Libby said pacing the floor. "Don't you see Gwyneth. You didn't trust us, after all George has done for you, you blatantly lied to us and to everybody else, especially Father Michael, those at the funeral and those who were closest to you. Who else knows?"
Gwyneth stood standing at the fireplace looking into the ashes.
"We all do," Sarah interrupted. "We were all there and we all saw what happened. We saw how Nana was in one of her states, she was out looking for Lucky at two o'clock in the morning. Richard had Father's shotgun thinking he was back at Gallipoli, and he shot her. In the flash from the barrel we saw Nana die."
"But the body was found under the tree…oh, I see, another lie," Libby almost shouted.
"Linda, does Linda know as well?"
"Yes, I know," Linda said walking in through the door. "Sorry. I overheard the conversation. "Yes, I saw it all as well Libby. I'm truly sorry, I really am. I'll understand if the offer to help Richard no longer stands, but you must know that nobody wanted what happened after Mrs Thomas died. It was a case of making the best of a bad situation, surely you understand that?"
"I don't know what to understand anymore other than a lifelong friend who has taken advantage of my husband's good fortune has betrayed us."
"Now hold on Libby," Gwyneth said turning to face her. "Nobody has taken advantage of George or you. You paid a fair price for a share in Llanon and Ballinger's Mill. It was strictly a business transaction. It's right enough that Sean and I needed the money but we didn't take a handout and certainly nobody took advantage, let's be straight about that."
Libby went white and started shaking, looking as though she had been mortally wounded. She took a step closer to Gwyneth.
"Well the high and mighty Gwyneth Murphy has come down a peg or two I must say. Butter wouldn't melt in your mouth, oh no. Always the dutiful wife while that so called husband of yours has been sleeping around for years," she said vindictively.

"Do you think I don't know that?" Gwyneth snapped back. "And who are you to talk anyway, when it all boils down to it, you're nothing but a conniving, gold digging prostitute who spent most of her life on her back, where's that ever got you?"

"Well at least I own damn near half of Llanon and Ballinger's Mill with my faithful husband, that's where it's got me. What have you got, nothing, certainly not a faithful husband? Your name's not even on the titles, nor on any bank account. For all the years you've been here, you've got nothing to show, nothing at all. I wouldn't be surprised if Moonyeen Wu has got more out of your marriage than you have."

"At least I've still got my son," Gwyneth shouted out in absolute anger.

No sooner had she said it than Libby crumpled in a heap on the floor with her hands covering her face, shaking in convulsions of tears.

Chapter Nineteen

**

It was on a glorious Sunday afternoon in early December when Dickie Fleming sounded the klaxon as he pulled up outside Sarah's boarding house. Sarah, wearing a white lace dress and a large broad brimmed hat with a matching handbag, half ran outside excitedly.
"Oh Dickie, you got your uncle's car," she said clutching Dickie's arm, "I didn't think he would let you have it being brand new."
"Uncle Stephen's a good stick really, besides he can't be bothered running it in so he wants me to knock up a few miles so he can drive like a madman later on. It's a Studebaker, he read about one being driven on the Parapara Highway all the way to Raetihi in only four and a half hours so he was impressed. He's retiring in a year or so and that's the sort of thing he wants to do, motoring I mean."
"Even so, it's very generous of him. It's, it's so big and shiny. It must have cost a king's ransom. Look at the leatherwork and the huge seats, you could get a whole family in there."
"Yes, that's the idea," Dickie readily agreed. "It's a tourer, that's what it's designed for."
"I love the royal blue colour too and the white tyres, it looks so grand, it'll certainly turn heads."
"Yes, a flashy American car all right, but I must admit it looks good, and it does go rather well. It has a six cylinder engine you know," Dickie said with a broad grin as he hopped out and opened the passenger door for Sarah.
"Jump in love and we'll go around Oriental Parade and the Miramar Peninsula, maybe stop at Scorching Bay for an ice cream. What do you say to that?"
Sarah stopped in her tracks.
"Dickie!" she called out in surprise.
"What is it?"

"You called me 'love'. It's the first time you've ever done that."
"Sorry, you don't mind do you?"
"No, I suppose not, but I don't want you doing it in public," she said secretly pleased and smiling to herself as she climbed into the car.
Dickie shut the door behind her. "I'll take the roof down if you like so we can drive with the wind in our hair. Would you like that?"
"Perfect," Sarah agreed pulling the sides of her hat down over her ears while turning to look at Dickie and crossing her eyes. "If the wind changes, you'll stay like that," he told her and they both laughed out loud. "I know, we can drive through the tram tunnel," he announced.
"But we're not allowed," Sarah laughed.
"All the more reason to do it then. Besides if we wait for a tram, we can follow it through. Everybody does it. I've seen them and I've always wanted to give it a go."
"As you say," Sarah laughed. "Now drive on Jeeves," she called out above the noise of the engine, "an ice cream at Scorching Bay it is."

**

"Any word from your mother?" Dickie asked as they drove around Evans Bay.
"No, not since she fell out with Auntie Libby."
"But that was several weeks ago. Do you think she's all right?"
"I'm sure she is, somebody will be in contact if anything serious happens. I thought Mother might telephone but her end is at Auntie Libby's house, so I suppose they're still not talking."
When they arrived at Scorching Bay, the sun was shining brightly, and the beach was quite crowded with picnic makers. Parking the car on the grass, Dickie turned the engine off.
"The sea looks beautiful," Sarah mentioned.
"You go and find a good spot on the beach. There's a blanket in the back if you like," Dickie suggested. "I'll go and get the ice creams, I see there's a bit of a queue already."

Sarah shook a dark green and blue tartan blanket and laid it out on the hot sand. She looked about her. Families with small children were playing on the beach, making sandcastles, or playing beach cricket and paddling in the surf. All around there were people at play, seemingly without a care in the world.

"Here you are," Dickie said after a while. "Two large vanilla and strawberry cornets. You'll have to hurry, they're starting to melt already."

"Thanks," Sarah said taking hers. "It's funny isn't it? Not in a 'funny' funny way but in a funny odd way."

"What is?" Dickie asked.

"Us being here, like this, sitting at the beach on a beautiful day enjoying ourselves when right now, over on the western front, our men are fighting for their lives in the rain and the mud. The war's in the balance yet all I can see in front of me are people enjoying themselves as though the war doesn't exist."

"It does for lots of them in many ways" Dicky said. "I expect if you asked any one of them they will know somebody who's been killed or maimed, family or friends, this is their escape probably, at least for a while, a search for some sense of normality in these dark and turbulent times. Later on today they'll all have to go home and face their realities. Look at me, I'm here and relatively healthy, apart from my leg of course but the reality of war is never far below the surface."

"Yes, of course, sorry Dickie, I didn't mean to rake up bad memories."

"Of course not, but oddly enough there are some relatively good memories as well and you have to hold on to those."

"What do you mean?"

"Well, you get close to your mates, none closer than Theo. He and I were together for a long time. We chose to do that so we could do some good rather than kill. Regardless of the unspeakable conditions, surely, we must have helped somebody. Theo was so gentle and always thinking of others, not just us but the Turks as well. He recognised everybody as a person. Plus his mule, Apollo. He went everywhere with that moth eaten, half crippled beast, I swear they loved each other. Did you know that just before Theo found the animal half dead from shrapnel, he saw a butterfly on a thyme bush? He told me to be careful not to harm it when all around us men were dead or dying from the mortars and machine guns. Theo didn't deserve to die like he did. He went to the hills on a quiet sunny Sunday, well at least it was quiet for Gallipoli. He went to offer a prayer of thanks for his blessings, for being alive, that's the sort of man he was, and yet he never came back. Instead, he was machine gunned along with Apollo. But you grew up together on the Mokau River didn't you so you know all about him of course"

Sarah took Dickies arm and gently rubbed his shoulder. "Yes but it's always good to hear the different things, different perspectives. He had a way with animals. The war has a lot to answer for. My father's right in many ways, blaming the politicians. Don't you go mentioning Winston Churchill when you're with my father, or you'll never hear the end of it."

"Why would I be around your father," Dickie asked. "Are you trying to entice me to Llanon?"

Sarah turned and smiled at Dickie realising exactly what she inferred. Without speaking, she said what she wanted with a cheeky smile.

She turned back to look out to sea. "You see the lighthouse on top of the Orongorongo Hills?" she asked keen to change the subject. "That was the original lighthouse built over fifty years ago. The lighthouse keeper was Mary Jane Bennett. She was New Zealand's only female lighthouse keeper, she must have been a strong woman."

"You admire strong women don't you?" Dickie asked.

"Yes of course, I grew up with strong women. You should have met my Auntie Atarangi, Auntie Ngaire's sister. She was a suffragette and helped women get the vote. I'm sure there wouldn't be a war if women were politicians."

"Couldn't do much worse. You'd have to include the Russians in your statement though. It hasn't helped they've pulled out of the war," Dickie mused.

"Yes," said Sarah coming back to reality. 'If Kerensky signs the armistice with the Russians, the Germans will put everything into a spring offensive. With what I've seen coming off the wires at the newspaper, it's not good. The American's need to commit more numbers, then actually do something useful. It doesn't help they won't side with us or the French, it makes me so angry. They made a song and dance about going over to Europe but won't actually fight. We still haven't recovered from Passchendaele, and we need more men urgently. Everybody expects a major German offensive in a few months when the snow melts and as you say the Russians pulling out hasn't helped. Bloody Bolsheviks don't realise quite what they've done, and to think I had some sympathy for them at the start."

"I don't think it pays to dwell on it too much though Sarah," Dickie said, staring into the distance.

"Sorry Dickie, I just can't help it. Our men must be suffering so much. I keep thinking of Tama, wondering if he's alive."

"I expect he is," Dickie answered. "I only met him very briefly of course at Chunuk Bair. He seemed to be a natural soldier, the sort of man others go to for courage and leadership, a man's man. Theo spoke of him very highly, Richard too of course."

"Let's leave the conversation on that note, shall we?" Sarah slapped Dickie's shoulder with the back of her hand.

"Hey," Dickie called out in mock pain. "Any more of that and I'll call you 'love' in the middle of Lambton Quay."

"You wouldn't dare," Sarah laughed. "Now come on Jeeves, you can drive me home. Let's go back along the south coast through Island Bay. We can follow a tram back through the tunnel and unwind how we came in."

**

Sarah walked into the Evening Post offices ready for her shift just as Mr Harris came out of his office looking quite distraught. "Listen up everybody!" he shouted. "More bad news I'm afraid. We've lost a lot more men at a place called Polderhoek. Five hundred injured or so and around a hundred dead."

"There's no bloody end to it," said a voice from the back.

"I can tell you that's not how we're going to lead the story" Mr Harris insisted. "Here's the guts. The First Canterbury and First Otago Battalions went in on a chateau held by the Germans, but the attack failed. A lot of our men died from our own artillery fire, but we won't be reporting that of course, we'll keep it to ourselves."

"We did the same at Gallipoli," Sarah added, "Colonel Malone from Stratford…"

"Yes, yes Miss Murphy, that's enough of that talk, the rest of you check details and get on with the story. You Paul, I want a first draft in an hour. Miss Murphy, I want you in my office now."

Sarah shut the door behind her as Mr Harris stubbed out one cigarette and immediately lit another. He took his glasses off and rubbed them with his handkerchief.

"Too much bad news like this will kill morale here, you know that. I want you to get some good news stories to lighten the mood of the paper, go and see what you can find?"

"Good news, from the western front?" Sarah questioned.

"That's what I said wasn't it? You've got the nose for it. With Passchendaele, and now this Polderhoek business, the public won't take it too kindly . We don't want to rouse anti Empire feelings born from frustration either. It's bad enough on the home front now with this six o'clock closing. What's a working man to do in the evenings for God's sake? Now go and find a good news story, you've got two hours, there's a good girl. Oh…and the latest Gazette's just come in, you might want to start there, nothing posthumous mind, we don't want to rub salt in the wounds. Not a good choice of words but you know what I mean."

Sarah sat down in a dark corner with the list of names. For a brief moment she considered how only yesterday she was carefree and driving around to the beach with Dickie. Now she understood the mood of the people she saw on the beach as she was one of them and how Dickie was right about the effects of the war never being far away. She shook her head to get rid of her thoughts and started reading down the list.

Cronshaw, Robert, Greg.
M.M.   Gunner. NZ Field Artillery.
            L.G. 12th December 1917.
For bravery in the field.

Taylor, John, Francis.
        MID.   Lieutenant, 1st Bn, N.Z. Rifle Brigade.
        L.G. 28th December 1917.
For conspicuous gallantry and devotion to duty. During the Messines attack when all the other officers had become casualties, this man took charge of a railway construction company. Under heavy shell fire from a determined enemy he assumed command and gathering the men, he ensured the tasks were completed. Again on the night of 21st August 1917 during wiring operations in the front of outpost line at La Basse Ville he displayed great courage setting a good example to his men while carrying out his tasks conscientiously.

Heta, Arapata, Hoani.
DCM.   Sergeant, 2nd, Bn, Auckland Regiment
        L.G. 26th November 1917.
For conspicuous gallantry and devotion to duty. All the officers of his company became casualties and he was the only sergeant left. He at once took command and under heavy machine gun fire, made repeated attempts to capture enemy strong points but was held up by uncut wire. He displayed the finest qualities of leadership and initiative.

Gotobed, Michael, Phillip.
MM.   Private, 2nd Bn, Otago Regiment
   L.G. 15th November 1917.
For conspicuous gallantry and devotion to duty. On 3rd July 1917 during an attack on an enemy pillbox, this man was one of a bombing section and when the N.C.O. became a casualty, he immediately took command. Leading his men he endeavoured to work around the left flank of the pillbox while bombing his way forward under heavy machine gun fire. He consolidated his position which he held until a new line was dug through. His conduct throughout was splendid and he showed great powers of leadership.

Sarah stopped at the next on the list taking it in. She sprang up and went into Mr Harris's office.
"This had better be good Miss Murphy," he said looking up over his glasses.
"It is," Sarah said wiping away a tear. "It's damned good Mr Harris."
"Let me see."
He scanned the list stopping where Sarah had circled.

Ratahi, Tama, Wirimu
   DCM.   Sergeant, N.Z. 3rd Wellington Bn.
   L.G. 28th December 1917.
For conspicuous gallantry and devotion to duty. On 3rd December 1917 during an operation outside of Passchendaele with the First French Army and with the majority of his men becoming casualties from an aerial attack, this man, on seeing the wiring operation had failed, went into open land under heavy machine gun fire. On doing so he ensured the telephone wires were connected to establish communications. His conduct throughout showed exemplary courage and leadership.

"What about it?" Mr Harris demanded. "A valiant deed but heroes are ten a penny at the moment, what makes this one so special?"

"Because I know this man, Tama, he was a lifelong friend of Theo Twentyman, the man I spoke to you about when I first came here, the man with the mule."

"Yes I remember, so this Tama Ratahi knew your friend, Theo Twentyman?"

"Yes of course, the three of them, Tama, Theo and my brother Richard, had their last drink as civilians together, they joined up together. Theo is now dead, and my brother is shell shocked to the point of dementia. But Tama now has a Distinguished Conduct Medal."

"That could be a good story," Mr Harris said staring out the window and thinking. "His parents?"

"Wirimu and Ngaire Ratahi. They live on the next farm to my parents."

"Do they hear from their boy? Does he write?"

"No, not that I know of. Writing has never been Tama's strong point."

"So they may not know about this DCM?"

"Possibly not."

"When did you last speak with them?"

"Two or three weeks ago."

"Can you get in touch with them quickly?"

"Maybe. Theo's parents live in the original house at Llanon, they have a telephone now so maybe they can relay a message to Wirimu and Ngaire to call back."

"Do it now Miss Murphy, tell them to reverse the charges of course. I want to hear what their reaction is to their boy getting a DCM. We can run a story of a Taranaki boy doing well, its good human interest and it'll bring hope to a lot of families who are in the same boat."

Sarah almost ran back to her corner of the office in her enthusiasm to make the call and let Wirimu and Ngaire know Tama was not only alive and well but was a hero. She put her hand on the heavy black handset hesitating before she picked it up to dial the exchange. Then she started thinking, how should she break the news? Should it be up to her to say what happened when Mr Harris clearly said he wanted to speak with Wirimu? What if Wirimu or Ngaire didn't want to speak? She let go of the handset and weighed up all the pros and cons.

"Have you made the call yet?" Mr Harris' voice boomed out.
'No, no, not yet" Sarah stumbled.
"Make it, don't dilly-dally."
Relieved her choices had been made for her, Sarah started the call to the Wellington exchange. Twenty minutes later, the telephone at George and Libby's house rang without any answer.
"Nobody home!" Sarah called out.
"Keep trying, you can work tonight if need be, there's a better chance they'll be home then anyway."
Two more times Sarah called and each time she felt more reticent. This wasn't her news to give but it was already decided that it should be. Her mind was no more made up now than it was before. The more she thought about it, the more she became uncomfortable talking to George or Libby and asking them to go and see Wirimu and Ngaire to tell them the news and call the newspaper back. It wasn't their way, both were quiet people who would reflect on Tama's achievement privately. Sarah was torn between the job she desperately wanted to do and family loyalties. She stayed at her desk until seven thirty and decided to make one last call. George's voice eventually answered. "Hello,"
"Hello, Uncle George, it's, it's Sarah here, Sarah Murphy."
"Sarah, are you all right?"
"Yes, yes of course. How are you and Auntie Libby?"
"We're all good."
"Mother and Father?"
"They're well."
There was an awkward silence.
"Uncle George. I have news of Tama."
A silence followed, then Sarah realised the implications of what she had said.
"Oh it's all right" she blurted. "Its good news but I need to talk with Uncle Wirimu and Auntie Ngaire."
"Wirimu and Sean are in New Plymouth at the auction, we're selling off some Jersey heifers. Do you want me to get Ngaire if I can?"
"Would you please, Uncle George?"
"Of course. She needs to know, especially as you say if it's good news. Can I ask for a hint?"

Sarah hesitated.
"You must promise to keep it to yourself,..." she hesitated. "...Tama's been awarded a medal, a Distinguished Conduct Medal, for bravery. The citation is inspiring. I shouldn't have told you and you must keep it to yourself, but you see it truly is good news."
"Indeed, it's enough to know he's alive. How's Dickie?"
"He's doing well at the Public Works Department. He still wants to become an architect though. Uncle George, you don't have to answer but how are things between Mother and Auntie Libby?"
"Strained at best."
"Are they talking?"
"When they have to. We still have the farm to run and School Farm takes some working out at times."
"And Richard?"
"About the same. Sean took his rifle back thank goodness, but Richard still prowls around at night. Sometimes he's gone for days at a time, we don't know where to be honest. Listen Sarah, I'll walk over to Te Kainga and see Ngaire, I won't say anything other than it's good news about Tama. I'm sure she'll come running. Do you want me to get your mother before I go?"
Sarah thought for a while.
"You'd better not, the newspaper's paying for this call so I need to make it strictly business."
"Of course. I'll go over to Te Kainga. It'll be an hour or so before Ngaire can get here though."
"Thank you, Uncle George, and tell Ngaire to make sure the charges are reversed so the newspaper pays for the call."

**

"So how did it all end up?" Linda asked the next morning after Sarah recounted the story.
"Auntie Ngaire was ecstatic of course, as you would expect. She didn't care about the medal; it was enough to know Tama was alive"
"Naturally, of course she would be, and the interview?"

"It didn't happen," Sarah told her. "Auntie Ngaire wouldn't have it. She said that Wirimu should know first and if there's any interview, they should both be there."

"That's as it should be but I bet that went down like a cup of cold sick."

"He was quite upset," Sarah confirmed. "He saw it as the good-news story he so desperately wanted."

"And how do you feel about it all?" Linda asked.

"I was quite proud of Auntie Ngaire to be honest. I agree, it's a personal thing not everybody wants to share, not at first anyway. Both Auntie Ngaire and Uncle Wirimu put a lot of store in being quiet achievers. It's who they are as much as anything, they are very humble people. They'll talk about it in their own time."

"Did you ask about Richard?"

"Of course, he's just the same apparently, he wanders a lot. Father has his shotgun back."

Linda got up and walked around the room, she walked gently shutting the door to make sure Mrs Chard wasn't listening.

"I've been thinking Sarah. Work at the hospital is getting bad. I mean, there are so many more soldiers coming in now with limbs missing or other horrendous injuries, or like Richard not even knowing who or where they are. Quite frankly I'm not sure if I can take much more, there's just not enough time to spend on them to do some real good and sometimes I do more harm than anything else, getting their hopes raised by chatting with them for a brief moment. Sorry to say that for the majority, the rest of their lives will be a formidable hurdle they just won't get over and I can't bear it much more."

"So what are you saying Linda?"

"I have a proposal for you, well, for Richard really but I need your blessing first."

"What is it?" Sarah asked totally intrigued.

"Truth to be told, it's not a complete idea really, not really thought out, more half an idea which still has a way to go."

"Linda, it's not like you to be so vague, spit it out no matter how half-baked it is."

**

There was a tense atmosphere in the parlour of Sean and Gwyneth's house at Llanon

"So let me understand this properly" Sean said to Linda.

"You're prepared to give up your work at Wellington hospital to come here to Llanon just to help Richard?"

"Yes, that's it in a nutshell," Linda answered. "Although it's not 'just' Richard as you put it."

"Who else is it then?" Sean wanted to know.

"It's everybody I suppose, including myself. I see what Richard's state of mind is doing to you as a family. It's happening all over New Zealand; you see Richard and his compatriots are a lost generation if we do nothing."

"But the hospitals are for that surely?" Sean said.

"To some degree. They fix the physical wounds as best they can but it's the mental wounds which take time. That's why our men are shuffled through as quickly as possible because there's always more wounded coming in ready to take their place, it's a bit like a conveyer belt in many ways."

"Why would you do this?" Gwyneth asked briskly "Are you saying we don't do a good enough job with Richard as it is?"

"No, not at all," Linda replied. "But most of us here saw what happened with Richard and Mrs Thomas." Linda realised she had struck a sore point. "Sorry," she said.

"It's because I want to make a difference, I want to test my ideas of connecting with Richard and people like him to be brutally honest. I'd like to help Bronwyn as well. I know she has a bond with Richard, and I'd like to get to know her better to help reach Richard. I understand that you once offered me the job, as a paid position I couldn't accept that now, why should I?"

Sarah turned to face everybody. "Can't you see what Linda is offering is a fresh start in some ways. We've all been bogged down with everything that's been going on over the last year, this may be a way of breaking that. The war cannot go on forever and we need to face the future together, as a family. With Linda's help, Richard may come right, then we will grow and move on to a more certain future than we have now."

"You're sounding exactly like your grandfather," Gwyneth said. Linda took Sarah's hand and gave her a nervous smile.

"Where would you stay?" Sean asked.

"Don't be absurd," Gwyneth interrupted. "She'd stay here with us. It's our son she'd be helping. Sorry Linda, I don't mean to speak as though you're not here."
"No offence taken."
"Well I for one think it's a good idea," Gwyneth said.
"I agree," Libby added. She looked directly at Gwyneth. "And I also think it's time to move forward, in more ways than one."
"Sean?" Gwyneth asked.
"Who am I to stand in the way of my son's recovery?"
"Then it looks like we all agree?" George looked around the group.
"We do," Gwyneth said. "And it would be good to have another pianist in the house, perhaps you could accompany me sometimes Linda?"
"I'd love to Mrs Murphy."

Chapter Twenty

**

Tama didn't know much about the attack. He was left behind when the remnants of his platoon advanced after the direct hit from the shrapnel bomb. Totally confused and barely able to hear anything other than the unrelenting roaring noise in his head, he staggered through bomb craters or lay for some time where he fell in the mud, hungry, wet, and chilled to the bone with barely the strength or the will to continue. There were times he fell over bodies, either shot, blown to bits, or simply drowned in the mud. At times, he would pummel his ears with his fists and scream his lungs out to try and stop the living nightmare which filled his consciousness above the ever-present noise of war as the ground vibrated from big guns. Several times he staggered into artillery batteries, but the men were always too busy to take notice of just another soldier. It was only good fortune that kept him away from imminent danger. On the third day, hallucinating and lacking the will to do anything but welcome death, he blundered into two soldiers huddling in the remains of a barn.
"Bugger me mate, watch it will you? I thought you was a bloody German, damn near shot you I did," said one.
All Tama heard was a dull noise rising and falling behind him when he turned and fell.
"Jim? Is that you Jim?" he found himself trying to shout above the noise in his head.
"He looks a bit rough Stevey boy," the soldier said looking at his companion.
"Yeah, well you ain't no oil painting either Dave, has nobody ever told you that?" Steve replied. "Who you with matey?" he asked turning to Tama.
Tama looked over. "Jim?"

"No mate, I ain't no Jim. I reckon he's gone over to the neighbours to ask 'em to turn the noise down a bit so we can have a cuppa in peace."

Tama closed his eyes and let exhaustion take over.

"What's wrong wiv 'im then?" Dave asked.

"Same as all of us," Steve said. "Sick of the ruddy war and sick of being bloody well shot at I reckon. Here Davey, we'll drag him up 'ere, see if we can get some char down his neck, might do the trick, it usually does."

The two men dragged Tama's limp body up to the wall just as some stones fell off the top and tumbled down onto him as if to warn him away.

"Careful," Dave said. "Don't want to damage this fine property do we, s'pect the farmer will be well dogged off with the Germans as it is."

"Who's he wiv then?" Steve asked.

"Noo Zealander by the flashes. There's a few about wiv the Aussies. I've seen 'em before."

"'e's a bit black for a Noo Zealander en 'e?"

"Frigged if I know," Dave said. "Must be one of them Aboriginals or Māoris, they're all the same anyway."

"What we gonna do wiv 'im then? Tea break 'll be over soon."

"Let's leave 'im here, behind the wall, 'ell be safe enough, or as safe as 'e can be given the extenuatin' circumstances, like the friggin' war. Best get another cuppa down his laughing gear Stevey boy."

After some struggle, Tama managed to swallow some hot tea and it felt good, reviving his spirits to some degree. Squinting his eyes, he watched the men starting to pack their equipment together. Steve looked at him. "'ere Davey, that char seems to 'ave done somethin'. 'e looks right perky 'e does."

Dave walked over to Tama. "Can you 'ear me mate!" he yelled out.

"'alf the friggin'' German army can 'ear yer" Steve said with a smile.

"You just keep sorting the gear," Dave told him. He turned back to Tama. "Jim said for you to stay here! Have you got that?"

"Ay?" Tama questioned, screwing his face up as he concentrated to hear.

"Jim said for you to stay 'ere, behind this wall where you'll be nice and safe, see?"

Some of the message got through to Tama who smiled a faint smile.

"Kia ora," he muttered.

"Whatever," Dave said. "Come on Stevey boy, let's go and sort out these bloody' Germans so we can all go 'ome."

The two men threw their packs on their backs, picked up their rifles and walked out from behind the wall. Steve turned around for a last look at Tama. "Good luck mate" he shouted out giving the thumbs up.

At last and finally on his own, Tama finally found the luxury of relinquishing all care and let himself slip away into unconsciousness.

**

"Take it easy with him." Tama heard a faint but melodic voice cutting through his private comfort as he became aware of his body being shaken. He looked up at a canvas roof flapping in a breeze against a blue sky and turned his head to one side to see where the voice was coming from, but the sun was in his eyes.

"Careful now," he was told as he tried to move. "Don't want you doing any more damage to yourself."

"What...what....?"

"It's all right, you're well behind the lines in a field dressing station. You were brought in yesterday after spending God knows how long buried in rubble."

Tama knew something was strange but he couldn't work out what. He was mystified by where he found himself and what was intrinsically different. It was a strange feeling he couldn't shift. He let himself fall back on the bed which in reality was nothing more than a few planks set on sandbags.

"Not the Hilton mate but we're under a bit of pressure you see." The soft lilting voice came back to his consciousness.

"Welsh?" Tama asked.

"I am," came the reply. "Captain Geraint Jenkins, pleased to know you I am sure. But you're not Welsh though are you?"

"Māori, Maniapoto from Mokau in New Zealand."

"There's nice. I've heard New Zealand is a lovely country. Where's this Maniapoto?"

"It's not a place, it's my tribe, in Taranaki. Tama went into deep thought. "Captain Gareth Jenkins?" he said out loud.

"What about him?" Geraint Jenkins asked.

"You know him?"

"Never heard of him, but then again there's a few of us Welsh people here you see. Who is he then, this other Captain Jenkins?"

"Good man. Met him at Chunuk Bair," Tama said surprising himself at his clarity of thought.

Geraint Jenkins raised his eyebrows. "You've been through a bit then so you have."

"You said I was found buried under a wall?" Tama asked.

"That's what the ambulance boys told me."

"How'd they know I was there?"

"You were lucky you see?"

"How?"

"Well, lucky the old woman knew you was there."

"What old woman?"

"There was an old woman with a couple of kids standing on the rubble waving at the stretcher bearers. Got their attention she did. Strange thing seeing an old woman out here, especially with the nippers, but this is war and after three and half years you get used to seeing strange things so you do."

"What did this old woman look like?" Tama was getting anxious.

"No good asking me, see one old woman you've seen the lot really."

Geraint Jenkins saw Tama looking at him strangely.

"All respects of course," he quickly added.

Tama suddenly realised. "I think I know. She was my tupuna wahine, my grandmother," he said as he swung his legs over the side of the bed.

He was silent for a minute thinking things through.

"I can hear!" he called out loud. "That's it, the noise has gone. I can hear, the kuia, the old woman. Don't you see? It makes sense, she took away the noise in my head and led the stretcher bearers to me."

"If you say so," Geraint Jenkins looked at Tama strangely. "Haven't had a bang on the head have you lad?"
"No. My Tupuna wahine, she's my father's mother, my grandmother."
"So you said. What's she doing here in the middle of all of this then?"
"It's not like that. She passed many years ago, but she comes back in times of need."
"You sure you didn't have a bang on the head?"
"She did the same to my father after his ship was wrecked before I was born. She brought him back from near death."
"Well as I said, you get to see some strange things in war so who am I to judge? Oh and before I forget, there's someone looking for you. You're not to leave until you've been seen, that's an order by the way"
"What? Who?"
"Not sure, top brass though. He'll be back later today or tomorrow. I've got things to do, stay where you are for a while eh, you're just exhausted, that's all, no injuries," Geraint Jenkins said as he turned and walked away.
Tama sat on the side of his bed looking about him. All around were wounded and dying. He felt a fraud as he didn't feel there was anything wrong with him, quite the opposite and he felt strong with a new sense of purpose so he decided he would help while he could. He spent the afternoon walking around the station, talking with the wounded and doing what he could to give them some encouragement. He helped to change bandages and played cards, but mostly listened to the stories of others appreciating how lucky he was just to survive. Two days passed and he became asked for by the men as he gave them a confidence they needed. Those who could walk, sought him out just to be with him. It made Tama feel warm, to be wanted and he felt a camaraderie he had been missing. He was able to talk freely, especially with one man in particular, Sapper Private Peter Trewinnard, a short, tubby man with a round balding head and kind eyes. He had lost a hand and was waiting to be taken back to England.
"The straw that broke the camel's back, losing your friend like you did," Peter said the next morning at breakfast when Tama confided about how he felt after the attack at Passchendaele.

"You lost your young friend, so you lost your hope in any future for a while. A man needs to know there's something to work towards. Your mate was just one more death but sometimes it only takes one drip of water to overflow the bucket when it's already full," Peter said. "And as for your grannie, you wants to come to Cornwall, that's normal down there, spirits, knockers we call 'em sometimes. You see there's more we don't understand than what we do in this life," Peter went on. "We don't question it you see cos we just know. It's not like it's gonna do you any harm is it? Your grannie sounds a good sort, and as for those two kiddies she's got with her, why wouldn't she have them? No harm can come to them cos they've already passed and they want to help as much as your grannie does. They'll be family you see."
Tama was silent, trying to work it all out but got nowhere.
"You've lost your hand but it doesn't seem to let it spoil your outlook," he said.
"No reason why it should either," Peter replied. "I'll be back with my wife and kiddies in Port Isaac before I knows it, lucky I'd say, me."
"Port Isaac. What's that like?" Tama asked.
"'taint nothin' but a tiny fishing village all tucked between the hills on the Cornish coast, but I reckon it's the closest place to heaven that I knows of, I ain't leaving after this lot" he said waving his arm around, "I can tell you that for nothing."
"What you do there, for a living?"
"Fisherman. Crabs mostly, and pilchards of course, needs them for a gazer pie you see."
"Gazer pie?"
"Stargazer pie to be right. Mana from the gods is a stargazer. Beautiful brown flaky pastry, with spuds and eggs and the pilchards all looking out the top of the crust like they do. Gazing at the stars they are you see like every seaman does cos getting back 'ome depends on it. T'aint nothing better boy. A finer meal you won't get anywhere, it brings the sea to the table it does."
"I'll remember that" Tama said full of interest. "So what'll you do with only one hand then?"

"I'll be back on the boats in a month," Peter told him. "It's in the name you see. I was born Peter from 'im as was in the Bible. Saint Peter, the fisherman of men. Who knows what I'll do, maybe I'll find somebody with the other hand missing and we can make a pair," Peter said chuckling as his eyes disappeared in the laughter lines of his face
Tama looked up to see Geraint Jenkins approaching.
"A popular man you are, I'll be sorry to lose you," he said.
"What do you mean?" Tama asked.
"There's a Lieutenant Huntley from divisional here to see you. He's waiting in my tent now, you'd better look sharp."
"Let me know how you go lad," Peter said lifting a cup of tea towards Tama before he put it to his lips.
"I will," Tama replied with a smile.
Geraint Jenkins looked at Tama strangely.

**

Lieutenant Huntley was a small man and impeccably dressed in his uniform with the spring front leggings, Sam Brown belt and leather shoulder strap. The red tabs of the gorget patches on his collar and red band on his cap immediately identified him as being from divisional command. His tunic carried the red brassard with a silver fern emblem on his right arm and he had NZ/STAFF emblems on his shoulders. Tama took a second to take it all in, momentarily stunned by the official trappings.
"Sir," he managed a salute.
"Sergeant Tama Wirimu Ratahi?"
"Yes sir."
"At ease sergeant. You know who I am?"
"Yes sir," Tama replied.
"Then you must be wondering what this is all about?"
"Sir."
"Well it is my duty, and my pleasure to inform you that you have been awarded a distinguished conduct medal, a DCM."
"Come again...sir."

"On the third of December last year, outside Passchendaele, your platoon were laying cables with the French when your section were involved in an aerial attack. Your platoon, along with the French, took significant numbers of dead and injured including the officer who was to connect the wires to make the system operational. On your own, you went out under fierce machine gun fire to complete the task started by the French officer which you did successfully. That single act of bravery meant vital communications could be maintained, communications I need to say sergeant, which saved many lives."

Tama looked at Lieutenant Huntley in disbelief. "Yes sir, I suppose I did sir. But if it wasn't for the covering fire from our own line, I would never have made it. It was one of the French, Henri-Émile Dechambeau who deserves a medal."

"Nevertheless, your individual action saved many lives and for that, you have been awarded the DCM. We should have told you earlier of course. However, General Sir Alexander Godly confirmed the medal be awarded a while ago and I must advise that it has already been posted in the London Gazette and probably the New Zealand Gazette as well. It is possible your family may already know of the honour you have earned. You will appreciate the operations surrounding Passchendaele meant the normal processes in these matters were interrupted. Allow me to be the first to congratulate you, Sergeant" Lieutenant Huntley said taking Tama's hand. "You will appreciate that the awarding of the DCM means a one-off payment of twenty pounds and an extra sixpence on any army pension."

"Twenty pounds?" Tama asked.

"Yes Sergeant, twenty pounds, but I expect it may be a while until you receive that. There is to be a parade of sorts here this afternoon. General Sir Alexander Godley himself will be here to award your DCM medal ribbon along with two military medals to be awarded to other men. I have other news as well."

"Sir?" Tama managed barely making sense of what was being said to him.

"You may not know yet but the II Anzac Corps is now a part of the XXII Corps and you are being withdrawn to a reserve area at Staple, west of Hazebrouck for a well-deserved rest and training."

"Training sir?"

"Yes, for the big push. Since the Russians have signed an armistice with the Germans, we are expecting an all-out offensive from the Hun. Possibly as soon as March. But we are prepared Sergeant, we have new weapons and new tactics. Tanks in particular, we have more tanks coming in every day. Anyway, congratulations again Sergeant Ratahi, it is men like you who will help us win this war."

"Sir. Thank you, sir," Tama replied taking the officer's hand.

He left the tent trying to take the news in. He felt he had to tell somebody, so he went straight to see Peter Trewinnard, but he wasn't where he was before. Tama looked around but he was nowhere to be found.

Searching out Geraint Jenkins, Tama asked where Peter was.

"His body was taken away first thing," was the response.

"What do you mean 'his body was taken away'?"

"Peter Trewinnard died of septicaemia late last night."

Chapter Twenty One

**

The sun, unexpectedly warm for early May, shone through the window onto the concrete laundry tub and a lazy breeze gently fanned out the net curtains as Sarah folded her washing.
"Miss Murphy!" Mrs Chard called out. "I have somebody for you to meet."
"Just coming Mrs Chard" she muttered under her breath, less than impressed about the interruption.
"Hurry up Miss Murphy, I don't have all day."
Giving up on finishing her task, Sarah put her clothes to one side and walked into the front room.
"Fay," she called out seeing Fay Carrington standing by the side of Mrs Chard
"You know each other?" Mrs Chard uttered.
"Yes, yes we do" Sarah replied.
Fay interrupted before Sarah could say anything else. "Well here's a coincidence and a half" she said feigning shock at seeing Sarah. "It was a very long time ago, in New Plymouth" she insisted as she rolled her eyes towards Mrs Chard and frowned at the same time.
"I was going to say we have a new boarder but as you may already know, Miss Carrington has been in England nursing our boys back to health and giving them religious instruction as well. Isn't that splendid?"
Sarah was momentarily taken aback. "Religious instruction?" she said.
"Her father was a man of the cloth you know," Mrs Chard said with a beaming smile.
Sarah hesitated for a moment watching Fay dilating her eyes and nodding slightly towards Mrs Chard standing behind her.
"Of course," Sarah said. "Fay, it's so good to see you back safe and sound. I trust you are well?"
"Yes, perfectly thank you, Sarah."

"Where was your father preaching now, I can't quite remember?" Sarah asked pointedly.

"Pahiatua," Fay replied with a well-practised lie. "Pahiatua's such a small town of course, my father was a travelling minister you see, he would go all over the place, up to Mangatainoka, and Woodville or down to Mauriceville and Opaki then back up home again. Quite the traveller."

"Gosh, you would hardly ever see him," Sarah answered.

"Well enough of this chatter," Mrs Chard interrupted before Fay could reply. "Miss Carrington is taking over Miss Bryant's room, so you two will have plenty of time to talk I'm sure."

Sarah went back to the laundry until Mrs Chard was in the garden, then she dashed around to Fay's door, knocking urgently.

"Just what are you playing at, lying to Mrs Chard like that?" she demanded as soon as Fay had the door half open. "I know your father wasn't a minister, quite the opposite even if half the stories are true."

Fay looked around and pulled Sarah into her room. "I had to say something to get the edge so I would get in here. I wanted so much to be back here with you and Linda, people I considered friends as we were at Jimmy Brown's. I didn't know Linda had left."

"She's back home, my home that is, at Llanon, helping out with my brother's recovery. But what are you doing back here? The war's still going isn't it? What's going on Fay? If you consider me to be a friend, you'll tell me the truth. Did something happen in Egypt?"

"Well no, not Egypt," Fay said sitting down. "I was there for several years. It was good in some ways, every day was busy and the men were grateful, just to be away from the front lines. I liked the work, it meant something. I was in Heliopolis, at the Aotea convalescent home for two years but then moved to a hospital near Hazebrouck. That became too close to the shelling so we were evacuated back to England, to Hornchurch at first and then Brighton."

"That's a lot of travelling around Fay, why didn't they keep you in one place? Nurses don't move around that much, at least not once they're in England? I know about Hornchurch, I've been reading about the work there. Brighton's for officers though, isn't it?"
"You have always been a good detective, Sarah."
"That's why I'm at the newspaper. So what happened?"
Fay shuffled around in her chair.
"The truth mind, I'll know if you're lying."
"There was one officer, a major. He was a good man but a lonely man."
"And a married man?" Sarah asked.
Fay looked up at Sarah ignoring the question.
"We talked a lot, he made me laugh and we got on well. One thing turned to another and, well, you can guess."
"That's terrible Fay, but I suppose in some circumstances understandable, not that I condone such behaviour of course. What happened to this major?"
"As soon as he found out I was pregnant, he pulled a few strings, and well, here I am."
"What about the baby then, how long ago was this?"
"I 'lost' the baby Sarah, the same as I lost the others."
"Others?" Sarah questioned.
"You wanted the truth?"
"Yes, yes of course" Sarah said, totally absorbed.
Fay got up and walked around the room nervously fiddling with some string she picked off the table.
"You see I've always had an attraction to older men," she confessed. "I, I don't know why but I think it's because of my father, or lack of a father perhaps."
"But your father was, well, let's say…"
"He was a pig," Fay interrupted. "A vicious, drunken pig who deserved to die like he did. I hope it was a slow and painful death."
Sarah was lost for words. Fay sat by her, taking her hands.
"I've never told anybody this before Sarah, nobody, do you understand?"
"Of course."
"I'm relying on you to keep it to yourself" Fay told her. "It has to end somewhere."

"What does, what has to end?"
"It's no secret my father was a philandering drunk who used his fists, not only in the pub but, well, on Mother as well."
Sarah put her hands to cover her mouth.
"There's more to it. When he came home drunk which was most of the time, well…I don't know how to say this, but well, let's say that if he beat my mother senseless and couldn't have her, he, uh… he would have me."
Sarah stood up staring at Fay in shock.
"You, you mean he would rape you, his own daughter?"
"You put it so bluntly," Fay said. "He called it his party time but it wasn't a party for me I can tell you."
"But your mother must have known what was going on?"
"She did, but if she tried to do anything she'd be knocked senseless by his fist or anything he could get his hands on. He hit her with the iron once. He knocked her out cold and left her on the floor with a bleeding head."
"How long had this been happening Fay?"
"Years. I don't know how many exactly but from when I was a little girl. That's why I wanted to be a nurse, to try and make people better so I would feel better myself, only it didn't quite work out. That's why I wear my heart on my sleeve I suppose."
"So what stopped your father?"
"A year or so before I went to Egypt I found out I was carrying my father's child"
"God alive," Sarah gasped out loud.
"Exactly. So, one night, I went with a man, a filthy stinking man from the port so I could divert the blame away from my father. I don't know why I wanted to protect him, but I did. I realised I couldn't have the baby so I decided to have an abortion."
"An abortion? Who would possibly do that?"
"An old woman in the back of a filthy shed by the port."
"But it could have killed you."
"It nearly did, I bled for a week and was very frail as you can imagine."
"And your father?"

"He didn't care, he didn't even recognise what had happened. A week or so after the abortion he came home, drunk as usual and wanted me again. Only this time something was different, I fought back, I was desperate you see and the pain from the abortion was all the more real. It gave me the strength and the courage in a funny way. In the fight, a candle was knocked over and the house caught fire. I managed to scramble out and ran. Father was too drunk and as I'm sure you know, he died, thank God. I know it's wrong to say, but it was the biggest relief of my life I can tell you. To know the nightmare had actually ended was such an incredible feeling of elation. It took some weeks to sink in though even now he still comes back in my sleep."

Sarah was stuck for words, dumbfounded, she just sat staring at Fay.

"I know. It's hard to take in isn't it? I can still hardly believe it myself so for somebody like you who comes from a really nice family, it must be totally unbelievable."

Fay wiped her eyes and Sarah struggled for words, adding to the tense silence between the two with Sarah not knowing quite what to believe and Fay feeling spent after telling the one person she trusted of her past life, if indeed a life it was.

"After that I did go to Pahiatua for a year," Fay went on. "I stayed in a home for unmarried mothers way out in the back blocks and I worked there as a nurse and general lackey to the young mums."

Fay looked directly at Sarah

"I wouldn't blame you at all if you didn't believe me. So, to answer your question why did I lie about my father? It was to cover the shameful truth and to try and find some sense of decency, however fabricated it may be to at least put up a pretence of being from a good family."

**

"I spy with my little eye...something beginning with B." Bronwyn was playing her favourite game with Linda. She had become a different child since Linda arrived at Llanon and they spent most days together walking and talking.

"Birds?" Linda said looking down the hallway towards the river.

"No not birds," Bronwyn laughed.
"Bush?"
"No."
"Boiling water," Linda guessed again pointing to the range.
"No, that's BW," Bronwyn said still giggling.
"Bank?"
"Bank?" Bronwyn asked.
"The riverbank of course," Linda told her.
"Good guess, but it's wrong."
"All right. I give up."
"No you can't give up, you're not allowed."
Linda looked around the kitchen. "I know, bricks."
"Yes, bricks, the bricks on the chimney," Bronwyn squealed with delight.
"That was a good one. I can see you are getting far too good at this game," Linda mocked
"It was my friend's idea."
"Your friends are very clever."
"No, they told me about some bricks a little while ago when they all fell over."
"Your friends fell over?"
"No," Bronwyn laughed out loud. "The bricks. They fell over when a bomb went off making the bricks fall on him."
"Fell on who? Where was this?" Linda asked. She had become accustomed to such conversations about the imaginary friends Bronwyn constantly talked about. Nobody took much notice with so much happening, they were only too glad of a diversion from the very real family tensions for such a vulnerable young girl.
"In the war," Bronwyn said. "A German bomb exploded, and the wall fell over burying him, but it's all right because he was saved."
"Who was saved?" Linda asked becoming quite serious.
"The soldier."
"What soldier, Bronwyn?"
"Uncle Wirimu and Auntie Ngaire's soldier. Auntie Wairingiringi was there with my friends and they saved him."
A cold chill went down Linda's spine. This was the first time Bronwyn had ever mentioned any names.
"You haven't mentioned any Auntie Wairingiringi before now."

"No. She likes to stay quiet and watch us play."

"Watching who play? What are the names of your play friends?"

Bronwyn fidgeted playing with some wooden building blocks for a while.

"The boy is Robbie, and the girl is Caryl," she muttered. "But you mustn't say anything or they'll be angry, you must promise me Auntie Linda, you really, really must promise." This was the first time Linda had seen Bronwyn so anxious.

"All right, I promise," Linda said. "Let's get this right. Your Auntie Wairingiringi and your friends, Robbie and Caryl saw the soldier, Uncle Wirimu's and Auntie Ngaire's soldier, be buried in bricks?"

"Yes, that's right, but he's all right now because the Germans couldn't see him so he was saved after Auntie Wairingiringi showed them where he was."

"And this soldier, where is he now?"

"He's fighting, of course. He has a very pretty piece of material on his jacket that the soldier in the flat hat gave him."

"What material?"

"It's on his chest."

"What does it look like Bronwyn?"

"It's dark red with a blue middle. Uncle Wirimu's and Auntie Ngaire's soldier is very proud of it," Bronwyn said. "You do promise not to say anything, ever, don't you Auntie Linda?"

"Yes, of course I do."

**

"It's absolutely fascinating," Sarah said getting into the tram with Dickie.

"The war?"

"What else? The House can't talk of anything but the war, our men have covered themselves in glory at Auchonvillers Ridge and Colincamp. Now there's a real feeling of optimism, especially now the Americans have released men to actually fight with us and the French. The tide of war is turning to our favour and at last the Allies have the upper hand now the dreaded German spring offensive has failed. I know we lost the land at Passchendaele, but the Germans lost a great many men, far more than us, over a quarter of a million if what I hear is right. Now Germany's lowered the age of conscription to seventeen to make up numbers."

"Yes. Two Germans are being killed for every allied soldier, so now they're sending innocents to war eh?" Dickie asked rhetorically.

"You're beginning to sound more like a good socialist every day" Sarah told him. "But you were an innocent of war once Dickie, all our men were. I hear there are British fifteen year olds still volunteering, lying about their age to get in the action while they can, young boys still wet behind the ears are going over with rifles to fight tanks."

"But we have more tanks," Dickie replied. "And we can make more tanks and guns faster than ever before. The Germans can't because of the blockades so now they are being starved of materials as well as men."

"I wonder how Tama is," Sarah mused not really listening.

Dickie went quiet as the tram slowly rumbled on past Pigeon Park.

"Dickie!" Sarah almost shouted out. "Let's get out at Courtney Place and walk along Oriental Parade to the tea house, the one right on the sea front, I do so love it there."

"Very well, there is something I want to say anyway" Dickie replied. Sarah looked at him sideways.

"It's no good raising an eyebrow to me Miss Murphy, my lips are sealed."

"Then how can you say what you want to say?"

"Don't be pedantic or they'll be no tea cake for you," Dickie teased. Sarah let out a giggle and Dickie squeezed her hand as they walked against the autumn chill.

**

Sarah stared out the window of the tea house, watching the waves breaking on the grey sea for a full ten minutes. "A penny for your thoughts," Dickie said interrupting her daydream.

"Sorry," Sarah apologised. "I was just thinking back to the Britannia Tea Rooms in New Plymouth when Nana owned it. I used to help out, especially on a Saturday, I quite looked forward to spending time with her. We were very close then. I had to save two Welsh cakes for Matron, God help me if she came in and we had sold out. People used to come especially for Nana's Welsh cakes. Mine weren't too bad but I must say that Nana's had the edge. I haven't had one in a long time. Perhaps I can convince Mrs Chard to use her kitchen."

"You can make some for me if you like," Dickie suggested.

"Yes, that would be good, you can give me your considered socialist opinion Mr Fleming. Are you all right? You look a bit nervous."

Dickie looked about the room, it was empty but for an old woman in the corner. He sat forward in his chair taking Sarah's hands.

"Listen Sarah. It wasn't meant to be like this."

"What wasn't Dickie? What's wrong?"

"Nothing's wrong. I've been thinking, that's all. Well more like planning something but I just need to come out with it now regardless."

"Come out with what?" Sarah asked with some trepidation.

Dickie looked about the room again and then back at Sarah.

"Will you marry me, become my wife…Sarah?"

She sat in her chair in absolute silence, looking into Dickie's eyes as nerves got the better of him. "I…I…I can provide for you, really I can. Uncle Stephen's retiring soon and there may be a promotion and…and…"

"And nothing," Sarah cut in. "I'm quite capable of providing for myself thank you very much."

Dickie looked down at the tablecloth dejectedly.

"And, yes, of course I'll marry you Dickie Fleming."

Sarah leaned over the table and kissed him on the cheek.

"Now you can call me 'love' in public, darling," she whispered.

Chapter Twenty Two

**

Gwyneth took Sarah into the bedroom at Llanon on the morning of the wedding. "I have so much enjoyed the last six months. Not only to see you and Dickie married of course, he's such a wonderful and caring man, I couldn't be happier for you both, but so many good things have been happening lately. Linda is making inroads with Richard, he's even had a few meals with us, Bronwyn is such a help of course, she and her 'friends'. With the war ending and the armistice signed we have a bright future again, it's hard to believe our men will be coming home. No more war news is hard to believe, I have to pinch myself."
"I know," Sarah said. "I don't think anybody in Wellington has slept for three days with all the celebrating going on. There were so many people out in the streets dancing and waving flags, even policemen. Many were crying with happiness. I was hugged at least a dozen times and even kissed once or twice walking along Lambton Quay. Mr Harris even gave me a hug. It's absolutely unbelievable in so many ways."
"I think it's been the same all around the country," Gwyneth agreed. "I hear Stella Ratcliffe didn't close the Mokau Hotel for days. Life is looking up for us here at Llanon as well, and a lot of that is down to you Sarah, so before we start the proceedings for today, I just wanted to say, 'thank you'. Not the least for bringing Linda into our lives to help Richard. She has been a godsend I can tell you. You Sarah are a strong woman, and you have given me such strength, more than you will ever know. Just knowing that you have your own life, and now you will be sharing that with the man you love and making your own way in the world is an inspiration to me."
Sarah started to get teary.
"I just cannot wait for grandchildren," Gwyneth told her.

Sarah's face fell and she looked away. "I've been meaning to tell you Mother, ever since Dickie and I became engaged."
"Tell me what?"
"Dickie and I won't be having children."
"Of course you will."
"No Mother, we won't, I can tell you now."
"Why ever not?"
"His injury you see, the bullet went into his groin, and…"
"Oh love, I am so sorry, I should have thought."
"No, you couldn't have known. I know what grandchildren would have meant to you and Father as well, especially with only Richard to carry on the family name."
"Enough said Gwyneth. Now we need to find your father, we have a little something for you. No doubt he's already started breakfast."
They walked into the kitchen where Sean was just taking some bacon out of the pan and putting it between two slices of bread.
"You'll spoil your appetite," Gwyneth chided. "Is the front lawn set up all ready?".
"That it is," Sean answered. "Wirimu, me and George have been doing nothing else for the last two hours so we have. Tables and chairs, and the altar, all set up just as it was when we got hitched."
Sean took a long look at Sarah. "You are a beautiful young woman," he told her stepping over for a hug. Sarah held back a little.
"I've told Sarah we have a surprise for her," Gwyneth said.
"We'll sit over by the piano," Sean suggested, "before it all gets too busy. It's seen a lot of history this piano. It came up from Dunedin in what seems like a hundred years ago."
"Thank you very much Sean Murphy," Gwyneth mocked." "I hope that's no reflection on me?"
Sean said nothing.
Gwyneth opened up the keyboard. "This is especially for your Nana who wouldn't have missed today for the world so I know she'll be watching from above," Gwyneth said as she played *Canon Lan* very softly.
"That's beautiful Mother."

"Well your nana is here in more ways than one," Sean said taking an envelope off the top of the piano.

"You'll remember when she sold the Britannia Tea Rooms, she promised to put the money from the sale into a trust for you and Richard?"

"Yes, I remember, I wish she hadn't done that. It was her money to enjoy," Sarah said.

"Well she'll be enjoying it now. Open the envelope" Gwyneth suggested, smiling broadly.

Sarah, still a little tearful and shaking slightly, took the envelope. "What is it?" she asked.

"Take it out and you'll see for yourself," Gwyneth told her. "This is your wedding present from Nana. You see true to her word she put the money in trust, half for you and half for Richard. It was to be paid out on your twenty fifth birthday or when you were married, whichever came first. So as I said, this is your wedding present from her."

Sarah gave out a gasp as she looked at a cheque for three thousand pounds. She immediately burst into tears.

"Mother, this is more money than I ever thought. It's enough for a house in Oriental Parade, a really nice house."

"That's for you and Dickie to decide Sarah. You can give him the news yourself, it's just that your father and I wanted this moment to be private if you understand, a special moment for you from your Nana. We both have a wedding present to give you both later on after the wedding. Now put the cheque away nice and safe then go and get yourself ready for the ceremony. There'll be a boat load of people arriving in a few hours with Father Michael and Dickie will be over from Te Kainga soon enough looking like a new pin. I'll go over to George and Libby's to check on his parents."

"How long do you have for your honeymoon now?" Gwyneth checked before she left.

"I'm not sure exactly," Sarah said. "Mr Harris approved the two weeks I applied for so I know where I am, but he also said not to rush back. I'm not sure what he meant by that but it sounded good to me."

**

Tama walked past a soldier sitting on a pile of rubble and looking across the desolate landscape. He lit a cigarette and turned to look at Tama.
"Ciggy mate?"
"No thanks, I don't" Tama replied.
"You must be the only one then," the soldier remarked. He hesitated as he drew on the cigarette, enjoying the moment and then blew out some smoke rings in the still air. "Strange eh?" he said to Tama.
"Unbelievable," Tama responded. "The noises have changed, the light has changed, even the air seems different, everything. It's like being drunk but it's not, all at the same time."
Tama took in the endless mud, the barbed wire and rotting bodies. Remnants of ruined buildings still standing, against all odds, now almost defiant against the German tanks and artillery which dotted the landscape, silent in the mud. Machine guns lay abandoned in nests or bomb craters dripping water in the light November drizzle. Instead of being surrounded by the clamour of war, Tama heard the single delight of a blackbird singing in a nearby tree. It had only been saved from the ravages of war by a stone wall which had previously been a part of somebody's home. Most of the leaves had fallen, leaving only a few, withered specimens hanging precariously off the branches. The bird flew to the ground after a few minutes and pecked at some worms in the grass around the tree's base then flew away taking Tama's attention to the German army. Only days ago he thought them unassailable, but now they were being rounded up and marched in small columns of prisoners towards a common point where they were held captive. In the diffused light, only the uniforms separated the victors from the vanquished.
"It's unreal, eh?" the soldier said. "I 'haven't heard so much as a rifle go off for half an hour."
Tama remained silent.
"Where you from then?" the soldier asked.
"New Zealand."
"It'll take a few days for you to get home then?"
"Ay. You?"
"Bangor, northwest Wales".

The two men looked around again still in awe of the peace.
The Welshman broke the silence. "Who'd ever have thought it? That we'd ever be here to see the last day of the war and the first day of peace. Seeing all these bodies reminds me of a song we have back home, he said half singing. *"All around see dead and dying, friends and foe together lying."*
"Men of Harlech" Tama said smiling to himself as he picked up the rest of the verse. *"All around the arrows flying. Scatter sudden death.* I know it well. A good waiata I grew up with.
"That's good you know the proper version," the soldier said. "But there's no arrows flying anymore is there. Very glad I am of it too if you know what I mean."
"I know," Tama replied. "It's good just being alive without having to kill to stay alive, not being frightened of showing your face to the world, not being scared of living or terrified of dying. It's a freedom I never realised I had before the war."
"A bit deep for me that is mate, but freedom's what we've been fighting for isn't it? Well I'd better get back," the soldier said. "I just wanted to take five minutes to look at what peace looked like, to take it all in." He took a last draw on the cigarette and threw the dog end into the mud.
"Captain Gareth Jenkins!" Tama called out, suddenly remembering. "You know him?" he asked.
"There was a Captain Gareth Jenkins who was my CO at Gallipoli if that's your man, 'bout five six, a quiet spoken, well-mannered caring sort of man."
"Sounds like him," Tama said. "Is he…"
"Alive? He never got off Chunuk Bair."
"A lot of good men never did so he's in good company," Tama said quietly.
"The thing is you see," the soldier said awkwardly. "Captain Jenkins went the same way as your Colonel Malone."
"How do you mean?"
"He was killed accidentally, blown to bits by New Zealand guns."
Tama felt sick in his stomach.

**

For the next three weeks, Tama, with the entire division marched towards Germany. The atmosphere started as one of levity amongst the allies but as the columns of men approached Germany, a solemn air took hold and at the German border the New Zealanders were stopped.
"What's up?" one soldier called out.
"Ain't lettin' us in," came a reply from towards the front.
"What do you mean 'ain't lettin' us in? It's bloody Germany en it? We beat 'em fair and square and now they got the gall to say we can't come in, what's the guts?" he yelled out.
"The guts is sergeant," a passing officer said, "is that for you Kiwi's the war is over. You are being sent back to England and from there you will be shipped home to New Zealand."
"I thought we were going into Germany."
"No," the officer replied sharply. "No native troops will be used to garrison Germany, those are the rules."
"So we're going home?"
"Eventually yes, but first you must go to England, that's the process."
"When?"
"As soon as you get yourselves to Dunkirk where a ship will be waiting to take you back for eventual demobilisation. Your officers will give your orders."
"So it's over then? It's really over?"
"Yes soldier, now you can go home to your wife and children."
"That's when the fighting will start all over again," the man next to him said and a chorus of laughter rose up.

**

Dickie and Sarah stood in the front room of a spacious villa looking out over Oriental Parade to the bay and the harbour beyond.
"Our very own house," Sarah said. "Isn't it wonderful darling? I just can't believe we bought this place."
"Well it's not everybody who walks into the bank with a cash offer like we did is it?" Dickie replied.

"Indeed not. Thank you Nana, thank you Nana, thank you Nana," Sarah repeated over and over, spinning around with her arms stretched out. "The first thing I shall cook in the oven are Welsh cakes. Oh Dickie, it's all so lovely with the sun streaming through the windows and the garden." Sarah ran over to the bay window.

"Every time I look out here across to Oriental Parade I shall count my blessings. We can watch the people promenading while we sit here in our very own home. Isn't that wonderful? See how even the sun is sparkling today, just for us, I think it's a welcome present, it's like Theo is giving us his blessing."

Dickie looked awkward for a moment

"I love this place almost as much as I love you Dickie Fleming" Sarah said throwing her arms around him.

"Well as much as I would love to stay here with you, we both need to leave for work soon," Dickie told her.

"First day back after a month away, it will take some getting used to. I do hope Mr Harris isn't angry but he did send a telegram agreeing to me extending my leave. It's been a wonderful month Dickie and your parents were so hospitable."

"Waiheki was the best though," Dickie said putting his sandwiches in a bag. "The bach was perfect for just the both of us, I can't wait to see the photographs. But all good things come to an end, and we both need to get going, else we really will be late," he said looking at his watch.

"You are such a slavedriver, Mr Fleming."

"And you are the most beautiful of all slaves," Dickie said kissing Sarah. "And don't forget we're seeing the bank manager at one o'clock sharp to sign on the dotted line to finalise our share of Llanon and Ballinger's Mill."

"Yes," Sarah agreed. "It was very generous of Mother and Father to give us ten percent of both as a wedding present."

"It takes some thinking about, especially now," Dickie said. "Our men will be back from the war in a few months and there'll be a call for good timber. You father did the right thing replacing the steam plant when he did, we'll be sitting pretty in another year or so, mark my words."

**

When Sarah got to the Evening Post offices, she expected to see Mr Harris to thank him for his generosity in letting her extend her honeymoon. She walked in full of anticipation, keen to see her colleagues and share in the excitement surrounding the end of the war. She was greeted with a lukewarm response.

"I didn't expect to be greeted back with open arms," she said to Paul "but I haven't seen the office this quiet for a long time, what's happening?"

"Not sure," Paul replied. "Old man Harris has been in his office with the door locked for over an hour."

"Who's with him?"

"Men from the Repatriation Office we think."

"What could they possibly want?"

"Our jobs Sarah for goodness sake."

"How? Why?"

"They're looking to find work for our boys when they get back. The place will be crawling with returned servicemen soon enough, haven't you heard, there's fifty six thousand coming back in six weeks, all looking for work, I don't fancy your chances of keeping your job, being a woman."

"What's that got to do with it?"

"Everything Sarah, surely you know that."

"Mr Harris would never allow such a thing."

"You haven't heard then?"

"Heard what?"

"Your precious Mr Harris is leaving."

"Leaving, he can't be!" Sarah exclaimed, shocked at the news.

"Well he is, I can assure you."

"Why?"

"His boy, Brian came home last week."

"So early, but that's a good thing surely."

"Is it? He was in a hospital ship. He's totally blind and his lungs are burned out from the mustard gas, he'll take some looking after I can tell you. The old man is leaving so he and his wife can look after their boy as best they can. Apparently, it'll take a few years for him to die at home. God help them, that's all I can say."

Sarah burst into tears and ran from the office. She wanted to be alone so she almost ran to the Government Building and up the three floors to the women's toilet. She ran into the cubicle slamming the door behind her and cried her eyes out.
After a while there was a knock on the door.
A woman's voice called out. "Excuse me Miss Murphy, but are you all right?
Sarah remained silent.
"I say. Miss Murphy, are you all right?"
"It's Mrs Fleming now, and yes I'm fine thank you," Sarah shouted out, annoyed at being disturbed.
"Well if you'll pardon me saying so, I understand you are not all right. Ronnie from the desk asked me to enquire after you."
"Ronnie?"
"Yes, apparently you nearly knocked him over as you were rushing up the stairs, he could hear you crying from the second floor he tells me."
Sarah smiled and wiped her eyes. She opened the door slightly to see an elderly woman in a long, light brown overcoat and matching hat. She had a kind, motherly face and the two women smiled slightly at each other.
"Bless him. Can you please tell Ronnie I am fine and I will be down shortly to apologise? Sorry, I must look a real fright."
"Not at all dear, and yes Miss…sorry, Mrs Fleming, I will pass your message back to Ronnie."
"Thank you Mrs…"
"Mrs Massey."
"Thank you Mrs Massey. I am much obliged to you," Sarah replied without thinking.
She spent some time in front of the mirror before she heard a clamour from downstairs. She opened the toilet door and the noise of shouting and celebration could be clearly heard so she made her way back down. She stopped on the second floor looking over the banister. The corridors were packed with people, all laughing and shaking hands. The old men with cigars were slapping each other on the back and somewhere in the noise, Sarah could hear the chink of glasses being raised. She went down to the ground floor and edged her way through the crowd to the front desk.
"Hello Ronnie," she had to almost shout.

"Mrs Fleming. Are you all right?"
"Yes, yes Ronnie, I'm fine thank you."
"It's just that we were worried about you."
"We?"
"Yes. I saw you running upstairs very upset and heard you crying. Mrs Massey saw you as well so I asked her to make enquiries given where you were."
"Mrs Massey? Do I know Mrs Massey?"
Ronnie smiled and took Sarah to one side away from the crowd.
"She knows you, Mrs Christina Massey," he laughed, "Mrs Christina
William Massey, the wife of our Prime Minister."
Sarah went deep red. "Mrs William Massey," she gasped putting her hands over her mouth. "She knows me? Don't be ridiculous."
"Mrs Massey knows more than you think. She's been watching you for a while, reading your articles, she likes what you write."
"She knows I'm a reporter? Well a reporter of sorts. Why didn't she say something?"
"The wife of the Prime Minister would never befriend a reporter, it's just not the done thing, even if you are a woman. But that's why she likes you of course, she admires your pluck if I may say so without speaking out of term," Ronnie said in a low tone.
"Of course" Sarah said embarrassed at her own naivety.
"Would you like a seat?" Ronnie asked seeing Sarah shocked at what he had told her."
"No thank you, now what's all the noise about?"
A wide grin appeared on his face.
"The House has just been informed that the entire New Zealand Pioneer Corp are coming home as a complete battalion on the *SS Westmorland* in mid-March. They'll be back home by May."
"Oh that's wonderful news," Sarah said throwing her arms around the embarrassed Ronnie. She looked up and caught sight of the clock above the reception desk.
"Oh my goodness, look at the time." Saying no more, she ran out the building as fast as she could go and back to the office.

"Sorry Mr Harris, I need a longer lunch break, you can take it out of my wages. I have to be at the bank ten minutes ago. Dickie will be angry by now," she garbled running back outside.

**

"Mr Harris is leaving," Sarah said to Dickie as they patiently waited outside the bank manager's office in a cold and austere hallway.
Dickie looked at his watch. "I was rather hoping this wouldn't take long, I told Uncle Stephen I would be back in an hour."
"Yes, I shall be in trouble as well, it was bad enough getting here. Did you hear what I said about Mr Harris leaving? He has to look after his son."
"Yes," Dickie replied. "Uncle Stephen is leaving as well."
"Really? Why?"
"He's very close to retiring so he thought if he left in a month or so his assistant can move up so there'll be a new place for a returned soldier."
"Did the repatriation department suggest that?"
"Apparently, they were around last week. The thing is a few men left the office to sign up but their places were taken by men who were injured in the war so it's the same thing really. The only job that will become vacant is the secretarial position because Jill's getting married when her fiancé returns."
"Really? The repatriation people were in the office today as well," Sarah said. "Paul seems to think I might lose my job to a returned soldier."
"I don't think they would allow you to apply for the job at my work," Dickie said looking straight at Sarah.
"No, I wouldn't want it anyway. It wasn't me I was thinking of."
The manager's door opened. "You can come through now Mr and Mrs Fleming."

**

Beads of sweat dribbled down the side of Ngaire's face as she raked the fire in the range on a hot March afternoon. "I just wish Tama would write, or at least the army would let us know when to expect our men back."

"I'm sure it won't be long until you hear something," Linda replied. "Sarah mentioned in her letter that they are all safe in England, in a military camp waiting."

"Waiting for what? That's what I want to know."

"A ship home of course. There's fifty five thousand of our men to bring back. It takes some organising."

"Yes, I know," Ngaire answered. "It's just that Tama never writes and waiting for the army to do anything is like waiting for paint to dry."

"I'm sure they are doing all they can."

"Atarangi would say the same thing."

"She's your sister isn't she?" Linda asked.

"Ai. I must write to her soon, I just never get around to it."

"And you wonder where Tama gets it from?"

Ngaire looked at Linda for a minute realising what she had said, they both laughed.

"So how are you settling in at Llanon?"

"Good, I think. It all seems to be working out, but Richard will be a work in progress for some time."

"You are doing good work Linda, it's not many men who would have somebody like you to watch out for them."

"It's just that I think we owe our men a debt of gratitude we may never repay. I can do a lot more here with Richard than I could in Wellington Hospital. Bronwyn is a big help, she and Richard seem to have an understanding.

"Bronwyn's a special girl, a very special girl, as indeed you are," Ngaire said.

"Well I'm not sure about that," Linda replied. "I'm not making much progress at the moment. Richard went off on one of his walks yesterday, he'll be gone for two or three days."

"Nothing wrong with that Linda, it's good medicine I'd say, something we could all learn from perhaps."

"Maybe you're right Ngaire," Linda said thoughtfully. "I do wonder where he goes though, perhaps I could follow him one day?"

"Why?" Ngaire asked. "You'd never keep up, he's as fit as a buck rat. Besides, we all have the right to have somewhere private, somewhere we can all go when life gets a bit too much. God alone knows what's going through his mind. You keep doing what you're doing Linda, reaching out to him, that's all you can do."

"Maybe I am getting a bit ambitious," Linda admitted. "But I know I am helping in a small way."

"More than you realise I think," Ngaire added. "It's a big relief for Gwyneth, you being here for Richard, and Bronwyn come to that."

**

On a chilly March evening, along with one thousand men of the Pioneer Battalion, Tama marched towards the British merchant steamer *SS Westmorland* bound for New Zealand.

It took three hours from when they arrived at the quay side to be processed and shuffle their way forward to the ship for more processing before embarking on the voyage home. Tama took notice of the exact time where he had one foot on the gangway and one of the quay and he stopped for a second to remember Richard and Theo, wondering what happened to them both and whether he would ever see them again. For a reason he couldn't explain, he wanted to turn around and go back. His mind was confused with one part telling him he was going home after four years of war, the other telling him that because those years had cost him so much of his life, he had to stay. He looked at the hundreds of faces behind him, all eager to get on board and his mind was made up for him as the sheer pressure of men pushed him up the gangway.

His mind went to Mokau as the smell of the smoke from the ship's funnel blew down and once again he remembered the times he went to New Plymouth. All of a sudden, the last four years disappeared as though wiped clean.

Once aboard, he leaned on the railings looking over the port side choosing not to speak with anybody, trying to remember all he had been through and make sense of it, even wondering whether he should be going home at all. He checked his pack as he had done many times to make sure the war-torn penny worn by Jim Manuel was safe. After another hour, the ship's siren sounded and Tama leaned forward on the rails and watched the dockers let the ropes go. With the sea water swirling between the ship and the pier, the *Westmorland* was slowly eased away from her berth by a tugboat, then suddenly, the cables were released and the *Westmorland* was under her own steam and heading out to the open sea. Tama watched several lights flickering on the shore but even they relented to the darkness as England and all it stood for and after all it had cost, became a dark shape fading away into the distance. A light drizzle started to fall as Tama turned and headed for his bunk.

**

"But we don't know which ship, if any, Tama's on" Wirimu said over Sunday dinner at Llanon. "Ngaire and me have talked about this for a while and for all we know he may stay in England. I hear many men are staying on to travel around to go sightseeing, to see what they went over for in the first place."
"He'll be where he'll be," Sean said. "I'm picking he'll be finding it hard to leave. If a man spends a lot of blood and loses a lot of mates, that ties you to a place so it does. It'll live in his heart and his mind for the rest of his life."
"Not like Richard though," Gwyneth quickly interrupted more to put Wirimu and Ngaire's mind at ease. She could see they felt uncomfortable not knowing where their son was, nor when he was due back.
"Besides," Gwyneth added. "That didn't stop you from leaving Ireland all those years ago did it?"
"No of course not," Sean said. "But a man never forgets these things."
A silence followed.

"How's the milking?" Wirimu asked keen to lighten the conversation.
"Going good," George replied.
"And the pumps?"
"Best thing we ever did," George said. "What do you reckon Sean?"
"Ay. I'll give you that. They certainly save a man a lot of work."
"Women as well," Gwyneth muttered.
"We'll be heading into winter in a good state," George said. "The pasture's improving all the time and with a bit more sunshine we can't go wrong."
"School Farm's doing well too," Libby added. "The books have never looked so good and the school has about a hundred pounds in the account so we could look at a few more improvements maybe?"
"When's the next lot of kerosene arriving George?" Sean asked bluntly. "We're getting pretty low and damned if I'm going back to milking by hand."
"There's some arriving over the next few days on the *Heron*."
"It's about all she carries now," Sean said, "kero and a few passengers.

**

"I've been thinking" Dickie said over breakfast. 'With Uncle Stephen retiring, there's a chance of a promotion."
"So what does that mean exactly?" Sarah asked.
"It means I can do some more serious drafting work, bordering on architecture almost. I'll be helping to design schools and railway stations, that sort of thing," Dickie explained between eating his toast. "If I can prove myself over the next several years, who knows, perhaps I can start training to be an architect?"
"That would be perfect," Sarah said pouring a second cup of tea. "It'll give more work to the returned soldiers as well."
"Yes, that's the idea. This is Mr Harris's last week at the newspaper isn't it?" Dickie asked.

"Yes, it will be sad to see him go but he and his wife need to focus on helping their son, poor man. I'm not sure about his replacement, Mr Armstrong, he's called in several times but he doesn't seem as kind as Mr Harris, he has a look about him I don't trust."

"That's a bit unfair isn't it if he doesn't even start until next week?"

"Maybe so," Sarah said, "but it's not only me saying it."

"Nevertheless, you need to give him a fair chance."

"Dickie?"

Dickie gave out a groan and looked at Sarah sideways just as he bit on some toast.

"A while ago you mentioned there may be a secretarial job coming up at your office."

"The advertisement is in the newspaper this Saturday. Why?"

"Mr Harris has a daughter, Annie, he mentioned her a while ago. She wants to be an architect as well but will never get the chance, simply because she's a woman. Could she apply?"

"If she can type seventy words a minute accurately and write shorthand, she will do well in the test. But it's purely secretarial, nothing to do with drafting or architecture."

"That doesn't matter. At least she would be in the right department for future opportunities."

Dickie looked at Sarah disapprovingly.

"Could you put in a good word for her?" Sarah asked.

"But I don't even know the girl."

"But you know Mr Harris and he has been so good to me, could you help please; pretty please darling," Sarah pleaded taking Dickie's hand.

"No promises but I'll talk to Uncle Stephen. He'll be pleased if he doesn't have to pay for an advertisement. But this Annie will have to pass the tests like anybody else if Uncle Stephen agrees to interview her".

**

Wirimu went down to the riverbank with some timber and nails to repair the jetty. He looked about him on what was a warm autumn day. The sunshine lit up the foliage on the tree ferns as they hung over the water on the river bend. For several hours he knocked out the old timbers and replaced them. Halfway through the job he heard a steamer heading downriver from Ballinger's mill. It passed Wirimu, slowly chugging its way to Mokau and then on to New Plymouth with a full cargo. As it passed, the horn blasted out and Wirimu waved out to the men on board.
"Do you be needin' any more timber?" the captain yelled out.
"I've got nigh on sixty tons," he joked.
"Kia ora. I've enough here." Wirimu returned the comment with a big smile as he held up a small length. The steamer carried on slowly on its way downriver.
Another hour passed and Ngaire appeared at the top of the riverbank.
"Dinner's ready in ten minutes, come and clean up."
"But I've nearly finished," Wirimu called back.
Ngaire gave him the kind of look that made him drop his hammer immediately.
"Coming," he shouted out.

**

"Another hour and I'll get the jetty finished," Wirimu said at the table.
"Shh…" Ngaire responded. "I can hear the *Heron*, she's slowing down."
"It'll be David dropping off more kero, I'll go and help," Wirimu told her, putting down his knife and fork.
"You'll do nothing of the sort," Ngaire snapped. "You'll sit down and eat your kai. David Stockford will leave the kero on the jetty like he always does."
"Ay". Wirimu resigned himself.
As he finished his meal, he looked up as a figure slowly appeared at the top of the riverbank and walked toward the house. After a few seconds he pulled out his handkerchief and dabbed his teary eyes.
"What's wrong with you?" Ngaire asked.

"Turn around," he muttered.
"Have you gone mad?"
"Just turn around will you?"
Ngaire looked at Wirimu who was openly crying as he moved around by her side, putting his hands gently on her shoulders. "What is it?" she demanded. Just as she turned, Tama, wearing his uniform and with his pack slung over one shoulder appeared at the open door carrying two kerosene tins.
"Where shall I put these?" he asked.

Printed in Great Britain
by Amazon